EARTHBOUND

EARTHBOUND

Portals of Tessalindria Collection: Book 5

F.W. FALLER

KIRRINATH
PRESS LLC

The Portals of Tessalindria Collection: Book 5

Copyright © 2024 by Kirrinath Press, LLC

Print ISBN: 979-8-9894805-5-5

EBook ISBN: 979-8-9894805-6-2

Cover Design by Brandi Doane McKann

Interior chapter art by Emrys Fir

=======================================

DEDICATION

To all those who
struggle to see themselves
for who they really are

Tessalindria

Portman

Doth

Vann

Toplan

Werenvar

Hartana

The
Vorsian Sea

North Strand

Immerland

LORA

Dorfrand

Tessamandria

Kimura

Fuxteen

Gulf of
Mythinia

The Lengar Sea

Wendolan

MANNA

Morlan

Vindarill

Crown of
Tessalindria

Mythinia

Horrinane

Narel waste

Farhantra

Coralill

The Moorman Narrows

Moorman

Ialag

Otalla

Vindor

NASHA

0   2   4   6   10

Daysmarch

The Great Southern Sea

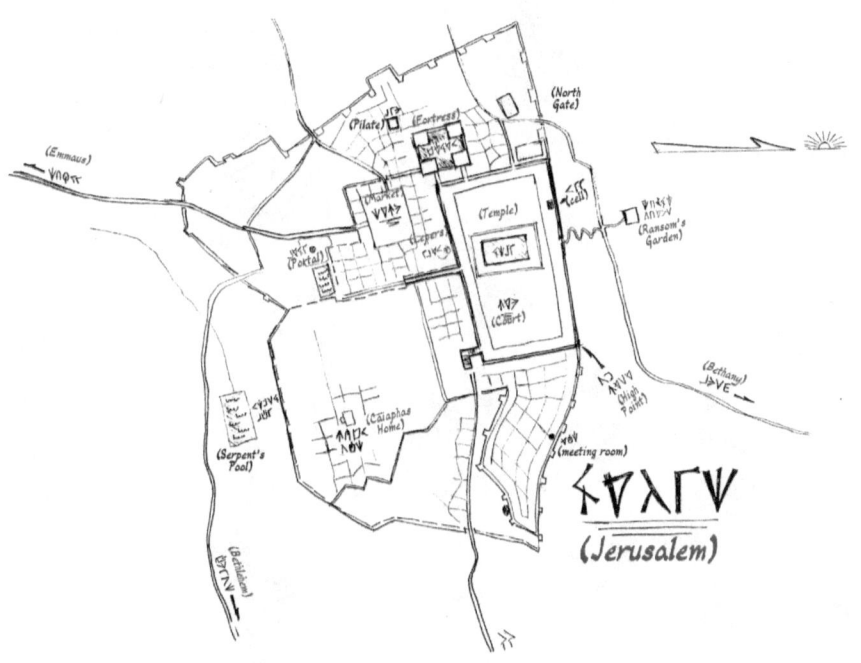

(North Gate)

(Pilate) (Fortress)

(Emmaus)

(Market)

(Temple)

(Portal)

(Steps)

(Ransom's Garden)

(Court)

(Bethany)

(High Point)

(Caiaphas Home)

(meeting room)

(Serpent's Pool)

(Bethlehem)

(Jerusalem)

CONTENTS

A Prophecy   XIII

1. Nowhere   1

2. Portal   23

3. Master   39

4. Jerusalem   51

5. Romans   61

6. Lepers   73

7. Temple   87

8. Betrayal   95

9. Prison   103

10. Manna   111

11. Eladrim   117

12. Arrest   127

13. Vishtoenvar   141

14. Escape   153

15. Tomb   161

16. Jail   173

17. Freedom   181

18. Portal   187

19. Westward   191

20. Emmaus   197

21. Darkness   201

22. Gate   209

23. Resurrected   213

24. Barabbas   223

25. Training   235

26. Pilate   245

27. Confrontation   263

28. Future   275

29. Arrest   283

30. Insurrection   293

31. News   303

32. Conspiracy   315

33. Differences   323

34. Cell   335

35. Escape   345

36. Bethlehem   355

37. Oasis   375

38. Northward   393

39. Home   403

40. Emergence   413

About the Author   419

Also By ...   421

Contact   427

A PROPHECY

"Born of the lioness of Mooriman,
    a link in the chain of Rizerand,
    hidden by distance from all the splendid
    aspirations of the mankind.
    In abuse, he does not stumble in psadeq,
    nor fail in hakapa.
    In rebuke, he does not falter,
    but brings rebuke upon us all,
    and by his trials, are we shown
    the path through trial.

    In life, he lifts the hand of the oppressed,
    and gives us hope.
    In death, he holds the hand of those
    who have died while living.

    Purified through the crucible of youth,
    and forged under the hammer of Asolara
    on the anvil of the NarEl Waste,
    so shall he emerge with the light of all life.

Through the portal he is called, and from
that darkness, he comes in strength,
to stand against those who rule the mankind with fear.

Like bitterleaf in the parched lands,
a deep root that finds water in the wastes,
he brings forth a drop for our tongues
and healing for our vorns.

With bread from the stones of the desert,
in his hunger he feeds us all;
On the path through dry lands,
he shows us hidden water.

With the gentle hand of the healer,
that sets the bone without reproach,
we are healed of the scourge of narmatan,
and made whole without wholeness".

Volenkarta Sin
Uliya Alnar

"'After his suffering, he showed himself to these men and gave many convincing proofs that he was alive. He appeared to them over a period of forty days and spoke about the kingdom of God.'"

Acts of the Apostles 1:3
Luke, the Evangelist

Chapter One

NOWHERE

"Faithful is the friend that leads you from death to life."
Journey to the infinite
Karendo Marha

Who are you, Mael?

It wasn't a new question, but recently it had resurfaced with an urgency Mael could no longer ignore. It broke into his concentration more frequently now, disrupting his work...his precious free moments when he would rather not think about it. It plagued his dreams while sleeping and his dreams of life while awake.

Who are you, Mael?

The flax blade for Jaris glowed orange as it lay just below the surface of the coal in the firepot—the final heat of the night. The blade for the town's weaver would cool in the bin of wood ash beside the forge, and Mael would do the final shaping with a file in the morning.

A north wind pounded the wall of the smithy with splatters of rain, shuddering the timber frame and clattering the shingles. With a vicious slap, the shutter on the window by the door freed itself from its restraint and slammed cross the window.

Mael glanced quickly down at the glowing blade, hesitated, then jumped toward the door.

The rain soaked his pants legs and his back before Mael got the shutter properly refastened. He bolted back to the forge.

His face fell at the sparkle of burning steel...two hours of forging lost in an instant of inattention.

"Who are you, Mael?"

He crossed his arms and watched the sparks with vacant eyes that reflected the inner emptiness that gnawed his vorn. "Burn well," he muttered as picked up the tongs to remove the blade from the fire. He examined the ruined edge briefly, before dropping it into the slack tub. It groaned as it hit the cold water and sent up one last gasp of steam as it sank into the blackness.

Mael pulled the door to the smithy closed behind him, shutting the burned blade out of his sight and mind. His fingers ached from the cold rain as he fumbled to secure the latch. With his hat tipped down against the wind that drove in off the harbor, he stepped off the stone stoop into the dark, muddy street.

"Who are you, Mael?"

Erolin's shape materialized in the rain in front of him, startling him out of his frustration. "Hey," she said.

Mael shook his head as he started toward home. "What are *you* doing here?"

"I felt you needed encouragement."

"And how did you *feel* that?"

"Be careful, Mael," she said.

"I burned another blade."

Erolin nodded. "It's not the end of the world," she said, "or the end of your life." She strode beside him as he slogged through the muddy puddles. He tipped his head down against the anger of the wind driven rain.

"Fada will be angry."

"Your father was young once."

"I am twenty-three—been making blades since I was seven, Erolin! I shouldn't be burning them."

She didn't respond.

"The chimney doesn't draw properly in the wind," he said into the silence, "and the coal cokes differently when the air is this wet."

"Your time is coming, Mael."

"You've said that before, but you know I can't leave." He glanced sideways to see her leaning into the wind, eyes straight ahead. "Matar's death left no one except me to take over for fada."

"Your father knows the prophecies, Mael. He trusts Mah'Eladra."

Mael shook his head. Cold beads of water dripped off his hat brim onto his shoulders and the rivulets snaked down his sleeves into his pockets. "I know the prophecies too."

Erolin nodded. "They're why I'm here, Mael. As a guardian of the ancient ways—this is my duty." She had explained her role as a Pistisine before.

"The prophecies are vague and distant—timeless," he said. "When I read them, they can mean anything—about anyone—at any time."

"I followed your mother here, for this purpose."

Mael stared straight ahead. "I'm tired—the son of a free slave, destined to live my life as a free-slave. My friends are married, have homes and children, but I still serve like a child in my father's smithy."

"Do you think your friend's lives are simpler and more pleasant because of those things?"

They'd had this discussion before. The honest answer was no, but something burned inside—a passion he couldn't identify. There was more—somewhere—somehow. He sometimes wondered if there was something wrong with him. No one he knew felt the guiding forces behind his life that drove him without mercy.

"And the answer doesn't lie in the temple," Erolin said, "but you know that already."

Mael nodded. "They treat me like I can't understand. I want to understand and I think I do, but they can't answer my questions."

Erolin frowned. "Their vorns have become hard and they've stopped listening. You must live what they teach, but not what they live."

"If they would read the book honestly..."

Erolin nodded.

"How is it that no one else sees this□"

"There *are* others, Mael."

"And where are they?" He despised the desperation that flooded his voice, and he knew he had to be careful.

"You will find them...*in time*...in a place you don't expect."

Mael wasn't so sure, but he knew it was pointless to pursue Erolin's vague allusion. Statements like this felt unfocused, like the prophecies. He wondered if *she* even knew what they meant.

"Would you like to come in for something to eat?" he said as they paused by the front door of his house. "You're always welcome."

She smiled. "I know, but not tonight, Mael."

He stared into her eyes, clear as crystal, and gray as the haze over Farhantra harbor before dawn. Her copper hair, cut just above her neckline, was soaked, and dripped onto the forest green scarf

bound closely around her neck. The twenty-year age separa-
tion couldn't diminish the severity of her youth, somehow held
in stasis by the force of her life.

"Are you sure?"

"Another time, Mael."

He hugged her. "Another time," he mumbled as he turned
toward the door. "Another time."

He slipped through the door and looked back. Erolin had
vanished. It was often like that. She came and went with the
fluidity of a ghost. To this day, he wasn't even sure, where she
lived.

Erolin wore a startling, severe beauty that rivaled any
woman he knew, except perhaps his mother. At nearly the same
age, his mother's endless burden of supporting a family that
registered as nothing on the social ladder of the community,
had faded her natural beauty.

Erolin appeared only a bit older than himself. Perhaps it
was the Pistisine life and her knowledge of the way the world
worked that kept her young. He liked her—was attracted to
her—but their lifelong relationship kept him from thinking of
her as anything but his guardian and mentor.

"And who are you, Mael?"

A fair breeze from the northwest had cleared the air during the
night. Asolara breached the horizon behind them as Mael and
Fada walked together toward the smithy, skirting the puddles
that remained on the road.

"I'll forge a new blade for Jaris first thing," Mael said.

Fada nodded. "What happened?"

"I was tired." He refused to excuse himself with an explanation about the shutter.

"Thinking about something else?" His father's deep voice accepted his answer with no hint of accusation.

"Things aren't going well at the temple."

Fada stopped. Mael turned to face him. Fada's eyes shone in the early light of dawn—black as the coal that fired the forge, but luminous and large in the deep sockets above his chiseled cheeks behind the graying stubble of his beard. "You have to stay true to the Tessarandin, Mael, even if no one else does—even the priests."

"You've said that before." Mael turned to continue walking.

"It's important."

Mael shook his head. "I feel like I should go somewhere else. I come to the smithy and forge the same things again and again: Hooks, pokers, kitchen knives, scythe blades☐pins and feathers for the quarry... I go to the temple every day, and every day it's the same. I have questions—they think I'm too young to understand so they don't answer—I think they don't *know* how to answer and that's offensive to them—I go home and sleep—I come back to the smithy..."

"You're destined for great things, Mael." Fada's confidence made him shudder.

"You keep saying that. Erolin says that. Mada says that, of course. All mother's think that their sons and daughters will be great someday."

"In your case, it's true."

Mael shook his head. "Maybe. But who *am* I, Fada? All the great men come from great places: Tessamandria, Vindor...Mythinia...Mooriman. They're born into great families." Mael hands thrashed about from his emotion. "They're trained in the great schools. Farhantra is a flea on a horse's shoulder—off the edge of nowhere—a Mooriman outpost—an afterthought. The streets are mud. The only stone is in the temple and the presidatory's palace!"

"Be wise, Mael." Fada shook his head. "The pride of the mankind wants us to believe that all that is important—it's not."

"How do *you* know?"

"The Tessarandin tells us."

Mael frowned. "The priests read the Tessarandin, and they're as greedy and selfish as the Mooriman Highborns."

"We have to be different, Mael. We have to try to *live* it." Fada entered lecture mode.

"Yes, and what do we have? We're abused, then discarded like kitchen compost on the manure pile! We can't go to the schools..."

"Good morning, Aanaris," his father said to the older woman who waited at the door of the smithy. "Your shears are ready. I'll get them as soon as we're inside." He unlocked the door, ushered Aanaris in and then waved to Mael.

Mael slipped past his father's broad shoulders and the eyes that bore into him. It felt more like entering a prison than a place to work and serve. He would serve this morning. After lunch, he'd go to the temple again.

The temple!—the dim possibility of escape. The priests shunned him, but they allowed him there, the singular bastion of power and authority that tolerated members of the underclass in Mooriman society. Though jaded by the escalating conflicts with the priests, the temple still offered Mael a ray of hope, illuminating a larger life that burned inside.

Mael stood before Elleth and the five other priests on the steep stairway to the Kirrinal temple. They towered above him. Standing straight and two steps above him in their long blue robes and their silver brocaded sky blue bonnets. The high priest stood in front of him.

"I don't understand why you make this so complicated, High Priest."

"You are too young to understand, Mael. We've been through this before."

"I'm capable of understanding anything that you can explain," Mael said, "but this doesn't make sense. It seems that you—all of you—would rather hold onto your way of life than hold to the noble truths. You, yourself, have said that the noble truths don't bow to tradition and the culture of the mankind."

Elleth's eyes narrowed. "Someday you'll appreciate the teachings more fully."

Mael shook his head. "If Mah'Eladra want all of the mankind to live out the Kirrinath, it can't require years of schooling to understand. Most of us will never have the luxury of such an education. We work for our bread, and honor Mah'Eladra by the sweat of our hands."

"How little you know—and you would teach us, Mael? It's taken us years to understand it so we can teach others what Mah'Eladra want."

"But what you are teaching—me and others—are simply rules that can't encompass the intent of the Kirrinath. The Kirrinath can't be reduced like this; it has to be lived out with wisdom—in the vorn—not from a rulebook. The evil intent of the mankind will find ways around any rule. Rules give the appearance of restraint, but are powerless to confine the unruly." Mael paused. The High priest clenched his jaw and glared.

"The mankind has proven over and over," Mael continued. "that they don't want to, and cannot live by, rules. No collection of them can guide us properly. They breed guilt and failed obedience, and you and the others, use that guilt to enslave us to your will and the will of Vishtoenvar."

Elleth's eyes stormed. "Are you saying that we don't teach the will of Mah'Eladra? Such impudence is born in ignorance—and arrogance. We only listen to Mah'Eladra."

"You hear Vishtoenvar, who desires only to enslave and master the mankind for his rebellion."

"You know nothing of Vishtoenvar!" Elleth said. "It's blasphemy to attribute the work of Mah'Eladra to him."

"I've met Vishtoenvar." Mael replied. "I've felt his chill. I've tasted his hatred as he conspires to master the mankind. He promises comfort and to help us, but works only to enslave those who do not serve Mah'Eladra fully."

Mael continued: "I feel his chill here. You hate me because I stand before you with truth. You haven't found fault in what I say, but you conspire against me. We've known each other long, yet still you won't listen."

"Vishtoenvar would not show himself to you!" Elleth replied.

"He has—and he does to you! You listen to his voice, yet speak to me of obedience to Mah'Eladra. Which is a greater blasphemy□"

Elleth stared at him as the muscles on the side of his jaw pulsed.

Mael knew he spoke truth, a truth so brutal that it could not be said with the compassion he desired. Years of struggling for compassion and patience had failed to change the conversation. His compassion remained through sheer stubbornness, but Elleth, and the priests that followed him, stood at the threshold of his patience.

Even so, Mael wasn't sure it was his place to deliver this message, but the words came from deep within, from a reserve that he knew must be from Mah'Eladra. Elleth and his acolytes glared silently at him.

Mael turned and walked down the steps. He knew, somehow, that his last words would catalyze a conspiracy against his life.

Three days passed—long weary days sharpening knives and truing scythe blades for the harvest. He forged a set of identical hooks for a Mooriman noble who would point out inconsistencies and demand reduced payment. Mael couldn't refuse by law. A large chandelier that his father had designed and forged for the entrance to the presidatory's palace had to be riveted together—tiring, tedious, but exacting labor.

A neighbor had split the edge of his felling ax when the handle broke and the head hit a stone. Removing and refitting a new steel edge into the head took most of one afternoon.

The rhythm of the huge double-chambered bellows, once the breath of life to Mael, felt more like a death rattle now—long wheezing breaths that kept the fire alive for another round of nails for the addition on the back of the town bakery.

He could do three nails in a heat: forge the point, cut the nail and drop it into the jig, four blows to square the head and repeat—five hundred times—three hours of tedium while his mind worked overtime on his frustration with the priests.

He hadn't been back to the temple. He hoped the extended hours in the smithy would alleviate his growing anger, but the rote work left his mind free to enlarge his vexation with this tiny, claustrophobic town while the huge, unexplored world surrounded it.

Who are you, Mael?

On the third night, he and fada worked late. "You've been working hard," Fada said as he locked the door to the smithy. "And no break for the temple?"

"I won't go there. I'm no longer welcome."

His father sighed. "It's your *life*, Mael. I see it in your eyes. I feel it in your vorn. You resonate to a vornal beat I have seen in few others. The smithy is work—but the temple is life to you."

Tears pushed up into his eyelids. "There has to be more," he said through clenched teeth. "Something bigger. Something more—real."

"Where would you go?" his father asked.

"I don't know," Mael said. Opening his mouth to speak clarified his thinking. "Tessamandria—Kinvara," he said. "I've heard the temple there is the greatest in all Tessa. Perhaps Vindor. Study at the school of Asha Vindor under the scholars there—Maybe to the stones of Ordrathan..."

"Then you should go." His father's whisper wavered.

"What?" Mael had heard it clearly, but wanted to hear it again.

"You should go."

"But how?"

"There are regular trade ships out of Farhantra to Moori-man. You know this. From there, there are routes to Horrinaine and south to Vindor."

"I meant, how can I leave you here—the family?"

"Koltar's an able smith. I can make him my apprentice until you return. We can make it work."

"What if I don't come back?"

His father smiled. "If we can make it work while you're gone, we can make it work if you stay gone."

Mael stared straight ahead, unable to speak further.

"I have watched you the last three days, Mael. You need to go. Mada spoke with me and she knows better than I that it's time. She's known a long time—since you were born. I didn't want to know, but I see it now."

They paused on the front step before opening the door to the house. Fada stepped forward and wrapped his arms around Mael, leaning into the hug with his chin above Mael's shoulder. "We would miss you," he said as he compressed the breath out of Mael's lungs.

Tears sprouted from Mael's eyes. He couldn't speak. He wrapped his arms around his father's chest and returned the squeeze. His breath rolled forth in the chilled night air. The stars danced before him. He had never felt this way in his life that he could remember. Fear sought to eclipse his elation but a deep resolve welled up to overwhelm both.

He fell into a fitful sleep that night, as he stared out his garret window into the infinity of the deep sky.

"Who are you, Mael?"

Someone shook Mael's arm. He struggled to open his eyes. Meekar's pale half-light, filtered by the trees outside his window, offered him barely enough to see.

Erolin hovered over him. "Mael...Mael!" She spoke close to his ear. The urgency of her voice brought him to full awareness.

"What time is it?" he said. "What are you doing here?"

She held her index finger over her lips. "Come with me!"

"Where?"

"No time! Get dressed—traveling clothes."

Mael swung his legs out of his blanket to the floor.

Erolin was dressed for the woods—a dark tunic with a hood—leather leggings and soft leather footwear bound up around her calves. Her belt carried a leather water pouch opposite her long knife in its leather sheath.

"Quickly! We're traveling light."

"Do I need anything else?"

"No time—come!" She leapt to the open window, and slipped through it onto the low roof over the chicken coop. Mael followed. She turned back to him with her finger over her lips. He nodded.

She dropped over the edge of the roof, landing silently on the ground, then grabbed her staff she'd left against the roof post and took his hand to lead him away from the house.

At the back gate to the goat pen, she stopped and crouched down, pulling him down and cupping her hands to his ear. "No time for goodbyes," she said as she pointed toward the front of the house. Shadow figures on horseback dismounted quietly. Mael counted six.

Erolin pulled him through the gate and closed it silently before moving into the shade of the lemon tree. She pointed up. Two shadows swept over them toward the house. Gulls! Mael felt the chill as they moved overhead. It vanished as they passed out of site.

Erolin started out toward the tree line into the woods. They moved quickly, like shadows in the scant light, their dark hooded tunics shielding them from eyes that hoped to catch him in his house.

When they reached the trees, Erolin pulled him into a copse of dense undergrowth and then turned, with her finger again to her lips. They crouched behind a rotted log and watched.

Torches flared. Voices drifted across the field—loud, angry voices. The torches were in the house now. His father yelled; his mother screamed. Chaos ensued. The torches entered his room in the garret.

"Who are they?" Mael whispered.

"Temple guards—and a couple priests." Erolin yanked him to his feet.

It had all happened so fast. Mael hadn't been aware of his senses, but now, plunging along in the darkness on Erolin's heels, he became suddenly aware of a vornal darkness that surrounded them.

Erolin stopped. Mael ran into her. "Do you feel it?" she asked.

Mael nodded. "What is it?"

"Messenger gulls!" Erolin waited as she caught her breath. "They're tracking us."

He shivered. "Ever felt it before?"

She nodded. "Many times."

"Where are we going?"

"I'm taking you to the portal."

"What□"

"To the portal. Elleth has ordered your arrest. It's time to leave."

Mael's mind reeled. "How far is it?" was all he could say.

"Two daysmarch."

"You know the way?"

"Several ways!"

"They have horses."

"We'll go where the horses can't!"

"What about the gulls?"

"We'll do the best we can."

They stuck to rocky backwoods trails, where horses couldn't follow. They waded up streams, to cover their passage. They climbed trees and leapt onto cliffs from the branches, tracing along the tops of rocky outcrops to find other trees, which they used to climb down.

Erolin paused frequently to listen, though Mael didn't know what she was trying to hear. She often tensed into high alert. Mael had never seen her like this: focused, aware and so quick to make decisions. That night, they slept in a shallow cave that she had found, with no fire.

"Mael," she said in the darkness, close beside him.

"I'm here."

"I'm afraid," she said. Her voice quivered.

"You? Afraid?"

"Yes."

Mael didn't know what to say. He had never seen Erolin fear anything.

"Mah'Eladra told me to bring you to the portal. There's a secret entrance that's unknown to the priests and they're guiding us there."

"Mah'Eladra⊓"

"Yes. I'm to see you safely into the portal—"

Mael waited in disbelief.

"I'll not be coming with you."

"No!"

"It has to be this way, Mael."

"You have to come!"

"I can't."

"Why?"

"The portals move to the will of Mah'Eladra. They've made it clear that I can't go with you. I've implored them. Since coming to Farhantra, you've been my life, Mael, and I want to go with you. But they won't allow it." Her voice wavered with emotion that Mael had never felt from her. In the utter darkness of the cave, he could see nothing. She sniffed.

"Why are you afraid?"

"I am going to die defending you into the portal."

"What⊓"

"We're in great danger, Mael. I won't escape."

Mael's mind reeled. "Are you afraid of death?"

"Yes." She said in a hushed whisper.

Mael sat stunned.

"...and no."

Mael shook his head.

"Mah'Eladra have been good to me, Mael, and I don't fear the infinite, or to climb the golden stair into the deep sky—but the violence of dying at the hands of the priests..."

"We don't have to do this."

"We do. You have to go into that portal and you must do it alone."

"We don't have to do this *now*. We can hide until it's safe."

"No Mael, there's an appointed time."

Mael's mind raced. Emotions flooded through him.

"I love you, Mael." It was barely a whisper. "I have since you were born."

"Why are you telling me this now?"

"So that you know. I cannot bear the thought that you might not know."

Tears sprouted in his eyes and rolled down his cheeks. He reached out and groped for her hand. When he touched it, she pulled it back.

He had always loved Erolin in a way that was genuine, not selfish, but never thought to tell her. "I—I—" Why couldn't he say it?

She sat quietly in the darkness. He could see nothing, but her felt her nearness.

"I—have always loved you too." He stammered a whisper.

"I know."

They sat for a long time without words.

"We have to sleep," she said. "Tomorrow's another long day."

She said nothing more.

Mael couldn't will himself to sleep. He lay for a long time on the leaves they'd brought into the cave. He wanted to touch her—He was afraid to touch her. The slow, rhythmic breath of her sound sleep filled the darkness. He didn't remember falling asleep.

Water dripping from the vines that hung from the brow of the cave woke Mael from his fitful sleep. Erolin sat in front of him. "Eat," she said as she handed him a dry biscuit. "And drink." The water skin was in her left hand. "We have to hurry."

Any emotion from the conversation in the dark was gone, or perhaps hidden behind the mask of her role in his life.

"How far today?"

"A full day," she said between bites on her biscuit, "but tonight we can rest if we make our goal."

"Our goal?"

"Come, we have to go." She stood up and shouldered her pack.

Mael glanced out as he stood up. A drizzling fog obscured the view beyond ten paces.

"A good day for traveling," Erolin said. "The woods are wet and protected by the fog. The gulls won't be able to track us. Come."

Mael slogged along behind her as she pressed through the woods. It wasn't long before he was soaked. His teeth chattered from the shivering. He wasn't convinced that this portal idea was good, especially in light of the revelation the night before. His mind burned with a strange understanding that he had never felt.

He wasn't ready to leave. He'd made no farewell to his family, fada especially. He knew somehow that both fada and mada would understand his leaving, but his sudden disappearance wasn't the way it should have happened.

New feelings for Erolin twisted through his thoughts—feelings he had never had before, but restrained by her opaque stride as she walked in front of him, pausing now and then to make decisions on their path.

With odd turns—ups and downs, they twisted through wet thickets that tore at his clothes and made him wetter and colder.

They paused for a quick lunch. Erolin offered no crack in her veneer. Late in the afternoon, the clouds pulled away and the slanted rays of Asolara warmed the air as they filtered through the canopy.

They pushed through a thick growth of bushes covered with plump red berries he had never seen before. "Don't touch the fruit," Erolin said.

They emerged from the berried bushes into a stand of slender trees, each the thickness of three hands, and perfectly straight as they towered up to a dense green canopy ten paces above them.

The ground in front of them sloped down for about fifteen paces and ended at the edge of a pond. The surface of the water was as flat as glass and reflected the trees on the other side like a mirror.

Just before the water, the land leveled and cleared. A small ring of stones graced the center of a clearing with a fire burning in it. To the side was a neat stack of firewood.

Erolin led him to the fire and sat down, pointing beside her for him to join her.

"What is this place?" he whispered as he sat down on the moss in front of the fire. "And how is the fire burning? Were we expected?"

Erolin nodded. "We were."

Mael shook his head.

"This is the Shihou Margah, Mael."

"Margah□"

Erolin nodded.

"Like the Grand Elia Margah in the Crown?"

"Well—in concept yes," Erolin smiled, "but hardly the same scale."

"So what is it then?"

"There are many margahs, Mael. This is a small one. They're hidden around Tessalindria—refuges for the Eladra in their work. Most of the Mankind don't know they exist. Most of the Mankind are forbidden to enter them."

"But we can?"

"We have been given permission."

"By whom?"

"The Eladra."

Mael followed her eyes into the fire. "The Eladra are real? They're still here today?"

"Very real and very present."

Mael's mind raced to Erolin's assertion. He wondered why, if what she said was true, that he had never seen one. He feared asking more. He knew the legends of the Eladra: the servants of Mah'Eladra who had filled Tessa with wonders for the mankind to enjoy. He knew the stories of Vishtoenvar's rebellion, and the scorching of the NarEl waste, but he never assumed the Eladra were still present.

"We're safe here," Erolin intruded into his thoughts. "The priests that chase us are forbidden. We can sleep in peace. We have food, and the fire to warm us."

Mael looked around. The mirror lake was only five paces from them. "It's beautiful," he said.

Erolin nodded. "We're forbidden to touch the water—or to drink it or to eat any of the fruit in the margah. Those are the only restrictions we have."

"Why?"

"It just is, Mael. It's this way in all the Margahs."

They fell silent again.

"Is the portal nearby?" he said after a time.

"Very near."

She leaned forward and opened her pack, drawing out her last bits of food: two small raisin cakes, an apple and two small dried fish wrapped in a piece of linen. As she spread out the linen, another apple appeared with two small glasses, already filled with an amber liquid.

Mael startled. "How did you do that?"

Erolin ignored his question and handed him one of the glasses. She took the other into her own hand, and raised it in a toast. She smiled as the glasses clinked together. "To life and all that it means."

"To life," Mael echoed as he sipped the liquid. It rolled like gold over his tongue, a strong, smooth aromatic that burned as it coursed down his throat. He felt it all the way down into his stomach and suddenly felt the effect on his vorn. His mind cleared. The aromas of the moss and trees intensified into a hyper-sense. "What is it?" he said.

"Amberviol," she said.

Mael took another sip.

"It's an ancient gift to the mankind from the Eladra, to sharpen the mind and senses in the times of great stress...like today."

They stared into the fire, sipping the strange elixir until it was gone from both glasses. Mael tingled. The subtle sounds of the fire heightened and the wind in the trees made it feel as if they were talking. He looked at Erolin. Every strand of hair and each small detail of her face stood out against waning light of the day and the fire. The grayness of her eyes sparkled. She looked up.

"What?" she asked.

"About last night..."

An odd hiss on the other side of the fire arrested his intended words. A giant materialized from the hiss. Erolin stood up. Mael jumped to his feet.

"Welcome to Shihou, Mael, son of Dilarna."

The huge warrior's hair fell like gold over his shoulders. Burnished greaves adorned his shins and his forearms bore gleaming bronze bracers. Leather armor shrouded his torso and loins, and his belt bore a scabbard housing a short sword with an ornate silver hilt across his right hip.

Mael stepped in front of Erolin.

The giant sat down. Erolin grabbed Mael's arm and pulled him back. "This is Vishtalar, Mael. Your guardian."

"Guardian?"

"Sit down, Mael." Erolin reseated herself on the moss.

Mael sat down.

"Vishtalar has been your guardian from the beginning, though you have never seen him."

"Eladrim?"

Erolin nodded.

"Since the beginning? Like when I was born?"

Vishtalar smiled. "Since before you were born."

"When I was imprisoned for not making that dagger for the Mooriman Highborn?"

Vishtalar nodded. "It could have been a lot worse."

Mael's hand involuntarily moved to the scar across his right cheek. He held up his right hand. "When they took me to work in the quarry or when they crushed my hand?"

"They would have done more. I restrained their abuse."

Mael stared at the giant.

"Erolin has told you about your journey?"

"Some."

"Do not fear, Mael."

Mael stared into the fire. "I am trying. There's a lot to fear."

Erolin stirred. "I told him what I know."

"I know," Vishtalar said.

"Does it have to be this way?" Mael said. His voice trembled.

The giant nodded.

"I'm not ready."

"Readiness is not a requirement."

"Will you let Erolin die?"

"That is not my province."

Erolin looked up at Mael and shook her head as if to say 'don't ask that question.'

"Are we truly safe here?"

"In the Shihou Margah, you are beyond the reach of any evil. You should rest now. Tomorrow is not far ahead. I will be with you."

Vishtalar vanished with a hiss.

Mael still felt the heightened effects of the Amberviol. "How long does this feeling last?" he asked

Erolin smiled. "A while. You'll still feel it tomorrow."

"About last night..." Mael said.

"I should not have said those things," Erolin said as she stared into the fire.

"But you did."

"Yes and it's true—but I cannot talk of it further at this time. We need rest for tomorrow. We're safe here. Sleep now. In the morning you'll go through the portal."

"Erolin—" The rest of the sentence stalled in Mael's mouth. He looked down and shook his head as he reached for one of the raisin cakes. "Thanks for the food—and the Amberviol," he said.

Chapter Two

PORTAL

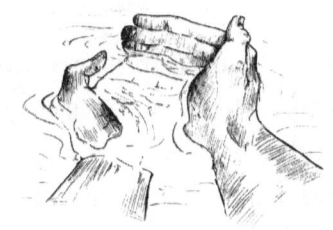

"The purposes of Mah'Eladra are clarified in waiting."
The Essences of Corritanean Wisdom
Hispattea

Dawn came quickly in the margah. No bird song graced its appearance. No breeze moved the branches of the trees. It seemed as if the world had stopped.

Erolin divided what was left of the food and they ate in silence.

The circumstances trapped Mael's mind in an endless loop of futile thoughts: His own journey, Vishtalar's role in his life, Erolin's death, images of the portal...all coursing randomly through the pathways of his mind.

Who are you, Mael?

Erolin stood up. "It's time." She offered Mael her hand. She pulled him to his feet as if he weighed nothing. "The portal is over here," she said.

Mael followed as she moved up the slope to the right. She left everything behind except her staff and her sheathed knife.

She led him about twenty paces to a small dip in ground, nestled into the woods. "Here," she said.

At the bottom of the dip, a small square opening lay between two boulders, shrouded with moss that had been undisturbed for years. "I'll go first," she said into his ear. "You follow. No talking."

She entered feet first, squirming into the small opening and dragging her staff behind her. When she'd disappeared, Mael sat down and imitated her entrance.

By the time he had worked his way in, Erolin was holding some sort of greenish light that barely illuminated the cave. The ceiling was low, but they could almost stand up. She held her finger to her lips. Mael nodded.

They crept along in the near darkness. At one point, Erolin stopped and cupped her hands over his ear. "Around the next corner—the portal. Quiet."

Mael followed closely as she crept into the vaulted chamber. She stood up. As she did so, torches flared and they both shielded their eyes from the sudden light.

"We were expecting you." The unmistakable graveled voice of the High Priest.

Erolin stepped in front of Mael. "And we you," she said.

"The protection of the Margah doesn't extend here," said the High Priest.

"The protection of Mah'Eladra is everywhere," Erolin countered.

Mael's eyes were adjusting to the light and he dropped his arm. A pace behind him, a vale of smoky, black ink, restrained by some unknown force into a vertical wall, twitched in the torchlight.

The High Priest stood in front of them in his thick, blue robe. The polished silver of his headdress gleamed orange in the glow of the torches. The drawn sword in his hand crossed down in front of his knees—tense—like a drawn bowstring waiting to loose an arrow. Mael studied the scowl on his face.

Behind the High Priest stood four more Kirrinal priests, their hands gripping swords that pointed down at the stone floor, all dressed in their full priestly regalia. Readiness glinted in their eyes below their blue and white turbans. Four temple guards stood behind them. Burnished helmets gleamed in the light from the torches they held. Their dark, vacant eyes betrayed willing obedience to the slightest utterance from the High Priest.

Erolin stood slightly in front of Mael, her staff ready in both hands, with the stout end protectively angled in front of his chest.

"If you enter the portal you'll die," the High Priest said.

A subtle indignation mixed with fear flooded Mael as the priest spoke—then a sudden strengthening of resolve to stand against his hypocrisy. "Should I prefer to face death by your sword, Elleth?"

The priest's eyes narrowed. "You know the legends, Mael. You've blasphemed the gods. Your death in the portal will be eternal and painful in the hands of Mah'Eladra. If you die by my sword, your narmatan will be released and you will only face oblivion. If you live, you know that no one will listen to a disfigured son of an Otallan dog!"

The black nothingness of the portal shifted behind Mael. Legends of the inky surface spoke of cold terror for those who entered; passage to an unknown place and time. To Mael, the blackness warmed his back in spite of his fear.

"He lies," Erolin said through her teeth. "I've been through the portal. It's not death, even for those who are imperfect."

The priest's eyes stormed. "She's the liar, Mael. She's been lying to you since birth. You know that. We all know that. She pretends to be a Pistisine Guardian, but has no education. No knowledge. She'll die with you for her impudence and then, what will either of you gain?"

Mael shuddered at the words as the fear swept over him again—the fear of death—cold and empty.

The priest tossed his head to one side. The other priests spun their swords up into attack position as the High Priest slowly lifted his sword up in front of his eyes. "You have such potential, Mael." He examined the blade. His dark eyes glittered with anger as they coursed along its edges. "You'd be a valuable addition to the temple, if you'd renounce the foolishness she's used to ensnare you. We wouldn't have pursued you, if we didn't think it worthwhile to rescue you. Your stubbornness is pitiful!

"Now you have a choice—" The priest peered past his blade into Mael's eyes. "Reject her and join us—throw yourself into the infinite torture of the portal—or die by my sword."

Mael stared back. His vorn, deep in his core, ached for those of the priests. It could be so much more beautiful. He ached more so for the guard's excusable ignorance. He hurt for Erolin, for he knew her fate, and none of the three options would avoid that.

Death from the priests' swords would end his life, but there was more to learn—something else he had to do. Joining in the hypocrisy of the Kirrinal temple worship, even in the hope to help them change, was futile. The priest had given himself into the service of Vishtoenvar to a depth from which there was no escape. The unknown of the portal was the only path out.

The priest's voice chilled. "Choose the manner of your death, blasphemer!"

The words rose up, almost against Mael's will: "I choose life!"

The priest moved fast, but Erolin was an instant ahead of him. His descending blade severed her staff at the thick end, glancing far enough to the right that its tip only slit Mael's right palm on the way down. The other priests moved in behind him, four swords arching down on Erolin who shouted, "Go, Mael!" She stepped in front of him.

Mael reached out, grabbed the back of Erolin's tunic and sprang back into the warm darkness. His last memory of his beloved mentor was her fall under the descending blades of the priests. He was not fast enough to avoid one last thrust from a sword that pierced her body and then ran through his left hand. He let go and yanked his hand off the sword as he stepped farther back. All sound and light disappeared. Pain flooded over him as he stumbled backward in the utter nothingness of the portal.

Three—four—five steps back—he tripped on something and lost his balance. He expected to fall hard onto the rough, stone floor, but it vanished beneath him. He cried out as he fell into the darkness that swallowed his voice, somersaulting out of control into a soundless abyss.

Elleth's eyes fell to the task of wiping the blood off his sword with the hem of his robe. The blood on the thick, blue wool angered him. *By the throne of Vishtoenvar* . . . In front of him, crumpled and bloodied on the floor, lay the charlatan Pistisine, slaughtered by the other priests. He turned to them as they wiped down their own swords.

"We're rid of her, Highness," said Tanar without looking up from his task.

"You were supposed to slay *him*, not her!"

"We tried, highness. *You* tried—she was in the way."

"We should never have let him get here."

"I think your first stroke injured him, highness."

"Injury wasn't the objective," Elleth said. "The master wanted him dead."

"I don't understand why Vishtoenvar didn't just kill him when he had the chance," Arth said.

"Vishtoenvar has some arrangement with Mah'Eladra, even as he denies they exist. He speaks in riddles when I'm with him; vagaries and fragments that I don't understand—he never gives me details."

The priests sheathed their swords and straightened their bloodstained robes.

"Why was Mael so important that all five of us had to come after him?" Dargan said.

Elleth let out a deep breath as his scowl deepened. "Vishtoenvar wanted to be sure we ended it."

"What happens now?" Arth said.

Elleth shook his head. "Let's go." He turned to the captain of the guards. "How do we get out of here?"

The captain saluted. "Follow me, Highness."

"What about the woman?" Arth paused over the bloodied corpse in front of him.

Elleth's eyes narrowed. "Throw her into the portal!" he said as he turned to look at the captain.

The captain lowered his eyes. "She should be burned in Eshen, Highness."

Elleth's eyes flooded red. "She's a blasphemer. She deserves no such honor."

"If you wish to treat her like this, do it yourself."

"You defy me?"

"With all respect, Highness, it's *your* teaching that requires Eshen for any of the mankind. If you want her thrown into the portal, do it yourself."

"It's forbidden that a priest of Kirrinal should touch a person so dishonored in death. Her blood would defile me." Elleth stared into the captain's eyes.

The captain remained unmoved. "Her blood covers your robes."

"The blood of the sword doesn't defile us. The blood of her flesh would. Into the portal!"

Their eyes locked for a long moment.

"I'll report this to the commander, captain. You know your disobedience to the will of a Kirrinal high priest won't bode well for you."

The captain didn't move.

"Do I have to cross swords with you?" Elleth said as he reached for his blade.

The captain's eyes fell in disgust. He nodded his head to the other guards. "Into the portal!"

The three other guards stepped forward. They stooped over Erolin's remains and took hold of her clothing, trying to avoid touching her flesh. Their hesitance showed their distaste.

With two swings, they tossed her into the dark wall. The darkness roiled as wispy fingers of black shot out and wrapped themselves around the ankles and wrists of the guards. They called out in panic, scrambling back from the portal. The wisps retracted into the wall, which writhed momentarily before calming into the sooty edifice it had been when they arrived.

The guards trembled as they moved back from the darkness, wiping defiled hands on the backs of their leggings.

The woman's severed right hand lay near the edge of the blackness. "That too," Elleth said.

The captain scowled, took two steps forward and sent the hand into the black wall with his boot. The wall swallowed it without a sound.

Elleth looked up. "Well done, Captain. Well done. You'll find that it's much simpler this way."

The captain scowled as he turned to the passage leading away from the portal. "Follow me, Highness."

Elleth stood alone in the sanctuary of the Kirrinal Temple. He liked the elliptical shape, and the high vaulted ceiling with a circle of windows around the base of the arched roof. His eyes moved down from the intricately painted ceiling to the narrow balcony that circled the room. Thirty stone columns rose from the polished floor to support the balcony with room behind each for three men to walk abreast. A large eight-pointed star in a blood-red stone adorned the center of the polished, gray marble floor.

He shivered in the cold breeze. It was always so, even in the hottest part of the summer. The air moved as if it were sweeping in from the ends and exiting the ceiling above, but he had never found any openings beside the ornate double door at one end of the ellipse.

Vishtoenvar had summoned him here as he entered the city. He had been riding all night and still wore his blood-stained robe. He stood on the center of the red star and waited. That was the protocol.

He tumbled the anticipated conversation through his mind, rationalizing answers and his defense of any possible attack from the dark Lord. It was delicate business and fraught with pitfalls as these conversations always were.

The light shifted as Vishtoenvar entered the room. Elleth had no understanding of how this happened, but his presence was undeniable. He didn't speak—protocol.

The wraith appeared like a vague shadow as he descended to the floor and snaked through the columns—cold smoke that left a chill with no odor. "Tell me how you fared with the young Mael."

The hiss came from behind Elleth and raised the hair on the back of his neck. He dared not look.

"Oh lord, you know these things."

"Speak, priest. Use *your* words." The voice penetrated him, close and cold.

Elleth shuddered. "He escaped Farhantra with the help of the charlatan."

"I warned you about her."

"Yes. We underestimated her treachery."

"Your pride clouded your judgment. Do you think I warned you to no purpose?" The gray mist twisted twice around Elleth and paused just in front of him, almost materializing as it posed the question. Elleth looked up and it vanished backward away from him "Answer me!" The command lingered in the air before him.

"You warned me Lord. You did."

"And you didn't move to intercept them?" The voice descended from the dome above Elleth, moving backward as it whispered.

"We did—I did—with four other priests and four temple guards."

"And?"

"They escaped into the woods. The charlatan knew paths where the horses couldn't follow. We tracked them with messenger gulls and the soldiers and horses followed us."

"But you didn't catch them!" What should have been a question was whispered as a statement from somewhere in the colonnade to his left.

"We didn't catch them."

The wraith moved more slowly, circling and coming in closer with each turn. The traces of mist touched Elleth's hands and ruffled his robe. He tried not to flinch.

"We guarded the two entrances to the caves that we knew about. They got in somewhere else."

"Did you find out where?"

"We are searching for it. The woman must have known."

Vishtoenvar wrapped around him closely, then suddenly pulled away. "You don't know that they entered the portal?"

"No. We *are* sure. I saw Mael enter, but we cut down the charlatan as she defended him. My sword cut his hand. Arth may have injured him also."

The wraith spiraled upward toward the high vault. "And the Pistisine, what happened to her body?"

Elleth trembled. "We threw it into the portal."

All motion stopped. It was as if the lord had left the temple, but Elleth wasn't sure. He held his breath.

A sudden downward blast of the wraith's presence forced him to his knees. "Fool!" The voice thundered from all sides at once as if the entire temple had shouted it. Elleth dropped his head and covered his ears with his palms, waiting for a physical blow that never came. Vishtoenvar disappeared without explanation; no direction; only the empty fear of disappointing the one who kept him in power, and the vague sense that the matter wasn't finished.

As suddenly as he fell, Mael stood again on solid stone. The queasy feeling of free-fall vanished, but it was still dark and quiet beyond his experience. He stomped his foot. The shock rippled up his leg without sound. He waved his hand in front of his face. Nothing. He touched his cheek, with fingers sticky from the gash across his right palm.

His left hand throbbed as the blood dripped from his fingers. He still felt the coarse texture of Erolin's tunic. Tears streamed down his face into the darkness.

He knelt down to avoid the risk of falling again and inched forward, patting his hands along the unseen floor in front of him.

They ached from the injuries but he knew no other way to navigate the unknown before him.

After about five paces, the air changed on his hands and then his face as he emerged into a more ordinary darkness. He could hear again, but there was still no sound. He breathed deeply to stabilize his feelings. "Hello?" His voice reverberated off close walls—a small chamber—or perhaps a corridor.

He sat down on the stone floor, and tucked his hands into the folds of his tunic under his armpits. They needed attention. He had to do something—perhaps he had to do nothing. The clear voice of armatan spoke in his vorn, that deep inner composite that formed the core of every Tessalindrian. "Wait, Mael. What happened was not an accident. The purposes of Mah'Eladra are found in waiting."

Erolin's image filled his mind. She was ready. Her death had been swift at the hands of the High Priest and the temple guards, perhaps not even long enough to recognize the pain of it. Her sacrifice meant something to history, but Mael sensed it only vaguely, a ghostly image through smoky glass.

She had served him and his family since before he was born, but she never spoke of her purpose nor the reason for her presence. Her selflessness had taught him truths and showed him paths that he would never have seen without her and it saved his life in this one, final heroic action.

Her death was now far in his past, or perhaps deep in his future, possibly removed from him by millennia in either direction, and by some distance—some place on the other side of the world. More tears wet his cheeks from the imagery of her last moments.

Mael waited. He pinched the skin of his hands together to stop the flow of blood, but his shallow breath and the dizziness told him he was weak from its loss.

The sensory deprivation of his tomb heighted his awareness. The first slight sound brought him to full attention—a small scrape, somewhere to his left—several light taps, as if someone were on the far side of a solid stone wall. Another scrape and more taps, then a sudden grinding that lasted but a moment—another grind and then a faint light opened into the darkness.

Mael rose carefully. He shuffled toward the light. The light was darkness beyond the crack, but even Tessalindria's night was bright compared to the darkness of the portal and this tomb.

With a sudden burst of motion and grinding stone, a doorway opened before him.

"Mael! Come!" Vishtalar!

Fresh air from outside washed over him as he moved forward. "Come! Quickly!"

He paused at the narrow opening. Vishtalar took his wrist and yanked him through. The opening ground closed behind him. He whirled to look. A round stone, the thickness of the length of his forearm and taller than he was, rolled back over the opening and sealed it shut against the solid rock behind it.

Vishtalar took his shoulders in his hands and looked down into his eyes. "You are safe now, Mael. And you are here." He smiled before dropping his hands. "I must go, but I am nearby."

"Wait! Where am I? And when?"

"You are *here*, Mael! Now!"

"What happened to—" The giant smiled and vanished with a hiss, leaving him alone in the night with many unanswered questions and an unbearable grief. He wept for Erolin. He wept for his loneliness. He had never been so alone in all his life.

The tears subsided after a time and he looked up. Thin tree limbs snaked over him occluding most of the sky, but Tal hung low over the horizon. A white gravel path glimmered in the darkness, and led to where he might see the sky. The stars would tell him where he was.

In twenty paces, the path rose and he came into an opening. He was in a garden, but stood where the shadows of low buildings that surrounded it and the short trees occluded the horizon. In spite of the thin crescent of Tal's light overhead—wait! It wasn't Tal. Its light was more yellow and the markings on its surface weren't the same. It was larger, and not as bright.

His eyes roved to the stars—thousands of stars, all different in brightness, points of light that spangled the sky with their glory, but it was all different—no familiar patterns. He looked for Elgatora. They were nowhere to be seen. Without Elgatora, Vitorinda should be visible with his spear—or Allizar. If he couldn't see Nolaran in the turtle's leg he should be able to see the Hellscor ring...

Nothing! *Where* was now the greater mystery. *When* remained opaque.

A small grassy area to his left offered him a place to sit and wait. His mind roiled with questions. It took discipline and courage to wait when every thought called for action.

He sat cross-legged in the cool grass, and leaned forward with his elbows on his knees to think. As he dropped his chin into his palms, he gasped as his short thick beard stabbed at his wounds. He looked more carefully in the faint light. The wounds weren't bleeding but his heart pulsed under the painful, half-dried furrows in his skin.

The skin of his right palm had been sliced by the priest's sword from the base of his thumb to his little finger. Dark sticky blood smeared over the rest of his skin, and it was tender.

Blood still oozed from the puncture through his left hand, and it ached terribly. He licked the back of his hand, gently cleaning the backside of the wound from the outside edges with the softness of his tongue. Clean water would be best, but...

Clean Water! His mind leapt to the intense thirst as the sound of running water invaded his awareness. He stood and moved toward it.

A trough of wood carried a flow of water from the base of a low hill until it fell into a shallow pool carved into a wide flat stone. It

ran over the far edge of the stone and disappeared into a bed
of white gravel.

Mael fell to his knees in the gravel to get a drink where the
water dropped off the stone. His thirst raged and he gulped
the water. *Slowly*, he reminded himself as he swallowed several
times. He could drink more, shortly. He pushed his hands gently
into the cool water and then jerked them out as the water
flowed over the wounds. He pushed them back into the flow
again—past the pain, rubbing them gently to loosen the dried
blood.

"What are you doing?"

Mael startled, standing quickly and turning to face the voice
three paces behind him.

The man stiffened. "Master?" The man's surprise was shaded
from any light by the hood of his robe that fell from his shoulders nearly to the ground, loosely bound about the waist with
a cord. He carried a short rake and a hand shovel.

"I was just getting a drink—and washing my wounds. I am
master of nothing—no one," Mael said.

The man's shoulders relaxed. "You're defiling the pool with
your blood!" he said as he looked down at Mael's hands.

"I was catching only the water that flowed over the edge."

"Where're you from?"

"From Farhantra—on the east coast of Morlan, on the Vorsian Sea."

The man moved the shovel into the hand that held the rake
and reached up, pulling back his hood. The shock of gray hair
like a lion's mane descended into a full beard. His eyes remained
shaded by his thick eyebrows. "What's your name?"

"Mael."

"Mael..." The old man processed the name. "I'm Klopas.
That's an unusual name. I mistook you for someone else."

"It's my childname, given me by my mentor when I was young." Memories of Erolin flashed in front of him again. He gritted his teeth to force them back.

Klopas nodded and pursed his lips. The details of his face became clearer as he stepped toward Mael, weathered with years, with deep creases from his nose down around his chin. He was tall, more like an Eladrim warrior than a man. "May I see your wounds?"

Mael startled. Klopas's lips didn't move with the sound of his words. "What is this place?" Mael asked.

"The garden of the dead—where we bury those who die." The sound was clearly coming from his lips, but the lips formed something else. "I'm the gardener." He waved the shovel and rake to indicate the surroundings.

"It's a beautiful garden," Mael said.

"I keep it so."

They stared at one another. The eerie feeling that something was wrong flooded over Mael's vorn. Klopas was the first contact out of the portal. It couldn't be accidental. Nothing was accidental, but something was off.

Mael offered his hands to Klopas. "I was injured by a priest," he said. "This hand is just a gash—but the sword went all the way through this one."

Klopas laid down his tools and stood to full height. "May I?" he asked as he gestured to see the wounds up close.

Mael nodded. Klopas leaned in for a closer look and straightened the fingers of Mael's left hand. He stood up straight and looked into Mael's eyes. He was closer now and still holding Mael's fingers. "A priest did this?"

Mael was now sure that his lips had said something other than what he heard. Mael nodded. "The wound, yes. The crooked fingers are from several years ago."

Klopas muttered an epithet that Mael didn't understand. "Sometimes they're worse than the soldiers," he said.

Klopas looked down again and probed the palms of Mael's hands gently before he looked up into his eyes. "What work do you do?"

"I'm a blacksmith and a farrier—like my father."

"We need to find the healer," Klopas said as he shook his head, "or you may never smith again."

"The healer?"

Klopas dropped Mael's hand and stooped to pick up his tools. "There are many doctors in the city, but none are like the healer," he said as he turned away. "Come. He's often in the garden east of the city when Asolara rises."

Mael hesitated. His thirst rose up before him again. "May I get another drink first?"

Klopas stopped and faced him before nodding to the stone.

Mael knelt and took several more swallows from the flow. He would need more, but it could wait.

Chapter Three

MASTER

"By all accounts, he was an ugly man."

The Antharan Lie
Ontalar

Cleopas made his way through the market, leading Mael north around the fortress and out the northern gate of the city. Mael labored to keep up behind him. "You're limping," Cleopas said.

"Yes."

Cleopas stopped and turned. Mael looked up into his eyes. It was a bit lighter now and Cleopas could see Mael's face more clearly. His left eye didn't focus where it should. It drooped down awkwardly, similar to the master, but it was the master's right eye that was lazy. "I can walk slower, if you like. I didn't know ..." He glanced down at Mael's feet.

"It's an old injury from a quarry when I had to labor there," Mael said.

Cleopas nodded.

"We couldn't afford the better doctors."

Cleopas turned and walked more slowly. Mael strode up beside him.

"I figured a farrier smith would be honored," Cleopas said, "that he would make a good living."

"My father is a free-slave. He was a Mooriman slave, but he was freed when he married my mother and helped colonize Farhantra."

Cleopas had never heard of these places. "A free-slave?"

"He is free to practice his trade, but has few other rights. My father begged his wealthy patrons for help with my foot—the ones who brought him their horses for shoeing. They laughed. Our friend Hannorah did the best she could, but my foot never healed properly."

"How old were you?"

"Twelve."

"Perhaps the healer can help."

Cleopas explained that if the healer were in the garden, he would most likely be in his favorite spot, under the olive trees where the eastern and southern walls formed the corner. They were almost there.

Cleopas stopped. "When you see the master—the healer—you must be prepared. He's not like any other you've ever met."

"In what way?"

"You'll see." Cleopas stared into Mael's eyes. "He'll look through you, but only in kindness, as if he sees only your soul."

Cleopas paused, wondering if he should continue. There was something about Mael's face and eyes that were different. Everyone's face and eyes are different, of course, but this was different in a peculiar way that made him seem not human. In the light, he noticed that when Mael spoke, his mouth appeared to form different words than he heard.

"Hannorah, in Farhantra, was like that," Mael said, "an old friend of the family."

"Well," Cleopas continued. "The master isn't one that you would be attracted to naturally."

"In what way?'

"You'll see. Don't shy from him. He's an extraordinary soul." Cleopas turned to lead the last few steps. "Come."

Mael followed a step behind Klopas. As they came around a corner in the neat gravel pathway, Klopas stopped and straightened his arm in front of him. He nodded up the slight rise toward the large twisted tree in the corner of the garden.

On a small stone bench sat a solitary figure, back straight, both legs comfortably off the bench with both feet planted on the ground. His hands rested on his knees, palms up, his head erect, and his eyes staring in front of him. He wore a gray robe that fell down below his knees. His unkempt hair, too short to hang naturally, tousled in all directions. Mael couldn't see his face because of the gathering brightness above the garden wall behind him.

Klopas raised his index finger to his lips.

They waited.

Nothing moved—no wind, no birdsong—no leaf stirred. Everything waited. For what?

"Come, Mael." The man turned to look straight at him. The dry, raspy voice commanded his attention. "Come sit with me. I've been waiting for you."

Klopas shifted uncomfortably and lowered his arm, staring at the man in surprise.

"Klopas, my friend. Leave us for a time."

Klopas nodded. "As you wish." He took several steps back before turning and vanishing around the bushes that hid the path.

"Come, Mael," the healer said. "We won't be alone for long."

Mael walked slowly toward the healer, who took his hands from his knees and shifted his body to the right to make room for Mael to sit beside him.

The healer waited until Mael sat down. Mael breathed deeply and waited.

"You've come a long way to be here," the healer said. "And I've eagerly awaited this time."

Mael stared straight ahead.

"Look at me, Mael."

Mael turned to look into the man's eyes for the first time. He shuddered. His left eye drooped and didn't focus at Mael. A scar across his right cheek dropped down to interrupt his beard. He smiled. One of his front teeth was missing.

"I am Ransom," the man said.

Mael wanted to look down, but couldn't. "Ransom," he echoed. "I've heard that name—in the ancient histories."

"You're here so you can learn its meaning."

"You know where I'm from?"

"You came through the Kana Portal on Tessalindria, to be with me in these last days."

"Last days?"

"You will learn." Ransom paused.

Mael waited.

"Let me see your hands."

Mael turned his hands palm up. Ransom reached out his left hand and cradled Mael's right in it. With his right index finger, he wiped a tear from his eye and then traced a small circle around the wound in the dried blood. Ransom sniffed and Mael looked up. More tears were running down his cheeks. He wiped them with his finger again and again stroked the wound. Mael watched the wound close up. It burned for a second, all the pain focused into that instant. A deep purple scar was all that remained.

"The other ..." Ransom rasped and sniffed through his tears.

Mael moved his left hand into Ransom's left. Ransom sniffed again and wiped his tears with his finger. This time, he approached the wound directly and plunged his wetted finger into the hole in Mael's hand.

Mael gasped and tried to pull it away, but Ransom's grip was unbreakable. The pain shot up his arm and tears leapt to his eyes. When Ransom pulled his finger out of the wound, it closed behind it, leaving the same purple scar. All pain was gone. Ransom held his hand immovable.

Mael shook. He looked up into Ransom's eyes.

"May you never join with one who would do this to a brother." The husky voice swelled with passion and power. Ransom dropped his hand and stared out over the garden.

"The mankind is ever cruel. Brother against brother in jealousy, anger, selfishness, war, fear, envy and resentment. It must never be this way with you, Mael. You'll suffer, as I will, but it is not your place to exact the justice of Mah'Eladra. Each will face that in their time."

Mael watched his lips. He spoke true. There was no shifting as with Klopas. Ransom knew Mael's language and issued it flawlessly.

Ransom turned to him. His eyes bore deep. "You are called to something much larger than this, Mael." Still the eyes held. The overwhelming weight of complete bonding with Ransom pressed on his vorn. The tears formed and flowed, but he could not turn his eyes away.

"You must leave your world behind, Mael. Leave its sadness and pain."

"I don't know if I want to. I didn't want to come here. My family is there. I lost my best friend. I don't even know where I am." A wave of despair punctuated his last sentence.

Ransom's face softened. "I know." His eyes bore into Mael. "You'll find healing here with us, Mael, and make new friends. But now, Asolara rises, and there will be others seeking me. Come."

Ransom dropped his hand and rose, as if he knew what was about to happen. Two men ran up the path and burst around the corner of the bushes that had occluded them. They stopped short when they saw Ransom standing. Mael remained seated on the bench. "Master," one of them said, his eyes shifting back and forth between Mael and Ransom. "We've been looking for you."

"You knew I would be here, Bieter."

"Everyone is waiting, Master."

"The crowds can wait. I want you to meet a new friend." Ransom turned to look down at Mael while the other two stared at him. "Mael, this is Bieter and Chiahn. They are brothers, if you notice. Chiahn, Bieter—this is Mael."

Mael rose as the two approached him. They each shook his hand, astonishment never leaving their eyes. His hand tingled from the freshly healed wound as their strong, scarred hands gripped his. Both were huge men; Bieter the larger of the two.

"Take him with you Chiahn. Mael has come a long way and the journey has been painful. Find him some water for his thirst and give him breakfast. Introduce him to the brothers. Show him the city. Though he is from far away, each of you shall treat him as a fellow Serealite. The table where you eat is shared with him. Where you go, he goes with you. You will understand in time."

Chiahn nodded. "Come," he said as he turned halfway to the path and held out his hand.

Ransom looked at Mael and nodded toward the big man.

Chiahn waited until he came along side before he started down the path. "Where did you come from?" Chiahn asked as he looked down at him. Chiahn's eyes, hooded under thick eyebrows, rested beneath a brow furrowed by thinking and exposure to the heat of the day, but Mael watched his lips. It was the same as Klopas—the peculiar misshapen syllables.

"I am from Farhantra, on the coast of Morlan, west of Moori-man."

"Never heard of it."

"It's a small city." Mael sensed that Chiahn wanted to walk faster. "Sorry about the limp," he said.

Chiahn shook his head. "I know the feeling."

"Really?"

"Before I found the master, I was a fisherman. It can be dangerous. We got caught in a storm, and in trying to save the boat I broke my knee. It never healed quite right."

They rounded a corner in the path. In front of them was the gate in the wall around the garden. In a few steps, they would be through it.

"How do you walk now?"

Chiahn stopped and looked into his eyes. "When I met the master, he healed me. I don't know how. He just does things like that."

Mael looked down at his hands. Chiahn followed his eyes. "Ahh," he intoned. When Mael looked up, Chiahn smiled and nodded knowingly. "They look new."

Mael nodded. "Sword wounds from the temple priests."

Chiahn closed his eyes and shook his head, then flicked back the dark hair that fell over his eyes. "A tough lot. They'll change when they meet the master." Chiahn turned toward the gate. "Come, see the city."

They stepped through the gate and stopped. Mael had never seen anything like it. Across the shallow valley, city walls gleamed in the light of Asolara. He had not noticed them in the darkness when Klopas had brought him here. Farhantra was tiny and quaint in comparison. High on the hill in front of them across the valley, rising up behind the wall, was a magnificent stone building.

Chiahn followed his gaze. "The temple."

"What is this city?"

"Chershalem!" Chiahn smiled. "The city of kings."

"You have a king here?"

"There are many that would like to be king in Chershalem, Mael. Right now, the Ermans think they own it, but they'll be driven out." Chiahn's eyes looked out over the city to the distance. "It belongs to the master, and he has come here to claim it."

Mael looked down. He pictured Ransom in his mind. Ransom couldn't be a king. Kings were handsome. Ransom wasn't someone that the crowds would accept. Mael knew this from his own experience.

Ransom's lazy eye and the hair lip; the scar on his cheek; the missing tooth—his broken hands were not those that would hold a scepter. This wasn't a king. A kind and powerful healer, yes, but not a king.

"You can't doubt, Mael." Chiahn put his arm around his shoulder. One day this will all be ours when the Master takes the throne. In the meantime, let's find some water and clean clothes—and *breakfast!*"

Chiahn's peculiar emphasis on breakfast made Mael smile. "Breakfast would be nice—and some water."

Judas wasn't happy about the addition to the breakfast table—another mouth to feed and an ugly, toady looking one at that. The master kept bringing people and every day it cost them more. He understood the sympathy, but it was not helping their cause to be collecting the lame and deformed without healing them. This Mael stranger was a frightening replica of the master himself, although shorter. If he had not seen his face, he would have taken him for a boy, but he was clearly more than a boy. How could one person be so broken so young?

He had seen the master heal the lame. Why didn't he heal himself—or this Mael or Phillip?

Thomas slapped him on the back. "C'mon, Judas, eat. You've been in a foul mood these days, but you shouldn't go without breakfast."

Thomas was likable enough, with a quick smile and whiter than average teeth, exaggerated by a slight overbite. His light brown eyes penetrated in a way that made Judas always feel like Thomas could see inside him, in an uncomfortable way.

"Not hungry." Judas shrugged off Thomas's hand.

The action attracted the stranger's attention. Mael stopped eating and stared at him. He stared back, not wanting to yield to the intimidation of this odd little man.

"What's your name?" the stranger asked without breaking eye contact.

"Judas."

"Funny name." Mael smiled as if he were trying to make a joke. It wasn't funny.

"'Mael' is also a bit odd around here."

"That's true," Mael acknowledged. "I'm not *from* around here."

"Your accent is strange too." Judas offered a wry smile.

"Do the words you hear match what you see from my lips?"

It was an odd question, but perhaps expected. Judas had noticed something peculiar about Mael's speech but hadn't identified it. "Say something else—where did you say you were from?"

"Farhantra. Across the sea—a Mooriman colony."

Judas's jaw dropped. Mael could not possibly have said the words he heard.

"That's why I asked," Mael responded.

Mael leaned over his plate to take another bite of bread without breaking eye contact. "No one here, except the master, has lips that say what I hear," he said around his food.

A change of topic was in order. "When did you arrive, Mael?"

"Last night."

"On a ship? From the coast?"

"I don't know exactly. I woke up in the garden of the dead and the gardener, Cleopas, introduced me to the master."

"You just woke up in the garden?"

"I was in a cave and fell through a hole and ended up in a cave in the garden. It's hard to explain."

The others at the table listened carefully. Judas shook his head. *Where did the master come up with these people?*

"I don't know how it all works, Judas, but I have faith that I am supposed to be here, at this time. Perhaps you would understand if you allowed your heart and mind some room to see things differently. The truth is not always obvious, but it is still truth."

Now that Judas was aware of the lip thing, it was all he could see. Mael's words were unnerving enough without the odd twists of his mouth.

"I'm getting used to it," Mael said.

"What?"

"The lip thing."

Judas shook his head. Jerusalem was an expensive place to feed all the followers who were not going to contribute to the cost, but Judas saw the master in Mael's eyes. It made him feel guilty without accusation.

"How old are you, Mael?"

"Twenty-three."

"And do you have a trade?—some way to earn money?"

Mael looked down at his hands. "I'm a blacksmith. I know the fire and the iron, the horse and the shoe. I know blades and steel.

That is my trade." He closed his hands and rested his fists on the edge of the table as he looked back up at Judas. "I think I have been brought here for something else...but I am not sure what."

No one at the table moved. Judas eyed Mael uncomfortably. "I hope this is all true," he said as he looked around the table at the others. "We may yet have need of a bladesmith..."

Before any more could be said, the door opened and the master strode into their midst. "We are going to the temple this morning, brothers. Mael will come along and see the city. Thomas, he's to stay with you."

Judas watched as the master turned to Mael. "Did you find water and enough to eat, my friend?"

Mael nodded. "I did, thank you." He lowered his head as he spoke.

The self-confident Mael from the moment before had vanished in the presence of the Master. Judas's anger spiraled up inside him; or perhaps it was resentment. Jesus had called him 'friend'. This ugly little foreigner was already something that he had never felt he was.

Chapter Four

JERUSALEM

"There is no smell like the smell of a city."

Knowing Life
Taharal Minnas

Mael walked beside Domas as they made their way into Chershalem. Mael liked Domas. He liked his smile and his easy conversation. From their brief acquaintance, this direct and thoughtful
man had seen much and accepted most of it at face value, with
a peculiar caution about new ideas. His light brown hair parted
in the middle, adding emphasis to his facial symmetry, with a

streak of white that ran from his forehead out over his left ear. It swept back behind his ears and hung just above his shoulders in a careless way that said he paid little attention to it. Thick eyebrows and piercing light eyes added an unnatural intensity.

They entered the city north of the great temple through a gate with armed guards who seemed to stare through them as if looking for something untoward. By the time they got inside, the streets thronged with people. Mael had never seen crowds like this, nor had he experienced the intensity of the dry, dusty air. They passed a fortress of sorts with armed guards lounging outside each entrance, and then turned south down a narrow canyon street. The crisp sky formed deep shadows of mid-morning, that added a chill as they passed through them, a chill that would vanish by mid-day. The odors of animal dung, spices, baking bread and heavy perfumes washed over him as they walked into a broad, open market.

Keeping up with Domas's longer legs challenged Mael's stamina. "Stay with me, Mael," Domas had said. "If you get lost, go to the temple. I'll find you there."

A festival of some sort moved through the crowds. People jabbered in strange languages that he didn't understand. Everyone was large, and strong. They jostled and shoved, each with his own mission: buying, selling, arguing, and bargaining—many moved toward the temple like Domas and he.

Mael pushed up beside Domas. "That fellow, Chudash, who sat across from me at breakfast—"

Domas looked down with a smile and nodded.

"—He seemed irritated that I was there."

"Chudash gets that way, on occasion," Domas said, "but more so since we came to Chershalem."

"Was I eating too much?"

"What?" Domas stopped and stared down at him.

Mael looked up into his eyes. "He had an attitude towards me."

Domas laughed. "He can be like that." He started walking and Mael had to skip-step to catch up. "We've been together for some time—we all have our thing, you know."

"Our thing?"

"We're all different, Mael."

"I know that—"

"Chudash was rough when he first fell in with us, but he's changed a lot. Spending time with the master and his teaching does that. It's a bit hard to explain." Domas paused. "Let's just say, he's come a long way. Sometimes his old ways show up to haunt him—like all of us."

They pushed through the market, weaving around the merchants selling cloth, peaches, lamp oil, bread and chickens, but even in the dense crowd, they were alone in their conversation. The bright colors of the stalls and awnings and overpowering odors of people, animals, fresh fruit and flowers shifted with the non-existent breeze as they swept along.

"How far is it to the temple?" Mael asked as they navigated a narrow passage between two rows of tables covered with bright colored fruit.

"Not far now," Domas cast over his shoulder. "A couple hundred paces to the bridge to the western gate. You want anything to eat before we get there?"

"I'm thirsty again...this dust—"

"We'll find some water then. Did Chudash give you any money?"

"No."

Domas shook his head. "Everything costs something in Chershalem. Chudash knows that." Domas stopped and reached into his cloak. "Here," he said as he removed his hand to reveal three small copper coins. Take these."

"What does Chudash have to do with it?"

"He's in charge of the master's treasury. He should have given you something for the day in the city."

"What are they worth?" Mael asked as he eyed the coins.

"What do you mean?"

"What can I expect to buy with these?"

"Three coppers?"

"Is that what you call them?"

"You really have no idea, do you?"

Mael shook his head as he looked up.

"That should be enough for a day's worth of food—and water.

A sudden movement to his left flashed over his hand. Mael closed it by reflex from the slap on his open palm but the coins vanished as a young man's bare arm disappeared into the jostling crowd. He looked up at Domas.

His father's eyes stared down hard. "I gave you the money for bread!" The eyes were stern. "For Yander's eighth!"

"I know, fada." Mael's eyes fell with his fada's tone. "It happened so fast...."

"Do you know who it was?"

Mael paused. "Yes."

Fada descended to one knee and put his hands on Mael's shoulders. "You know we don't have much, Mael." His gentle voice wavered between anger and frustration. "Every coin, every dendra—we can't just let others take it from us."

"I know."

"You're eleven, now, Mael. You need to start standing up to bullies."

He looked up into fada's eyes. "The Mooriman soldiers steal from you all the time, Fada." He dropped his eyes, ashamed to reproach his father, but what he said was true.

Fada's eyes closed as he breathed in, as if to calm his vorn. "The Mooriman soldiers steal because they can—" He paused, as if reflecting on the parallels to what had just happened. Mael waited.

"I am a free slave, Mael. You know that," he continued slowly. "By law I can't protest the fare of the Moorimans—so they cheat me."

"That's why we're poor, fada, not because someone snatched coins from my hand."

Fada closed his eyes as a tear slid down his cheek. "Do you know who took them?"

"Yes." Mael wrapped his arms around his father's neck and pulled fada's bearded chin onto his shoulder. "I think that perhaps this person needs them more than us, today."

"My son—" Mael felt the sobs his father tried to suppress. "Where do you get such compassion?"

"We have what we need, fada. Mah'Eladra provide for us every day in ways we don't expect, but it's always enough. We've never been without what we need. We'll never live like the governor, or even some of the other blacksmiths, but we live in the shadows of Mah'Eladra."

Fada pulled back from his embrace and shook his head, his hands still on Mael's shoulders. He stared into Mael's eyes. "You speak wisdom beyond your years, but it's true. We've never starved. The shadows of Mah'Eladra are always longer than that of Mooriman."

"I know." Mael wasn't sure how he knew this, but at eleven, impulses from beyond his experience rose up inside him more and more frequently.

"Your armatan, Mael, reminds me to remember the blessings."

"Yander's birthday will be special, even if we don't have special bread. She'll understand, Fada—if you do."

Fada stood and wiped the tears from his eyes. "It's time to go home." He took Mael's hand.

Mael loved Fada's hands—hard and worn, with callouses that boasted of his extraordinary work in the smithy, yet gentle, to the finest touch that made his work the envy of Farhantra. All the nobles came to him, and all the nobles cheated him, but he always delivered work for which there was no compare.

They headed home for his sister's eighth birthday; a big occasion. Erolin would be there to celebrate with them. Mael knew that she would ratify the loss of three small coins and less special bread as being in the will of Mah'Eladra.

Domas stared back at Mael. "A day's bread and water, Mael!"

Mael startled from his memory—"Yes, that's what you said."

"Don't you resent the theft? Chudash is gonna be furious." Domas turned to continue walking. "C'mon."

Mael fell in behind him. "Of course I resent the theft, but I don't understand the circumstances of the thief. Perhaps he needs it more than me." They took a few steps forward. "Why does Chudash care so much about the money?"

"He's like that—and he worries about it too much."

"What does the master say about money? What does *he* teach?"

"He talks about it a lot—mostly about how dangerous it is for us—how easy it is to be captivated by it—how bad it is when money becomes too important."

"I think he's right."

Domas looked back over his shoulder. "Really now. And why's that?"

"I grew up without much. My father is a blacksmith for the Mooriman noblemen who live in our town. He's very good. One of the best."

"Of course a son would say that!"

Mael ignored the tease. "They all like him and he does good work, but they cheat him. He can't do much about it, being a free-slave."

"A free-slave?" Domas tossed over his shoulder.

"He was a Mooriman slave, but when he married my mother, they gave him some freedoms. He practices his trade and makes a living, but he has no other protection. They swindle him without recourse. The Moorimans take full advantage of this."

"Curious."

"Maybe—but fada makes sure that we're thankful for what we do have. We have learned how to be satisfied. We have each other—even when everything else is taken away."

"Each other?"

"My family: Mada, Fada, me, my younger sister, Yander, my younger brother, Matar, until he was killed—and there was always Erolin."

"What happened to Matar?"

"He was trampled by the Mooriman cavalry in an accident." Mael stopped and looked up.

Domas had turned to face him. "That sounds like something the Ermans might do."

"Ermans?"

"The Ermans—the soldiers..."

They started walking again. The crowds thickened.

"I just got here last night, Domas. I've not seen much."

"Well, you will know them when you see them. They're bigger than most of us."

"Bigger⊓"

"They look bigger, at least."

"Like the ones at the fortress?"

"Yes, like them."

Shouting erupted, exciting the crowd around him. Mael strained to see but being shorter, all he could do was start running with them. They surged toward the bridge to the temple. Domas held onto his shirt. "What's happening?" Mael shouted.

The intensity grew. They ran, tripping and catching themselves on the uneven cobblestones as the crowd surged up the bridge. The shouting swelled and the crowd started cheering.

The pavement leveled as they passed through the gate and sprawled into a large courtyard, filled with people. "It's the master!" Domas yelled as he tugged Mael's shirt. "C'mon!" Domas urged, dragging Mael along, his feet barely able to keep up. Behind the masses, the temple rose up from the pavement, an imposing edifice of stone, wood and gold.

The shouting continued, interspersed with loud crashes and the sound of coins falling to the stone courtyard. People sprinted in different directions. Small, nimble animals ran helter-skelter across the stones as gray birds fluttered through the crowds. People crawled on the ground, gathering coins, pushing each other out of the way and kicking at each other for the silver and copper scattered on the pavement.

Domas stopped suddenly and pulled Mael up beside him as they came to an opening in the crowd. The master, in his grey one-piece tunic stood barefoot in the middle of the opening. Overturned tables, potsherds and torn open birdcages littered the stones around him. Terrified animals skittered through the open space.

The people quieted suddenly, watching the master. He stood motionless. In his left hand, he held a bundle of cords that lay out in front of him like a whip. Men in fancy clothing, their heads wrapped in blue and yellow headgear stood behind the broken and upended tables, bewildered by the scene. Behind him, people still crawled on the ground gathering coins in the shelter of the crowd.

A line of guards emerged from the tall temple doors. Mael gasped—temple guards, like those from the Kirrinal temple in Farhantra that had chased him into the portal. The swords, staffs and leather armor on their shoulders and shins, and heavy leather tunics were almost the same. Dispassionate faces and dark eyes hid behind the nose bridges of their polished helmets.

They stopped in a line, about five paces from where the master stood. He turned to face them. They parted as several priests emerged from the temple to walk between them.

"How dare you!" the obvious leader accused, shaking his fist at the master.

"I dare only as Mah'Eladra have told me."

"You blaspheme—again."

"You have turned the temple of Mah'Eladra into a robber's den."

The High Priest turned purple.

"You profit and line your robes with the sacrifice of the masses, and you think the mighty ones do not see? You call for sacrifice, which is right and good, but then use that to accumulate wealth for yourself!"

The High Priest turned to the guards. "Arrest him! Bring him to me!"

The priests turned back as the guards drew their swords and started toward the master.

The master turned and strode toward the crowd that surged forward to meet him. His face showed no fear. As he approached, he looked directly into Mael's eyes for a moment then turned. Mael didn't see exactly what happened, but the Master vanished into the throng.

"Come with me!" Domas pulled him back into the crowd and bent over to Mael's height. "I've never seen him do anything like that." He whispered. "That's one sure way to get himself in trouble."

Chapter Five

ROMANS

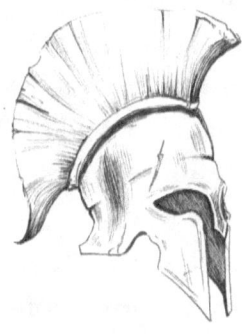

"The second thousand paces is more about humility than about distance."

The Middle Way,
Pratoraman

Marcus sat on his travel bag, his feet flat on the cobblestones, and his forearms resting on his knees. Sweat dripped off his nose from the late afternoon sun, doing its best to remove all incentive from the journey before him. Cassius sat beside him equally dispirited by the heat.

"We shoulda left earlier," Marcus grumbled to the ground between his legs.

"It woulda been hotter earlier," Cassius muttered as he wiped his brow with his forearm, without taking his eyes off the road. "Besides, Claudius had us working, remember?"

Marcus snorted. "I'm a Roman legionnaire. Polishing the hinges and door knobs on Claudius's villa—'Caesar's work' he called it." He spit on the ground in contempt.

Cassius ignored his grouse. "What do you suppose is so important in Jerusalem that we need to be there tonight?" he asked.

"Religious zealots," Marcus said. "Pilate's concerned about the garrison being understaffed, from what I've heard, especially with crowds gathering here for the festival." He paused and looked at Cassius. "Wouldn't be so bad if we had horses."

"Or even a cart. Legionnaires don't get horses, in case you haven't noticed."

"Oh, I've noticed," Marcus said as he stood up, arched his back and yawned. "S'pose we better move along."

Cassius sighed as he pushed himself to his feet and reached down to grab his duffle.

Marcus squinted down the road and shaded his eyes with his hand against the low sun. "By the favor of the gods, Cassius. Look."

Cassius looked down Marcus's extended finger. Two men walked toward them on the road from Jerusalem. He smiled and dropped his bag. "Sometimes the gods favor us Romans just a bit too much," Cassius said.

"If the gods were favoring us, they would not have sent us to this flea-bitten inferno to do military service."

"True, but they left us the locals." Cassius grinned.

Marcus stepped out into the road. "Ho there, good fellows!"

The two men walked toward them. The taller one looked at him and nodded.

"Where are you headed?" Marcus asked with a smile.

The tall one flicked his hand down the road. "Bethany."

"Well, we need your help."

The men paused. The tall one was obviously Jewish, but with lighter hair and piercing light brown eyes. The smaller one had darker skin than the Jews and his eyes were set a bit too far apart and one of them drooped horribly. His hands were disproportionately large—an ugly runt of a man.

"How can we help?" the tall one offered.

"Well, we have to be in Jerusalem before sundown," Marcus said, "and we need your help carrying our bags."

"We're going to Bethany."

"Now you're going to Jerusalem." Marcus left no room for rebuttal. "What are your names?"

The tall one shook his head. "I'm Thomas. This is my friend Mael."

"You know Roman law?"

"About carrying your bags? I do."

Marcus waved to the bags. "One for each of you."

"It's thirteen stadia to Jerusalem," Thomas said, "The law only requires us to take it eight."

"Ah, you *do* know the law—eight's a good start." Marcus waved to the bags again. "Be quick now, you wouldn't want the garrison commander disappointed in us for being late." Cassius smiled and stepped back from his bag, waving the small one to it.

Both men stooped to take the bags and, without any hesitation or apparent resentment, turned toward Jerusalem.

"We'll walk behind," Thomas said as he nodded to Marcus to take the lead.

They started down the road. Marcus gave Cassius a smirk, but the look on Cassius's face was far from amused. "What's the matter?"

Cassius tipped his head back toward the two men behind. "That was too easy," he whispered. "In this heat?"

Marcus raised his eyebrows and shrugged.

After walking about a stadium in silence, Marcus's curiosity overcame him. "Where are you from?" he asked.

"Galilee," Thomas said. "A bit north of here."

"Ahh, we know Galilee," Marcus said. "We marched through there on the way here." He looked over his shoulder at the one called Mael. He hadn't spoken yet. "And you?"

"Farhantra," Mael said, "on the western shore of the Vorsian Sea."

Cassius glanced at Marcus and shrugged. Mael's accent wasn't something Marcus recalled hearing before. "How long've you been here?" he asked.

"Arrived in the middle of the night."

Marcus looked back at Mael. He should have been struggling to carry the heavy bag, but he showed no sign of fatigue or frustration. "Ever been here before?"

"Never."

"Do you know the Roman law about carrying our bags?"

"I could guess."

Marcus stopped and turned to face Mael. "You're willing to just carry our bags because we asked you to?"

Mael looked him in the eyes. There was no fear or anger. "You have a law that can compel me to carry your bags, because you're a soldier!"

"Yes, eight stadia."

Mael didn't flinch. "How far is it to the Garrison in Jerusalem?"

Marcus looked at Cassius. "About twelve now, is my guess," said Cassius as he looked back at Mael.

"Then we'll carry your bags there," Mael said.

Marcus glanced at Thomas, who shook his head in puzzlement. Cassius smiled. "Sounds good."

Marcus turned back toward Jerusalem. He wouldn't make any effort to change the little man's mind. They walked in silence. Marcus wasn't sure whether he was annoyed or resentful. Normally the Jews resented the Roman carry law, but these two didn't seem to mind at all. The little one seemed eager about it. They walked on in silence. Passersby wagged their heads in disgust or spit onto the road in contempt. It was nothing new for Marcus and he ignored the antipathy, choosing to revel in the fact the he was not carrying his bag.

"What do you do for a living, Thomas?" he asked over his shoulder.

"I was a farmer—well, my father is a farmer—in Galilee."

"And what is a farmer from Galilee doing in Jerusalem?"

"I've been traveling with a man named Jesus."

"The Nazarene prophet?"

"You know him?"

"He's causing a lot of trouble for us Romans. I think he's the reason we were ordered to Jerusalem."

"He's not a troublemaker."

Marcus turned to face Thomas, who looked up into his eyes. Cassius stopped also. "Anyone who gets into the middle of the Jewish community and stirs it up is trouble for us Romans."

Thomas nodded. "Why do you Romans need to be here? Many resent your presence."

"We feel that! And you? Do *you* resent our presence?"

Thomas kept his eye contact. "Makes little difference to me. I've come to help Jesus. The Jewish leaders are more trouble to me than you Romans. I just don't understand *why* you're here."

Marcus turned and continued walking. "Many of us don't know why we're here either. I'd rather be home working on my father's vineyard."

Something Marcus couldn't identify was different with these men. Cassius interrupted his ponderings. "And you, Mael. What do you do?"

"My father is a blacksmith—and a farrier."

"Seriously?"

"Yes."

Cassius turned to face the little man. "Show me your hands!" he demanded.

Mael dropped the bag and held out his hands to Cassius. They were rough and gnarled beyond the age of Mael's face. Two fingers on the left hand twisted into an unnatural shape that spoke of an injury long ago. Both hands had purple scars in the palms. Marcus watched Cassius look up into the little man's eyes. "What are these scars? They look new."

"I was wounded by the Kirrinal Priests as I was escaping to come here—swords."

"Kirrinal? Never heard of that."

"Kirrinism is the religion of my people."

"And why did they injure you?"

"I don't know. I had many discussions with them and then many arguments. They didn't want to know the truth. They would have killed me, but I escaped."

"How're you so sure of the truth?"

"The noble truths are not something that change. They shouldn't be twisted the way the priests did."

Cassius changed the conversation. "And the fingers?"

"It's an old wound," Mael said looking up, "the result of standing for the truth."

"Is your version of truth worth so much to you?"

"Truth doesn't have versions."

Cassius shrugged. "Perhaps."

Marcus tugged on Cassius's sleeve. "Let's get going, or we'll be late."

—⊲⬧⊳—

Mael trudged behind the Erman soldiers. Gassis and Margas were engaged in a discussion of their own, so he slowed a bit to give them some distance. The bag *was* getting heavier. His fingers ached but he knew it was right to finish his service, in spite of the pain.

Domas walked quietly. Mael looked at him. "Are you alright?"

Domas smiled. "Yeah, but tired—and we'll be late for dinner."

"You hungry?"

"We didn't have much for lunch after you lost your coppers."

Mael shrugged. "We'll be fine. I've been hungry before."

Domas nodded. "Your fingers—it wasn't an accident, was it?"

"No."

"Someone did that to you?"

Mael nodded.

It was two days after his fourteenth birthday. Mael attended the local school in Farhantra where, by law, as the son of a free slave, the school allowed him to attend classes where the Mooriman highborn males were educated.

He sat in the back of each class. He could only listen and wasn't given any of the materials that the other boys were provided. The teachers tolerated his presence, along with two other sons of free-slaves, but otherwise the teachers and the others ignored him.

Mael liked school, in spite of the treatment by the Mooriman boys. He enjoyed learning math, science and history. Since books were hard to come by, even for the wealthier boys, most of the teaching did not require them. He learned by listening carefully, but was forbidden to join in any discussions. Mael discovered he had a better memory than most and he always knew all the answers, though they never returned tests to him as they did the others.

That day he wore the medallion that his father had made him for his birthday. It was an exquisite piece of work, all iron from the forge. About the width of two fingers, the fine iron shapes swirled through it and flowed into one another to form a simple, but beautiful, whole. His father had polished it to highlight certain surfaces, leaving others to the black oxide that normally emerged from the fire. It hung from a thin leather strap around his neck. He felt important—and bold.

He sat in the back of his philosophy class, listening carefully to the instructor. The discussion that day was about the Kirrinath, the foundational teaching of the wholeness of thinking for most Tessalindrian cultures. Mael had no little knowledge of this topic, having learned from his father and Erolin, who read to him regularly from her father's copy of the Tessarandin.

As he listened, he became aware of the false understanding promulgated by his teacher. He didn't know exactly how he knew, but something in his fourteen-year-old noga shifted to a certainty that the teaching was false.

He stood up. No one noticed except the teacher, who paused to stare at him. The pause was just long enough for the other boys to turn and look.

"Sit down, Mael."

"I cannot."

The teacher's face darkened. "Sit down, or I'll have you removed."

"I must stand to correct the teaching you are providing for the others," he said. "The eight points of the Kirrinath cannot be separated from one another as you're saying. They form a wholeness and understanding; each point is dependent on accepting each of the others. This is born out in the form of the Kirrinath star, where each of the points join in the center in unity as a whole." Mael stopped to look around. Fear in the others showed more clearly than the hatred. He trembled from his own fear, wondering if it made any sense to challenge the teacher. "What I'm saying is true," he continued. "It's born out in the Tessarandin."

The teacher strode toward him, weaving between the other students. "Sit down!" he said.

Mael trembled and closed his eyes, fearing the assault of the teacher. He did not know where the next sentence came from. "I stand for what is true."

The teacher stopped in front of him. Mael didn't move. "What is truth?" the teacher chided and then, without warning, he shoved Mael backward, sending him sprawling onto the floor before stopping hard against the stone wall of the classroom. Mael stood up with his back against the wall. "Truth is truth!" he said as he stared at the teacher.

The other boys crowded in behind the teacher, who stood with his hands on his hips. With a swipe of his hand toward the door of the classroom, the teacher exclaimed, "Throw him out!"

The boys surged past the teacher and surrounded Mael, howling with glee. Mael knew he wouldn't resist them. They would be too strong and too many, and Erolin's teaching about no retaliation echoed through his fear. They grabbed him and hauled him to the door as the rest of the class chanted encouragement. "Throw him out! Throw him out!"

Someone opened the door. Someone else yanked his father's pendant from his neck. "No," he cried.

They threw him down the steps outside the building and he tumbled down the stone stairs. He was laying on his back trying to get his bearings when one of the boys approached him. He put his hands on the stone terrace and tried to sit up. The boy lifted his foot and stomped on his hand, smashing it to the stone.

Several bones cracked. Mael rolled over on the stone, bringing his injured hand under the protection of his body. Tears sprouted from his eyes, but he didn't cry out. He curled into a ball on the cold stone, expecting more abuse, but it never came. The crowd retreated in laughter behind the fog of his pain.

He lay still a long time. His hand was bleeding, and two of his fingers were broken. Dark bruising swelled them. He couldn't feel them properly.

He stumbled home. They took him to Hannorah, the best healer in Farhantra that would help the underclass. She did her best to rearrange the bones and bandage the wounds. It was several months before he could hold a hammer. He never went back to school. His hand was not the same. He never knew what became of his pendant.

"What happened to them? Were they punished?" Domas's words cut through the fog of his memory.

"I don't think so. I never found out."

"You never wanted revenge? Or restitution?"

"Vengeance just passes on the suffering. Erolin taught that a chain of suffering ends when the last one in the chain refuses to pass it along. The one who did this was ignorant of the basic principles about what is true."

They trudged on. Domas was thinking. "Who is Erolin?"

"A mentor from home." Mael felt the choke swelling in his throat.

Domas looked over at him. "How do you know so many of the things that the master teaches, if you haven't been with him before?"

"I didn't know he taught that."

"He uses different words, but the idea is the same. He's forbidden us to retaliate, even if the other person is evil and unwilling to change or listen. Did you forgive this person?"

They approached the gates of Chershalem for the second time that day. They looked different than they did in the morning when they were the lit by the orange rising of Asolara. The glow of the sky where Asolara sank behind the city made the shaded walls darker.

"Not forgiving isn't an option," Mael said to Domas's question.

"Even if the person has no intent to change?—if they're not sorry?"

Mael stared straight ahead. "This is one of the hardest disciplines. Mah'Eladra have made it very clear that it isn't my place to pass judgment on another of the mankind. I want people to change, Domas. There's a greater chance that they will if I absorb their hatred. It is a great cornerstone of the Kirrinath."

"But your hand—"

"A small price to pay for psadeq."

The guards stopped Thomas and Mael at the gate. Thomas struggled not to resent it. He had already sacrificed his time and efforts to help Marcus and Cassius carry their bags, and he was tired. He dropped the bag.

Marcus turned to face the Jewish guards that accosted them. "They are with us," he said as he strode back to the gate. Thomas knew the guards wouldn't defy a Roman soldier.

"How far have you carried their bags?" said one of the guards.

Thomas looked him in eyes. "Thirteen stadia."

"You know they can only demand eight?"

Mael stepped forward. "We know the law. We chose to give them thirteen. Their commander ordered them here. We decided to help them because the bags are heavy."

Cassius and Marcus watched from behind. The guard's eyes flashed back and forth between Mael and himself. "Is this true?"

"Yes." Thomas said.

The two guards exchanged whispers. When he stepped back in front of them, he asked. "Are you followers of the Nazarene?"

Thomas hesitated.

"Yes," Mael said. "Does that matter?"

Thomas squirmed. Mael had been here one day and had more courage than he did.

"We've been told to arrest any followers of this man."

"Why? What have we done?" Mael said. "You would arrest us for a kindness done to our Roman friends?"

The guard's face betrayed his anger, but he hesitated, glancing between Marcus, Cassius and the small strange man who challenged him.

"No, we'll arrest you for being followers of the Nazarene."

Mael held out his hands. "Take us then."

The guard hesitated, bewildered by this strange, ugly little man with broken hands who offered no resistance. Marcus stepped between them. "They're with us. You will *not* arrest them."

The guard looked up into Marcus's eyes. "We have our orders."

"It won't go well for you if you arrest servants of the Roman Garrison."

A long moment hung between Marcus and the guard. Finally, the guard retreated to his post, muttering to the others. "Let them pass."

Thomas exhaled as the fear slid off his shoulders.

"Come," Marcus said. He reached down to grab his own bag. "We can take these from here."

Mael laid his hand on Marcus's stooped shoulder. "No, we'll finish the task." Marcus looked up as Mael continued. "Your kindness in defending us is not unnoticed."

Marcus stood up straight, staring down at Mael. His face softened. "Come along then. We'll find dinner for you at the garrison."

Thomas bent to pick up Marcus's bag and glanced at Mael. He wasn't sure if Mael smiled or smirked, but he knew exactly what it meant. There was a lot more to this little man than he first thought.

Chapter Six

LEPERS

"All healing is in the gentle hands of Mah'Eldadra."
Science and the Vorn
Fillaranda Darenton

Dinner at the fortress was passable for Mael, and plentiful, with some kind of meat in a gray, tasteless gravy with boiled potatoes and undercooked beans that desperately needed salt. There was copious ale, which Mael refused. Domas tasted it then privately declared it undrinkable. Eating with the Ermans made Domas uncomfortable.

The faces of the other soldiers betrayed their curiosity as Mael and Domas sat with them for dinner, but they made no issue of it. They talked, laughed, and uniformly complained about having to serve in Chershalem. To a man, they would rather be back at home, wherever that was. When the discussion turned to dealing with rising problems because the appearance of the Nazarene prophet, they shrugged or frowned, and quickly changed the subject. They were bored and frustrated by their appointment to this "dirty little nowhere city".

Margas and Gassis were gracious hosts, introducing them to the commander, but avoiding comment on their involvement with the master. It's not clear whether he would have cared. They sat with Mael and Domas until they finished dinner. Resentful servants, employed by the garrison, cleared the tables. More than one servant had scowled at him and Domas on varied trips to the table, as if their presence there represented some sort of betrayal.

They left the fortress in the dark. "Be careful," Margas warned them. "The streets here can be a bit rough at night—but maybe not so much for you." He apologized for not being able to house them. "Erman law forbids it", he said. They left the fortress into the darkness.

"I think we should try to go back to Pethny," Domas said. "The others are probably wondering where we are."

"We shouldn't go back through the same gate though," Mael said. "The guards—"

Domas nodded. "There's the gate across the temple courtyard—the one they call Golden. We've come and gone through it a couple times with the master. We'll have to cross through the temple court to get to it but I think it's shorter back to the road."

Mael had a superb sense of direction, but the canyon streets of Chershalem and the unfamiliar stars confused him. They had been let out of the fortress in a different place than they entered and had passed through the empty market. Tal, or whatever moon it was here, had just risen but it was only a thin sliver. The taller parts of the buildings bathed in the last glow of twilight, which made the streets feel even darker, and everything looked different in the darkness without the crowds.

"I think we're lost," Domas said, with a nervous quiver in his voice. "By now we should have found the bridge leading up to the temple."

The streets were nearly empty. Those who were out, gave them wide berth with palpable fear. They could see the massive temple walls. "If we move toward it, we will eventually find a way in," Mael said.

"You lead, Mael."

Mael turned at the first street that led up toward the wall. Within fifty paces, the dark imposing wall of the temple rose in front of them. They toiled along in the shadows of the wall. "Is there a gate on this side?" Mael asked.

"There's the gate we went through this morning, but it's all different in the dark without the crowds."

Mael nodded.

Domas smiled. "Seems like a long time ago, but it was just this morning that we were there."

They picked their way along in silence, working slowly to avoid the bushes and rubble that had accumulated at the bottom of the wall. Domas led.

He stopped suddenly, throwing his hand out in front of Mael.

Mael looked over his arm. The light of a fire illuminated the wall and the circle of bushes around a small clearing at its base. The indistinct murmur of voices rose from four figures seated around the flames. The murmur hesitated and evolved into a slow chant, accompanied by the tinkling of bells.

Domas gasped.

"What is it?"

One of the figures on the other side of the fire stood up.

"Lepers!" Domas said as he started to back up, pushing Mael back with his arm. "They are not supposed to be here—not inside the walls of Chershalem!"

"What?"

"Lepers! Leprosy!" Domas's voice trembled.

Mael understood the chant now. It echoed what Domas had said. "Leper... Leper... Leper... Leper ..." as the little bells kept ringing.

"**Help them.**" A hoarse whisper of many voices all at once, spoke in Mael's ear.

"What?" he said aloud.

"They're lepers," Domas said.

"**Don't be afraid—you can help them!**"

Wherever it came from, it echoed in his head with an undeniable reality. Mael ducked under Domas's arm.

Thomas's fingers slipped off Mael's cloak as he tried to restrain the little man. "Mael! Stop!" He watched helplessly as Mael stepped into the light of the fire. Those seated around the fire startled—a second one stood up. Mael paused two paces from the closest man.

"I have come to help," he said.

The lepers looked at one another, bewildered by the offer. "You can't help us," said the man who'd stood first.

"What's your name?" Mael asked.

"Who's asking?"

"I am Mael."

"Are you the Nazarene?"

"No."

"You look like him."

"I'm not him."

The man assessed the situation thoughtfully before answering Mael's first question. "I'm Saul, son of Jonah," he said. He pointed to the other men. "Judah, Simon, and Aaron. I am sure you mean well, Mael, but you can't help. We're lepers."

"I was told I *could* help."

"Do you know what leprosy is?" Saul asked.

"No."

Saul closed his eyes and shook his head. Judah and Aaron laughed. Simon poked the fire with a stick sending a shower of sparks into the air.

"No one can heal leprosy," Saul continued. "It would be wise of you to stay clear. That's why we ring the bells—a warning to you."

"What are you doing here?" Mael asked.

"We're waiting. We've heard that the Nazarene healer may be able to help us. We expect he'll come to the temple again in the morning."

"Is there a gate to the temple nearby?"

"About a hundred paces behind me there is a bridge leading to a gate. About two hundred paces beyond that there is a stairway that leads up into the corner of the gentile's court."

Mael threw his thumb back over his shoulder. "Thomas and I were hoping to go through the temple court tonight."

"You can't enter the temple. The gates shut at sundown and won't open 'til an hour before sunrise."

Thomas remained in the shadows. He knew about leprosy. He knew there was no cure. Even though he had seen the master heal several lepers at once, he was sure Mael could not. Mael knew nothing about the danger he faced.

Mael took a step toward Saul whose long brown robe covered his knees and completely sheltered his hand in its folds. Thomas could see the disfiguring marks of the disease on his cheeks.

"Show me your leprosy." Mael's voice was half command, but laced with compassion.

Saul hesitated and looked straight at Thomas as if asking permission. Thomas didn't move. He wasn't sure if Saul could actually see his face in the shadows. Saul turned back to Mael and slowly pulled his right hand from the folds of his cloak and stretched it out. In the light of the fire, Thomas could see the stubs of his fingers, decayed and dark in the orange light.

He watched as Mael bowed his head and brought his hands to his face. Thomas could not see, but it looked as if he was wiping away tears from his eyes with his fingers. Then suddenly he straightened and reached out with his hands. Before he could touch Saul's hand, Saul withdrew it slightly, a startled look cascading over his face.

"Do you want to get well?" Mael asked in a voice husky with emotion.

"I do," Saul said, "but I'm afraid."

"Do not fear!" Mael reached back and wiped his eyes again, sniffed and cleared his throat. "Come, let me touch you."

Thomas looked at the other lepers, transfixed at the scene before them.

Mael stood with his hands out, palms up, his tears glistening on his fingertips. Saul extended his hand slowly without taking his eyes off Mael's face. Mael took Saul's hand between his own and held it for a moment, before slowly drawing both his hands back toward him. Thomas couldn't see well, but Aaron and Judah gasped and Aaron jumped to his feet. Mael dropped his hands, but Saul lifted his hand up into the light for all to see his restored fingers.

Saul's hand then went to his face, feeling for the scars that had been there moments before. His eyes filled with wonder as both hands groped beneath his robe. He looked up at Mael, his eyes glistening with tears, then fell to his knees and bowed his face to the ground. The others stood still. The world stopped except for Saul who wept and kissed Mael's feet. "You *are* the Nazarene!"

Mael was shaking. "No, Saul, I am not—it wasn't me. It wasn't me. It was Elohim. Stand up!" he bent down and took Saul's head in both hands and lifted him up. "Stand up!"

Saul stood up straight and threw his arms around Mael's neck as he wept into the little man's shoulder. The tears formed in Thomas's eyes with a choking joy that he couldn't contain, but he dared not enter the scene.

Mael extricated himself from Saul's embrace. He turned to Judah who was trembling. Thomas could see both of their faces. "Do you believe?" Mael asked.

Judah shook his head. "I do—and I don't. Help me believe!" his voice trembled as he fell to his knees.

Mael stooped to one knee. "Let me see your feet."

Judah sat back to expose his feet. Mael gently pulled back Judah's cloak. Judah closed his eyes. The feet were black with the infection and deformed beyond recognition.

Mael hesitated and looked up for a moment before stooping and scooping the soil from beside the fire into both hands. He leaned over and spread the soil onto Judah's legs, massaging it into the blackened skin, between the toes and all around the ankles, as far up the legs as the infection extended. "Bring me some water!" he said in the same husky, emotion-laden voice. Saul grabbed a skin of water that was sitting to his left. "Pour it over his legs!"

Saul uncorked the skin and poured the water over Judah's feet. It looked for a moment as if the water was boiling, but as it flowed away, Judah's skin looked like that of a young man. Judah's hands went to his mouth and he cried out. "Elohim, Elohim!", then he jumped up and leaped around and hugged Saul, who was stupefied by the change.

A wave of horror, perhaps agony, spread across Mael's face, and he stooped as if he was suddenly burdened by a heavy load. It lasted only a few seconds before he straightened again.

"Come here, Thomas!"

Thomas startled, like waking from a dream.

"Come here, Thomas!"

He stepped out of the shadows and drifted toward Mael.

"Simon, do you believe?"

"I do." Simon said.

"Show us!"

Simon pulled up his cloak to reveal his scarred and darkened legs, from the knees to the ankles and around his heels. When he pulled up his sleeves, his forearms, and wrist showed the same.

"Spit on your hands, Thomas, and draw the poison off Simon's hands."

Thomas looked at Mael, who was staring at him with an intensity he had only seen in the master.

"**Don't be afraid, Thomas!**" It wasn't Mael's voice, but some other. It sounded like five voices whispering in perfect unison and it sounded old, like ancient men, dry and husky with age.

Thomas looked down at his palms, and spit into them, then reached out. Simon was looking into his eyes. He hesitated.

"**Do not fear!**" It was a command he couldn't disobey. He reached out, laid his hands on Simon's forearms near the elbows, and then pulled them slowly back toward him. He trembled, but whether it was fear or anticipation, he couldn't tell.

As he pulled his hands back the flesh on Simon's arms revived, and when he reached the fingertips, his hands fell, as if pulled down by a weight he couldn't hold. His body shuddered with a pain he'd never felt before, as if every part of his body was rebelling: his bones, and muscles, his head and eyes. He trembled under its weight and his eyes teared involuntarily. He turned to the fire and as the weight of the disease fell from his fingers into the flames, the pain vanished.

Simon leapt at Thomas and embraced him. He struggled to extricate himself from the embrace, but when he saw Mael smiling over Simon's shoulder, he relaxed into it. Mael turned his attention to Aaron, who stood frozen with fear—amazement overwhelmed his face.

"Tell me, Aaron," Mael said as he stared at the frightened man. "Do you now believe?"

Aaron opened his mouth but there was no sound.

Mael put his right hand on Aaron's shoulder. "May Leprosy never plague you again!"

Aaron started shaking violently. His teeth clenched and he fell to his knees. Mael took both his upper arms in his hands and lifted him to his feet. Aaron opened his eyes, stepping back from Mael, then sat down abruptly, facing the fire, staring into it as if nothing had happened. "I never would've believed," he said absently, "I never would've believed."

Mael sat down beside him and the others followed. Thomas stood aloof, not sure what to do. Mael looked up. "Sit down, Thomas. The danger is past. Enjoy the fire with us."

Aaron shuffled over a bit to make more room for him to sit down. It was still hard to believe what he had just seen. Saul had shed his robe and was sitting on it. He kept staring at his hand that held a stick while he played with the fire. "What do we do now?"

"The law requires that you go and show yourself to the priests," Thomas said. "Show them that you've been cleansed." He looked over at Mael who sat quietly, staring into the foundation of the temple as if no one else in the world was there. "You should do that tomorrow," Thomas continued.

"How will we explain what happened?" asked Simon.

Mael stirred and looked down. "Tell them *exactly* what happened: that you were hoping to see the Nazarene and be healed by his touch, but by the power and the mercy of Yahweh, you were cleansed in the night, because that is what has happened. Your faith in their power has healed you."

"But what about you?" Aaron asked. "Surely you had a hand in this."

"Your faith in the master's healing touch had you here in defiance of the city laws, waiting by the wall of the temple. He has healed you through that faith. They spoke to me to tell me how—as they spoke to Thomas when you were healed, Simon. We are but servants who came here to quicken your faith. Now I must sleep. The journey here has been long—and surprising."

Thomas watched as Mael pulled his cloak around him. He simply laid down where he had been sitting and closed his eyes. The others looked at Thomas. He shrugged, smiled and shook his head.

Saul stared across the fire at him. "I don't think I'll be able to sleep for a while." He grinned and touched his healed face again with his newly restored fingers. "I will never forget this—ever. It's been twelve years."

Mael woke before the others. He vaguely remembered murmured conversations long after he'd laid down. The fire was out. The faint light of dawn barely eclipsed the stars above the towering wall of the temple, and a heavy dew frosted the cloaks of the other five men hidden inside them.

He shivered in the chill air and stood up, eager to stretch his legs and rebuild the warmth in his body. He walked south toward where Saul had suggested they would find a gate. The going was slow, as there was no path immediately against the wall where the shrubs and rubble kept him busy with their avoidance.

He pondered what had happened. It came so fast. He'd never had that experience. The voice kept coming to him, telling him exactly what to do. He knew he was supposed to be afraid of the leprosy but did not know why. The thick, husky, multiplied whisper gave him no time to consider his fear.

He was as surprised as the others at the effect of his obedience, and wondered whether, if he had grown up with this scourge, his fear and conditioning to the way leprosy enslaved the culture would have prevented his simple submission to the voices. Perhaps that is why Thomas wasn't called to participate until after seeing two healings.

The pain of the healings surprised him. It was as if he absorbed the suffering of each man as the leprosy left them and flowed into his vorn. It had been intense, but also blessedly short, allowing him to move on. He guessed that Domas had felt the same.

"Is this why you have brought me here?" he asked aloud. "I've always tried to walk in the way of the Kirrinath," he continued, "but this is new."

He paused as he kept walking. His thoughts swirled through his life along the path by which he arrived here in the strange city of Chershalem, with the strange people and strange diseases.

He kept walking. He knew enough about Mah'Eladra that they would answer in time when he asked a question. His mind drifted back to Erolin. She had taught him this:

"They always answer your questions, Mael," Erolin said. They sat together on the dock overlooking the harbor at Farhantra. The brilliant beams of Asolara thrust upward into the vermillion sky to the east. He had risen early for his morning walk and she had found him wandering the docks. Erolin had repeatedly insisted that this was the best time to find Mah'Eladra.

She couldn't explain why. Her mentor had told her this and she had been encouraged to test it for herself. She became convinced of this and had made it a point to convince him. "You won't know this until you test it," she challenged.

"But I thought they were everywhere at all times. Why would morning be so special?"

"There are things we know, Mael, not because they make sense or because we can rationalize them into our sense of things, but because we have observed them to be true. Armatan isn't born in rational thought, but in experimental obedience to Mah'Eladra."

"I'm not sure what you mean."

"You've been learning about science in school?"

Mael nodded.

"You see or hear something about how things are, and you ask 'why?' You propose an answer and then set about seeing whether your answer is consistently true. It's no more complicated than that.

"Long ago, I was challenged that the best time to hear the voice of Mah'Eladra was in the morning, before the day was cluttered with all its demands. I found I had more control over the mornings. If the first expectation of the day was at sunrise, I could get up before sunrise and nothing else demanded my attention until then."

Mael looked at Erolin as she stared out over the harbor. Her copper hair hung straight down, ending in a ragged cut just above her shoulders, and her bangs hung down barely above her eyelids. Her gray eyes reflected the light of the sea, and her finely featured nose had a small scar from the bridge down to the cheek from some time-distanced injury.

"In addition," she continued, "I think that there is something about the way our lives are broken into days. The Tessarandin teaches that each day has its own fullness. It is not too long and not too short, but just the length that we can live it well, if we decide to do that. Then we have the night, where we rejuvenate in sleep, to face the next day with its challenges. Finding and listening to Mah'Eladra at the start of the new day, sets the course of the day *rightly. Yesterday is gone—tomorrow is beyond the horizon—asking for today to be well lived is enough."*

"And how did you test this?"

"I think that Mah'Eladra hear us at all times. There are days when I ask for their voice all through the day, but I found over time, that the requests I make in the morning are more likely fulfilled in the day. I think it has to do with psadeq. They want our attention. They want our vorn to be in step with their El in us. Morning says to them that we want them first."

"Do you seek them every morning?"

"It's a discipline, not a rule, Mael. I make the time every morning, but if something happens to interrupt it, I don't worry. There are times and circumstances that don't allow us to be rigid about such things."

"Have you heard the voices of Mah'Eladra. What does it sound like?"

Erolin smiled and turned to look at him. "I think it's different for different people—and maybe different at different times. Most times I do not hear a distinct voice, but rather, if I wait, it comes as a clearing of my head until there is only one thought that emerges as their voices. When I am obedient to that thought, it proves itself true."

"Have you ever actually heard a voice?"

"That has been rare."

"What do they sound like?"

"It's hard to describe, Mael, but for me, it sounded like a whisper of many voices—perfect in unity and demanding beyond any other thing one can know."

Mael waited as he picked his way along the wall. It was the first time he had heard the husky whisper, and it was, as Erolin had described, clear and compelling beyond resistance. He had obeyed the voice each time, and the results were startling. If Domas's fear of Leprosy was any indication of its reality to these people, then this was surely a miracle beyond Mael's understanding and it was deeply satisfying to have been part of it. It was as if Mah'Eladra had wanted to heal these men all along and needed an obedient conduit through which it would happen.

If these men could live by his simple obedience, why did Erolin have to die? Where was the voice when he needed it at the portal? Perhaps he could have done something other than try to pull her into the portal with him. Mael shook his head.

It wasn't long before he came to the stone bridge that Saul had mentioned. It spanned the shrubs and rocks with graceful arches, rising up from the land above him, but there was no access to it from the ground near the wall. He turned around to go back to Domas and the healed lepers.

"Is this why you brought me here?" he repeated aloud. This time he was careful to think of nothing else. When he tried to think of nothing, his head swam with a thousand thoughts, swirling around one another. As he walked and waited, it began to slow down. The flow of thoughts subsided until suddenly there was only one thought remaining, and it was very clear. "*You are here to learn what you will become.*"

Mael knew he would only know what it meant in the course of time. The meaning might remain obscure, but the thought itself was wholly unambiguous, and he put it firmly into the place he had in his mind for things he had to ponder.

Chapter Seven

TEMPLE

"Mah'Eladra are several, and Mah'Eladra are one."
Tessarandin, Book 1

Thomas scolded Mael lightly. "You should have told us you were leaving." His thin lips curled into a half-smile.

"You were asleep, Thomas—you *and* the others. You were up late."

Thomas nodded. "True."

"We worried that perhaps you had gotten lost," Saul added.

When they had gotten up, Mael was gone. Judah was already awake, and he had woken the others. Eager to get into the temple courts, they had packed their meager belongings and started off along the wall, concerned about what may have happened to Mael.

"I take time every morning, before others are awake, to find Yahweh." Mael explained. "If I had woken you—any of you—then I would have been distracted."

Thomas wasn't convinced, but had to admit to the simple logic of the little man's argument. He had seen this in the master. "We are headed to the gate. Simon is eager to find the priests, even if they are unlikely to be there until the third hour."

They remained quiet as they walked briskly toward their goal. Morning seemed to be a time to be quiet and Thomas knew that once inside the temple courts there would be no respite. He wondered if the hawkers who had been selling their goods in the temple would be back after the scourging they got from the master. He guessed that they would. There was too much money to be made and today they would be ready if Jesus came after them a second time.

They passed under the arches leading to the gate in the western wall. In a short while, they came to the stairway up to the southwestern corner of the temple courts. There were others already waiting on the stairs.

Saul leaned over to Thomas and whispered. "It's been twelve years since I've been able to stand in a crowd freely. It's almost uncomfortable."

Thomas smiled. He still hadn't fully absorbed the idea that these men, not twelve hours before, would have been unable to stand shoulder to shoulder with a crowd like this, much less be inside the walls of Jerusalem at all. From what he saw the night before, he was still a bit uncomfortable. The images of the four lepers around the fire was still too raw to be obscured by a single night of cold, restless sleep.

A murmur swept through the crowd as the inner bars lifted inside the gates. The huge gates opened slowly, swinging noiselessly back to provide space enough for six men to walk abreast through the opening. The crowd surged forward, entering into the vast empty court and fanning out. The merchants were back, their cages of animals neatly stacked, sitting behind their tables waiting for the eager crowds.

They headed toward the temple, the small band clinging together in spite of the newfound freedom of the healed lepers. Thomas knew this was right. The master often spoke of gratefulness, and he suddenly recalled one of the master's stories:

"There were two men in a town. One was a leper and the other suffered from weak eyes. Each day they offered sacrifices to Elohim and asked for healing. A prophet came into town and healed both of them. The second man rejoiced and went home to tell his family. The leper left everything and followed the prophet to the next town."

Thomas looked at his new friends, so eager to find the priest and celebrate their healing and he looked over at Mael. No hint of presumption or triumph tainted his bearing.

Mael looked back at him. His eyes told Thomas what they needed to do. Thomas stopped. The lepers stopped also. "We'll leave you here, brothers. Find the priests when they arrive and tell them you've been healed. Mael and I will find the master and then we will return with him if he is to be here today."

Saul stepped forward, holding out his restored hand to Thomas. Thomas hesitated but took his hand. Saul pulled him into an embrace. "Twelve years," Saul muttered over his shoulder, "I never thought I'd hug anyone again." Saul stood back. "Thank you!" Thomas watched as Saul turned to Mael and embraced him also. "I'll never forget you!"

"Never forget Elohim," Mael said. "It is they who healed you."

Saul smiled. "I'll never forget."

Each of the others hugged Thomas and Mael in turn. "When you find the master, bring him to us so we may follow him also," said Judah. "We have waited a long time for someone worthy of following. It is hard to follow as lepers—but we've been healed!"

Thomas nodded as another of the master's stories came to mind:

A king and a prophet lived beside each other. When the king went for his daily walk, people gave him berth because he was the appointed sovereign. When he stopped to turn and look, no one was following.

When the prophet went for his daily walk, and stopped to turn and look, many people followed behind him.

Which of the two was a true leader?

The answer was obvious: "The prophet, of course."

The master had smiled. "So it will be among you. In the days to come, you will know the leaders, because they have followers. You must offer your obedience to appointed leaders, but follow those who truly lead."

"We will tell him of your healing and bring him to you." Thomas promised. Mael nodded.

They left the lepers behind and headed for the Golden gate on the far side of the court. Thomas hoped to intercept the master and the others on their way back into Jerusalem.

Mael walked along-side Domas as they descended the steps outside what Domas had called the Golden Gate. It faced east out over a deep ravine and the serpentine road leading down into the valley was already seeing the flow of pilgrims upward toward the temple. Domas was quiet. Mael let it be.

Mael wondered what he would say to the master when they found him. He didn't doubt that he had acted appropriately in responding to the voice, but he knew his place and hadn't intended to offend anyone by his actions.

When they got to the main road, Domas turned to him. "I am guessing the master is in the garden if you want to find him," he said as he pointed up the hill to the east. "I am going back toward Pethny to find the others. I'm hungry again." Somehow, Domas knew that Mael needed time to be alone with Ransom.

Mael nodded. Domas stepped forward and embraced him. "It's been quite a night."

"Indeed, it has—Domas?"

"Yes?"

"I think it best that we do not share about Saul and the others—at least not at this time."

Domas stepped back from the embrace. He pondered Mael's suggestion and nodded. "It's going to come out at some time, my friend, but I will honor your request."

"The stuff about the soldiers and the fortress and all that. That's fine."

Domas smiled. "That is a great story. The brothers will be envious, I think, but not envious of a cold night on the streets of Chershalem after we got kicked out."

"Thank you, Domas. I'll see you soon."

Domas turned and started south along the road toward Pethny. Mael paused for a moment and breathed deeply. The fresh morning air was laden with fragrances that came from the garden up the hill in front of him where Asolara still hid behind its trees. He shivered once before starting up the path into the garden.

Ransom was in the same place he had found him just one morning before. With closed eyes, he knelt facing east, murmuring something that Mael couldn't understand. Mael waited, sure that this time between Ransom and Yahweh was sacred.

Ransom stood up. "Good morning, my friend!"

Mael bowed his head. He wasn't sure why, but it felt appropriate.

"Come and sit with me, Mael." He pointed to the stone bench where he sat the day before. "As always, the others will be here soon, but we need to talk." Ransom sat down and nodded to the spot beside him. "Come, Mael."

Mael sat down. They were beside each other but it felt like he was looking into the master's eyes. He had never felt this before. What was it?

"When you healed the lepers, how did it feel?"

"You know about that□"

"I know all things, Mael, especially those that come from Elohim."

Mael shook his head. "Was it your voice that I heard? It sounded like many."

"We are several, Mael. A unity in plurality, but we speak as one. Just as you know us as Mah'Eladra, you already know about this."

Mael nodded. "I tried to do exactly as you told me."

"You did well, my friend. Most of those through whom we speak are not ready to obey."

"How could one *not* obey? It was so clear."

"You know the answer to that, Mael."

Mael turned to look at him, but Ransom's eyes were somewhere distant, staring off toward the wall of Chershalem and the temple.

"The Kirrinal priests, who chased you into the portal," Ransom continued, "have heard our voice, but their vorns are so twisted by their tradition and the teachings of Vishtoenvar, that they do not listen. Our voice becomes distant and hollow, and devoid of meaning to them."

Mael tried to absorb what the master said.

"Are you surprised, Mael, that I know of your trials on Tessalindria?"

"Yes."

"We know all things, Mael. Though Tessalindria is far from here, and the scholars and thinkers of this world deny that there is other life in places outside this world, there is more. We created it. Should we not be aware of it?"

Mael was simultaneously surprised and not so. "The philosophers of Tessalindria think that there is nothing beyond the deep sky, and many of them deny that even the deep sky is real."

"Yet you *do* know that the Kirrinath supposes the vastness beyond the deep sky?" Ransom wrapped his statement into a question. "And the Tessarandin, if read openly, presupposes the same?"

The sudden clarity of the words coalesced into an image that Mael should have identified on his own, but hadn't. The answer to his request from earlier that morning by the wall flooded back to him: "*You are here to learn what you will become.*"

"Do you know why I was brought here?" he asked as he turned to face Ransom.

"Yes."

"Do you know what I will become?"

"Yes."

Mael desperately wanted to know details, but it would be inappropriate to ask. He had to wait. Already the path was clearer in a certain vague way.

"You will learn, Mael, and you must not fear what you learn. If I were to tell you all at once, you would be afraid. but I *will* tell you this: I had to discover who I was. It was painful at times and the pain is not over, even now. To discover it all at once would have been too much to bear. Do you remember when I healed your wounds, yesterday morning?"

"Yes."

"Do you remember the intense pain of healing for that small wound, all at once?"

Mael *did* remember. He remembered crying out and he remembered the tears, and he remembered the relief that followed.

"Do you remember the pain you felt in healing Saul—and Judah and Aaron?"

Mael nodded.

"There will be much pain along the way, and you cannot endure it all at the same time. Such is the path to discovering who you are. Last night you tasted the power that is available through unquestioned obedience when you hear the voices of Mah'Eladra. You will see greater things than this, and greater pain with it. Come, the brothers are approaching."

The master stood up as the murmur of the brother's voices rose from the path below the garden. It sounded like they were arguing about something.

Chapter Eight

BETRAYAL

"The vision of the mankind destroys wisdom; By rash action, does
one prove his foolishness."
The Essences of Corritanean Wisdom
Hispattea

John struggled to believe Thomas's story. Being conscripted
by the Roman soldiers was plausible, but being invited to dinner
at the fortress?—and the story about the lepers? Thomas had
promised the strange little newcomer that he wouldn't tell. John

didn't like that. If a miracle of that scale had taken place, the master would know anyway and it would be odd that the other brothers shouldn't know also.

When they had arrived at the garden, the master and the new-comer were together. Perhaps the little man had told the master what had happened.

There was no time to worry about this now. They were nearly to the Golden Gate. As soon as they entered the temple courts, the crowds would besiege them as they always did these days. With the narrow escape from arrest the day before, John wondered what was in store for them today.

"Do you suppose we will see your leper friends?" he asked Thomas, forgetting that the newcomer was right behind him.

Thomas frowned and glanced over his shoulder. John followed his eyes to see the newcomer smiling at him. The little man shrugged.

Thomas relaxed. "They'll probably find us. They want to meet the master."

"Everyone wants to meet the master."

"True, True," Thomas nodded. "They were hoping to find him today anyway—so they could be healed."

"Weren't they healed already?"

Thomas nodded. "That was before Mael and I met them."

They passed through the gate into the court with hundreds of others. "What do you think they will do with the master if they find him?—the priests, that is."

"They can't do much in a crowd like this," Thomas said.

"Are you afraid for him?"

"Not for him, so much, but what happens to us?"

"We'll have to see."

Thomas nodded. John was about to ask if he was ready for that, when a disturbance in the crowd arrested his attention. Four men, dressed in dirty white robes burst through the crowd and stopped in front of the master, falling to their knees in front of him. "Thank you for healing us," one of them said as they bowed their heads.

"Stand up!" The master motioned with his hands as he spoke. They rose to face him. "I have heard the story of your healing. Your faith has made you well."

"We want to travel with you, master."

"What is your name?"

"Saul."

"Saul, you must go to the priests first, as is stated in the law, and show yourself to them, as proof of your cleansing. When they have blessed you, come and follow me."

"The priests haven't arrived."

"They'll be here soon. There are many preparations for the feast that they need to oversee today."

The crowds surged around Mael toward the Master. There was no hiding now that the healed lepers had identified him publicly. Mael joined the brothers as they formed a close circle around him as if this were a common event, begging the people not to press in so hard. "Chaizus, Chaizus of Nazareth," the crowd shouted as more came running.

Most of them were bigger than Mael. As he struggled to stay in the circle, he noticed Chudash nearby, also outside the circle. Mael was about to call out for help when Chudash turned and moved away from the crowd. Something wasn't right. His face bore an intense gravity, like one on a mission, a mission quite separate from that of the master and the other brothers. Mael followed him.

As they moved away from the master, the crowds thinned and Mael dropped back and moved to the left so that he would not be following right behind.

Chudash headed north, to the right of the temple and toward the long portico that spanned the width of the courtyard on the north. He entered the central arch of the portico. Mael entered through the left arch and lingered behind one of the pillars.

Priests filled the portico. They helped each other adjust their vestments as they chatted casually and smiled at one another.

Chudash approached one of them. From his robes and the headpiece that he wore, he was the most highly revered, the one who had confronted the master the day before—the chief among the priests.

Chudash bowed and then straightened. The priest's face became grave. He shook his head. Mael couldn't hear the words and could not get closer without being noticed. Chudash and the High Priest argued. Chudash repeatedly pointed out into the courtyard and the priest kept shaking his head. They came to an impasse and stared at each other. The priest made a final gesture.

Chudash's frustration darkened his face, but he nodded. The priest turned to one of the lesser priests and said something. The young priest left. When he returned with a leather pouch in his hand, he handed it to Chudash. Chudash knelt down and started to open it.

The High Priest knelt in disgust and laid his hand over the leather bag, closing it and lifting it, locking his eyes into Chudash's as they rose together. The High Priest pointed to the courtyard. Chudash shook his head and turned, stuffing the sack into his robe. He glanced around before exiting through the main arch.

Mael waited for a moment. When he turned to leave two priests blocked his path. Behind them were four temple guards with swords drawn.

"What are *you* doing here?"

"I'm with Chudash—he was just talking to the High Priest." He started to walk toward the arch, but the priests and guards moved in front of him.

"Kiephus!" one of them called.

It did not take long before the High Priest stood in front of him, looking down. "No, this isn't the Nazarene—not the one we want. He *does* look like him, but he's not." He turned to Mael. "What're you doing here?"

"I followed Chudash."

"You heard our conversation?"

"No."

"Do you know what it was about?"

"I couldn't hear."

The High Priest weighed his honesty for a moment. "What did you see?"

"You were arguing."

The priest nodded. "Anything else?"

"You gave him money, but didn't let him count it."

The priest smiled as he looked at the priests that had surrounded them. "An honest man, at least." He looked back at Mael. "You look familiar." His eyes probed Mael's vorn. "Were you in the crowd with the Nazarene yesterday—when he chastened the moneylenders in the courtyard?"

"Yes, I saw that."

"Were you *with* him" The priest's eyes grew dark.

"I heard the commotion and came to see what it was about. I saw him slip into the crowd when you tried to arrest him."

Exasperation lit the priest's face and his dark eyes stormed. "Are you one of his followers?"

Darkness and fear swept in around Mael. He wanted to tell the truth and he wanted to shade it to avoid the trouble descending on him. The fear pushed him toward the a subtle desire to escape..."I only arrived the night before last—from Farhantra, on the western side of the Vorsian Sea. I have only just met this man, but I *would* be his follower."

The priest looked around at the others. He probably needed no approval from his cohorts, but he seemed cautious. He looked back at Mael and their eyes met. For a long moment, the man in front of him stared into him, locked in the process of deciding his fate.

"Arrest him. Put him in one of the cells along the eastern wall. Don't let the Ermans know. Don't let him talk with anyone. I will let you know when he can be freed." The priest never broke eye contact. "You'll be safe, but we cannot let you interfere with our plans."

"DO NOT BE AFRAID. THEY WILL NOT HURT YOU!" The voices were crystal clear.

The moral victory of standing with truth did not dissuade the consequences. Two temple guards stepped forward and grabbed Mael. "I'll go without resistance," he said.

Judas made his way back to where Jesus was handling the crowds. It had been hard to find a moment where he could work out the arrangements, but the intensity of the crowds during the feast had given him good cover. Thirty silver sovereigns would make a handsome addition to the treasury.

Jesus didn't seem to care that much about where the money came from and where it went. There was always enough, but barely, and Judas always wished there was a bit more padding.

The foolish priests had played into his game. They couldn't arrest Jesus publicly because of the crowds. Even if they did, Jesus would surely escape again as he had numerous times before. He was destined to rule, and neither the Romans nor the Jewish establishment would be able to interfere.

He wished he'd had time to count the silver. Caiaphas's interference in his efforts to do so angered him. He would have to do that later. The weight of the uncounted silver in his cloak hung heavy on his mind. It felt like betrayal, but it *was* for the better, and the priest wouldn't dare to shortchange the contract.

The number of followers increased daily, and the treasury was lower than it had ever been. The women who accompanied them and provided most of the money for his work seemed to be lower on funds, and were having difficulty keeping up with the rising numbers that came under the sway of the master.

Of particular distaste was the short little one that arrived just yesterday. Mael, he called himself, but Judas doubted that was his real name and there was something about him—his size, or perhaps the width between his gray eyes and the way he stared through him when they talked. His hands were unnaturally large and scarred. Maybe it was his lazy eye—there was something—

"What's happening," he asked Peter as he rejoined the group. "I got separated."

Peter laughed. "He just healed another lame man." Peter pointed. "I love the way they dance about whenever he does that. Look at him!"

Judas followed the line of Peter's finger. The old man was shouting and jumping up and down like a child. "I can stand! I can jump! I can dance!" Jesus smiled. Another beggar turned mouth-to-feed. Judas forced a smile.

Andrew doubled over with laughter and James grinned from ear to ear. Bartholomew slapped Judas on the back. "Cheer up, Judas," he laughed. "This is what we came to see, isn't it?"

Judas wanted to say no. What Judas wanted was to see the Romans squirming under the hand of Jesus's authority. He wanted to see them walking out of Jerusalem because they were no longer needed. He wanted the High Priest and all his cohorts to realize that their way of life was over and they would all be serving the master. Judas would be there, of course, treasurer of the new kingdom, with the wealth of the temple fully in his hands.

Thomas came up beside him. He looked worried. "Have you seen Mael?" he asked.

Judas looked around quickly. The quirky newcomer was nowhere to be seen. Even with the throngs that swarmed around Jesus, it would have been easy to spot him. "No—I got separated for a bit, but no—I don't see him."

The look of concern on Thomas's face intensified. He moved on. Judas liked Thomas. Thomas was cautious and thoughtful, not always buying into the way of the master, but adopting it with caution, as he understood it. The little Mael would have to fend for himself. He was a latecomer anyway—not part of the core that would rule with Jesus.

Chapter Nine

PRISON

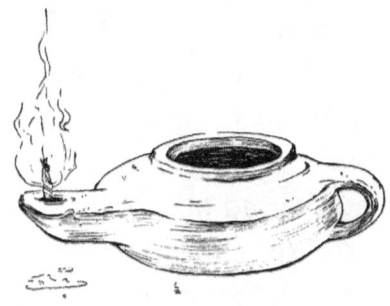

"The prison cell breeds reflection; In the mind of one imprisoned is born anger or change."

Old Mythinian Proverb

Mael shuffled along between the two guards through the chambers of the portico, then right along the eastern wall of the temple. They weren't far from where the golden gate entered through the wall when they descended several sets of stairs into the darkness below the sunlit courts.

The noise of the crowds fell away. Mael's curiosity surfaced. "Are you both from Chershalem?"

"Be quiet!" one of the guards said.

"My name is Mael."

"Shut up!"

They walked a bit farther in silence. "I'm going with you willingly. I have no ill feelings."

"Be quiet, little man!"

"It's alright to be civil."

This time the guards ignored him. They lit a torch from a sconce on the wall and descended another set of steps.

"What are your names?"

They walked in silence until they came to a row of empty cells.

"This one!" One of the guards stopped and pointed at the door. The second guard removed a key from the pouch on his belt and opened the door. They waved Mael into the cell. Just before he shut the door, the one with the key said. "My name is Joshua."

The other guard cursed. "Shut the door, fool!"

The door slammed shut, leaving Mael in darkness except for the faint light of the torch through the tiny barred window on the door. The key turned in the lock as the guards argued about whether Joshua should have given his name.

The light faded and Mael was in utter darkness.

He sat down on the cold stone floor.

"DO NOT BE AFRAID. WE HAVE MANY IN THIS CITY."

The voice seemed to echo from the stone walls of the cell, and it faded into a slight hiss. A faint light that he could barely see materialized into Vishtalar before him. He was glowing faintly, but the dim light was welcome in the darkness.

"Stand up, Mael. I have brought you food and water to strengthen you." Vishtalar held out his hands. In one he held a clay jar and in the other a small basket covered with a linen cloth. "Eat, drink and be strong. You have nothing to fear."

Vishtalar set the basket and the flask on the floor of the cell, then cupped his hands together and put them down to the floor. As he opened them, a small oil lamp stood between them, already lit. "Do not let the lamp go out, Mael. When the oil is finished, you will be freed."

Mael nodded.

"Eat and wait, Master Mael, but do not fear."

With the same slight hiss, Vishtalar vanished. The flame flickered and almost went out, then revived into a steady, unwavering light for the cell.

Mael uncovered the basket. In it were two small dried fish and a round flaky disk of flatbread. He laid one hand on the fish and the other on the jar. "Thank you," he whispered.

Mael ate the bread slowly. It was sweet, tasting of honey and a flavor he had never experienced before. It crumbled in his hand as he broke small pieces off the disk. The cold water had a slight essence that, combined with the bread, seemed to fill him quickly. He ate both of the salted fish leaving half the bread.

After his eyes acclimated to the darkness, the oil lamp provided enough light to explore his cell. It was about four paces square and featureless except for the mortared cracks between the stones. The stones on the wall opposite the door were massive—the eastern wall of the temple.

In the far-right corner was a chamber pot and a small three-legged stool. A woven, woolen mat lay on the stone floor, barely big enough to lie on without some appendage hanging off the edge. The solid wood door had a small opening in the bottom and a window about the size of his face at the height too high for him to see out. The yellow flame of the lamp warmed the walls with its light, but did little to dispel the chill from the stone that robbed his body of warmth.

It was far more pleasant than the one previous time he had tasted the timelessness of prison:

At twenty-one, Mael was considered to be full-grown. He was a man according to the law of Mooriman, and recognized as such by all who saw him. He was slightly taller than his father, long and thin with sinewy strength born from hours in the smithy forging iron to support the family. Had he been allowed to participate, he would have been a handy match for any contestant in the traditional wrestling matches where most Mooriman highborns proved their strength.

Late one afternoon, after fada had left, Mael was cleaning up the forge, spreading the fire and sprinkling it with water to prepare the coke for the next day. He was about to clear the clinker from the bottom of the firepot, when the door to the smithy opened.

A high-ranking officer of the Mooriman court strode into the dimly lit area just inside the door. Two soldiers stood quietly behind him. Mael laid down the fire rake. "May I help you?"

"You're a smith, are you not?"—more a sneer than a question.

"I am, but my father is the proprietor here, and he's gone for the day."

"But you are a smith also—a blade smith?"

"Yes, your honor."

"I need you to make me a knife. I'll wait for it."

"Your honor, it would take me at least three hours to make any knife, and one that is worthy of your stature, would require twice that, at least."

"I will wait."

"I'm closing the smithy. It's been a long day, your honor. I'm sure we can accommodate you tomorrow."

Mael started to turn away, but the man reached out and grabbed his arm. "You don't understand. I'll have this knife tonight."

The breath wreaked of bad wine. Mael glanced over the man's shoulder to the two soldiers. They remained impassive. He knew the consequences of resisting the demands of the highborns. They ruled the city with absolute authority, ruthless and cruel in their desire for control.

"What would this knife look like?"

"The blade would be this long." The highborn held his palms about two hand widths apart. "Pointed at the end—sharp point, with both sides sharpened. I need a hardened hilt, at least the width of my hand."

Mael looked down at the floor, a sign of respect. "A dagger?" he asked.

"Look at me, boy!"

Mael looked up into the man's eyes and was met with a swift and brutal slap to the side of his face.

"How dare you look at me like that!"

Mael steeled himself. "We—my father and I—will not make daggers your honor." His father's reputation was well known and well respected, even among the Moorimans. There was no man in Farhantra, high-born or otherwise that would demand weapons from his father's smithy.

"Insolent pig!" the man bellowed, grabbing Mael's tunic and drawing him up close. "Do I need to slap you again?" His foul breath flooded around Mael's face.

Mael looked up into the man's bloodshot eyes. He remembered being neither angry nor frightened, but rather beset by a deep compassion for a man with no control over his anger and no respect for decency in the mankind.

The second slap was harder than the first. The blood rushed to his face. He turned his head to expose his other cheek. Erolin had told him this was the proper response to such a challenge. He'd never tested it.

The man shoved him back just a bit, still holding his tunic, and struck him on the other cheek with a vicious backhand. The sapphire stone in the highborn's ring cut a deep gash from his cheek bone to his chin. The man shoved him backward, as blood spilled from the cut.

The blood released the remorse in the highborn. "I'm sorry, I'm sorry." There was a genuine emotion in his voice until Mael looked up, his hand trying to hold back the blood. He looked into the high-born's eyes. As quickly as the remorse had appeared, it vanished into the stone-faced cruelty that precipitated the aggression.

The high-born turned on his heel and strode between the two guards. "Take him to the prison," he muttered. "Now!"

The guards stepped forward and grabbed Mael's arms. Mael knew he could not resist—it would make things worse. He walked between the two soldiers as blood spilled down his beard and dripped onto his tunic. At one point the guards stopped. One of them handed him a small square of linen from his pack. "Hold this on your face."

They threw him into the cell in the Mooriman fortress over-looking the harbor of Farhantra. When he entered, three rats in the corner scurried into a hole at the base of the wall. The door slammed and locked behind him.

Before the darkness descended, he assessed his situation. The cell was filthy with mold and dirt as well as filth from previous occupants. A pile of grimy rags occupied another corner and there was nowhere to sit, except the bare dirt floor. A thin slit in the stone wall, higher than the reach of his hand, filtered a gray light. No one knew where he was or why.

He lived in that cell for three days and nights with no food or water, until two guards came and freed him without explanation.

Mael's hand involuntarily moved to the scar on his cheek that cut down through his beard. After two years, it was still tender to the touch and stretched tight whenever he smiled or laughed.

He wondered what happened to the highborn who inflicted this on him. He wondered what happened when this man went back to his family and about the pain that he likely inflicted on his wife and children. He wondered why the highborn wanted a dagger and why he wanted it so quickly and what he must have felt the next morning when he woke up from his drunken stupor to face another meaningless day as a Mooriman highborn in the desolate outpost of Farhantra.

Mael was sure that the Kirrinal priests had nothing to offer such a man, though he likely visited the temple regularly as all highborns did.

No, Mael's current situation was tame. Yes, he *was* in prison and wasn't free to be with the brothers and Ransom, but he was unhurt and he was clean.

Mael had barely slept the night before. He laid down on the woolen mat and, after several attempts to find a comfortable position, fell asleep curled up in a ball with his cloak pulled tight around him.

Chapter Ten

MANNA

"Give us today, our daily bread..."
Jesus of Nazareth

"Where do you suppose he really got this stuff?" Joshua asked as he navigated the first turn on the stairs leading up to the temple courts.

"I don't know," Elias responded. "He said Vish-something brought it to him. I didn't quite get the name."

"Sounded like an angel from the way he described it." Joshua's hands trembled as they carried a basket and a finely crafted earthenware flask that still had some water in it.

"I don't think the High Priest is going to like this." Elias's words belied Joshua's sense of foreboding.

Joshua nodded, though he knew Elias wasn't watching. "Not one bit. Are you sure no one entered the cell?"

"If they did, it wasn't on my watch!"

"I'm not accusing you, but we're going to have to explain this." Joshua said.

They ascended the next flight of stairs in silence. One more to go before the level of the court. Elias stopped and Joshua turned to look at him. "We should have brought the lamp I think." Elias said.

"Perhaps." Joshua breathed deeply. "We brought everything else. He insisted that he keep the lamp burning."

"Caiaphas isn't going to like *any* of this," Joshua said as Elias started up the stairs again. "—not one bit."

Elias frowned. "Yeah, you said that."

"I mean it!" Joshua said. "He's an ugly little toad, isn't he?"

Elias snickered. "Short, eyes wide apart, that scar on his cheek messes up his beard and did you notice the scars on his hands?"

"Did you see the *size* of his hands?" Joshua smiled.

"Like frog hands!"

"Seems like he's had it rough already—and the lazy eye and the limp—which of us should explain this to the priests?"

"You should, Joshua. You're the ranking guard, at least you always say that when the good things happen."

Joshua shook his head. "*You* opened the door and found this stuff—"

"Because you *ordered* me to! C'mon, be a man, Joshua."

They came around the corner to the open chamber where the priests were adjusting each other's garments before their morning appearance in the courts. Today was big—two days before the feast and all the priests were on duty to wander the crowds that flooded into Jerusalem from all over.

The High Priest wasn't hard to find. He wore his appointment as High Priest with an air of overbearing importance. Joshua didn't want to face him.

"And how is the prisoner?" the High Priest asked as Joshua approached.

"He's fine, Highness, but we found something interesting."

The High Priest cocked his head. "Interesting?"

"We found these in his cell, Highness." Joshua held out the flask and the basket, still covered with the linen napkin.

"How did he get them?" The storm gathered as the priest looked into Joshua's eyes.

"He said someone gave them to him. He said his name was Vish-something but neither of us heard it clearly."

"It's very difficult to just give something to someone locked in a guarded temple cell."

"We were on duty all night, Highness, and no one entered the cell—or even in the area we were guarding outside. We're quite sure of that."

The High Priest's eyes narrowed. "How is that possible?"

"We don't know. He said something about Eladrim—We heard that clearly, but have no idea what he meant."

"What is in the basket?"

"We didn't look." Joshua handed the basket to the High Priest.

The priest lifted the napkin. He gasped and dropped the basket to the ground and stepped back as the contents spilled on the pavement. "Is this some kind of joke?" he stormed as he looked up.

The basket held some sort of flakey bread in it but it was crawling with maggots. "It's not a joke, Highness," Joshua said as he stepped back. "We just retrieved it from the cell and brought it here.

Other priests heard the exclamations and gathered in a small circle. "It's unclean, Highness," one of them said.

"I know it's unclean!" the High Priest said. "Have it cleaned up! Now!" Two of the younger priests darted from the group. "What's in the flask?" The High Priest looked up at Joshua.

"We don't know Highness—we didn't check." Joshua handed him the flask.

The priest cautiously lowered his nose to sniff at the contents before he straightened, his eyebrows raised in surprise. "Ceremonial incense! Where could he have gotten this? It's forbidden except in the temple worship."

Joshua lowered his eyes. "We don't know, Highness—and there is one more thing."

The priest looked up.

"When we entered the cell, there was a distinct smell of myrrh, and sitting in the middle of the cell, on the matt was a small oil lamp, with a single flame. He wouldn't let us take it or extinguish the flame."

"He wouldn't *let* you□"

Joshua looked down, flustered. "Well, he convinced us not to take it. He said he was told to let it burn all the way out. We tried to reason with him, but—well, we left it with him, not thinking it was that important."

The High Priest closed his eyes. Joshua expected a torrent of anger, but before the priest unleashed it, the ram's horn sounded, heralding the start of the day in the temple.

The priest's eyes flew open and he looked straight at Joshua, his eyes ablaze with passion. "We don't have time to deal with this now. Both of you—" He looked back and forth between Joshua and Elias. "Go to that cell and stand outside it. Be sure no one else enters, not even you! Give the prisoner no food or water. Don't unlock the door! Do you understand?"

Joshua nodded.

"Do you understandn" the High Priest repeated.

"Yes, Highness!" Joshua and Elias answered in unison as they stood up straight and saluted.

"Let him keep his lamp," said the priest as he turned away, "but nothing else!"

Joshua stood at attention while the priests filed out of the chamber. He dropped his shoulders. "This isn't the way I was planning to spend the last day before the feast," Joshua said. He smiled weakly and shook his head. "Anna will be furious."

Chapter Eleven

ELADRIM

"They come on the wind, they leave like a mist, but while they are here, we know their presence."

Deep Sky
Irokandolar

Elias hadn't intended to spend the day standing guard at the cell, either. They had gone straight back to the prisoner to double down on the access to his cell. The other cells were empty. The Romans insisted on keeping all prisoners, even those arrested by the priests.

Occasionally, they would keep someone for a short while, but Elias was mystified why the High Priest had decided to keep this odd little harmless criminal? He wasn't even sure what the crime was, unless it was being too nice to your captors.

When they arrived back at the cell, there was another basket outside the door covered by a napkin. Beside it were two small earthenware flasks of water. Elias looked at Joshua, who shrugged.

He pushed the basket aside with his foot and peeked through the small barred window into the cell. The little man sat in the middle of the room staring into the lamp flame. He leaned forward with his elbows on his knees and his chin in his hands. Another basket and water flask sat beside him.

"Are you alright?" Elias asked.

"I'm fine," The prisoner said without moving.

Elias waited to see if there would be anything else, then turned back to Joshua. Joshua had lifted the napkin off the basket. Two flat, round wafers of flakey pastry glistened as if they had just been collected off the grass after a damp night and were still wet with dew.

"What is it?" he asked.

"I dunno," Joshua said, "but we best leave it alone." Elias had nodded, but after several hours of standing quietly in the silent halls, his gnawing hunger was getting the better of him.

"This was meant for us, don't you think?" he said to Joshua while nodding at the basket.

Joshua sighed, "I dunno. I don't think the High Priest would appreciate it."

"The High Priest is not here to say what we can and can't do other than stand guard. After all, *he* didn't provide for us—we both missed breakfast."

Joshua nodded. "You think it's safe?"

Elias turned and peered into the cell again. "Did you leave this bread for us?"

The little man nodded. "Vishtalar thought you might be hungry and thirsty."

"What is it?"

"I don't know, but it tastes good."

Elias paused.

"Who is Vishtalar?"

"A friend."

In the whole conversation, the prisoner hadn't moved. Elias stepped back from the window. "I am going to try it," he said. Joshua nodded.

Elias bent down and took one of the small loaves. As he broke it, it crumbled in his hands. He handed half of it to Joshua. "You first."

Joshua shook his head.

"Alright." Elias raised it to his nose and sniffed it, then touched with with his tongue. His eyes lit up. "Like honey, slightly spiced."

Joshua did the same. "Coriander!" he said. "Very good!"

They ate both cakes and then tasted the contents of the flasks. "The High Priest said this smelled of ceremonial incense," Elias said. "Whatever it is, I'd love to know how to make it."

Joshua licked his fingers. Elias couldn't imagine that one small cake would replace two meals missed guarding the prisoner, but he was full. He peeked through the window in the door. "What is this stuff?"

"I don't know."

Elias sighed. "It's gone now," he said to Joshua. "Back to work."

They stood guard for several hours. Elias guessed it was getting dark outside, but had no way of telling. They dared not leave their post and their idle chatter ran thin with the boredom.

"It's frustrating that we are so cut off from ..."

A sudden, thin hiss from behind the door arrested Elias's words; a sound he had never heard before.

"What was that?" Joshua exclaimed as he jumped to the window in the door. Joshua stared for a moment and then backed away with a panicked look on his face. He waved Elias to the window.

The prisoner was standing now, with the light of the single oil flame illuminating him from the ground. Opposite the little man stood a giant, dressed in leather armor with eyes like the sky and long straight hair the color of bleached straw. He had a belt about his waist that held a short sword in its scabbard. The bronze bracers and polished greaves reflected the light from the flame and cast an otherworldly radiance about the cell. He looked like a Roman soldier, but bigger and different.

The soldier spoke, but no sound came from his mouth. The prisoner responded as they stared at each other.

"What's happening?" whispered Joshua. "What are they doing?"

"They're talking but there's no sound... They just sat down facing each other with the lamp between them..."

"No sound?"

"Shhhh..." Elias strained to listen through the small window.

"Should we go find the priests?"

"No! He'll be gone before they get here, and they wouldn't believe us anyway."

"You think he's an angel?" Joshua said.

"Shhhhh!" Elias stepped back from the window to let Joshua try.

Joshua stepped up and listened. "Nothing!" he exclaimed.

"How did he get in there?"

"He must be an angel. *They* can do things like that."

"Learning always precedes understanding"
Vindorian proverb

Mael stood up when Vishtalar appeared. He'd been waiting a long time, pondering his situation and listening for the voice. The oil in the lamp must be getting low, and he struggled to be patient while the flame continued its steady burn. Now his giant friend was there, in the cell, standing opposite him in the feeble light.

He wondered for a moment if this Joshua and the other guard were able to see Vishtalar. They hadn't believed that he had visited earlier that day and had made no comment when they discovered the food he had left, other than asking if it was for them.

"Are you safe, Mael?" the giant said, his voice echoing off the stone walls.

"I've been adequately taken care of."

"Do not look at the door. Mah'Eladra have shut their ears so they cannot hear us. Sit."

Mael sat down as Vishtalar joined him on the floor across the flame.

"They will come for you soon, Mael. They cannot harm you, because you are protected, but they will take you with them to see. You must go with them—this is a time to learn."

"I'm learning much, but I have many questions."

"I will tell you all I can."

"Where is this place? Where am I? It doesn't feel like Tessa."

"It is another world, Mael, like Tessa but *not* Tessa."

"Why was I brought here?"

"Because you must learn who you are before you go back."

"What should I call this place?—this world?"

"The inhabitants call it Terra, or Earth. It has been hidden from those on Tessa, so it has no name to you."

"Hidden?"

"This world has been set apart from all the worlds created by Mah'Eladra because of the battle that is raging here. We have been forbidden to come here so we know little of what is happening."

"Then how are *you* here?"

"I am your guardian, Mael. I have special dispensation to continue to protect you while you are here, but no one else may come from outside. There are Eladrim who belong here and work among these people as we do on Tessa. The mankind here calls them 'angels'. There are also NarEladra; they call them 'demons.'"

"How long will I be here?"

Vishtalar paused and looked up at the ceiling briefly. "I cannot say, but you will be here until you have been readied to return."

"Will it be painful?"

"I do not know, little one."

"Ransom, the one they call Chaisus—he is special in some way, right?"

"Yes."

"In what way?"

"I am not permitted to answer that, but you will learn."

Mael thought for a moment. "The people here—do they know about Mah'Eladra? They speak of Elohim and Yahweh, and sometimes just use the word God as if they are talking about the same."

"Those are their names for Mah'Eladra."

"They don't know anything about the Kirrinath?"

"They were given a code, long ago by a man who learned it from Yahweh. It is like the Kirrinath only different—it is for Terra alone. It was written and collected into a book. They call it 'the law', 'the book of the law' or sometimes 'the books of the law'.

"Like the Tessarandin?"

"Similar, but more like the Kirrinath and the Tessarandin folded together. The law embodies the same concepts as the Kirrinath, but they think about it differently, and just like the Kirrinath, there are groups that see its implementation into life very differently."

"Like the difference I see between my understanding of the Kirrinath and that of the Kirrinal priests?"

"Yes, like that. And the people are fractured, even in the midst of great sincerity and fervor."

Mael paused before his next question. "The High Priest of the temple and the other priests—are they sanctioned by this law?"

Vishtalar nodded. "And you must submit to them, Mael, for they represent Yahweh to the people. You must do as they say, but do not do as they do."

Mael understood. "This is hard. I sense a cruelty and defensiveness that does not deserve such honor."

"They are sincere, even as they are misguided," Vishtalar said. "They have been entrusted with the protection of truth, but they are subject to all the failings of the mankind."

Mael sat and thought. "Why would Mah'Eladra do things so differently here on Terra than on Tessa?"

"There are mysteries for which we are not given answers, Mael. Perhaps if you get a chance, you can ask Ransom."

"He would know?"

Vishtalar nodded.

"How would he know when you don't?"

"You will understand after you learn. Learning always precedes understanding."

Vishtalar stood up. Mael knew it was the end of the conversation.

"Thank you, Vishtalar."

Joshua watched as the giant disappeared.

"Gone," he muttered to Elias. As he turned to take up his position again, the giant hissed into place not three paces in front of them. He was standing tall with his sword drawn in front of him. Joshua froze.

"I am Vishtalar," the giant rumbled. His voice surrounded Joshua. Joshua started shaking.

"Do not fear, Joshua. Do not fear, Elias. You have done what you were tasked to do. Elohim has shown favor on you and will protect you. When asked, you must tell the truth about what you saw without fear, and you will be given the words that you need."

Vishtalar sheathed his sword and stepped forward to kneel down. After taking the basket and the two flasks, he stood up. He looked into Joshua's eyes. Joshua wanted to close them but he couldn't. He couldn't even blink. The blue eyes shone like sapphires. "Farewell!"

The giant vanished with a hiss. Joshua's body released from some unseen stiffness and he almost collapsed. He gasped for breath.

He looked over to Elias who was in a similar state of recovery. Both bent over with their hands on their knees, breathing deeply and dealing with the overwhelming sensations of what had just happened.

They hadn't even had time to talk when the torchlight of an approaching entourage and the murmur of voices invaded the stillness of the prison.

Joshua jumped to the window on the door and looked in. The prisoner sat on the floor—just as before. As he watched, the flame on the lamp flickered and went out and the cell fell into darkness.

He stepped back from the door and resumed his guard position. "The light just went out." He whispered.

The entourage that carried the torches rounded the corner. Four soldiers from the temple guard surrounded the High Priest. Four other priests trailed behind them. They drew up in front of Joshua.

The High Priest stepped forward. "How's the prisoner?" he asked, looking straight at Joshua.

"He's safe and fine," Joshua responded. "His lamp went out not a moment ago."

"A moment ago?"

"Yes, Highness, as soon as the light from your entourage was seen in the hall."

"How do you know?"

"I was watching. A last check before you arrived."

"Has anyone been to visit him?"

Joshua hesitated.

"Well?"

"Yes, Highness, he had a visitor."

"But you did not let him in!"

"No Highness, he appeared from nowhere in the cell. A tall warrior, dressed for battle. We did *not* open the door, but we heard him arrive."

The priest's face turned ashen. "Did they talk?"

"Yes, Highness, but we couldn't hear the conversation. We tried, but neither of us succeeded."

"Was there anything else?"

"Yes Highness, when we arrived here, there was a basket with loaves in it and two flasks of water. The prisoner told us that it was for us because we had nothing to eat."

"It was outside the door?"

"Yes, Highness."

"Did you eat it?"

"Yes, Highness. We were hungry—and thirsty."

"There were no maggots□"

"No, it was sweet, and crumbled into flakes in our hands. It tasted like honey—with coriander."

The priest's face turned a shade whiter and his eyes bespoke anger and horror. "Where is the basket now?"

"Vishtalar—the warrior—appeared in front of us—outside the cell. He told us his name, but we were like dead men before him. We couldn't move. He gathered the basket and flasks and told us to tell you everything. He vanished just before you arrived."

The priest closed his eyes and shook his head as if the shaking would rid him of some truth he didn't want to face. Joshua's knees trembled.

The priest opened his eyes. "You've done nothing wrong. Both of you: take leave of this place and go back to your families. Don't tell anyone anything of what you have seen here, is this clear?" He looked from Joshua to Elias and back—several times.

"Yes, Highness," they said in unison.

Chapter Twelve

ARREST

"The Illusion that we must conform to the customs of this world is only and exactly that: an illusion."

The Middle Way

Pratoraman

The report of the guards troubled Caiaphas, but not enough to dissuade him from his purpose. He'd come too far and couldn't turn now. He didn't want to believe, but had no reason to doubt that they thought they were telling the truth. He'd never seen an angel; he didn't even believe that they existed, but had no reason to contest the experience of his guards.

"Open the door," he commanded. One of the guards stepped forward with the key to the door and opened it. Caiaphas motioned for two of the guards with torches to enter first. They moved to either side of the door so he could enter between them.

The little prisoner was standing with his back to the wall opposite the door. "High Priest," he said as he bowed slightly before looking up.

"My guards told me that you had a visitor."

"Yes Highness. Vishtalar is an Eladrim guardian. He told me that you might call him an angel."

"What was he doing here?"

"He came to make sure I was safe; that I was not being mistreated. He brought me food and water. We talked about my purpose here."

"And what was the food he gave you?"

"I don't know, Highness. I've never tasted it before. It was sweet and slightly flavored."

"Many years ago, there was a bread given our people to keep them from starving in the wilderness—" He paused to see the prisoner's response. The little man gave no hint of recognition.

Caiaphas changed the subject. Time was short. "The robe," he called as he held out his hand.

One of the priests stepped forward to lay a gray linen garment into the prisoner's hand. "Take off your clothing and wear this."

The prisoner nodded.

"Do you know what it is?"

The prisoner shook his head as he dropped the robe to the floor and started removing his own tunic.

"It's a cloak that is worn by prisoners, to identify them. If you try to escape, we will quickly find you."

The new information had little effect. When the prisoner stood fully naked, he bent to pick up the robe. He slipped it over his shoulders, and pulled it around in front of him.

Caiaphas knew that the prisoner would have to hold the single woven piece of cloth closed to keep himself covered. If he used his hands for anything else, it would expose him to the public, but the little man seemed unconcerned about the consequences of wearing the robe.

"I have forgotten your name," Caiaphas said.

"I am Mael."

"Come Mael. You'll accompany us to find your master."

Chudash's voice seethed with anger toward Mael. "What is *he* doing here?"

"We caught him yesterday when you came to collect your silver." The High Priest showed no sign of caring.

"Highness, he can't come with us!"

"Why not, he's in a prison robe. He's not caused any trouble since we arrested him."

"This wasn't part of the deal."

"That you were careless enough to not know that he followed you wasn't part of the deal either. Besides, I want him to see what happens to your master."

Chudash cowered under the forcefulness of the priest, who showed no reluctance to belittle him. He shook his head and glared at Mael. Mael stared back, undaunted by the intimidation.

Mael had done nothing to cause Chudash shame. He hurt for Chudash, who had put himself in this situation for some small sum of money. Erolin had always insisted that money should never be the driving force in the nature of a relationship. The power of money was rot in the fabric of any society. Money was a fine servant, but terrifying and deadly to those who let it master them.

The priest stood up straight. "Tonight we have the opportunity we need," he said. "The crowds sleep and offer no hiding place. We have one who came forward to lead us to where he is hiding." He waved at Chudash. "We may only have one chance," he said as he turned back to the gathered group, "and this must be accomplished before Shabbat, for obvious reasons.

"We're subject to Roman law so there may be complications, but we must start. Chudash will lead you. It will be dark, and even with torches it may be difficult to see. Chudash will kiss the one we seek. You must arrest him before he slips away.

"Malchus will lead you. He and the other priests will follow Chudash, the temple guard behind them, then the soldiers. Mael will walk with Chudash."

Chudash closed his eyes and shook his head. "No, Highness," he said. "No!"

The priest ignored him. "Chudash says that the one we want is outside Chershalem. You'll exit the courts through the Golden Gate and make the arrest at midnight. Don't light your torches until Malchus tells you. There is no moon, but the road is white to see the way. Keep all talk to a minimum. When you have arrested him, you are to bring him to me. Lead on, Chudash."

Chudash stepped out in front. Sadness overwhelmed Mael as they plodded across the courtyard together with the entourage of priests and soldiers close behind. Chudash's heavy steps and drooped shoulders showed the weight of his deceit. Mael knew this burden.

Fourteen is an age when boys will do things to one another without thinking through the consequences. Mael could claim a small handful of them in his neighborhood as friends. Though they were prone to trouble of their own making, they respected Mael's struggle to stay clear of inappropriate behavior. He often wondered why it was so compelling to make trouble just to see if they could get away with it, because they seldom escaped, and the consequences were always unpleasant.

Mael also had antagonists, and there were none worse than the sons of the Kirrinal priests. The privileged place of their families, their access to the protection of the temple, and the faulted presupposition that they were better than others left them many opportunities to misbehave with less consequence.

Mael remembered the day well. Someone had stolen a silver Kirrinath star from one of the pedestals that adorned the gates of the temple. It wasn't large, but the value of the silver was significant and because it was from the temple, the theft was also an offensive blasphemy.

Mael had spent many hours at the temple. His back and forth with the priests earned him no small respect, because few other young men were interested at all. It also earned him a reputation as one who was unafraid to challenge their practice of the Kirrinal religion. Recent conversations had turned adversarial. The fundamentals were right, but the need for the priests to maintain their image and control over the temple, often guided how they put it into practice.

Mael was one of several young men identified as possible suspects in the theft of the star. They were all boys whose families were most likely to benefit from the significant value of the silver.

Three sons of Kirrinal priests had specifically accused Mael, claiming they had an eyewitness who had seen him take the star with details about exactly how and when.

Mooriman law was specific under such circumstances. Seven suspects of similar stature to that described by the accusers were lined up and the witness asked to identify the offender in person. Once identified, the accused was sentenced.

The 'witness' turned out to be one of the few friends from school who had shown Mael kindness and respect. Mael stood in the lineup as Voltar walked slowly down the line looking each of them in the eye. After two passes, he stopped in front of Mael and touched his shoulder. "This is the one."

His mother cried out. His father stood stone-faced and ashamed beside her as she wept. They led him away in chains, sentenced to work in the pit mine where they quarried stones for the buildings of Farhantra.

The quarry was horrible—filled with slaves and criminals. The bad food was meager and the violence of those who kept order, notorious.

On the seventh day, one of the stones they had loaded on a cart bound for the Presidatory's new mansion, slipped off the cart as the horses lurched it forward. It landed on Mael's right foot, crushing his toes. They carried him back to his bed in the bunkhouse, but offered no treatment for his foot. He cried himself to sleep that night.

The next day they released him from the quarry. During the night, the Kirrinath star had been returned to the pedestal, and the magistrate ordered his immediate release.

He limped home. Hannorah came immediately, but she could do little except clean the wounded foot and bandage it.

A year later, Voltar confessed to Mael that he had been paid by three sons of the priests to accuse Mael. The silver they gave him had been consumed by unexpected family expenses, and they were no better off than before the betrayal. He begged Mael for forgiveness.

Mael remembered Voltar's vornal agony as he explained how the framing had been arranged, and the misery of his life since that day. They embraced and wept together.

"You don't have to do this, Chudash," Mael whispered as he recalled the agony of wrestling through his forgiveness of Voltar. "You know the claims against him are false."

Chudash remained stone-faced and unrelenting. Mael knew the torture—the mixture of agony enflamed by pride—the persistent awareness of what was right and the pain of yielding to it.

They passed through the gate and down the serpentine road toward Pethny. Across the valley, in the faint light of the stars, he saw the hill rise up against the horizon with the garden where he had first met the master. Were they going to march all the way to Pethny?

"How much did they pay you?" he asked.

"It doesn't matter now," Chudash said.

Mael waited for several steps. "Was it worth it?"

"We needed the money for the treasury."

Mael waited again. The thin prisoner's robe did little to keep him warm against the night chill. The tread of the men behind him disquieted his vorn.

"He'll escape anyway," Chudash said at length. "He always does, and we will be thirty pieces better off."

"Not everyone escapes a false accusation, you know."

"*He* does."

They reached the bottom of the valley, but instead of turning toward Pethny, Chudash led them up onto the path into the garden. Why would the master be in the garden at midnight?

At the garden gate, Chudash stopped. "He's in here," he said to the Malchus. "There will be a few others, but they may have a couple swords."

Malchus raised his hand as he turned to face the others. "Light your lamps," he said. He smiled as he turned back to Chudash and Mael. "Lead on."

Thomas pried his exhausted eyes open. "'Can't you keep watch with me for one hour?'" It was the third time that the master had rebuked them for falling asleep. The night with the lepers, the long days in the crowded temple courts and the throngs of people wanting to see Jesus were enough to tire anyone.

The Passover meal with the brothers was emotionally exhausting. Jesus had told them so many new things that he hadn't fully understood and the wine hadn't helped. Thomas wanted to sleep.

When they left the room where they had the meal, he thought they were going back to Bethany. He wasn't sure what the detour into the garden was all about, but Jesus told them to wait for him—and to pray. No one was able to stay awake.

"Look," the master continued, "'My betrayer is here." As he said it, Thomas noticed the torches. There were many of them. The sound of the tread was not the footfall of peasants or priests, but that of soldiers and this many lights at midnight in the garden meant it was no small army. Jesus had assured them that the two swords they had brought would be enough. Thomas wasn't so sure.

The brothers stood up as the lights came into view. Jesus stood in front of them as if he knew what was about to happen. As the crowd drew closer, Thomas was horrified. Judas was in the lead. He had left the dinner early, possibly offended by something the master had said.

Beside Judas was Mael. Thomas's anger flared for a moment until he realized that Mael wore a prisoner's robe—which would not have been his choice.

As they drew near, Judas approached Jesus. "Greetings, Teacher," he said, then stepped forward and kissed Jesus on the cheek.

"Judas! You'll betray the son of man with a kiss of affection□"

Before anyone had time to react, two of the temple guards seized Jesus by the arms. Peter drew his sword and swung it at the man leading the group, cutting off his ear.

Jesus shook off the guards and knelt to pick up the ear, then, helping the priest's servant to stand, he placed the ear back on the man's head. "Put away the sword!" he said, "If you draw the sword, you'll die by it. You don't think that I could call on my Father, and he'd send more than seventy thousand angels to help? But if he did that, how would the prophecy about this be fulfilled?"

All time stood still at the obvious miracle. Thomas wondered what the leader must have been thinking—or Judas!

Jesus turned to the leader. "'Am I leading a rebellion that you came out to arrest me with swords and clubs? I've been teaching in the temple courts—publicly—and you didn't arrest me, but this hour of darkness—this is your time.'"

The leader nodded to the guards, and they grabbed Jesus once again. This time he didn't resist.

"RUN MAEL!" The husky voices were clear in the mayhem. Mael startled and hesitated. "RUN!"

As Mael started to move, a hand reached out from behind him and grabbed his cloak behind his neck. He struggled for a moment and then releasing his hands and throwing back his shoulders, he left the cloak in the hands of the guard. He fled naked into the bushes, ignoring the scratching against his bare skin.

Others fled also, crashing through the foliage of the garden with occasional cries of pain. Mael stopped to catch his breath and listen. No one pursued. Apparently, the priest had acquired his prize and the rest of them were of little interest.

Mael moved cautiously back toward the garden. The dark shade of the trees made it hard to navigate. The panic of running away had been much easier. When he reached the edge of the clearing, one lone figure remained, fallen on his knees, sobbing. Chudash!

Mael waited, listening to see if any of the others might still be nearby. He wasn't afraid, but wisdom demanded caution. After several moments, he crept out of the bushes and walked forward quietly. He was still naked, except for his sandals. As he approached, he found his discarded robe on the ground. He picked it up and shook it out before putting it on.

The sound aroused Chudash. Even in the darkness, Mael could see the tears in his eyes. He looked at Mael. "It wasn't supposed to happen that way!" He choked on the words.

Mael moved in close and knelt beside the broken man.

Chudash mumbled. "My friend...my master...what have I done?...what should I do?"

Mael said nothing, but waited patiently for the man beside him to come to a full awareness of his presence.

Chudash continued mumbling, alternately asking Mael and Yahweh for advice. He rocked back and forth on his knees, seeking relief from his grief.

Suddenly, his tone changed to anger: "Thirty pieces—thirty silvers—that's all they gave me." He looked up at Mael. "Was it worth it? Was it worth it?" He grabbed Mael's cloak and pulled him close. "What do I need to do, little man?" he begged. "Yahweh isn't listening to me now! What should I do?" Chudash's bloodshot eyes glinted in the gloom of the garden.

"Do you still have the thirty pieces?" Mael said.

"Yes!"

"If you give it back, it will lighten your load."

Chudash looked down. "They won't take it."

"Perhaps not, but it's blood money, Chudash. You don't want to hold it, and it will be no good for the treasury. I doubt the master would accept it."

Chudash fell silent as he continued to rock back and forth. Mael always felt intensely when others hurt, but all he could do was wait.

Minutes passed in silence—perhaps an hour. Mael sat still but looked up, watching the stars slowly process through the leaves in the branches that canopied the clearing. The cold crept into his bones and into his vorn, but still he waited.

"I would rather die than live like this." The slow, hoarse voice surprised Mael.

"You don't have to die, Chudash, at least not of your own choice."

"Yes—yes, I know—we'll all die someday."

"There's still hope, Chudash." Mael spoke as gently as he could. "Even if there were no hope, it's not your place to decide your death."

"There is no hope—their plan is to kill him."

"They will only kill him if Mah'Eladra allow them."

Chudash looked up at him, his eyes glistening in the faint light of dawn. "Who is this Mah'Eladra that you speak of?"

"It is our name for the one you call Elohim."

"Why do you speak of him in the plural?"

Mael was thankful for the distraction from the morbid hour they had just spent. "We have a teaching that says 'Mah'Eladra are several, and Mah'Eladra are one'. It was chosen long ago, that because the *several* is first, we honor them by acknowledging their several-ness."

"It's awkward," Chudash said as he looked back at the ground.

"For you, but not for us. It is awkward for me to speak of them as a single being. I think it is similar to when you call them Elohim."

Chudash fell silent again. "They will blame me. I know they will," he said at length.

"If something happens to the master, it will be because of the priests, or perhaps the Ermans, and not you, Chudash. You were a tool to set in motion what they want. If you had not volunteered, they would have found someone else—someone who has less chance of withstanding the accusations—less hope than you. You've been with the master and know his teachings about life. You are more prepared than any other to remain faithful. If the master is what you have claimed he is Chudash, then they will not be able to hurt him without permission from Mah'Eladra. It is still possible that he will escape from them as he has in the past."

"They will still blame me!"

"For what?"

"For being a traitor—for being a coward who caved in to the will of the priests."

"Did you notice, Chudash, that when confronted by the priests, the elders, and the soldiers, that all of us fled, except you."

"I fled too," he said bluntly.

"But you came back."

"So did you!" Chudash said as he looked up.

"Yes, because I saw you here weeping. Where are the others, Chudash? Are they not as much cowards as you, perhaps more so? Just different?"

Chudash looked up into the thin light of dawn on the horizon and his eyes brightened. "I need to return the money. Will you come with me, Mael?"

"They may arrest us, you know."

Chudash nodded. "I know that all too well."

The courts buzzed with intensity. "What's going on?" Judas asked the first person he encountered as they walked through the golden gate.

"They're taking the Nazarene to Pilate!"

"Why Pilate?" The panic rose again. His stomach churned.

"C'mon, Judas," Mael urged as he took his hand. "We need to get to the temple."

"Why Pilate? Why the Romans?" Judas asked again, but the man had already moved on.

The noise of the crowd was deafening. People ran past him, headed toward the corner of the court where the fortress of Antonia rose above the wall. None of the shouting made sense. The voices blurred into a wall of sound that pounded on his mind. What was happening?

"C'mon, Judas, first things first." Mael gripped his hand as he dragged Judas through the throngs of people running toward the fortress.

Judas stumbled as Mael pulled him into the vestibule north of the fortress, and it was only by the little man's strength that he managed to stay upright. They burst into the anteroom at the top to a wall of priests and the elders adjusting their vestments. They stopped short.

Mael dropped his hand and wrapped his prisoners cloak tighter around his body.

"What do you want, betrayer?"

Judas choked. Fear flooded over him and he couldn't speak.

"We don't have much time," the High Priest continued, showing no concern for Judas's fear or purpose. "The heretic is being taken to Pilate and we need to be there. Out with it!"

Mael nudged him. "Now, Judas!"

"I've made a mistake," Judas said. "A terrible mistake!"

The priest looked down at his own attire and picked a fleck of lint off his robe. "Ask me if I care!"

Mael nudged him again.

"He is innocent. He's done nothing!"

The priest stepped up close to Judas and raised his index finger in Judas's face. "He has blasphemed the Holy one of Israel—one too many times. We heard it with our own ears." He swept his hand around the group. Judas watched in horror as all the priests nodded.

"No, he's innocent! He came to restore truth to Israel. You *know* this!"

The priest shook his head. "He has an odd way of doing that, claiming he's the son of God." The priest continued to look for lint on his tunic. He looked up. "Now, be gone from here, unless you want to be condemned along with him."

"Why did you send him to Pilate?"

"Surely you know, betrayer: We cannot execute the heretic without Roman permission."

"I've brought back the money!"

"So? What is that to us? Do you think we *need* this money?"

Judas choked. Emotion boiled up from inside as fear, hatred, anger, helplessness—or perhaps all of it at once, coalesced into an indescribable oppression.

His tears made it difficult to see, but he reached into his tunic and grabbed the purse with the silver coins. He loosened the tie, and in an act of defiance, swung the purse forth so the coins sprayed out onto the stone floor. As they clattered and rolled between the feet of the priests—none of them moved.

"Suit yourself, betrayer. It's blood money now and can't change anything."

Judas turned in blind fear and started to run.

"Don't let the little one escape!" Caiaphas said.

Chapter Thirteen

VISHTOENVAR

"He exists in the lie that he does not exist."

Of beings
Mortag of Horinaine

Vishtalar stood at attention in his place on the rim of the Crown of Tessalindria, its eight peaks, in a vast perfect circle, glistened in the first rays of Asolara. He looked down into the center of the ring, into the crater of Grand Elia Margah. The golden stair, spiraled up from the center to vanish into the infinite blue of the sky.

Thousands and thousands stood with him on the rim of the margah, their bodies radiating a light brighter than the rays of Asolara that gleamed from their polished armor.

Rings of Eladrim princes on one knee with heads bowed filled the depths of the Margah. The warriors waited as the fierce beat of the Hallorian drums overwhelmed all other sound, as it reverberated from the rock walls, anticipating the arrival of Mah'Eladra.

Times like this were rare. It had been at least five hundred years since the last. It was never trivial, but Vishtalar had little knowledge of why they were called into assembly.

A ripple moved through the princes in the vale as they stood up and stepped back to form an opening in the center. Vishtalar looked up. Descending out of the crystalline sky beside the golden stair, was the visage of Mah'Eladra themselves. Perhaps he should close his eyes, but he couldn't.

The deep pounding of the Hallorian drums intensified as Mah'Eladra drew near. They were brighter than Asolara, eclipsing the glory of all that surrounded them and though there was no voice, it sounded like a great waterfall emanating from somewhere in the vale.

All around them, other creatures descended with them, their gold wings flashing in the brightness of their countenance. As Mah'Eladra settled to the floor of the margah, their robes spread out along the ground until they almost touched the feet of the Eladrim princes, who then bowed to touch them.

Vishtalar stood transfixed and unmoving, frozen by the presence of power and authority that lay before him. Mah'Eladra raised their hands and the drums fell silent. They waited. Nothing moved. The flying creatures had landed on the hems of the glowing robes and stood silent and tall between Mah'Eladra and the ring of princes.

In the timeless presence of the kings of all creation, Vishtalar couldn't count the minutes or hours that they stood in silence, until a new motion appeared above the rim. The presence that descended was gray—dark in comparison to the light of the kings, and surrounded with beings whose flesh looked like that of dead men, and whose eyes burned with intensity that could only be described as hatred. Each carried a red steel sword, bared for battle. The Nelaril! In the middle of them was Vishtoenvar, larger by his head and shoulders than any of the other Eladrim princes.

As the wraiths settled to the floor of the margah, the voices of Mah'Eladra rumbled out before them like the waters of Morahura. **"WHERE HAVE YOU BEEN VISHTOENVAR?"**

The dark lord looked up. "I have been out and about, visiting the distant places where the mankind no longer listens to you."

The Nelaril beat their swords against their shields. Vishtalar shuddered. Such impudence shouldn't be tolerated in the presence of the kings.

"HAVE YOU CONSIDERED MY SERVANT MAEL?" thundered the kings. The mountain shook under Vistalar's feet.

"You insult my legions. You have laid a hedge around him to protect him. Remove that, and you will see him fall."

"MAEL SOJOURNS NOW IN A DISTANT PLACE. WHEN HE RETURNS, YOU MAY TEST HIM, BUT YOU ALONE."

"There will be little contest!"

"AS WE SAID FROM THE EARLIEST OF DAYS, YOU MUST CHALLENGE HIM IN THE FORM OF THE MANKIND, BUT YOU MAY NOT TAKE THAT FORM UNTIL THAT TIME."

Vishtoenvar laughed, and dipped his head in a mock bow. "There is another I must attend to."

"BE GONE THEN!" thundered the kings, as they brought both hands down from above their head onto the ground. In the shock wave that followed, Vishtoenvar and the Nelaril were scattered like leaves in a storm. They shot upward, tumbling head over heels until they were out of sight in the blue of the sky.

All eyes turned back to the kings. They remained silent for a time and half a time. No breath stirred in the margah and no muscle moved on the rim.

Finally, in a gentle voice, the kings spoke, like a chorus of thousands whispering softly. **"Do not fear, my faithful ones. There are deeper things to know. Many of you have searched for them for a long time, but they aren't your province."** The kings laughed.

"Go now in peace. Be vigilant and trusting. Give strength to the weak and courage to the faint in their vorns."

Mah'Eladra rose from their seat, pulsing with power and strength. Warriors and princes fell to their knees, their eyes transfixed until the sky closed in around the ascending kings.

Mael yielded as the guards grabbed him by the arms. He couldn't leave the cloak behind.

"Put him back in the cell until after we deal with the blasphemer!" said the priest.

Mael didn't resist.

"You won't escape this time," said the High Priest. He nodded to the two temple guards who held him and then to a couple others who fell in behind and in front of him. "Make sure that he has no visitors—and no food or water!"

Mael had no intention of escaping. He had only run before because of the voice. He knew that if he heard the voice, no number of guards could hold him. If there was no voice to obey, then no strength on his part could free him.

They took him down the same steps, and stopped at a different cell. After pushing him through the door, they slammed it shut behind him.

The cell, like the one before was clean and cold, void of light except that which filtered into it through the tiny barred hole in the wooden door. Mael sat down on the mat to wait.

"What will happen to Chudash?" he asked aloud to the deafening silence. "And what will happen to Ransom?" His mind swirled with possibilities but none of them clarified. He imagined what might be happening with each of the brothers. Surely, after the time they had spent with the master, they would not abandon him permanently. Surely, they would return or be in the crowd that thronged to the fortress. Surely, they would be watching.

He breathed deeply. The key ground in the lock, followed by the hiss of someone materializing before him.

"So here you are, Mael." There was only one voice like that. "Trapped and helpless, without recourse, without protection, without any defense—abandoned by Mah'Eladra while your precious friend hangs himself in the valley."

"What do you want, Vishtoenvar?"

Vishtoenvar swirled around the cell, a half dragon wraith with a voice as cold as the ice on the sea north of Vann. "Not only that, but your Ransom, the one they call Master, has been condemned. We only need to entice the Romans to kill him. We're working on that."

Mael looked over to see one of the guards looking through the small window in the door. "Who're you talking to?" asked the guard. A hurried exchange of muttered curses followed a desperate attempt to open the door.

"Tell them the door is locked, Mael—that they cannot enter until I am through with you."

Mael remembered the first time he had come face to face with this NarEladrim prince:

The wraith swept across the dying coal fire and it flashed upward toward the leather skins that protected the smithy's roof from flying ash. "Do you know who I am, Mael?" The cold thin voice struck terror into his vorn.

Mael grabbed a fire poker and held it in front of him. He'd never seen anything like this before.

"Do you know who I am, Mael?" the wraith said again.

"No."

The creature was upon him before he could move, snatching the poker from his hand to send it clattering across the floor.

"Fool, you cannot stand against me! Do you know who I am◻" The anger and intensity burned its way into Mael.

He shuddered. "I do not." He stood helplessly as the cold wisps of gray mist swirled around his legs and curled up around his body.

"I am the morning star, the cherished son, the true leader of freedom from the oppressions of Mah'Eladra."

Mael shivered again. "What is your name?"

"You know my name!"

"How would I know your name?"

"Fool! You blasphemed my name to the priests in the temple, just today!"

A small caution crept over Mael. He knew he shouldn't speak the name and answer this beast. "If your name is so important, then say it yourself!"

The wraith shot up to the ceiling then descended upon him as if to crush him, but the blow never came. The implications dawned on Mael: with all the bravado, Vishtoenvar couldn't touch him. Somehow, he was blocked. For all the intimidation and swagger, this NarEladrim prince could do nothing except elicit his fear.

"You can't touch me, can you◻"

Vishtoenvar swept across the fire again and once again the flames shot up to the leather spark barrier, then he descended to wrap himself closely around Mael's body like a giant, frigid serpent.

Mael shivered, trapped and held helpless by this servant of evil. He shivered as waves of fear swept through him. suddenly there were words as tiny lights emerging from the darkness of terror. "You have no power over me that I do not yield to you in my fear. You have no authority over the mankind except to indulge them in their own self-absorption, greed, anger, selfishness, self-pity and shame."

Vishtoenvar's grip fell away and he flashed outward. An icy mist trailed behind the voice as it hissed its hatred and malice. "There are many of the mankind, many that surround you, that heed my voice," he said as he knocked over the tall ring mandrel. It crashed to the floor. Mael jumped.

Vishtoenvar swept over the hammer rack as one by one, the hammers tumbled into the air and clattered onto the stone floor. As he passed over the slack tub, the water exploded into the air like a cloud and vanished.

Mael was eighteen. He had seen such tantrums among his peers. As frightening as it was, this display of disruptive power was child-ish. "Prove to me your power by becoming like the mankind. I have heard that the Eladra do that."

"How little you understand, puny man."

"Teach me!"

The serpent mist drew up close in front of his face. "Mah'Eladra. They have given me permission to sift you like barley before the scales. At this time, I cannot touch you, but there are others who can. There are those of the mankind whose hatred I have incited against you and you will not be able to stand."

Somehow, Mael already knew this, though he wasn't aware that it was so deliberate. He'd tasted that hatred—the envy—the scorn. Instead of the default behavior of directionless men and women who didn't have the courage to live under the Kirrinath, the deliberate incitement by Vishtoenvar and his followers added a new conviction to his understanding.

"Why have you come to me?"

"Because in your arrogance you think you are above the others around you."

Mael had never thought that obedience to the will and the way of Mah'Eladra was arrogant. He recalled the expression from the Tessarandin: 'Woe to those who call evil good, and good evil.'

This twisted logic offended him. "The way I live is by choice. The decisions I make aren't accidental or convenient as they may be with others. I don't yield to the whims of other men, the eladra, the NarEladra or even you. This is not arrogance, but prudence."

"You impudent child!" the voice was no longer a cold whisper but a roar. The wraith expanded to fill the smithy as iron scraps from the floor and half-finished work on the table swirled in the maelstrom. Mael shielded his eyes and face and then as suddenly as it all started, the wraith vanished as the debris clattered to the floor.

Mael shuddered. His last sentences had come from some deep well that he didn't understand but they spoke a truth he'd never put into words. He stood still a long time, shaken, but unhurt by the savage tirade of the NarEladrim prince. He was sure he hadn't seen the last of this creature.

"You have no more authority here than you do on Tessalindria." Mael said to the wraith in his cell.

"Things have changed, little man—they have changed."

The guards banged on the door. "Open this door!" They shouted.

"Tell them!" Vishtoenvar hissed. "They can't see me."

"Tell them yourself. You should be able do that!"

Vishtoenvar swept around the inside of the cell and then vanished through the door. The clamor outside stopped suddenly and he re-emerged into the cell.

"What did you do?" Mael asked.

"They won't ask again!"

"Why are you here?"

"I'm here to let you know that you can't stand against me."

"I'm standing against you as we speak."

"You are being protected, you fool. Don't you see that?"

"My protection is from Mah'Eladra, because I do as they say. It is the promise given to all of the mankind. It's not unique to me."

"Do you not know who you are?"

"I am Mael—nothing more."

The wraith made two full passes around the cell before pulling up short in front of him. "Why were you brought here, Mael-and-nothing-more?"

"I was brought here to learn; then I will return."

"To learn what?" The voice softened suddenly. "Return to what?"

"I have yet to learn what I haven't learned."

"Then you're not ready for the contest."

Mael didn't ask what he meant.

"I have another to defeat, and when I do, I will return and you will learn, at that time, that I am the Lord of Tessalindria also. There is none to oppose me." He swept around the room two more times and then vanished up through the ceiling, leaving nothing but a train of cold air behind.

"Mah'Eladra will oppose you," Mael muttered to the empty cell as he exhaled in relief.

"Woe to those who call evil good, and good evil."
                                    Tessarandin, Book 3

Mael awoke in the darkness to a sense that the wraith had returned. "Behold little one," Vishtoenvar hissed as he circled the walls, his icy vapor trailing like smoke behind a fire. "The time has come, your Ransom is defeated, dying like a worm, a spectacle to the crowds, and powerless to save himself, lest his claim would come true that he can save others."

Mael had nothing to say. He knew, somehow that Mah'Eladra was bigger than that. There was something missing.

The wraith continued to circle, but closer and colder. "He is defeated and with him all his hope and all his heresies and foolishness that he could defeat me."

"But he is not dead yet?"

"He is moments away."

"Why are you not there to watch?" Mael spoke through his teeth that clenched in suppression of fear that Vishtoenvar could be right.

"Fool!" the wraith thundered. "I am here *and* I am there."

Mael wasn't sure that this was possible, but had no reason to dispute it from his own ignorance of such things. He remained quiet.

Vishtoenvar crept closer—ever closer, cold and circling like a snake suffocating its victims by denying their breath. "I'm here," he whispered, "because *you* are next. You don't suppose they put you in this cell for entertainment, do you?"

Mael wasn't sure exactly why he was in the cell, but he wasn't sure that this creature had it right either. His knees weakened as the cold tightened around him. This couldn't happen now. There was more to learn. He knew that. It wasn't his time.

"Be gone!" he shouted, throwing out his hands as if he could dispel the mist that tightened around him.

Suddenly, the room filled with blinding light from all sides as the hiss of engaging Eladrim warriors eclipsed the voice of the wraith. Vishtoenvar shrieked and started up toward the ceiling as twenty Eladrim hands grabbed hold of him, restraining his ascent. These were no ordinary Eladrim, but bigger and brighter than Mael had ever imagined, like princes of majesty and power. They pulled Vishtoenvar down, writhing and screaming as they sang together—words that Mael couldn't understand.

Mael collapsed to his knees and put his hands to his ears to hide the sounds. The cold energy of the wraith passed around him as the Eladrim pushed Vishtoenvar to the floor and then, with a single final shout of victory and a shriek of horror, Vishtoenvar vanished with the Eladrim through the solid stone floor of the cell.

The silence closed in around him and then, just as suddenly, the floor shuddered beneath his knees.

"What was that?" The panicked voice of one of his guards was distinct through the small window. Mael stood up.

The floor shuddered again, and this time dust and small debris fell from the stone ceiling. The walls trembled.

"This isn't good!" said the other voice.

With the third shudder, Mael lost his balance and tumbled onto the mat, as more dust fell from between the stones.

"Let's get outta here!"

"We can't leave the prisoner!"

"We're gonna die!"

Running boots signaled their retreat. Almost simultaneously, the doorway shifted slightly and the door flew open with a crack. It teetered for a moment, then dropped off its hinges and fell outward, pancaking to the floor with a startling slap.

Chapter Fourteen

ESCAPE

The infinite is the timelessness of the deep sky.
The deep sky is the infinite spaces beyond Tessalindria.

Passages
Oratanga

Mael peered out of the door into the torch lit hall. Nothing moved. The earth rumbled again and more dust fell from the ceiling.

Mael ran, navigating upward as well as he could remember, emerging suddenly into the portico to the east of the temple courts. He darted out into the courtyard. The surreal vision that greeted his entrance burned into his mind.

Rows of narrow benches stood in the middle of the court. Behind each stood one of the temple priests. Approaching each was a line of people holding animals and birds as the priests were chanting. The sky was dark, as if twilight were approaching, but the shadows were off. Asolara was high, but dimmed by some unseen mist, as if Vishtoenvar himself were masking her.

Overwhelmed, Mael slipped behind one of the columns of the portico. He was still breathing heavily from the run up the stairs. A man walked by carrying a small animal with white curly hair. "What's happening?" Mael asked.

The man startled and moved away, then stopped to look back. "You're not from here."

Mael shook his head.

The man came closer and peered at him. "It's the Passover." Spurred by Mael's blank stare, he continued: "You're not shrealite! What are you doing here?"

"I was in prison." Mael nodded back at the gate to the dungeon. "When the ground shook, the door opened."

"I have to go," the man said.

"What is happening to Asolara?" Mael asked as he nodded to the sky.

The man looked up and shook his head. "Odd, isn't it?" He scowled and stepped out into the court.

Mael peered around the column. The priests were slitting the throats of the animals as they were placed on the tables, and catching the blood in round silver bowls. When the bowls were nearly full, they passed them to other priests who stood in a line leading up the temple steps. Where was all the blood going?

Other priests were taking the dead animals and skinning them before handing the stripped carcasses back to those who had brought them.

There was blood everywhere. The animal skins were piled high at the end of the row of tables. Nausea turned his stomach and he slipped back behind the column with his back to it to rein in his sanity. It was all so horrifying.

Someone shouted, followed quickly by other panicked voices. He peered around the column. Priests ran out of the temple, their faces contorted with surprise, all but tripping on their long vestal garments, their silver blood bowls clanging down the steps around them. Some stopped to stare back at the temple entrance as their panic subsided.

A crowd hurried to where they stood. All Mael could hear amidst the shouting was "The curtain, the curtain!"

He decided to run, but someone grabbed his arm. Before he had time to turn, a hand clamped over his mouth.

"Don't run, Mael," Domas spoke into his ear. "Stop struggling!"

Mael relaxed.

"Are you alright?"

Mael nodded.

"Come with me!" Domas released his hand from Mael's mouth and towed him by the arm into the crowd.

"What's happening, Domas?"

They hurried along against the outer wall of the court under the portico toward the Golden Gate. "After we get out of the courts, Mael."

They passed through the gate in silence and without contest. The festival, the drama at the temple, and the twilit mid-afternoon sky, had rendered the guards uninterested in being guards. Domas and Mael started down the ramp outside the wall against the flow of people moving up to the temple, many of them carrying their sacrificial animals.

About halfway down the serpentine pathway, Domas spoke: "They've killed the master," he whispered. "He died just a short while ago."

Mael bent over and dry-retched in the middle of the road. Domas's hand pulled him up. "We have to keep moving. This is what they wanted all along, Mael."

"Who did it?"

"The priests—probably the Ermans also. The master troubled both of them."

"But he did nothing wrong!" Mael protested.

Domas's grip tightened on his arm as he picked up the pace. "The trial was a joke." Domas described what had happened briefly as they hurried along. The description of what Domas called crucifixion set off another wave of nausea. Domas waited patiently as Mael bent over to dry-retch again.

"Where were you, by the way?" Domas asked when he stood up.

"I was in prison."

"Before or after the betrayal?"

"Both."

Domas studied him for a moment. "C'mon, we need to keep moving."

"Where are we going?"

"Not sure—"

"Let's go to the garden," Mael suggested. They stood at the point where the path to the garden met the road to Pethny. "No one will be there."

Domas nodded. "You're probably right."

He *was* right. The path to the garden was deserted. By now, Asolara was out from behind the strange darkness, but it was hanging low over the city to the west.

"Prison was not my choice, you know," Mael said.

"I'm guessing it wasn't, but I am curious how you ended up there—twice."

Mael explained in as much detail as possible without touching on the visit by Vishtoenvar. When he was done, they sat in silence for a while, each processing his own thoughts. "Where will they burn the master's body?" Mael asked at length.

"What?"

"Eshen—the ceremonial cremation of his body after death."

Domas looked horrified. "We would never do that!"

"What do you do?"

"We wash and prepare the body and then it's buried. If you're rich, you might have a tomb or mausoleum."

"The master wasn't rich," Mael observed.

"No—not rich—at least in a money kind of way." Domas was looking out over the valley toward the city where Asolara swung low behind the temple. "He seemed to have everything he needed and wanted."

"Erolin always told me that that was true riches."

"Erolin?"

"She was a Pistisine guardian. Where I come from that was significant. She watched over our family and was always there to help. She taught me much about the Kirrinath and read to me from the Tessarandin whenever she could."

Domas looked at him and grinned. "I have no idea what you just said."

Mael looked at his friend. "The Pistisines were the guardians of truth from my world..."

"Wait! Are you saying you are from a different world? I thought you were just from a city I had never heard of somewhere."

"Look at me, Domas! Don't you see that I am just a bit different in too many ways to be from this place. Watch my lips when I speak."

"Yeah, I've noticed that...but never thought it would be another world. Where is it?"

Mael pointed at the sky. "I don't really know. Somewhere out there, I think—somewhere in between the stars at night, but I can't tell you where."

"That's impossible."

"I have been discovering that there is no limit to what is possible with Mah'Eladra—Elohim, that is."

Domas shook his head in disbelief. "And why did you come here?"

"I was brought here to learn, Domas, but I don't know what I am to learn. All I've learned so far is that the world here is just about as cruel as where I came from."

Domas shook his head again. Mael wasn't sure it was disbelief or frustrated agreement.

"When I have learned what I'm to learn, I'll go back."

"How did you get here?"

"I'm not sure I can explain it to you. Do you have time portals here on Terra?"

"Time Portals?"

"Gateways—like the gates of the temple—but when you go through them, you end up in a different place and a different time."

Domas sat staring out over the city again. "We have nothing like that here—it sounds impossible."

"On Tessalindria there are seven such portals. They are used to move people to different times and places to serve the purposes of Mah'El—Elohim. Many believe that there's an eighth portal, but no one knows where it is. Apparently, it's here on Terra."

"I'd like to see it."

Mael looked over at Domas who was staring at him. "Now□"

Domas nodded. "Unless it's too far to go before Asolara disappears."

Mael wasn't sure this was a good idea. He looked over at Asolara. "How long is that?"

Domas squinted out to the horizon. "Perhaps an hour."

"It's on the other side of the city."

"Show Him!" Mael startled at the clarity of the voices.

"Are you alright?" Domas stared at him with an odd curiosity.

"Yes. Come with me." Mael leapt to his feet. "Now is good!"

Chapter Fifteen

TOMB

*"If Mah'Eladra can make life from nothing
Can they not restore life to something?"*

It Is Said
Sessasha

Thomas stood up and brushed the dust off the back of his cloak. Mael's sudden intensity made him suspicious. "How far is it?"

"I dunno." Thomas towed Mael with him as they joined in the back of the procession. The women were weeping. "Where are we going?" he whispered to Andrew.

"Some rich man said they could put the master in his new tomb." Thomas looked down at Mael and smiled. "I guess it *is* possible for a poor man to be buried well."

Mael nodded.

"What?" Andrew asked.

"Never mind."

They walked behind the women, who were mourning audibly, with occasional wails and tears. They turned off the main road into the valley.

Mael nudged Thomas. "This is the way to the portal," he whispered.

"Down here?"

"I told you it was close."

"What are you guys talking about?" Andrew said.

"Never mind."

The procession stopped before a tomb cut into the solid rock. The round stone that would cover the entrance had been rolled back in preparation, and chocked to hold it.

Mael's eyes were wide with surprise—his mouth hung open.

"What?" Thomas whispered.

Mael just pointed.

"The portal□"

Mael nodded.

"Don't say anything!" Thomas whispered.

They stood still as those carrying the body lowered it to carry it into the tomb. Strips of linen wrapped the body from head to toe so it was impossible to see who it actually was, but Thomas had no reason to doubt. Two of the servants who had been carrying the body took the ends of the litter and stooped to enter the low opening of the cave. As they disappeared, a new round of wailing erupted from the women.

The rest of the group stood watching as they emerged from the tomb with the empty litter. "Close it," ordered the well-dressed man who stood by the door.

Two men stepped forward and knocked the chock from in front of the large round stone, and it rolled down, grinding against the rock wall behind it until it settled across the opening.

The patron turned to face the crowd. "It's an honor to me, to be able to serve Jesus the Nazarene in this way. But now there is little time to get back to your homes before sundown and the start of Shabbat." He snaked his way through the mourners as each turned to follow him.

As Thomas turned, Mael grabbed his sleeve. "I'm staying," he whispered.

"You can't stay here!"

"Why not?" The little man's eyes were solid and unmoving.

"Shabbat ..." Thomas pointed to the retreating women.

"I know nothing of Shabbat," Mael said, "but I need to stay here."

"Once the sun is down, we cannot travel."

"I wasn't planning on going anywhere."

"Why?"

"Respect."

"It's likely to get cold." Thomas could feel Peter, John and Andrew hesitating as they listened to the quick conversation.

"I can light a fire."

"You don't have a way to light a fire."

"Then I will be cold."

"Suit yourself." Thomas turned to leave.

"I was hoping you'd stay also."

"Me?" Thomas knew what Mael meant.

"Yes, you."

"Why?"

The little man looked deep into his eyes. "You're the best friend I have in this world, Thomas." His voice trembled, but he didn't break eye contact. "And you were one of the master's best friends also."

Thomas glanced at the brothers. Peter shrugged and Andrew shook his head.

John simply said, "He has a point."

Thomas glanced back at the setting sun. The others were some distance ahead already. He looked back at Mael.

"We spent the night with Saul and his friends," Mael said. "It was no colder than this."

Thomas glanced down at Mael's prisoner's robe. "It will be colder with no fire and less to cover you."

"Then we'll be cold."

"It might rain."

"Then we'll be wet."

Thomas paused the banter as they stared at each other.

"You also know we have no food." He said. He knew Mael's answer before he finished the sentence.

"Then you may also be hungry."

"What about you?"

Mael looked up at the sky for a moment, that odd little thing he did just before he did something unexpected.

"I have food you know nothing about."

Thomas startled at the reference to the master's saying. Peter, John and Andrew shifted noticeably.

Thomas glanced around. "I'll stay with you Mael." He said.

"Thank you, Thomas," Mael dropped his eyes and turned. He walked over to the stone covering the tomb and sat down with his back against it, pulling up his knees behind his arms.

Peter shrugged before ambling over to sit down beside Mael. It wasn't long before they were all sitting in a small circle. Darkness settled in fast with the new moon.

Peter wasn't cold, but he wasn't comfortable either. He was exhausted. Sleeping in the flat area in front of a tomb would be uncomfortable, and his conscience wouldn't let him sleep anyway after what had happened following the arrest. He sat with his elbows on his knees and his chin in his hands, wondering if he had the courage to talk about it.

"I denied the master this morning," he said at length.

"What☐" John gasped. Andrew looked up expecting more. Mael didn't move.

"I denied the master. I had an opportunity to defend him and I didn't. And that was in front of a servant girl."

Everyone sat quietly staring into what they wished was a fire in the middle of the circle, as Peter related the ordeal.

"Jesus warned me about the rooster. I've never wept so hard. I felt powerless. I kept promising myself that I wouldn't do that, after the master warned me last week."

"How did you know where he was?" Andrew asked.

"After I ran from the garden, I hid by the road and followed them back to Jerusalem. They took him to the temple. What a joke *that* was. I've never wept so hard," he confessed, shaking his head as tears filled his eyes.

"At least you followed them back." Andrew was staring at the ground. "I ran away from the path and over the north side of the garden. I stumbled running down the hill. Must have hit my head." He touched the side of his head gently. "Didn't wake up until this morning."

"Then what?" asked Thomas.

"I didn't even know where I was. It's all wild back behind the garden. Took me a while to get oriented and finally make it back to the city. Just in time to see the end of the trial at the palace."

They all stared at John, who looked up—surprised. "I fled back to Bethany, but I couldn't sleep. I spent the night wandering around the empty streets wondering why I didn't defend him—like I promised I would."

"Like we all did," Thomas echoed as he hung his head between his knees.

"He loved me more than I could ever imagine," John said. "I could not love him back—I got back just as they were leading him off to be crucified."

The darkness folded around them. The rocks were still warm, but Peter knew the chill would set in soon. "What about you, Thomas?"

"I ran north for a bit and waited. When I realized no one was pursuing me, I came back to the garden." Thomas looked over at Mael. "I saw Mael sitting in the glen with Judas—talking."

"Really?" Andrew turned to Mael. "What were you talking about?"

Mael stared out toward the temple, but said nothing.

"I dunno," said John as he looked at Mael, "but I found it a bit peculiar that you were with Judas when he betrayed the master."

Mael remained silent. In the last light of dusk, Peter could see the hint of tears in his eyes. He waited.

"What happened, Mael?" said John.

It seemed like a long time, but the master had taught them to wait at times like this. Peter could see the pain in Mael's face. Finally, the little man spoke:

"I saw Judas get paid in the temple for his betrayal. The guards caught me—and threw me in their jail. When it was time for the betrayal, they gave me this robe and brought me along." Mael's voice verged on breaking from emotion.

"When I fled, a soldier grabbed my robe. I left it behind." The little man rocked back and forth, his arms wrapped tightly around his knees. "I was naked and cold, so I came back to get my cloak. Judas was the only one who had come back. He needed my help."

"He betrayed the master!" Andrew's voice trembled with anger.

"He was sorrowful to the point of death. I tried to console him. He asked me to go to the temple with him—to return the silver. It was the least I could do. They captured me again and threw me in another cell. I was freed when the ground shook and the door flew open. I escaped up to the temple court. Thomas found me there. I don't know where Judas went. I hope he's safe."

The brothers exchanged glances. "Judas is dead, Mael," Peter said.

"How? Why?" Mael's voice quivered as he looked at Peter.

"He hung himself on a stake in the valley—down below the garden." Peter said.

He looked back at Mael. His head tipped back, his face up—eyes closed. Tears rolled down his cheeks. There was no sound, but his body rocked from tremors of hurt that rippled through him.

Something about Mael reminded him of the Master, able to take the darkness of man's behavior, and treat it with mercy and tenderness. Peter didn't know what to say, but he reached out and put his hand on Mael's shoulder. He could feel the sobs.

Mael hurt in his vorn. His feelings for Chudash wouldn't let go. The loneliness and hopelessness of this man, trapped in his selfishness, who would betray an innocent for money, swept over Mael. If the master had been available, he would have accepted Chudash, but the master had been betrayed, and while his innocence was being cruelly punished, Chudash could find no relief and had killed himself.

Bieter's hand landed on his shoulder. It was warm and strong, and it radiated empathy that he could feel, but he could not escape the pain of his own empathy with Chudash.

He sat for a long time. None of the others said anything as they waited in the gathering darkness. Soon it would be too dark to see anything except perhaps the stars.

"TELL THEM TO GET SOME WOOD."

Mael straightened and the tears stopped. "Go get some wood for a fire." He said as he wiped his eyes with the back of his hand.

"What?" said Handru.

"Wood for a fire—to keep us warm."

The brothers looked back and forth at each other. "Wood!" Bieter repeated. "Let's get some wood."

Handru shook his head.

"I think we should do what he says," Domas said as he stood up. Scrubby bushes and small trees surrounded them, and it wasn't long before they'd retrieved handfuls of twigs and small sticks.

Mael fashioned it into a nest—a small, unlit fire, and then sat back.

"Now what?" asked Chiahn.

"I don't know," Mael responded.

Bieter smiled and shook his head. "Are you going to light it?"

"TELL BIETER TO ADD ONE MORE PIECE."

Mael looked at the big man. "You light it, Bieter."

Bieter laughed. "How on earth should I do that?"

"Go get one more stick and add it to the fire."

"There is no fire!"

"One more stick, Bieter," Mael said.

Bieter stood up again and left the circle. He came back quickly with another small stick in his hand. He held it over the fire and hesitated.

"Add it, Bieter," Mael whispered.

Bieter dropped the stick up against the small pile of wood.

Nothing happened. Handru shook his head and chuckled. John stared at the small dark pile of wood.

Mael waited. Now what? The voice had been very clear.

Suddenly, a wisp of smoke spiraled up from the center of the fire. Domas gasped.

The breeze carried the smoke toward Handru who tried to wave it away from his face. Chiahn laughed and Domas joined in as Handru coughed and struggled with the smoke.

Then, just as suddenly, a flame appeared, deep in the pile. It burst upward, swallowing the smoke and burning outward until the whole stack of wood blazed. The brothers moved back from the heat. A warmth that came from someplace other than the fire, flooded Mael.

Bieter looked at him in astonishment. "How did you do that?"

"I didn't."

"You did *something*!"

"I did two things: I told all of you to get wood. I told you, Bieter, to light it with your stick."

Mael knew that they had all seen miracles from Mah'Eladra. From what Domas had told him, the Master often did things like this, and even more astonishing. He had raised people from the dead—several times.

"Tell me about the master's first miracle," Mael said.

The brother's glanced back and forth and Chiahn was the one who spoke: "We went to a wedding—in Cana—small town near home. He turned water into wine—really good wine, as I recall." The others laughed.

"Do you remember how he did it?"

Chiahn recalled the story in as much detail as he could, with the others interjecting clarifications.

"You say at first he refused his mother?"

Chiahn nodded.

"Said it was not his time?—then did it anyway?"

"I often wondered about that," Bieter said.

"Did he actually do anything, like wave his hand over the water or taste it?"

"No." Handru said. "He just told us to fill the jugs with water. When we came back, it was all wine."

They all stared into the fire. Mael noticed that it continued to burn without seeming to consume the wood. "Do you suppose he knew what he was doing? Or was he perhaps, just obeying the words of Elohim, and the result was miraculous?"

The question hung in the air over the fire. Mael could see in their eyes that they were all thinking. "Never thought about it that way," Handru said after a bit.

"I'm curious because, starting this fire may have seemed like a miracle. But all I did was ask you to get wood—and Bieter to add one piece."

"The fire doesn't seem to be burning down," Handru observed. Bieter nodded.

They sat for a while and stared into the flames. Domas broke the silence. "I am going to try to sleep. It's been a long day."

Chapter Sixteen

JAIL

"Ask honestly if something could happen,
Before explaining why it can't."

Science and the Vorn
Fillaranda Darenton

Thomas sat beside Mael, with his back to the stone. The dawn had broken chilly and gray, as a slight, windless drizzle fell on them. It was enough to make them damp, but not wet. The fire had died sometime in the night.

Peter, Andrew and John had left to find food, but Mael, cold, wet and tired, refused to leave. He stayed with his back against the stone. "I don't want anyone to steal his body," he said.

They had all woken an hour before dawn, cold and stiff. Everyone except Mael wanted to leave, and the argument devolved into a discussion about whether it was possible to break into the tomb and steal the master's body. Thomas had argued fruitlessly that no one would want to do this. Mael insisted on staying guard. Peter had proposed that since Jesus had insisted that he would raise from the dead—which he was not sure about—stealing the body would be a good way to make the Jews think that he had risen.

John was appalled. "If someone did that, it would be such a lie that whatever good the master had done would be defeated by it."

"No one raises from the dead after being crucified and then stuck with a spear like that," Thomas insisted. "Besides, it's been a full night, and even if he did rise, he would never be able to move the stone."

"Lazarus was dead for three days before Jesus raised him," insisted John.

....

In the end, Mael and Thomas stayed behind to stand guard.

Thomas revived an older topic that he had avoided while the others were there: "You're sure this is the place where your portal is?"

"Yes."

"If the portals are controlled by Elohim, then perhaps Jesus will go through the portal." Thomas was rather doubtful about the whole thing. "But where would he go?"

"Maybe to visit another world—or another time on Terra."

Thomas shook his head.

"I have never heard of dead people being taken through a portal," Mael said. "Either way, it will be hard for me to get back in there with this stone in the way."

"It would take five men to move that stone safely."

"Ah, but for the Eladra, it would be easy."

"Eladra?"

"I think you call them angels."

Thomas nodded. "From what I've heard, *one* of them could probably move the stone." He was getting used to the different words that Mael used, but a few baffled him. They reminded him of old Hebrew words, but they weren't quite the same. "I'm getting cold, Mael."

The little man stared straight ahead. "It's alright to be cold," he said.

Thomas wanted to leave, like the others, and find a warm, dry place and something to eat, but Mael remained implacable. "How long will you stay here, Mael?"

"Until someone else comes to stand guard."

"But no one else cares—no one's gonna come to guard something no one cares about."

"I care."

Thomas shook his head. "I'm very hungry."

"So am I."

Thomas shuddered. No escape. He leaned back on the stone.

"Someone will come soon," Mael said.

The first tread of approaching soldiers interrupted his comment. Thomas knew the sound. Roman soldiers had a way of walking together that all Jews knew well. "Soldiers!" he said.

Mael nodded, but didn't move.

Eight soldiers emerged from the cold mist. They approached the tomb without slowing until they stopped in formation about three paces from Mael.

"Have you come to guard the tomb?" Mael looked up but didn't move.

"Mael!—and Thomas! What are you doing here□"

Mael stood up. "We're guarding the tomb, Marcus. Have you come to guard the tomb?"

Thomas scrambled to his feet.

"How did you know?" Marcus asked.

"Someone needs to guard the tomb. The master shouldn't be left alone."

Marcus shifted and looked around. "He's dead, Mael. We've been ordered here to seal the tomb and make sure no one steals his body."

"Who would steal a body?" Thomas asked.

"The priests think that you—and your friends—might try."

"We've been here making sure that wouldn't happen." Mael said.

"The elders asked us to take that responsibility," Marcus said. "We brought four of our best down from the fortress and they'll stay here until we are sure that there will be no trouble."

"How long will that be?" Thomas asked.

Marcus smiled. "Apparently, his followers think he will be raised from the dead in three days. So, I don't know. But you tell me, Thomas, how long will *that* be?"

Thomas looked down. He wasn't sure. He had seen others raised, but that was by the master while he was alive. How would a dead man raise himself? He looked over at Mael, realizing that the little man hadn't heard any of what the master said on that night before his arrest.

Mael stared at Marcus. "You do realize, Marcus, that if Mah'Eladra—Elohim—decide to raise him from the dead, and walk out of that tomb alive, that no one from this world will be able to stop him."

Marcus startled at Mael's frankness then smiled again. "No, little man, I suppose that the gods can do whatever they want. We aren't here to stop a resurrection. We're here to prevent more ordinary men from creating a hoax by stealing his body."

Mael continued to stare into Marcus's eyes. "I hope you're here to see it when it happens, Marcus."

"Do you know when it will happen? I'll try to be here."

"Elohim never do things when you expect them."

Marcus shook his head and turned to the other guards.

Mael didn't move, so Thomas waited. The guards put a braided chord of woven yellow silk across the front of the stone, draping it back to the wall behind it. They sealed the cord to the wall with wax. Marcus produced some sort of disk from his tunic and embossed the seal. When he turned around, he said, "The seal of Rome." He slipped the disk back into his tunic. "Anyone who breaks this seal without the permission of the prefect will be executed."

He turned to the guards who had taken their posts in front of the stone. "Any guard who allows one of these seals to be broken, will be executed."

Thomas looked at the guards. Their faces showed that they understood, and took it seriously.

Marcus looked back to Mael and Thomas. "You two, come with me."

"I want to stay here," Mael said.

Marcus pursed his lips. "I'm not giving you the choice. We can't allow the guards here to be distracted, nor do we want any of the Nazarene's followers staying here—it wouldn't look good if the priests or elders came to check. Besides, we need to find you some real clothing. That prisoner's robe is gonna land you back in trouble."

"I didn't expect that I would end up in prison again," Mael confessed to Domas.

"Me either. We should've run when we could."

"And when was that, Domas? The guards surrounded us all the way back to the fortress."

Domas frowned. "At least they gave you some better clothing, even if it doesn't fit."

"It's also warmer here than outside—and they gave us breakfast." Mael smiled. "I've not had much to eat the last few days."

"I wonder what the brothers will think when they get back to the tomb?"

"The guards will explain what happened."

They were together in the same cell in the fortress. A high window in the wall with bars allowed them to see a bit of the sky. The cell was sparse. It seemed more like a holding place than a full prison cell.

They sat on the cold floor for a while in silence, but Mael was curious. "Domas, do you think that the master will rise?"

"He said he would."

"Yes, but do you believe it? I mean, really believe!"

"Well, I've seen some amazing things since I first started following him, but like I said before—he was alive when he did his miracles and I think that makes a difference."

"Bieter said you saw him raise a man who was dead for three days."

"Yes, but he died of—something not so specific. The master was brutalized; beaten. He wasn't very attractive to begin with, but after the soldiers scourged him and beat his head...and they nailed him to that cross...and then the soldier put a spear right through him—it's a little different..."

"I think he will rise, like he said." Mael said.

"And why are you so sure? And how does a dead man raise himself?"

"Maybe the miracles were all from Elohim, and they will raise him. Besides, I barely got to know him, but I am quite sure I was sent here to learn from him. Besides, if the portal is in the tomb, then he needs to rise so I can go home."

"I'm having a hard time with this portal idea."

Mael nodded. "It's there. Perhaps after the master rises, I can show you."

"How long do you suppose they will keep us here?" Thomas asked.

Mael looked up. "I have no idea," he said. "Does it matter?"

"Well, I don't want to stay here forever."

"When the master rises and leaves the tomb, there will be no reason to keep us here. Besides, isn't today what you call the Shabbat—is that it?"

"Yes, Shabbat. It's supposed to be a day of rest."

"How often does it happen?"

"Every week—the last day of the week."

"And you are restricted in what you can do—like how far you can walk? What else?"

"There are many rules about the Shabbat. How much work you can do, where you can travel, selling and buying things—stuff like that."

"Who enforces all the rules?"

"Well, it's supposed to be voluntary, but the religious leaders enforce it. If they didn't, a lot of people wouldn't live that way."

Mael remained quiet for a moment as he processed the idea. "I guess being in a prison cell is an easy way to keep Shabbat, isn't it?"

Thomas looked up to see Mael smiling.

"If keeping Shabbat is something people are forced to do, it's kind of like being in this cell. I don't know anything about your rules, but if I'm here, I can't break any of them, can I?"

Thomas shook his head. "I've never thought of that quite that way, but I think that's something the master might say. Either way, I'd rather not be here."

"Me either, but this is a good time to tell me the stories of your history. I want to understand."

Thomas smiled. "How much of it?"

"As much as we have time for. Since we have no idea about our time here, start at the beginning and tell me as much as you remember."

"The beginning is a long way back."

Mael shrugged. "If you run out of things to tell me, then I'll tell you about Tessalindria."

Chapter Seventeen

FREEDOM

"Shouldn't we be surprised by surprises?"
Foltar Masan, Comedian

Mael woke while it was still dark, but hints of dawn graced the small barred window above him. There was nowhere to go and, with Domas still asleep, no one to talk to. He sat and waited, reflecting on the history he'd learned from Domas.

They'd stayed up late, learning about the great fathers of armatan on Terra: Abraahm, Mosess, Josep and the great kings and prophets that shaped Domas's religion. It was complicated and made more so by many years of interpretation and infighting—not unlike the various offshoots spawned by interpretations of the Kirrinath on Tessalindria.

The story of the escape of the Sirealites from their slavery fascinated Mael in particular—the part about the Farro, the king who refused to listen to Mosess from Yahweh. According to Thomas, ten times Farro tried the patience of Mah'Eladra until Mah'Eladra decided to use his stubbornness to their own purposes and he was destroyed.

Domas's understanding was that Ransom had come to restore the truths of the teachings. The priests of the sect that currently held power and authority at the temple didn't want to hear those truths, and hardened themselves. Perhaps Mah'Eladra was using their hardness to his purposes. Mael had tasted this kind of behavior before with the Kirrinal Priests.

Domas had finally fallen asleep on the stone floor.

Mael had wrapped his cloak around himself hoping to revive a bit of the remaining warmth in his core. The twists and turns of Domas's story floated through his mind. This Terra, so different in its history, was not so different in the nature of the mankind, its stubborn rebellion against Mah'Eladra, and its refusal to listen to those sent to heal it. Perhaps this is what he came to learn: that he was not alone in vast places beyond Tessalindria.

The silence outside the cell broke with the unexpected and hurried approach of several guards. Mael knew they were coming for him and Domas. He crawled over to his friend and shook him. "Domas, wake up!"

Domas sat up as the bewilderment of sleep fled from his face. "What?"

"The guards are coming. Stand up!" Domas scrambled to his feet, instinctively brushing off his cloak while trying to arrange his unruly mop of light hair.

A face appeared in the small window in the door. A key ground in the lock.

The door burst inward and Margas strode into the cell followed by two soldiers with drawn swords. "Come quickly!" he said, his voice still husky with sleep. He stepped back through the door as the other guards moved behind Domas and Mael. The guards prodded them hurriedly toward the door with their swords. Margas strode down the corridor in the opposite direction of the stairway up into the fortress.

Mael had to skip-step to keep up with him. Domas stumbled, still groggy from sleep. "What's hap—"

"Shhhhh!"

After several turns into ever darkening hallways and descending two flights of stairs, they came to the end of a corridor with a small heavily barred door. Margas nodded toward it. The soldiers sheathed their swords and moved to lift the three heavy iron bars from the carved slots in the stone that held the door shut.

Margas turned to Mael. "Listen carefully, my friend. There's been a breach at the tomb. The body of the Nazarene is gone. The guards that were left there are on their way to be questioned by the priests. They're friends of mine—I fear for their lives." Margas's face scowled with concern in the near darkness of the hall.

"I know you had nothing to do with this, because you were here, but it's best for you to be gone. They'll have to blame someone."

With the last bar lifted, the soldiers grabbed the forged handles on the inside of the iron door and squealed it open on badly rusted hinges. The doorway revealed a wall with a narrow staircase leading up and to the left. "Run, my friends. Don't let anyone know where you were last night—at the tomb or here! Don't go anywhere near that tomb."

Mael nodded. "Thank you, Margas."

"Yes, thank you," Domas added as he cleared his throat.

Halfway up the stairs, the door screeched and thudded shut. The heavy bars dropped into place behind it.

The stairs emerged onto a narrow street with the wall of the fortress towering above them to the left. The street was still gray in the dawn and it was empty. He looked around. "Let's go!"

"Where?" Domas still seemed as if he was sleepwalking.

"To the tomb."

"Margas told us not to!" Domas protested.

Mael looked up into his eyes. "Margas freed us so we would not be a risk to him, don't you see? Of course he would want us to stay away from the scene of a crime against his fellow soldiers. It's going to be a nasty situation for the lot of them and he didn't want it complicated by our presence."

"I get it," Domas responded, "but we need to respect his request."

"Domas! Look at me!" Domas stopped and looked down into his eyes. "If the master is raised from the dead, we need to see it—we *want* to see it, don't we?"

"Of course, but—" The sentence died on Domas's lips. "Do we even know where we are?"

Thomas knew that the question was partly a stall, while he shook the sleep out of his head.

"We just got away from the fortress, Thomas. It shouldn't be hard to find out. C'mon." Mael grabbed his hand. "This way."

He shook his hand free. It made him feel like a child. Mael ignored the gesture and started down the alley. From the light of dawn, Thomas guessed they were headed west along the north wall of the fortress. It wouldn't be hard to figure out where they were and how to get to the tomb.

They moved quickly. Mael led west then turned south along the western wall of the fortress then cut west again just inside the Northern wall of the Second Quarter. The streets were empty. It was the first day of the new week, but the significance of Passover Shabbat still weighed on the city and Thomas knew they had several hours before the busy-ness would fully engage.

Within minutes, they descended onto the road headed west out of the city. The tombs would be on the left outside the wall. Thomas still wasn't sure this was a good idea.

Mael moved off the road to the right, ascending a slight rise where a small copse of trees allowed them to look down on the tomb without being too close.

Several soldiers milled around the entrance of the tomb as they talked with one another. The stone looked as if it had simply been pushed out from the tomb instead of rolled up the ramp it had rested on. It lay flat on the ground in front of the opening. "You think we should go down there?" Thomas asked.

Mael shook his head. "Marcus was right. It's not safe."

They watched for several minutes in silence. Thomas didn't know what to think. He was amazed and fearful, as well as filled with a curious hope, that the master had indeed risen.

A sudden commotion captured their attention. Two men, running headlong, as if racing one another, hurtled down the path toward the tomb.

"Peter and John!" Thomas exclaimed. "They don't even see the soldiers!"

They rounded the last turn. They saw the soldiers and Peter slowed down. John shot past him and with reckless fervor, leapt onto the rock and ducked under the low stone opening. Peter barreled in after him. The surprised soldiers barely had time to react. They shouted, but other than peer into the tomb after the brothers, they did nothing.

The quiet lasted but a few seconds before John and Peter burst from the tomb. John tripped as he leapt off the stone, but Peter grabbed him by his cloak without stopping and the two of them raced up the path. The surprised soldiers shouted after them.

Chapter Eighteen

PORTAL

"There should be an eighth portal. It's inconceivable that Mah'Eladra would stop at seven."

Deep Sky
Orokandolar

Domas leapt to his feet. "What are you doing?" Mael asked.

"Going with them!"

"No!" Mael objected, but Domas was already beyond the whisper.

Mael sat down to wait.

The long low rays of Asolara were just overtaking the tomb entrance when four more Romans approached on horseback. A quick conversation followed, and suddenly, all the soldiers abandoned the tomb to follow the horsemen back up the road toward the fortress.

Nothing else moved. An occasional passerby on the road interrupted the tranquility of the morning, but the tomb offered no further interest to any of them.

Mael stood up and brushed off the loose twigs and balsam needles, then picked his way down to the road, crossing only after looking both ways.

As he came around the last corner to where he could see the tomb, Klopas stood facing the entrance with his hands on his hips. His rake rested on his shoulder.

Mael approached the gardener. "Klopas?"

Klopas startled and turned. "Mael!"

Mael nodded. Klopas turned back to the tomb opening as Mael stepped beside him. "The Ermans make a mess out of everything they touch!"

"I don't think the Ermans did this, Klopas."

"Couldn't they just have rolled the stone up the ramp? No! They just blew it over. Gonna take ten men to put it back."

"The Ermans didn't do it."

"How do you know?"

"The Ermans guarded the tomb, under penalty of death, Klopas. It doesn't make sense. Four of them may die because of this."

"Well, whoever—I have to clean up!"

"There was no one here to see what happened?"

Klopas shook his head. "Not that I know of—except the soldiers, and they're not talking."

"May I look inside?"

"Sure. There's not much to see."

Mael ducked under the low arch of the tomb and stopped to let his eyes adjust to the shadows. The slab where the body should have lain was empty. Strips of linen lay neatly folded at one end.

As soon as he could see, he headed toward the wall to the right of the slab—solid rock, from floor to ceiling, all along the length of it. He felt it with both hands: black rock, but nothing like the blackness of the portal. Where had it gone?

As he turned to head out of the tomb, Vishtalar materialized in front of him. Vishtalar glowed with the cold white translucence of the Eladra. "Where are you going, Mael?" his lips didn't move.

"I wanted to see the portal." Mael confessed.

"It's not time to go home."

"There is more to learn?"

"There is much to learn. You have only started to know what you need."

"How will I learn?"

"Go out of this place. There is no need to seek the living in the place of the dead. Go with Klopas today. You will learn." Vishtalar vanished with a faint hiss.

Mael headed out of the tomb, shielding his eyes from Asolara that now bathed everything with its brilliance.

"Are you alright?" Klopas asked as he stared at him.

"Yes, I think so."

"I thought I heard voices...You look like you've seen a demon."

"It was an Eladra—an angel."

"What□"

"He told me to spend the day with you."

"With me?"

Mael nodded. "There is something I am to learn."

Klopas eyed him thoughtfully. "I am traveling today, but you're welcome to come along."

"I've hardly been out of Chershalem since I arrived," Mael said.

"It's a small place west of here—a few stadia. There is a merchant there that sells seeds that I like—it's worth the trip. I go every year about this time for the spring plantings."

"When are you leaving?"

"This afternoon. We'll spend the night there and get my seeds in the morning, then return. Meet me back here when Asolara is high."

Chapter Nineteen

WESTWARD

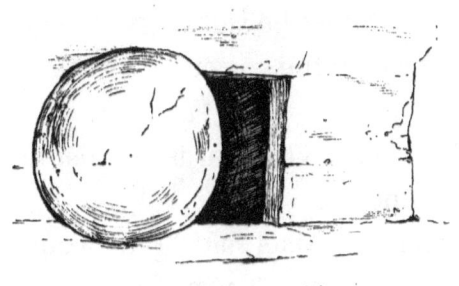

"Never let money divide a relationship."

It is said
Sessasha

Cleopas was curious: "Who was this angel who told you to come with me?"

Mael stared straight down the road. "A friend of mine."

"Wait—you are friends with an angel?"

"He started appearing to me recently—at times."

"What does he look like?"

Mael described the tall warrior with silver hair, a bit bigger than the Romans, dressed like a Roman soldier only different. "He often gives me advice that he seems to get from somewhere else."

"And he told you to spend the day with me?"

"Yes."

"Well, I guess there are stranger things. Never much believed in angels but with everything else that is going on—"

"Everything else?" Mael asked.

"The way the sun turned dark when the master died—right at the time that the priests were offering the sacrifices at the temple. The tearing of the curtain—the sightings of many of the holy men of old wandering through the streets of Jerusalem—I guess angels are plausible."

"It's very real, Cleopas. Vishtalar is not just my imagination."

"Oh, he has a name!"

"They all have names," Mael said. "Why wouldn't they?"

They walked on in silence. The sun was high in front of them, baking the dusty road, and adding a lazy ambiance to the quiet journey. A few travelers passed them on the left going the other way—nothing unusual for an afternoon traveling west from Jerusalem.

Suddenly, out of the haze two men crossed over from the other side of the road and walked straight toward them, engaged in an intense discussion. Cleopas put his hand out and grasped Mael's arm as they slowed down. The two men looked up, and moved quickly to the left, passing them without acknowledgement as they continued their discussion.

"The priests," muttered Cleopas.

"Why did they do that?" Mael asked.

Cleopas shook his head. "Call me jaded, but they're an odd lot. They look down on us while jealousy and envy mark their selfish perception of each other. They hardly get along, even though they are birds of the same feather, in reality. I'm surprised they're walking together."

He was about to explain further when Mael moved rapidly across the road. In the ditch lay a man, face down in the scrubby grass opposite where they walked.

Mael reached him first and laid his hand on him. "He's alive!" Mael rolled him over to expose his beaten face and put his ear to the man's chest. "Quick. Give me water."

Cleopas reached for his water skin. "Those priests walked right by him!"

Mael tore the hem from the bottom of his own robe, before looking up for the skin. He uncorked it, wet the torn cloth and rapidly dabbed the man's face. "He's still breathing."

Mael was nearly finished cleaning the blood and dirt from the man's injuries when he suddenly looked up at the sky. "What□"

"I didn't say anything." Cleopas was confused.

The little man looked down again. "Sit up!" he commanded.

The man groaned and then sat upright, a surprised look on his face. Mael was beside him on his knees. "Easy now—what happened?"

The man shook his head and looked back and forth from Mael to Cleopas. Fear descended onto his face. "I gave you everything I have."

Mael leaned back. "What happened to you?"

The man glanced back and forth one more time. "I was mistaken." His hands patted his clothing as he scrambled to his feet. "It's gone, all gone."

"What?"

"They took all my money!"

"Who?"

The man looked at them again. "Five men—stopped me on the road and beat me!"

"What is your name?" Mael asked.

The man stared at Cleopas. All the wounds on his face had healed. The man glanced back and forth two more times before lowering his defenses. "Josiah."

"I am Mael. This is Cleopas."

Josiah nodded to each in turn.

"Do you need money?" Mael asked.

"I was on my way to Jerusalem to pay my landowner. He threatened to evict my family if I don't pay by sundown. Now it's gone!" He wiped away the tears that were forming in the corners of his eyes.

"We have some money," Mael said as he laid his hand on Josiah's forearm. "How much do you need for your rent?"

"We do?" The words slipped out before Cleopas could stop them.

Mael stared at him. "Surely you brought money for the seed, and the inn—and dinner."

"Do *you* have any?" Cleopas resented this little stranger giving away his money—he hadn't brought an excess.

Mael looked back at Josiah. "How much?"

"Twelve drachmas."

Mael turned back to Cleopas. "We have to help him out."

"It will be hard to pay you back quickly," Josiah said.

"There's no need to pay us back."

Cleopas shook his head.

"Elohim will take care of us, Cleopas." Mael's eyes bore into him and wouldn't let go. Cleopas reached for his purse and dropped it into Mael's hand. He wasn't sure why. It was foolish—irresponsible.

Mael opened the purse poured it into his hand. "I don't know your money." He held it out to Josiah. "Take fifteen, how did you say—drachmas?"

"Whata" said Cleopas

"Fifteen will give him a bit extra for his family."

Josiah looked into Cleopas's eyes. "Fifteen," Cleopas said.

Mael smiled. "Go in peace, Josiah. Don't forget those who need it more than you."

Josiah bowed and then reached out to hug Cleopas. From the corner of his eye he saw Mael nod. Cleopas hugged the stranger.

Josiah stepped back. "I'll never forget this!" he exclaimed. "Never."

Josiah backed away on the road toward Jerusalem. It was then that Cleopas noticed another stranger standing not three paces from them, watching the transaction. He'd come up behind them from the city, unheard.

Mael nudged him. "I think the master would have done that," he whispered. It irritated Cleopas, but Mael was right. "The master would have given him twenty—maybe the whole purse."

"Your kindness was not unnoticed," said the stranger as he stepped toward them.

Cleopas sighed. "Thank you." He shook his head. "Let's go, Mael. I hope you are right, about us being fine. You gave away half my purse."

"Where are you going?" asked the stranger.

"Emmaus."

"Is it far?"

"Another two hours, maybe a bit less."

"Can I join you?"

Cleopas sighed. "As long as you don't ask for money."

The stranger laughed. "Your generosity to Josiah will be richly rewarded."

The stranger was a handsome man, slightly taller than Cleopas with the bearing of royalty. He was no commoner. When he smiled, his dark eyes sparkled and the crow's feet by his eyes attested to a pleasant life. "I have no money and no need of it," he said.

"Then come with us. I am in no mood to talk with Mael." Cleopas nodded west.

"It was a fine thing you did, Cleopas," Mael reiterated. "Even if he hadn't been robbed, he wouldn't have had enough to pay his landlord."

"How do you know?"

Mael shook his head and shrugged. "Just a sense."

They walked in silence for several hundred paces. The stranger seemed content with the company without words. "What were you talking about before you came across Josiah?" he asked at length.

Cleopas shook his head and rummaged back through the conversations. "Well, let's see...Mael here claims that he saw an angel in the tomb of the Nazarene, after the body disappeared."

"The Nazarene?"

Cleopas stopped. "Jesus of Nazareth—the one they crucified a couple days ago."

The man turned to face him. "Crucified? So, he's dead, right? What were you doing in the tomb?" he looked down at Mael.

"His body wasn't in the tomb. I think he rose from the dead. I wanted to see for myself."

"And?"

"His body wasn't there."

The stranger stared back at the horizon. "Who was this man?"

Chapter Twenty

EMMAUS

"When our vorns burn within us—when we feel the pull of deep things on our inner parts, we can be sure that the El of Mah'Eladra is working in us."

Irhandarin (The Journey)
Arafinda

Mael wasn't sure what to say. Klopas jumped in. "Were you just in Chershalem?"

The man nodded.

"And you haven't heard all the things going on there these last days?"

"What things?"

Klopas turned and started walking again. "About Chaisus, the prophet from Nazareth. A powerful man in his teachings and action. The chief priests and our rulers handed him over to the Ermans. They crucified him."

"Yes, you said that."

"Well, we had hoped that he was Israel's redeemer. Then today, some of the women who followed him came to the tomb and found it empty, except for an angel. And a couple brothers found it empty just like the women said, but they couldn't find him."

They walked a few more paces before the stranger spoke. "It must be him! Don't you see? Don't you believe all that the prophets spoke about the Christ, that he would come and suffer like this, and then go into glory?"

"I know nothing of these prophecies," Mael answered.

"Do you know of Mosess?"

"Domas told me about him—a little bit."

"He was the first prophet, the greatest. He gave us the law—the books of the law, and in them he made many references to the day, and the time, and the person of redemption..."

The stranger's eyes burned with a fire that Mael had seldom seen in anyone else. His words captivated Mael. For an hour and a half, he spoke about the history of his people, and the way that Mah'Eladra had guided them and talked about this redeemer, who would come and purchase back his people, and eventually the whole world. He told the stories of the prophets. Some of them Domas had mentioned, but there were many more. He talked of their suffering, and the way they were treated by men who should have loved them. His voice rose and fell with the swell of passion, as he described how Mah'Eladra cleared the path for this chosen one to come, and how he would suffer and eventually die for the sake of all others who live.

Mael listened. There was no place to interrupt the pageantry of the man's story as it marched through time, nor did he want to. The man finally stopped. "Weren't you going to stop here in Emmaus?" he asked.

Klopas nodded. "We are. We'll have dinner and stay the night then return in the morning. And you?"

"I am going on."

"But it's getting dark, it won't be safe."

"I will be fine."

"No. You must at least have supper with us. You have filled us in a way we could never repay. Please, at least let us extend this small kindness."

The man hesitated and then smiled. "Supper," he said.

Klopas knew exactly where they would stay. "Best supper in town and the prices are good." He scowled slightly at Mael as he mentioned the fare.

The inn was everything Klopas had said: warm and welcoming with a light ambiance of family about it. On the way to the table in the corner, they passed several families enjoying meals of roast birds and some meat with mounds of steaming vegetables and pots of fragrant stew.

Mael sat with the man to his left, across the table from Klopas. A quiet young woman brought in three mugs with a steaming pot of delicately spiced soup and a loaf of fresh bread on a board. After she had left, the man reached out and took the loaf. As he held it in his hands, he looked up. "Elohim, maker of all men and of this whole earth. We thank you tonight for the way you provide for us every day without judgment on us."

Then he broke the loaf in half, and handed the halves to Klopas and himself. As he did so, he smiled. Mael looked across at Klopas, whose face radiated surprise. He looked back at the man just as he vanished with a slight hiss.

"Elohim!" gasped Klopas.

"It was him!" Mael choked. "It was Ransom!"

"We should have known," Klopas said. "Didn't you feel the passion and the energy when he was talking to us on the road?—we should have known!"

A wave of energy swept over Mael. The fulfillment of spending more time with the master, which had waned since learning of his death, surged forward in his vorn. The fire of a hope lost and re-found, rolled out in front of him. "We need to go tell the brothers and sisters!"

"Now?"

"Yes, Klopas! We've just seen a man risen from the dead, the fulfillment of all the prophecies of which he spoke. They wouldn't forgive us if we withheld this news! Besides, we don't have enough money to buy your seeds anyway."

Klopas shook his head and scowled. "It'll be dark. The road will not be safe, but you're right—"

Mael slid across the bench toward the aisle, as Klopas dropped a couple small coins on the table to pay for dinner. Something fell on the floor. Mael stooped to retrieve a gold coin that he had not noticed on the bench. He gave it to Klopas.

Klopas blinked.

"Ransom must have left it behind," Mael said. "It certainly was not there when we came."

"Twenty drachmas! Cesarean Gold!" It was the first smile from Klopas that Mael remembered since leaving Chershalem.

Klopas tied off his purse with a flourish and slipped the gold coin into a pocket inside the vest of his cloak. "Let's go!"

Chapter Twenty-One

DARKNESS

"Evil seeks its prey in the dark places, and in the night where there is little light."

Journey to the Infinite
Karendo Marha

The light dusty road was wide and easy for Mael to see, even without the moon. The quiet darkness evoked a forbidding silence on any conversation for half an hour or so, but Mael was curious.

"Why do you suppose that he looked so different?" he whispered at length. "And the limp was gone ... and he was taller ..."

"I have no idea." Klopas's voice was hushed.

"Did you ever hear him teach about being raised from the dead?"

"I don't recall—I was not with him that much until the very end—last week, when he arrived in Chershalem."

Mael brooded as they strode along. He guessed that Klopas wanted to be in Chershalem, and off that road, as much as he did. It had taken them three hours to get to Emmaus, but at this rate, it might be a little over two to get back. Every once in a while, he had to skip-step to keep up with Klopas's stride.

"It may be," Klopas interjected, "that the body we saw was what he *would* have looked like."

"What do you mean?"

"Well, he limped from an injury. The scar on his face was from something else and who knows what happened to his nose and hands to make them crooked—and his missing tooth..."

"What about his lazy eye?"

"That's just it, Mael! All the imperfection of our lives—your deformities, for example, were inflicted by the abuse of this world. Perhaps in the resurrection that he taught about, we're to be fully restored to what we should have been."

"Perhaps, but even when he was talking to us—there was something different, and we missed it."

Klopas nodded. "His voice was clear and smooth, but it was typical of his teaching. You haven't heard him teach much, but after he came to Chershalem, I heard him teach almost every day."

"We'll have to ask him when we see him again."

"Do you think we will?"

"Do you think that if he is here among us, that he would not show himself again? Besides, I've got more to learn from him before I return home. I know that."

"How do you know that?"

"I've been told several times."

"And..." the sudden appearance of a dark figure on the road, not three paces in front of them, cut Klopas's words short. He stopped and grabbed Mael's arm. There were at least four others surrounding them. "What do you want?" Klopas stammered.

One of the five pulled a lit torch from inside a jar. The sudden illumination showed all five men to be masked, except for their eyes, and clothed all in black.

"We want all the money you have," said the one in front of him. He held a club in his right hand that rested loosely in his left. Each of the others had clubs also.

"We don't have much," said Klopas. His voice trembled.

"Give us what you have."

Klopas dropped Mael's hand and fumbled for his purse. As he pulled it out of his cloak, it slipped and dropped to the ground.

"Don't touch it!" said the leader. Klopas straightened.

"Kick it over to me."

Klopas pushed the purse with his foot, so that it stopped in front of the one who asked. He stooped and picked it up. "Not much here," he said as he hefted it in his hand.

"A few drachmas and several coppers," Klopas said.

"Certainly, travelers like you should have more."

"We would, except that on the way to Emmaus we met a man who had been robbed," said Klopas. "We gave him money to pay his landowner."

The robber raised his club and drew up close in front of Klopas. The tip of his club pressed up under Klopas's nose. "And why would you do such a thing?"

Klopas tried to step back, but one of the other robbers behind him shoved him back toward the leader.

Mael stepped forward. "Because we're followers of the Nazarene Prophet. It is what he taught us to do."

The robber hesitated and looked down at Mael. "I heard he was dead—crucified by the Ermans."

"He was, but he's come back from the dead. We saw him just this evening."

The robber glanced back and forth between the two of them, then settled on Klopas. "Is this true?"

Klopas nodded. "With my own eyes. I wouldn't have believed otherwise. It's why we're going back to Chershalem at this hour—to tell the others."

"The man to whom you gave money—was he badly hurt?"

Klopas glanced down at Mael.

"Answer me!" the club pressed up harder under Klopas's nose.

"He would have died—if Mael hadn't healed him."

The robber turned to Mael. "You healed him? How?"

"I heard a voice," Mael said. "I told him to sit up and he did—and he was healed."

Confusion clouded the robber's eyes—or was it fear?

"We gave him fifteen drachmas, to pay his rent," Mael continued.

"He only had seven," the leader said.

"He needed twelve. We gave him extra." Mael said.

The robber's eyes narrowed. "Why?"

"We had it, and he needed it more than we. It's what the master would have done."

The robber massaged Klopas's purse in his hand. "This is all you have now?"

"We had dinner at the inn," said Klopas. "That's what we have left."

The club moved so fast that Klopas had no time to move. The sickening thud came from the left side of his head and he crumpled to the ground without a sound.

"The master wouldn't have approved of lying, would he?" the robber said as he glanced down at Mael.

"No."

The robber nodded to one of his accomplices who stepped forward and fished into Klopas's tunic. His hand emerged with the gold Cesarean that he held up into the torch light.

"What is your name, little one?"

"Mael."

"Stay with your friend, Mael. He won't die but he'll need your help." The robber took a step back. "I have respect for your master. He was a good man—a man of psadeq, but I have little respect for those who claim to follow him and lie."

Mael nodded.

"Perhaps you can *heal* your friend."

"Perhaps," Mael said.

"Take him back to Chershalem. Don't stop along the way. We'll insure safe passage." With a flourish of his club, the other bandits vanished into the dark silence on either side of the road. He remained for a moment and then turned and strode off toward Chershalem.

Mael laid Klopas out with his sandals under his head and his own robe pulled over him to ward off the chill, then sat down beside him to wait and listen.

He wondered if Mah'Eladra was allowing discipline on Klopas for his deceit about the money and on himself for his silence when he should have spoken. He couldn't blame Klopas. His deceit was a natural response, but the natural isn't the way of Mah'Eladra. Mael knew that. This was a hard reminder.

Mael's mind drifted back to Erolin's last moments. Tears formed in his eyes. He wished he had time like this to be beside her; to have some hope that he could do something, even something as simple as putting her soft leather shoes under her head and hold her hand. Perhaps Mah'Eladra would have done something for her.

Klopas breathed with shallow, erratic gasps. Mael had cleaned the bruise with what little water they had and now he waited for something that would tell him what to do.

It was at least an hour before Klopas groaned and lifted his head, then dropped it back with a thud onto his sandals. He groaned again.

"Klopas!"

Klopas coughed twice and lolled his head back and forth.

"Klopas! Wake up!" Mael whispered. He gently slapped Klopas's cheek to wake him.

Klopas groaned and opened his eyes. Even in the dark, Mael could see the terror. "What ... where?" he stammered.

"Relax, Klopas—it's alright."

Klopas raised his hand up to touch the bruise on his head.

"Can you sit up?" Mael put his hand behind his neck and tugged gently. Klopas sat and hung his head down between his knees, to retch onto the ground before groaning again.

"We have to get you to Chershalem, Klopas."

"I can't stand, Mael—just can't." He retched again between his legs.

Mael wrapped his arms around him and hugged him. Tears ran down his cheeks. "What do you want me to do?" he said to the deep sky.

As if in answer to his plea, Vishtalar hissed into existence beside him. Mael stood up. The giant spoke quietly. "How can I help?"

Mael sniffed back his tears and ran his sleeve over his eyes. "We need to get Klopas back to Chershalem."

The giant stepped forward and knelt beside his friend. "Come, Klopas," he said as he scooped him from the ground like a mother lifting a newborn child.

"Can you heal him?" Mael said.

"Which way?" Vishtalar asked.

Mael pointed in the direction of Chershalem. "Can't you heal him?" he asked again as they started walking.

"Healing is the province of Mah'Eladra, Mael. We are forbidden—we are not able—we only protect and serve. Come along."

Mael had to trot to keep up with the Eladra's long strides. "How was he injured?"

Mael related what happened between breaths as he ran along side. He had just got to the end of telling about the encounter, when Vishtalar stopped. He laid Klopas on the ground and stepped over him, drawing his sword. His body began to glow and the pale blue light of the sword illuminated the road. Five dark figures stood across it, about ten paces in front of them.

Vishtalar stepped toward them. He was half way to meet them when the one in front dropped to one knee with his head bowed. Vishtalar stopped. The other figures dropped beside their leader.

"Speak!" Vishtalar's voice reverberated like thunder.

"We have come to make amends for our behavior."

"What is your name?"

"Barabbas!"

"What are your amends?"

"We will return the stolen coin, and four times its value—and see you safely to Chershalem."

"Shall I strike them?" Vishtalar spoke over his shoulder to Mael.

Mael hesitated. He had never been given such a choice.

"No. these , too, are children of the king."

Mael startled. "No, Vishtalar. Mah'Eladra find no delight in the death of the wicked. These too, are children of the promises."

Chapter Twenty-Two

GATE

"A pause to rest should not give us pause to consider retreat."
Passages
Oratanga

Cleopas's awareness returned slowly. The giant carried him with an ease and gentleness that defied reason. Mael walked along beside them, breathing heavily and skip stepping to keep up. The five bandits surrounded them, surveying the darkness as only children of the darkness can do.

"Where are we going?" Cleopas asked.

"Jerusalem," said the giant.

"They are coming with us?" he asked.

The leader of the bandits spoke. "We'll see you safely to the gates."

Emboldened by the presence of the warrior who carried him, Cleopas asked, "Can I have my money back?"

A rumble of amusement erupted from the giant. "You'll be well taken care of."

Cleopas shook his head. It still hurt. "Why did you steal it in the first place?"

"We're raising money for our cause against the Romans."

"And why would you give it back?"

"We promised you safe passage back to the city, and we kept watch over you while you were out. We saw how Mael cared for you. When Vishtalar appeared as he did, I realized—this was no ordinary thing."

"What is your name?" Cleopas asked.

"Barabbas."

"The Barabbas□"

The bandit chuckled. "One of them, but if you mean the one who was freed for the death of your master, yes."

Cleopas shook his head. "Why help us now?"

"We—I—have thought deeply these last few days; about what has happened. When I was in prison, I heard about your master, a man of integrity. When I was freed, I had no idea why—no explanation—but I was happy to be free. I sought out my companions." He waved his hand to the others in the group. "They told me how I was freed. It frightened me. For the first time in years, I took a step back to consider my path."

"And?"

"The simplest path was to just pick up where I left off. Why not? The Jews don't care about me. They just wanted Jesus. The

Romans never expected me to change anything. Why should I be different?"

They walked on in silence, as everyone pondered Barabbas's words.

"Then we ran into you—traveling alone at night—an easy mark. One of my men saw you collect the gold Cesarean at the inn, but we didn't know who you were, nor your affiliation with the Nazarene.

"When I saw it unfolding, and the appearance of Vishtalar, it closed the circle on my thoughts. It's time to change."

"My head still hurts," observed Cleopas.

"Yeah—sorry about that."

"You could have hit Mael," he said as he chuckled.

"You were the one who lied to me."

Cleopas nodded.

They were passing the master's garden on the right. "I think I can walk from here," Cleopas said.

Vishtalar stopped and lowered him to his feet. "I cannot go into the city tonight," the giant said.

"You can't?" said Barabbas.

"Not tonight. I will leave you here." With a hiss, Vishtalar vanished in the darkness.

Cleopas swayed back and forth on his feet. Mael took his arm as Barabbas stepped forward to give him a hug. "Sorry about the hit," he said in his ear as his arms embraced him. "I hope we can laugh about this one day."

Cleopas nodded as Barabbas stepped back. "We will leave you here, but we will see you again."

"I would like that, Barabbas."

"Leaving you or seeing you soon?"

Cleopas smiled. "Both."

Barabbas turned away from the gate and summoned his band with a wave of his hand. They vanished into the darkness within a few paces of leaving them.

"It's been quite a day, Cleopas," Mael said. "Let's find the others."

Cleopas nodded.

The gate to the temple would be shut. They made their way north to the gate in the city walls where they could enter late at night, even if it was in the watchful eyes of guards who had accosted them before.

Chapter Twenty-Three

RESURRECTED

"Come, eat. When the food is gone we will concern ourselves with life again."

Mirradach
The Tiger in the Tree

Thomas didn't believe—no, he wasn't sure he *wanted* to believe what he was seeing. The stranger had appeared in their midst. "'Peace be with you.'"

It didn't sound like the master, and he was taller and his face was unmarred. His dark eyes sparkled and his hair hung neatly down over his ears to his collar. His limp was gone and he stood erect and regal.

Thomas wasn't sure what to say. He was sure others wondered the same thing. "Is it you, Master?" he blurted out.

The man nodded. "It is."

Thomas shook his head.

"Come here, Thomas!" The stranger held out his arms for a hug.

Thomas moved toward him. "I want to see the nail holes, master!"

"Give me your hand."

Thomas extended his right hand and the man grabbed it with his left. "Put your finger here, Thomas!" He pulled Thomas forward, pushing his index finger into the hole that went clear through his wrist. Thomas tried to resist but could not. The master pulled his finger out and smiled, pulling him in closer and shoving his hand against his body, just above the hips. "Do you feel the hole, Thomas? Stop doubting and believe."

Thomas fell to one knee and bowed his head. "My lord!"

The master reached under his chin. "Stand up my friend!"

Thomas stood. The others stared at the master with their mouths open and slack.

A pounding on the door broke the awe of the moment. Thomas's heart skipped as the others gasped and looked around in panic.

"Do not fear," commanded the master. "Enter!"

Philip ran to the door, unbolted it, and pulled it open. In the arc of the lights stood Mael with his arm around the waist of Cleopas the gardener. Cleopas's left arm hung heavily across Mael's shoulder and there was blood on his face.

They stumbled into the room. Cleopas limped badly. John grabbed a stool and hastened it to where Cleopas could sit down.

"We've seen the Master!" Mael blurted out. "He's risen from the dead."

The master stepped forward. "It's good to see you again, Mael!—and you Cleopas." He stepped in front of Cleopas. "Look in my eyes!"

Cleopas looked up. The master swept his right hand over Cleopas's forehead and back over the bruise on the side of his head. "Be healed."

The blood vanished. Cleopas sat up straight and his eyes brightened.

"Your suffering tonight is not in vain, Cleopas," the master continued. "The world is changed because of it and many other's lives with it."

"It was Barabbas!" Cleopas stammered.

"I know."

Thomas looked around as a murmur of surprise rippled through the room.

"I told you before, my brothers and sisters—my friends—you will see even greater things than this if you hold to my name and do not shrink back."

"But I lied to him—about the coin you left for us."

"You will all fail, at times, and you will be disciplined—for what daughter, what son—is not disciplined? Don't fear, for you won't die until Elohim has so chosen. Discipline isn't pleasant when it happens, but it brings about righteousness, as it did tonight."

"What happened?" Thomas asked.

Mael stepped forward and stood in the middle of the group. He recounted the events of the trip to Emmaus, and about Barabbas.

The peculiar energy of his little friend rose and fell with his retelling of the story. His eyes sparkled as he looked around the room, individually connecting with each of the listeners.

"We wanted to surprise you with the news," he concluded, "but it's our surprise—the master is already here!"

Mael sat down on the stool that had been set forth for Cleopas.

"Don't be surprised at anything you see," the master rejoined after the pause. "With healings and other miracles, the Kingdom of Elohim will be opened to the eyes of the whole world. For anyone with eyes to see, let him see. For anyone with ears to hear, let him hear. Demons will be thrown down, for the prince of demons has already been imprisoned. Many of you will die for my name, but do not be afraid, for death also has been thrown down, and you will have eternal life."

The master stood up. "Come with me, Mael." He took the little man's hand and started toward the door. They vanished together with a hiss.

A flush of envy washed over Thomas—perhaps it was jealousy. He quickly retreated from it. *I put my finger through the nail holes! I felt the wound in his side. Is that not enough*

For Mael, it was like falling through the portal again. Ransom's hand gripped Mael as they floated in the darkness. Just as suddenly, they were standing again, with the cool, scented air of the garden surrounding them. The light of dawn shadowed the horizon and the damp grass tickled his feet.

"My favorite place on this earth," Ransom said. "Come."

They sat on the small bench in the darkness under the wide spreading olive tree. It's branches dipped low and almost touched Ransom's head.

"Do you have any questions, Mael?"

"Why did you bring me here?"

"To this garden or to this world?"

"Both—either."

"Do you know who you are, Mael?"

"You asked me that before—I am Mael and nothing more."

"That is true and not true. You are so much more, Mael, and you are here to discover that."

"All I have learned here so far, is that it's as dangerous here for me as on Tessalindria."

Ransom nodded.

"But I did hear the voices for the first time here..."

"Always be sure that you don't refuse the voices. For you, the first and greatest command is to love all others in hakape. The second for you is to always, always do what the voices say."

"What does it mean?"

"It means that your journey has started."

Mael sat for a moment. "How old were you when you first heard it?"

"I was twelve the first time, and sporadic after that until five days before my thirtieth birthday. Right after my immersion."

"Your immersion?"

"My cousin, Chiahn, immersed me in the river in a submission to psadeq with Mah'Eladra."

"What did they say?"

"They told me to flee to the desert. I was to eat or drink nothing until the test was complete. I had no idea what it meant, but I knew I couldn't refuse."

Mael nodded. "I know that compulsion. What was the test in the desert?"

Ransom looked up. "I can't tell you this, Mael," he said as he looked into Mael's eyes.

Mael looked down. "I have heard the voices several times already."

"Do they frighten you?"

Mael thought for a moment. "It's always startling—I'm not sure about fear—it's so compelling."

"There will be times when they will cause you to fear, but you can't give in to it."

They watched the vermillion sky creep up where Asolara would be. A lark in the tree overhead had started its morning song, and the gentle breeze rose to meet them, carrying the scents of blossoming trees and the dusty road from down the hill. Mael realized why Ransom liked it so much.

"Did you really die?"

Ransom smiled. "Yes, Mael, I really died, but death is not what most people imagine. The death we see here, the one that everyone thinks about, is simply the death of what you call the basa, your body. The rest of your vorn is very much alive."

"And what happened to you. Your basa is different."

"This is who I was destined to be. What you saw before was distorted by the world's abuse."

"We wondered that—what happened to the rest of your vorn?"

"Mah'Eladra took me to other places—to other times, long ago, by this world's accounting of time—to teach the disobedient ones."

"It was only a short time."

"In Terra time, yes, but in the infinite, a thousand years can be like a day here and a day like a thousand years. You know this from the portals on Tessalindria, don't you?"

Mael shook his head. "When we travel in the portals on Tessalindria, we end up in a different time, but it only takes a moment to do so."

Ransom paused. "But if you went through a portal to an earlier time and taught there for eight years, then came back through the portal to arrive only a day after you left ..."

Mael closed his eyes.

"When you go back to Tessalindria, if you arrive only a day after you left, would you have spent only one day here?"

"I understand." Mael breathed deeply before his next question. "Did you go through the portal in the tomb—to visit those lands and times?"

"Mah'Eladra do not need a portal. The portals of Tessalindria are only for Tessalindria."

"But I came here through a portal."

"You were driven into the portal, Mael. Those who pursued you think you are lost because they don't understand. Mah'Eladra brought you here and not to another portal there. Mah'Eladra oversee the portals and control them. They do what they will with them."

"And you have no portals here—like that?"

"Every world in this vast cosmos is different, Mael. Mah'Eladra never do the same thing twice. It is part of their nature as creators that nothing is ever the same in process or result."

"Why?"

Ransom smiled. "The Mankind always wants to know why, have you noticed?"

Mael nodded.

"They were created that way—it helps them make sense of their world, but sometimes the question must remain only the question. There are mysteries for which they may never have an answer, but in this case ..." The master looked up into the sky and paused.

Mael guessed he was hearing the voice.

"Here is a partial answer: Have you ever noticed that if something happens the same way several times, you start to expect that it'll always be that way?"

"Yes ..."

"When you healed the lepers, each time it was different."

Mael looked down and nodded.

"If each healing was done exactly the same, would you presume that this was *always* the way to heal a leper?"

"Probably," Mael admitted.

"Miraculous interventions into this world are the province of Mah'Eladra. The mankind turns the gifts given them into rules.

They use their science to make the miraculous into the ordinary and expected. Their science has its place—we gave it to them to make order of their worlds, to plant crops and make bread and build shelter and clothing—but it should never take the wonder out of the miraculous."

Mael noticed that Ransom included himself in Mah'Eladra. He hadn't noticed it before, but he now understood the alarm of the priests, who considered this blasphemous. To Mael, it was as it should be.

"We gave them the law," Ransom continued, "and they turned it into rules—in a surprisingly short time. Then they compounded the rules with rule after rule, because the intent of the perfect law did not satisfy their desires. They started making things up to codify the wonder of obedience into patterns. It became complex. They need lawyers to dissect it, and the commoner is left behind, ensnared by the lawyers and teachers who missed Mah'Eladra's intent."

"They've done that with the Kirrinath, on Tessalindria."

Ransom smiled. "The mankind is the same everywhere in the cosmos. On every world their struggle is the same, yet in this confusion, there are those who can be taught to live by Mah'Eladra's original intent and become free of the shackles of the patterns and their own narmatan."

They stared out to the east. Asolara crested the horizon, flooding the intervening landscape with patches of bright yellow and green between the vales of purple fog. It lit their faces with its warmth. The morning songbirds fell silent.

When it was fully risen, Ransom spoke again. "Are you hungry?"

"Very hungry—and tired," Mael said to Asolara.

Ransom turned to face him. Mael looked into his eyes. Ransom spread his hands over the bench between them and two small dried fish, a loaf of dark bread and eight olives appeared on a white linen napkin. At the last flourish of his hand, an earthenware flask appeared on the corner of the napkin with two small earthenware tumblers. He took the bread in his hand and without breaking eye contact, broke a piece off the loaf, and handed it to Mael, then broke a piece for himself.

"This is the bread of the covenant with me, Mael. Eat it."

They ate the bread together while they stared into each other's eyes.

Ransom then took the flask in his hand. "Would you like some water?"

Mael nodded.

Ransom poured water into one tumbler and handed it to Mael, then handed the flask to Mael as well. Suddenly, Mael understood.

He looked into Ransom's eyes. "Would you like some water?"

Ransom nodded and Mael filled his cup.

As Ransom raised his glass, he said. "Do this as often as you gather together, in remembrance of Mah'Eladra."

They drank the water together. It was sweet, with a light, distant fragrance that Mael didn't know.

Ransom waved his hand over the spread between them. "Eat Mael, and drink—then sleep."

With a slight hiss, he was gone. The weight of fatigue pressed down hard on Mael's gnawing hunger. He waited for a moment to reflect on what had just happened before he reached for one of the fish.

Chapter Twenty-Four

BARABBAS

Mael woke to someone shaking his shoulder. "Wake up, little one."

He opened his eyes then shut them tightly again from the brilliance of Asolara high overhead. He squinted. Barabbas! He shook his head as he shielded his eyes with his hand.

"What are you doing here, Mael?"

"I was exhausted."

"But why here?"

Mael swung his legs over the edge of the bench. "The master brought me here and we talked."

Barabbas sat down beside him. Only two others were with him this time. He could see them clearly without their headscarves. They looked quite different in daylight.

"Why're *you* here, Barabbas?"

"We're looking for the master and the brothers. Heard he often comes here."

"Yes, but in the early morning and sometimes at night."

"Do you know where the others are meeting?"

"I think so, but it's been a bit confusing lately where everything is. I don't know this city very well—still." He smiled.

"GIVE THEM SOMETHING TO EAT."

Mael looked up. "How?"

"What?" said Barabbas as he followed Mael's glance.

When Mael looked down, the napkin had two fresh loaves and two new tumblers. He looked into Barabbas's eyes as he picked up the flask. "Would you like some water?"

"How did you do that?" Barabbas said.

"I didn't. Would you like some water?"

Barabbas nodded. Mael poured from the flask into the glass. It was a deep red.

Barabbas laughed. "Can Abner and Joseph have some?"

"Of course!" Mael poured the wine into the remaining tumblers. "Have a seat," he said as he handed them to Abner and Joseph.

"How did you do that?" Abner asked.

"I didn't, I thought it was water—it was water earlier."

Joseph smirked as he sipped the wine. "Pretty good for water."

Barabbas stared at him.

Mael tried to change the subject. "Help yourself to the bread."

"Are you sure it's bread?" Barabbas reached for one of the loaves.

"Looks like it," Mael broke off a piece and handed the rest to Abner.

"Weren't there five of you when we met?"

Barabbas nodded. "Jacob and Simeon decided not to come with us."

"Why?"

"Not sure. They think I'm crazy—that we're crazy—trying to hook up with your clan."

"Where are you going?"

"To find the master and the others—like I said."

Mael shook his head. "Of course, of course."

"It's alright, you just woke up. Can you help us find them? They seem to be hiding."

"Wouldn't you be hiding if you had been through what they have?"

"Good point. We have to be careful for other reasons."

Mael looked up.

"I'm not interested in spending another night in any Erman cell; they weren't exactly happy about setting me free."

Mael nodded. "I'd be glad to help you find them, but you'll need to be patient with my ignorance of the city."

"We know the city pretty well. Especially the places we can go to hide if necessary. Been doing that for years." Barabbas smiled.

"We'll set out to find them as soon as we've finished this meal," Mael said.

Barabbas wasn't sure that this was a good idea. He expressed this to Mael as they walked back toward the northern gate where Mael had suggested they would enter the city.

"At some point, Barabbas, you will have to trust that Elohim's way works—in the longer term. You'll have trouble, for sure, but it's small trouble compared to your future life."

"I've always been a trouble maker—I know how to do that, and how to live through it. Living to avert trouble will be a very troubling work—for me—for us."

"You can't avert trouble, Barabbas, but you don't have to contribute to it."

"What if others make the trouble?"

"You don't retaliate, you don't reciprocate, you don't run—you extend your kindness instead. Let Elohim protect you. They are the perfect judge and you are not."

"There are some who would kill me if I did that."

"Perhaps."

Barabbas knew that this teaching was as strange to Abner and Joseph as it was to himself, though he guessed it would be more difficult for Abner.

Abner was a hard man, though faithful to a fault. Barabbas wondered if it was faithfulness that kept Abner from abandoning him, as had Jacob and Simeon. Abner was strong and fast, and had saved him many times through his quick response to trouble, but it was always at the cost of more trouble.

"What do you guys think?" he tossed over his shoulder. They trod along in the dust behind him.

Joseph responded first. "It's different, to be sure..." He paused, though it was obvious he had more to say. "What we've been doing hasn't worked out so well for us, but I wouldn't be here if I weren't willing to try something different."

Abner's vague assent was a simple grunt.

"We're coming to the gate," Mael said. "The Romans will have guards there."

"Why?"

"Just a hunch."

Abner grunted again and shook his head.

"If they stop you, be completely honest and don't threaten them," Mael said. "Smile in your honesty."

"Seriously?"

"I never joke about such things, Barabbas."

Joseph laughed aloud. Barabbas knew his nervous laugh well. "Alright," he said, "I'll be honest, and I'll smile."

"Good." The little man didn't even look at him.

Two Roman soldiers attended the company of Jewish guards. They stood on either side of the gate eyeing each entrant.

"Relax," Mael whispered. "If they stop us, relax even more."

Barabbas had never done anything like this, walking into the jaws of death, relaxed. "I'll try."

They were dressed in simple gray robes and carried no weapons. Barabbas had only a small purse with several silvers in it, and he was quite sure that Mael had nothing but the clothes on his back.

As they approached the gate, the Jewish guards whispered to each other. The soldiers noticed this, and the one on the left stepped forward from the shadow of the gate for a closer examination.

Barabbas nodded. Mael looked over at the soldier to the right and smiled.

"Stop!" They were almost past the soldiers. Barabbas knew he could run. He was good at it, but Mael already gripped his forearm. They stopped.

The soldiers came around in front of them. The taller one stared at Barabbas. "What is your name?"

"Barabbas." It took surprising effort, this honesty thing.

"I thought so—arrest these men!"

Abner cursed.

Two other Roman soldiers emerged from the shadows.

One of the Jewish guards stepped forward. "On what charge?"

"This man is accused of sedition."

"Isn't this the Barabbas you set free, in exchange for the death of the Nazarene?"

The soldier turned to face the guard. "You shouldn't meddle in the affairs of Rome, Captain."

Mael's grip tightened on Barabbas's arm.

"Your prefect released him in exchange for the death of one of our people. Unless you have new charges, you can't arrest him again. What has he done?"

"We have been told to apprehend this man!"

"By whom?"

"By the Prefect," said the soldier.

"Pilate?"

"He issued an edict only yesterday for his arrest."

"Then, by the laws of Rome, we appeal to your Prefect on his behalf," the Jewish captain said.

"You would defy us?" the soldier said.

"We are defying your right to defy Roman law, which you swore to protect when you took your oath as a soldier." The other Jewish guards had stepped up beside the captain.

Mael's grip tightened again. "Wait!" he whispered.

The two captains faced each other silently, locked in pride and determination. For the first time he could remember, Barabbas waited. He wanted to act—it was his way—but a new restraint held him. The Jewish guards and the Roman soldiers were fighting without swords. They battled over the Roman law and he was in the middle, without having to fight at all. When he breathed out, Mael's grip loosened.

"Take them to Pilate," said the soldier, as he turned away from the Jewish Captain.

The other soldiers stepped forward. "Follow us."

Four more soldiers emerged from the shadows and fell in around the four of them in a tight circle.

"Good to see you, Mael," one of them said. "What on earth are you doing with this brigand?"

"He's a friend, Marcus, and no longer the brigand that you suppose."

Abner fumed. This would undoubtedly turn out badly for all of them. Pilate sat on an ornate gilded chair on the Portico of his residence in Jerusalem. It seemed out of place, brought out so that the prisoners would not enter his house. Perhaps it was that they were Jewish. A woman, presumably Pilate's wife, stood behind him with her hands on his right shoulder.

As they drew near, Pilate rose and strode forward. "Barabbas bar Simeon!" he exclaimed as he faced the accused. "I had hoped that we would never see you again."

"I had hoped the same, your honor, at least not like this."

"What have you done this time?"

Barabbas looked him straight in the eye. "Nothing."

A puzzled look flooded Pilate's face. "Then why are you here?"

"We have not been accused of anything, your honor. We were arrested at the gate by your soldiers supposedly under an edict from you."

Pilate knit his brow in confusion and looked at the others. He looked straight into Abner's eyes. Abner could have strangled him were it not for the six soldiers that accompanied them and four others that stood immediately behind the Prefect. Pilate glanced at Joseph then blanched visibly when he looked at Mael. Mael stared at him.

"Who are you?"

"I am Mael."

"Mael what?"

"Mael and nothing more."

"Are you with these outlaws?"

"They're my friends."

"How long have you known them?"

"I met them on the road from Emmaus two nights ago. They brought me and my friend back to Jerusalem, keeping me safe from robbers along the way."

"Why would you travel at night from Emmaus? You must know it isn't safe."

"I'm not from here, so I didn't know this. We were coming back to Jerusalem to tell the followers of the Nazarene Prophet that we had seen him—alive—after his death and burial."

Pilate stepped back, his face ashen with terror. His wife gasped and backed through the doors behind the chair.

Pilate retreated to his chair and sat down heavily, shaking his head and looking at the floor.

He looked up. "I have heard the rumors of this 'Resurrection'," he said as he stood up to face them again, "and I am weary of the effect it's having on this city."

He turned to Barabbas in anger. "And you, you trouble maker, have you also seen this ghost?"

Barabbas bowed his head. "Not yet, your honor."

"Is it your hope?"

"If it's true."

Abner shook his head and looked over at Joseph. Fear filled Joseph's eyes. This wasn't going well.

Pilate paced in front of them, his guards watching carefully for any false move by the captives. "He was beaten nearly to death at the request of the priests and survived to make it to the place of the skull. We crucified him well. My best soldiers carried out the assignment. To satisfy your priests, we ran him through with a spear to make sure he was dead before sundown. We know he was dead."

He turned to Barabbas suddenly and stepped up to look him in the eyes. "You, Barabbas bar Simeon, know when a man is dead, do you not?"

"I do." Barabbas didn't flinch at the Prefect's intimidation.

"Do you think I don't□"

"I think you do."

"Then why do you hope?"

"Because a resurrection from death doesn't depend on how dead a man is, or the manner of his death. It is still a resurrection."

"Fool!" snapped the Prefect. He slapped Barabbas's face. Abner started to step forward but stopped in front of three swords held up by the guards. He stepped back, his eyes clouded with red.

"I wouldn't believe until I saw, and neither should you!" Pilate continued. "As to your offenses, you may not have done anything to warrant this immediate arrest, your history contains enough ..."

A slight hiss interrupted the Prefect's words as something materialized between Abner and Barabbas. It shimmered with light for a second and then settled into the form of a man, dressed in a white robe as the light in him faded.

Abner stepped back and so did the guards. Pilate paled and his jaw dropped open.

Mael laughed aloud. "Master!"

The man was tall and handsome—obviously Jewish. He stared at Pilate for a moment. "See and believe then, Prefect."

Pilate took another step back. "Who are you?" His voice trembled.

"I am Jesus, whom you crucified." He held out his wrists. "See the nail holes?" He lifted up the hem of his robe and swung his left foot forward revealing a similar wound to his ankle.

Pilate fell back into his chair as the soldiers stepped back, drawing their swords.

"Drop your swords," said the man. "There's no need for them."

Ten Roman swords clattered to the stone floor of the portico.

"Stand up, Pilate."

Pilate stood up.

"My followers come in peace, Prefect. They're no threat to you. They are part of a kingdom that isn't of this world, nor will it wage wars like the kingdoms of this world. This man, Barabbas, is a decorated criminal, having waged war against your authority by the ways of this world, but he is changed."

The man walked back and forth in front of Pilate.

"Your prisons are full of men like Barabbas, but all the prisons of Rome could not hold those who hate your occupation of their homelands. Your hope, in holding the ones that you do, is that they would change, and yet, when one, or a thousand others like him, do change or try to change, you refuse to believe in that possibility, and you punish them anyway. Does that make any sense at all?"

The words were resolute, powerful, and full of compassion and reason that struck Abner's heart. He'd never heard anything like this.

The man waited for an answer. Pilate remained silent.

The man continued: "Search your heart, Prefect. These men, who have chosen to follow me, are not your enemies, nor will you overcome them with your prisons, your swords, your spears or your crucifixions, because those things can only prevail over those who fear death. Death means a resurrection like mine to those who walk this path behind me."

The man stopped pacing and fell silent. Pilate looked back and forth between him and the prisoners, his face strained with the decision before him. The soldiers stood blank faced. There would be no answer from them. Silence reigned, as if no one could offer a solution to Pilate. His agony burned in his eyes, as they roved about helplessly.

Finally, he raised his hand and paused. No one moved. Darkness descended over his face. "Lock them all up!"

The soldiers scrambled for their swords, then surrounded the prisoners. Pilate turned and walked through the doors into his residence. The man reached for Mael's hand, and as he grasped it, they vanished together with a hiss as the soldiers closed around them.

Chapter Twenty-Five

TRAINING

"Come sit with me while we talk about life for a brief moment."
(Erengnira)
Tiger in a Tree

Mael and Ransom materialized together in the brilliant light of Asolara. They were standing on the corner of a high wall. Ransom held Mael's cloak with both hands as Mael's feet teetered on the edge. Behind him, the precipice dropped fifty paces into a ravine.

Mael panicked from the height and his precarious situation. Were Ransom to let go he would fall to his death. "Save me!" he cried.

Ransom pulled him back.

"Pilate will have to learn the hard way." Ransom brushed back the tears in his eyes with his sleeve. "So many of them insist on learning the hard way."

Mael nodded. He was amazed at the combination of fearless action and compassion that he saw in Ransom. Mael knew he didn't understand the situation well, but trusted that Ransom did.

"Have a seat," Ransom said as he sat down cross-legged on the wall. The top of the wall was three paces wide, but in spite of the relative comfort of its width, its height made Mael uneasy. He realized suddenly that they were on the southeast corner of the temple courts wall, and behind them and far below, still partially in the shadow of the mighty wall was the busy-ness of the temple. The crowds had thinned from the feast but people filled the courts, moving like ants building an ant hill.

"Sit," Ransom said again.

Mael took a step back from the edge of the wall, and sat down facing Ransom, who stared out over the landscape below. "It's beautiful, isn't it?" Ransom said without dropping his gaze. "At least from this level."

Mael turned to look outside the wall to the east and nodded. They could see a great distance from this height, and the patchwork of colored fields and roads, groups of houses and dots of trees, looked tranquil in the brightness of Asolara. Puffy clouds filled the sky with a laziness that defied words.

Ransom continued: "Yet down in the midst of that quiet, the vorns of men and women are wrenched in anguish and hurt. They are like sheep without a shepherd to guide them, and the shepherds assigned to the task are busy lining their pockets and stomachs from the fear of the sheep, whom they devour like wolves."

Mael waited for more as he continued to stare. The warm breeze flowing up the wall from the ground flowed over them, scented with flowers and bushes that filled the valley below. A hawk drew lazy circles above them, calling out now and then for some reason known only to her.

"You *do* know, Mael, that if I had dropped you off this wall, the Eladra would have caught you?"

"I like to think that is true." Mael said.

"It's absolutely true, Mael. But it's also true that if you tested Mah'Eladra in this, by jumping off yourself, this would be detestable to them."

"I think I understand."

"That is the true nature of armatan, what we call faith. That you know—that you are confident—but you do not need to test it. So much of this world—so many of the mankind, will not live without proof, but in testing for their proof, they violate the law of armatan, and the proof they want eludes them, so they doubt more."

Ransom fell silent again.

Mael waited.

Ransom looked around, roving his eyes about the countryside. "Vishtoenvar tried to convince me otherwise. He brought me to this very place and challenged me to test Mah'Eladra. He will also test you. You must remain true to what you know—what is taught in the Kirrinath. Use the Kirrinath to oppose him—don't try to stand alone against him. He's very clever."

"I know."

The conversation paused again.

"There was another test he gave me," Ransom said. "Very real at the time, but looking back, it was a bit foolish."

"What was it?"

"Well, we started out right here at the pinnacle of the temple, and he took me on a journey across the whole breadth of Terra. He showed me all the kings and kingdoms in the world. He promised me that if I would turn my allegiance to him rather than Mah'Eladra, I could have them all—rule over them all; all the wealth and power; all the splendor..."

"And why is that foolish? I think many would like that very much."

"Let me show you something, Mael." Ransom leaned forward and cupped his hands together in front of his crossed legs, and blew into them. He slowly opened them from the bottom and gold coins started falling onto the stone. After he had dropped about fifteen of them, he closed his hands and then opened them. They were empty.

He reached forward and brushed away the coins so they slipped over the edge of the wall. They clinked against the wall until they fell out of earshot.

Ransom looked up at Mael. "It's all ours anyway, Mael. It has been from the very beginning. All the gold, every talent of silver, every tiny copper, every cow, every goat and kid, and lamb and ewe—every waterfall and mountain. They're all ours."

"Alright," Mael admitted slowly. "And?"

"What wealth could Vishtoenvar possibly give me that I don't already have?"

Mael nodded. "The authority to rule over the mankind?"

"He rules over the hearts of many of the mankind. As a result, the kingdoms of Terra are full of evil: envy, jealousy, anger, murder, slavery, war, unfaithfulness, lying, deceit, adultery... He makes no effort to solve these problems and in truth, he perpetuates them to keep the mankind in endless distraction. Those problems can only be overcome if the vorns of the people were willing to change. Why would I want to govern unruly men, corrupted by their own wills, rebellious, selfish—who follow the teachings of demons that defy Elohim? Wouldn't I rather rule over a kingdom of those who truly desire to obey Mah'Eladra?"

"Does such a kingdom exist?"

"You call it the deep sky, Mael; we call it the Kingdom of Elohim. Now, the doorway into psadeq with Elohim, with Mah'Eladra themselves, will be opened here on Terra, to the mankind. It will be a kingdom that has no place, but will be in every land through the vorns of those in the mankind who choose to be part of it. It can't be conquered with the sword or spear, but will conquer other kingdoms from within, and the kings of this world will be powerless to frustrate its advance. They can kill the body, but they will not be able to kill the idea or the hope that it brings."

Mael looked at Ransom. "It will take an unusual king to rule over such a kingdom," he said.

"Mah'Eladra—Elohim—will be their king. Those who have ears will hear their voice and will come out and be separate, while still living in their midst. No one will say, 'Here it is!' or 'Over there!' for this kingdom will be infused into the nations. Because they will not wage war like the kingdoms of the world, those kingdoms cannot know how to defeat them."

Ransom swept his hand over the landscape. "Every land you see, Mael, to the fringes of Terra, will hear the message of this kingdom."

Mael followed the sweep of his hand. "What about Tessalindria? Will we hear this message? Can we be part of this kingdom?"

The master nodded. "When the time is right!"

A long pause followed.

"I have a question," Mael said.

Ransom nodded.

"You know all things. You knew I was coming here and how that happened."

Ransom closed his eyes and nodded again.

"Do you know what happened to Erolin?"

"Yes."

Mael waited. Ransom opened his eyes. "There are things that I cannot tell you, Mael."

"Can't or won't?"

"It's not that I am not able, Mael, but in the infinite wisdom of the creation, there is a wisdom that forbids certain things for the sake of psadeq. This is one of those things. To the one who wants to know, this may seem cruel, but Mah'Eladra are perfect in wisdom and I cannot tell you, for the sake of this wisdom.

Mael breathed deeply.

"One day, you will know. Then you will understand this wisdom."

They sat for several moments, staring out over the unchanging landscape. Mael wiped back the tears.

Ransom took Mael's hand and stared into his eyes. "I have something for you to do—and it's urgent!"

Mael sniffed. "Tell me."

"You must go to Pilate and tell him to set Barabbas and the others free."

"But..."

"There is important work for Barabbas to do, and a Roman jail is not a good place to do such business." Ransom's eyes wouldn't let go. "Promise me!"

Mael hesitated.

"LISTEN TO HIM—LISTEN TO US."

Mael shivered. It was all too clear, but before he had opportunity to open his mouth, Ransom's grip released and he vanished, just as he had at dinner in Emmaus.

Barabbas's irritation with Abner flooded his words. "Don't you think I know we're back in jail?"

"Of course you know it. We all know it!" Abner's anger flowed freely, as it had since the cell door closed. "I should have listened to Simeon!"

"Perhaps, but your raving about it now is not going to unlock the door! And it could be a lot worse!"

"Yeah, well it could be a lot better!" Abner growled.

"Can you two just back off a bit?" Joseph said.

Barabbas nodded and pursed his lips.

Abner's nostrils flared as he glared at Joseph.

"We're alive," Joseph continued, "and we haven't yet been condemned. We have no way of understanding what will come of this."

"Jail never ends well," Abner sulked.

"Have you ever been in jail for doing nothing wrong?" Joseph asked.

"No."

"So this is new for you, as it is for us also, Abner. We're not in prison; we're just in the jail. We have no way to know what will happen—and we saw Jesus—he showed up to defend us. That's rather extraordinary, wouldn't you say?"

Abner's temper subsided. "Some defense," he said glumly as he lowered his eyes.

"Did you see Pilate's eyes, Abner?" Joseph said. "He had no case. He was terrified when Jesus appeared. His pride got the better of him and he hardened himself. If history is on our side, that's not a good thing for Pilate."

"History?"

"Pharaoh? Moses?" Joseph said.

"Bah! That was two thousand years ago!"

"He has a point, Abner," Barabbas interjected.

Joseph smiled. "If Jesus is who he claimed to be—did you notice how he showed up, by the way?"

Abner nodded without looking up.

"If he is who his followers think he is, then we have a lot of hope, I would say."

"He got killed for his claims, did you notice thatⁿ"

"Abner!" Joseph stared hard at his friend.

Abner looked up.

"He showed up to defend us!" Joseph said. "He appeared out of thin air to argue our case. I am guessing Pilate wanted to crucify us, like he does every insurrectionist, but when Jesus showed up, his pride refused to let us go, so he just put us here. We haven't seen the end of this!"

"It could get worse in a hurry." Abner softened but wasn't ready to relent. "He vanished as quickly as he showed up, in case you didn't notice. How come he didn't take us with him—like he did Mael?"

"It could get better also," Joseph said. "And I have no idea about Mael. He's a curious one. He looks a lot like Jesus used to look."

"He's not from around here, that's for sure," Barabbas said, "but I like the little fellow. He has a curious innocence about him—likeable, don't you think?"

Joseph nodded. Abner shook his head.

"C'mon, Abner. Joseph is right. Let's not be too hard on the future. It just makes the present miserable."

Abner pursed his lips and acquiesced.

A slight hiss by the door startled all of them. They turned to see a tall figure dressed like a warrior facing them, the warrior who had carried the man on the road. "I am Vishtalar," he said with an accent similar to Mael's.

All three men backed up against the back wall of the cell.

"I come in peace. Do not be afraid, for Mah'Eladra has other plans."

Barabbas had never heard the term Mah'Eladra, but he knew exactly what the angel meant. He guessed that Abner and Joseph did also.

"Wait and do not fear, Barabbas!" He vanished with a hiss.

Chapter Twenty-Six

PILATE

"Bitterness solves nothing."
Old Otallan Saying

Pilate couldn't sleep—he was afraid to sleep. His mind refused to let go of the encounter with Barabbas and his men.

Barabbas was a Roman enemy, not an enemy of the Jews. When he questioned the soldiers about why they brought him to the palace, they confessed that the Jewish soldiers had insisted on it.

The appearance of Jesus's ghost haunted him. The ghost insisted that...what was he thinkingɒ...he didn't even believe in ghosts! He wasn't sure it was Jesus; it certainly didn't look like him, even before all the beatings.

After the changing of the guard at midnight, the palace's deathlike silence should have been comforting, but the fear wouldn't leave. More than anything, Pilate wanted to be free of the continual pressure of the responsibilities that smothered him ever since his appointment to Jerusalem. This wasn't his first sleepless night.

He nodded to the two guards at the entrance to his chambers. They were alert, but respectfully quiet as they nodded back.

The empty courtyard bathed in the silent light of the quarter moon that had ascended over the edge of the outer wall. The shadows of the columns that formed the portico were just becoming visible, and the white marble flagstones glowed in its light. The only sound came from the fountain in the middle of the court, as its water cascaded back into the pool at its base.

In truth, Jesus, or whoever it was, had been right. Of all his prayers to the gods, the one that repeatedly came to the fore was that the Jews would relent, and stop trying to overthrow him; that they could accept Roman authority. He didn't want to be here, but life in Jerusalem *could* be pleasant, were it not for the incessant assault of hatred by the Jews.

He kept to the shadows under the portico. After the second turn, he glanced back at the fountain. His heart skipped and he stopped. Were his tired eyes playing tricks? He rubbed them briefly. A small man—or something that looked like one—sat on steps at the base of the fountain facing the main entrance.

The man stood up.

Pilate looked around. The guards were at their posts. There was little to fear, unless the man had a sword or a knife. In his nightclothes, Pilate was defenseless except for his wits.

"Guards!" he yelled. His voice cracked with the tension. No answer.

The man opened his cloak and shrugged it off his shoulders. It fell to the ground. Even in the dim light, it was clear that he was naked except for a loincloth. He held out his hands with the palms up and stepped forward away from his cloak.

"Guards!" Pilate yelled again.

The man spoke: "They can't hear you, Pilate."

Fear surged through him. "Who are you?"

"I am Mael."

The little man from his confrontation with Barabbas! "What are you doing here?"

"I came to talk with you."

Pilate looked around. "How did you get in?"

"Through the gate from the front portico."

"My guards ..."

"Your guards didn't see me," the man interrupted.

"Guards!" Pilate's voice was more of a croak. No answer.

"I come in peace."

Wasn't that what Jesus had said, or whoever it was? "What did you say your name was?"

"Mael."

"Where are you from?"

"Farhantra, on the western shore of the Vorsian Sea."

Pilate stopped. "What do you want from me, Mael?"

"I've been told to ask you to free Barabbas."

"By whom?"

"Jesus, the Nazarene."

Pilate shuddered. "No."

"Why? He's done nothing to warrant the arrest."

"He has defied Rome."

"He has committed to change. As the master pointed out, isn't that what you want?"

"How do you know?"

"I've seen this change. I see his vorn. The master came to change people. Barabbas, condemned to death for his way of life, was freed by the death of the master, and that changed him. It will change many more."

"It's my job to defend Rome."

"The followers of the master are no threat to Rome."

"In his trial, Jesus admitted that he was a king," Pilate said, "and he had a kingdom. Any kingdom that defies Rome is a threat to Rome."

Mael hadn't moved. He stood in the pale light of the moon with his back to the fountain, his hands still spread, palms up.

"The kingdom of Elohim is no more a threat to Rome than I am to you."

"Are you cold?" Pilate wanted to change the subject.

"Yes, but I've been cold before. This conversation is more important than my comfort."

"You can put your robe on, if you like."

"Thank you." The little man stepped back and bent to pick up his robe.

"What makes you think that this kingdom is not a threat?"

"Because the master teaches that his followers would submit to ruling authorities. He teaches that Rome is an agent of the one God and has been appointed to keep order in this world. His followers will honor that and will not rebel. In return, it is your place to keep order and protect these people. They must be allowed to live out their convictions." Mael slipped his cloak onto his shoulders and shrugged it into comfort, tying his belt loosely before dropping his hands to his side.

"The Jews have been in rebellion since the day Rome arrived. Don't they worship this same God? Are you going to tell me that your God has changed also? Barabbas is a Jew and has been nothing but trouble."

"I don't understand the rebellion of the Jews. I've not been here long enough, but Barabbas will not be trouble if he changes."

"How can I know this?"

"You must start trusting somewhere."

"But with Barabbas?"

"Why not? If he can change, then who else could not?"

Pilate eyed the curious little stranger. "I will release him before the third hour."

"Thank you."

"Guards!" Pilate yelled. Two soldiers surged forward from the front door. "Escort this man out! See to it he doesn't come back."

They grabbed Mael by the arms and lifted him effortlessly off his feet, carrying him toward the door. He didn't resist. "Sleep well, Prefect," he said.

Pilate watched as they shoved him out the main door. He tumbled down the steps. When they returned, he was ready. "How did he get in here☐"

The guards looked at each other. "We don't know, Prefect. We didn't even know he was here until you called to us."

"Go back to your posts and make absolutely sure that he doesn't come in again; double up if you have to."

The guards saluted.

Pilate shuffled back toward the bedroom. The situation with this Messiah of Israel was becoming more complex by the day. He had no way of knowing whom to trust. The odd little man—Mael—was obviously a foreigner. What interest had he in all this? Why did he care? Aside from his striking resemblance to Jesus, at least before his crucifixion, he couldn't possibly be significant, but who *was* he? Perhaps in the morning he would get Claudius to investigate.

He slipped into bed. His wife turned over but didn't wake. Perhaps in the morning...

"They threw me down the steps," Mael said. "Fourteen steps—stone steps. I counted them and I think I hit every one of them on the way down to the street." Mael recounted his discussion with Pilate to Domas.

"I walked right past them on the way in so I'm not sure why they were so rough and so eager to get me out."

"That cut on your shoulder looks bad." Domas remarked just before he stuffed another pastry into his mouth.

"My knee hurts the most." Mael pulled up his cloak to reveal the bad bruise on his kneecap. "Hard to walk."

"Hardly noticed," said Domas.

Bieter sat down beside them with a plate of small biscuits and some butter. "You said that Barabbas was looking for us?"

Mael nodded as he dropped his cloak over his knee.

"Where is he?"

"He's in jail. Pilate threw him in there, even though the master argued with him about it."

"The master?"

Mael recounted the events leading up to the arrest.

Bieter shook his head. "He seems to be appearing all over the place. We have reports from many people who have seen him." He nibbled on one of his biscuits as he talked. "You think we can trust Barabbas?"

"Yes," Mael said. "He's sincere. Pilate said he would release him this morning. We need to be at the fortress when they let him out."

"You talked to Pilate?"

"He was just telling me about it," Domas asserted. "It's a great story..."

A slight hiss arrested his thought as Chaisus materialized by the door. "Good morning, friends!"

All eyes turned in wonder. They had all seen it several times now, but each time seemed as new as the one before. Mael smiled to himself. In a way, they were like children watching a magician, but this was no sleight of hand.

Chaisus took the seat nearest to where he had entered, beside Bartolmu and Chiahn. "There is much to do today," he said as he reached for the fresh loaf of bread in front of him. He then poured a glass from the pitcher of water mixed with some wine that sat on every table. He tore off a piece of the bread and passed the loaf to Bartolmu.

He raised both hands and looked upward. "Father, I am thankful for this flock that remains, that they will do greater things than they even know." He glanced around the room. "In remembrance of me," he said. He took a bite of the bread and chewed it slowly, his eyes roving the landscape of eyes riveted to him.

"In remembrance of your sacrificed body!"

Mael startled at the choral response as each took a small bite of the bread in his hand.

The master raised the cup of water-wine in his left hand. "To the covenant of my blood." He took a draught from the cup.

"We remember this new covenant of your blood," murmured the group.

Mael stumbled over his words as he mumbled along behind.

Bieter leaned over. "He taught us to do this the night he was crucified."

Mael nodded. "I wasn't there. What else did he tell you?"

Bieter turned to him and paused as his eyes studied Mael's face. "We were together from sundown until the betrayal, Mael. I can't remember everything he said."

"But you remember some of it—"

Chiahn smiled. "It's going to take a while to put it all together, Mael. We've been with him for three years. He gave us pieces of the puzzle all along, but that night he drew the picture in earnest. I'm not sure that we even understand all of it now."

"But I want to know. I've been sent here to learn," Mael protested.

"I have this feeling," Chiahn continued, "that just like each of us, you'll learn exactly what you are to know as you need it."

Mael retreated.

"There's a reason that you got locked away that night. Perhaps you weren't supposed to be there," Bartolmu interjected.

Mael breathed deeply and closed his eyes.

"If you haven't noticed, you've had several private sessions with the master that we've not been able to be part of." Chiahn smiled. "We're all a bit envious."

"And you were the one that was told to confront Pilate," Domas chimed in. "Why didn't he ask one of us?"

"I don't know," Mael confessed.

"It's been this way from the very beginning," Chiahn continued. "Each of us seems to have a unique place and is given special opportunities to serve. We've had to learn to avoid the envy and jealousy that is natural in that situation. But the master has his way about it, and we accept it."

Bartolmu smiled. "It's like your body, Mael. If your eyes and ears started arguing about who was more important, rather than listening and seeing, or if they became envious of each other, then a lot of things would go wrong in a hurry."

The master stood up and spoke over the murmur of the group. "Most of you have heard the rumors about Barabbas. He's been imprisoned by Pilate who has hardened his heart and won't release him yet—"

Mael startled. "But he—"

The master cut Mael short. "When he's released, he'll seek you out, and you must accept him. He's a murderer and a thief—a rebellious soul, and his insurrection has landed him back in prison, because Pilate refuses to acknowledge that he can change. Each of you know that you were the same, but you have been set free, and have been accepted in this new kingdom that does not define its future by the past.

"*There was a righteous man who wanted the fellowship of other righteous men. He set out on a journey to find those whose righteousness was like his own. After a long time, he returned home, having found no one like himself.*

"*In his loneliness, he called out, 'Are there no others like me?'*

"*There are thousands,*" *Yahweh said and opened his eyes to his own unrighteousness. Then he found many others like himself.*

"When Barabbas comes to you, you must accept him and his brothers. The rest of this world won't understand this, but if my kingdom were made up of those who are perfect, who did not need forgiveness, it would be a small kingdom indeed, and none of you would be in it.

"Go out in peace my sisters, my brothers. You will speak to the multitudes, and a few will listen. Your words will not come back empty. In a short while, I will no longer come to walk among you, but I will send one who is as powerful as I, to comfort you, just as I spoke when we last ate together. My kingdom will take root and no one will stop it. It will be like a tree, planted by a stream that draws its water from the deep and never fails to bear fruit."

He vanished with a hiss. The room was silent.

"**You must go to Pilate again.**"

Mael wasn't sure he would ever get used to the intrusion of the voice. He glanced quickly around to see if anyone else had heard it. The murmur of voices had continued as they turned back to their breakfast. Domas stared at him quietly.

"What did you hear, Mael?"

Mael stood up. "Pilate must let him go." He moved toward the door.

"I thought you said that Pilate would let him go this morn-ing," Domas whispered.

"Apparently not."

"I'm coming with you."

Mael wondered if he should refuse, but perhaps Domas had also heard the voice. "If you wish."

"That little man," Pilate said, "—the one who was here last night—he's in the courtyard by the fountain and there's some-one with him." Claudia's agitation spilled onto Pilate as his face darkened.

"I told him not to come back. I told the guards not to let him in—ever!"

"I told you my dream, darling. Give these men what they want and be rid of them or they'll be your undoing." Darkness and dread laced her words.

Pilate stood up from his breakfast and threw his napkin down onto the half-finished plate of porridge and quail eggs. "Flavius!" he yelled as he grabbed the flagon of ale.

His personal bodyguard trotted out from behind the screen in the corner of the dining area.

Pilate took a deep draught. It burned as it went down "Come with me!"

He kicked the chair backward and strode toward the court-yard.

"Be careful," Claudia said from some distance behind him.

Mael stood almost where he had the night before. Beside him was another man, taller and obviously Jewish. They stood unmoved as he strode up to them with Flavius close behind. The bodyguard drew his sword as they approached.

"We are no danger to you, Pilate, that you would draw your sword against unarmed men."

"What do you want?" Pilate growled.

"You said last night that you would free Barabbas."

"The morning is hardly over. How do you know I won't?"

"You've hardened your heart, Pilate. You slept well after I left and in your reflections this morning, you have decided to keep your prisoner."

"You can't know this!"

The little man said nothing. Pilate glanced at the other man, who stared at him, undaunted by his authority. His heart flickered in uncertainty as he looked back at the small stranger. How could he possibly have known about his decision?

"You can change your mind, Pilate." The little man's voice had softened. "No one needs to know. No one except the guards in the fortress even knows you have Barabbas."

"How do you know this?"

"You've told no one, because you know you must release him."

Pilate's hands trembled. Anger lingered close by, threatening to erupt. Other than the soldiers who arrested Barabbas, only Claudia had heard about it after she told him her dream.

"Your wife's dream wasn't an idle notion, Pilate. Listen to her. She has your best interest at heart."

The storm of anger overwhelmed him. "Get out! Now!"

Flavius stepped up beside him, his sword ready.

The two men didn't move. "We'll leave, as you wish. There is no need for the sword, Flavius. This time we will walk out as we walked in. I've no need of further injuries."

Flavius's sword fell to the ground.

"Come, Thomas."

The two men turned toward the door of the courtyard. The small one was limping.

Flavius scrambled to pick up his sword.

The heavy bronze doors of the residence opened for the pair as they strode out onto the portico. The two guards at the door stood stiff as javelins, as if they saw nothing. The doors closed.

Pilate shook his head. He turned to Flavius. "You dropped your sword␣"

"I don't know what happened."

Pilate shook his head. "Don't let them back in Flavius. Whatever you need to do—don't let them in! Is this clear?"

"As you command."

Thomas walked alongside his limping companion as they navigated the streets away from Pilate's palace. There was more to Mael than he had imagined. "What was the dream all about?"

"Pilate's wife had a dream last night. She told him just before breakfast. She said that he needed to release Barabbas. She begged him not to delay this decision, but he has hardened himself in his pride in the might of Rome. He won't do it."

"How do you know, Mael?"

"I don't know."

"How could you know something you don't know?"

Mael looked up at Thomas and smiled. "I honestly don't know," he said as he shook his head. "More and more, I am finding things that I know, and I don't know where I learned them. Things about myself, and others, that I can't remember how I should know them. Some of them are simple, like this dream. Others are much deeper."

"Such as?"

"I am forbidden to speak of some of them. It is not the time."

"What␣" Thomas had stopped. "Jesus said that a lot!"

Mael turned to face him. "There are deep things, Thomas—some of them do not belong to Terra—they are about my home world. Some of them belong here, but it is not time for others to know them."

"Who are you, Mael?"

"I am Mael, and—"

"I don't believe that!" Thomas said.

"I'm not sure I do either—anymore."

They walked on in silence. Thomas didn't even know where they were going or why. Maybe it didn't matter.

"Are you going to go back to Pilate again?"

"Yes."

Thomas refrained from asking when. Perhaps Mael didn't even know.

"Do you remember the story you told me about Moses, Thomas? How he went back to the king of the land asking to let your people out of their slavery?"

"Yes, it's one of our most loved stories."

"How many times did he go back?"

"Ten."

"Why?"

"Because each time, Pharaoh promised and then he hardened his heart and refused."

"You almost have it right, Thomas."

Thomas looked down. "I told *you* the story. What do you mean, I *almost* have it right."

"If you read it carefully, in the book of the law, you will find that in five of the ten times, it was Yahweh that hardened Pharaoh."

"What do you mean? How do you know this□"

"There comes a time, Thomas, when Yahweh will use a rebellious person to their own purpose. After Pilate has proven his hardness, Yahweh will harden him so that their way will be revealed. There will be an uprising. Pilate will be broken and Barabbas will be freed."

"How do you know?"

Mael smiled and shrugged. "I don't know."

"If you know this will happen, why do you have to confront Pilate? Just let it happen."

"Confronting Pilate is part of what must make it happen."

Thomas shook his head. "I give up."

"Don't give up, Thomas. Ponder these things, and they'll be revealed. Don't speak to the others about what I've told you. These words are only for you. After it has come to pass, you can tell this story to others."

Barabbas was tired of arguing. "Give it a rest, Abner. I am squarely with Joseph on this one."

Abner shook his head. "I can't believe that you're buying it!"

"I'm not buying anything. The gruesome death of someone else spared my life. That person—no one can explain what he did other than confront the priest and the teachers. Some of them are as bad as the Romans. You know that."

"So why would I listen or believe either one of them—or him?

The floor was a cold place to sit crossed legged, but there was nowhere else. Joseph listened to them argue. He had little to say and, like them, nowhere to go.

"I'm not listening to or believing either one," Barabbas continued. "I don't want to listen to the freedom caucus anymore either. Listening to them is what landed us here."

"No," Abner said. "What got us here was thinking we could just walk into Jerusalem through the gate in broad daylight, and not get arrested!"

"They accused us of the crimes we committed under the voice of the caucus, right? I'm not saying it's fair, but in their eyes, even if I've changed, I am still guilty."

"We should never have trusted that little runt!" Abner said as he shook his head.

Barabbas nodded. "He is a bit odd. But there's a new voice in the wind now, Abner, one that speaks of a hope and a future; one that offers us something different."

"And how's it going to be different for us, if we're rotting in this cell, or some Roman prison—or one of their copper mines."

Joseph sat up. "Grow up, Abner! You saw the angel—you saw Jesus confront Pilate—you've watched Jesus play to the crowds for several years. He's had much larger impact on all this than we ever had skulking around and provoking the Romans."

Abner fell silent. He looked down and picked at the dirt between the stones on the floor with a splinter from the straw mats they had slept on.

A hiss near the door interrupted the pause. Jesus materialized and landed squarely on top of the tin plates from the meager breakfast. The plates clashed together as Jesus deftly stepped to the side. Joseph laughed briefly, then all three of them jumped to their feet.

Jesus smiled. "Always a bit risky appearing like that." He bent over and stacked the plates and the spoons neatly by the door. "What are you talking about?" He brushed off his hands and looked up.

Barabbas waited to see if Abner would speak—the one with the greater complaint should confess it. Barabbas stared at Abner and waved as if to say, *your turn.*

Abner scowled and shook his head.

"We wish we had alternatives to this cell," Joseph confessed.

Jesus nodded as he looked into each of their eyes. "Well, don't let me interrupt." He looked down at the floor, found a suitable spot to sit, brushed it to clear away some of the dirt and sat.

Barabbas didn't know what to say.

"Will you join me? You can stand if you prefer, but I always find sitting is a nicer way to talk."

Joseph looked at Abner then Barabbas, then stooped to sit facing Jesus, a pace and a half away. With the size of the circle defined, Barabbas sat down. He looked up at Abner, who grudgingly sat down opposite him.

"Now, where were we?" Jesus said as he spread his hands in front of him. As they separated, a cloth napkin appeared on the floor with a small loaf of hot bread and four earthenware tumblers. "I am sure the prison food was adequate, but why settle for adequate?"

He took the loaf and broke it, handing a portion of it to each of them, then handed each one a cup. "Bread for the stomach, and wine to gladden the heart! Whenever you are together, do this to remember me."

They ate in silence. When they had drunk the wine and set down the tumblers, Jesus put them all in the center of the napkin, and folded it neatly over the top.

"The guards will love this!" Jesus smiled as he looked up at Abner. "Abner my friend, is this place so odious that you can't have even a bit of hope?"

Abner stared at the napkin.

"You have not even begun suffering as you will later if you choose to wear my name—if you choose to walk the path in my kingdom."

Abner shuddered.

"But that path is the path to eternal life. I am the only one who knows the way, and if you follow, I'll lead you there. All the others, the Romans you hate so much, the priests, the teachers of Israel, the caucus—they all walk on faulted paths. Their paths have a semblance of rightness as all the mankind has fashioned rightness, but they are illusions. They, too, will suffer in many of the same ways because they are part of this fallen world, but their suffering will be in vain, because their paths lead only to darkness."

Jesus paused. He gazed expectantly at Abner.

Abner sensed the pause and looked up. "What□"

"You will suffer no matter what you do, Abner. The mankind will see to that. Even good deeds fail to go unpunished." A faint smile flickered in Jesus's eyes.

"I believe that we can find contentment," Abner said, "but there are other ways to do that."

"Are you content now? You are almost forty two—have you ever been content?"

Abner pursed his lips then shook his head. "Not really—not yet."

Jesus's eyes grew soft. "Open your eyes, Abner!" he whispered. "Contentment and peace won't be found by pursuing them. They'll be found when you pursue righteousness, first with Elohim, but then with others here on this earth. You must set a priority on seeking the kingdom that is not of the earth, where no thief can break in and steal. The kingdoms of the earth fight and quarrel; they seek to destroy each other in war, rebellion, fear, retaliation, and an insatiable lust for power. You have tasted the bitter fruits of those kingdoms—even an apparent victory is bitter."

Abner fidgeted with the piece of straw.

"Follow me, Abner. It's as simple as that."

Jesus vanished with a hiss, leaving nothing behind but the tumblers and a few stray breadcrumbs.

Before any of them had formulated a thought into words, a key grated in the lock of the heavy cell door. Two guards entered. One of them stopped to gather up the plates. The other glanced at them and his eyes immediately fell to space between them. "What is this?" he said as he grabbed the napkin. The tumblers fell onto the stone floor. One of them broke in half.

"Where did you get this?" He demanded as he sniffed one of the cups. "Wine? How did you get this?"

Barabbas wasn't sure how to best respond. Joseph was looking at the floor, as if he were trying to ignore the intrusion.

"A friend dropped in with some bread and this wine," Abner said quietly. "A nice finish to breakfast. He left just as you were unlocking the door."

Chapter Twenty-Seven

CONFRONTATION

"One man standing in the way is worth a thousand who stand and watch."

Vindorian Proverb

Matthias sat opposite Jesus at the small, round table. A square plate of figs and grapes sat untouched on the table between them, as they both nursed mugs of cold water sweetened with honey.

"There is a lot more to be said about the future," Jesus said. "I'll be here for a while longer, but for now, there are still details to be worked out." He smiled. "What are your plans?"

"For the next few days? Or—the rest of my life?" Matthias hadn't really thought about it. The last several years had been so frenetic on the road with Jesus's entourage that he had never anticipated a time when he wouldn't be surrounded by that busy-ness. Now everyone was a bit unsure. Jesus came and went like a ghost and Matthias missed the steadiness of his presence.

Right now, Jesus sat across from him—very real and present. They had hugged when they met and all the illusion of Jesus as a ghost had vanished in that instant. The private audience was something he needed.

"The next few days," Jesus explained, "will continue to be surprising, because you, and the rest of the followers are not quite ready."

"Ready for what?"

"Ready for the rest of your life with me, Matthias."

"But you said you were going away!"

"I will, but I'll be with you. I told you all I'll send another to be with you, when I go away. He'll be in you, and will comfort and guide you. You must learn to listen to him as you listened to me, and to know that whenever you meet together, I'll be in your midst."

Matthias shook his head.

"Hard to grasp?" The master asked.

Matthias nodded.

"When it happens, you'll understand."

"I guess."

"There's no guessing. Your faith will not be secure if you're guessing."

Matthias looked up over the rim of his mug as he sipped. Jesus's eyes bore into him. He lowered his mug. "I have faith, Jesus. I wouldn't be here if I didn't. Help me where I lack it."

"That's why I'm here, Matthias," Jesus said as he reached across the table and took Matthias's hand. "We still have a few more days."

"How many is a few?"

"It's not for you to know these things, but stay with the others until the fire of my kingdom is ignited. Then new and wondrous things will unfold before you and..."

"Master!" Two shadows swept in over the table.

Matthias knew his private conversation was over.

Jesus stood up and hugged Thomas. Matthias struggled to his feet to embrace the strange little newcomer. "Sit with us, my friends," Jesus offered as he reached for a chair. Mael grabbed another chair from the next table and pulled it up.

"Been to see Pilate?" Jesus asked seriously.

Mael nodded.

"And?"

"He is hardened."

"What're you guys talking about?" Matthias asked.

Thomas explained the situation briefly between the four grapes he had taken from the plate.

Matthias looked at Jesus. "Do you think Barabbas has changed—really?"

"All of you will face this many times, friends," Jesus said. "You'll have to trust before you know. What if Barabbas hasn't changed? Suppose his behavior is a ruse? Should you treat him any differently? If you treat people according to your guesses, rather than in the uncommon love of compassion, respect and trust, then you'll be no different than the rest of the world."

"Pilate will release him," Mael announced suddenly, as if he hadn't heard the rest of the conversation. "But not today!"

"How do you know?" Matthias asked.

Mael stared straight into his eyes. "He's hard, but he'll be broken."

Matthias glanced at Jesus, who stared at Mael.

A commotion on the street interrupted the brief silence. Mael jumped up and ran from the table, dodging through the crowds. Jesus stood up and started moving after Mael. Matthias followed with Thomas close behind.

When they reached the place of the disturbance, the crowd parted to the sides of the street. Mael stood alone in the middle of the street with his hands up in front of him as if he were holding back the ocean tide. A chariot with two magnificent white horses stamped and snorted impatiently before him.

The charioteer flicked the reigns, but the horses seemed held back by the will of this deformed little man. A Roman official riding in the chariot rose behind the charioteer, to see what was holding him up. The crowd hushed.

Matthias gasped. "Pilate!" he muttered. He glanced at Jesus. Jesus stared calmly at Mael.

"What is the meaning of this□" Pilate said.

"You must release Barabbas!" Mael's commanding voice rose above the crowd."

"Run him over!" Pilate shouted.

Mael stood his ground. Both hands were out in front of him. The horses stamped, but didn't move.

Pilate's face turned purple with rage. "Run him over!"

"You must release Barabbas!" Mael said again.

Four soldiers marched up beside the horses.

The murmur of the crowd rose. "Barabbas? They have Barabbas?" It was soft, but it spread like fire driven by the wind.

Someone shouted "Free Barabbas!"

Mael looked at Jesus. Jesus stared back without emotion.

Mael dropped his hands and looked down.

Pilate sat down. The horses charged forward as the soldiers pushed the crowd back from the chariot.

Matthias didn't see exactly what happened, but the chariot swept forward with the horses. There was no way for Mael to avoid trampling.

"Free Barabbas! Free Barabbas!" the crowd chanted. More soldiers ran forward to protect the chariot.

The crowd closed in around the back of the chariot as it moved up the street. Matthias watched Thomas push through the crowds toward the spot where Mael would have been. Matthias struggled to follow.

"Free Barabbas! Free Barabbas!"

Matthias was right behind Thomas when they found Mael. He was face down on the cobblestones with his hands over his head. The crowd stared.

Thomas shoved them aside, knelt down beside Mael and rolled him over. Mael sat up and started brushing off his cloak. "I'm alright."

"You could have been killed!" Thomas exploded with anger.

Mael stood up. "Thomas!"

Thomas stopped and the crowd stilled.

"These are trained war horses, Thomas. They won't trample a man. The chariot is not low enough to harm one on the ground and its wheels are two paces apart."

"You're a fool!"

Mael looked up into Thomas's eyes. "That was Pilate's third warning," Mael said calmly. "Where is the master?"

Matthias looked quickly about the crowd. "I don't see him."

"We need to go!" Mael said quietly.

"Free Barabbas! Free Barabbas!"

Caiaphas frowned as he stood in a circle of his closest advisors outside the temple. "This may be an opportunity. We didn't start this one."

"Should we arrest the little one again?" Asher, the captain of the temple guard seemed eager for the task

"Mael? No. If he has turned into a rabble-rouser, let him continue. If the Romans want to deal with it, let them. This spat is between him and Pilate, right?"

"It always comes back to us, Caiaphas, you know that," Gamaliel interjected. "We always get blamed for the behavior of the crowds, regardless of our involvement."

"Perhaps I should talk to Pilate," said Caiaphas. "If we advocate to keep Barabbas in prison, then any public backlash will not be seen as incited by us. The followers of Jesus can be blamed."

"There *are* indications that Jesus's movement is not dying as we thought it would after his death," Gamaliel said. "We need to be cautious, but then, if Barabbas is let out, it might be more trouble than we anticipate."

"We had him let out before and he wasn't causing trouble," Caiaphas observed.

"Actually, High Priest," Asher continued, "we had him followed. He went back to the caucus. He laid low, but we think he was planning something. We know he was up on the Emmaus road causing trouble there."

"One would think that prison would've taught him something." Caiaphas shook his head.

"It seldom does, High Priest," Asher said.

Caiaphas looked around the group. "I'm open to suggestions."

"Pilate will listen to you if he thinks you're taking his side in all this." Ephraim Ben David was a small man, but well regarded for his wisdom in difficult situations. "He knows he needs your support to govern this city. The people today were agitated when they discovered that Barabbas had been imprisoned again.

"I was in the market this morning and I saw Pilate's face. He was terrified when the crowds started chanting. Perhaps you should talk to Barabbas first and then Pilate. If Barabbas agrees to cooperate with you, Pilate can release him and quell the unrest."

"You have a visitor, Barabbas." The guard pulled open the heavy cell door.

Barabbas stood up, shuddering off the stiffness of the cold floor and brushing the dust off his cloak as he straightened it. When he looked up Caiaphas stood in the doorway with two armed temple guards behind him.

"May we come in?"

Abner and Joseph scrambled to their feet.

Barabbas shrugged. "Do I have a choice?"

"If you want us to leave, we will, but perhaps you would do well to listen to our offer first."

"Have you come to offer us a way out of this cell?"

Caiaphas glanced at the other two men. "I have an offer for you."

"I won't leave without my friends. They've done less than I ever have and any deal that leaves them here would have to be predicated on false motives."

"My, My, such altruism."

Barabbas decided not to react. "What is your offer, High Priest?"

"Well, this morning there was a bit of a confrontation not far from here."

"Confrontation?"

"There is this little imposter of the Nazarene..."

"Mael?"

"You know him￭" Caiaphas looked up into Barabbas's eyes.

Barabbas nodded. "We're getting to know him."

Caiaphas studied him for a moment as he weighed his words. "He confronted Pilate publicly to have you set free," he said.

Barabbas looked back and forth between Joseph and Abner. "He's the reason that we're here, High Priest."

The priest raised his eyebrows. Barabbas told him the story of their encounter on the road from Emmaus, the arrest at the gate and the audience with Pilate.

"And why isn't the little one in here with you now? He was arrested with you, right?"

Barabbas nodded. "But he vanished with Jesus when Pilate sentenced us."

"Jesus?" Caiaphas took a step back. "The Nazarene?" His face darkened.

Barabbas nodded. "Yes, *that* Jesus," he said flatly. "He showed up as Pilate questioned us. Pilate was surprised, but angry, and put us all in here."

"Have you told anyone else you saw him?"

"Who? Mael?"

Caiaphas scowled. "Jesus!"

"We've been in this cell since that moment. No visitors until you."

Joseph shifted on his feet. "He showed up here briefly also."

Caiaphas turned to face him. "Who?"

"Jesus! He brought us some fresh bread and wine."

Caiaphas's face turned white then flushed with anger. "What is happening here￭" He scanned the faces of the three of them, his eyes darting back and forth quickly between them. "Have you become his followers?"

Barabbas spoke first. "We thought we'd give it a try. The way we were living before has been hard, and hasn't worked out as well as we thought."

"Tell him about the angel," Abner said.

Caiaphas's eyes darted to Abner.

"An angel showed up shortly after we arrived here," Abner continued. "He told us not to be afraid—easier said than done if you've ever been a Roman prisoner."

Caiaphas remained silent.

"We were brought here on no charges," Barabbas said. "Pilate just wanted us for crimes of the past. My goal is to change. If suffering in this cell is the price of change, then let it be so."

"May you rot in this cell," Caiaphas snarled. "I came here hoping I could go to Pilate to convince him to let you go; that you would cooperate with us, and cease your opposition to the Romans."

"We've decided to no longer oppose Rome, and we have done nothing that should keep you from continuing with that plan." Barabbas said, "But you never finished your explanation of the confrontation that brought you here."

Caiaphas paused as if he were unsure whether to finish the story. "The little one—"

"—Mael," Barabbas prompted.

"Yes, him." Caiaphas's eyes darkened. "He confronted Pilate publicly on your behalf." Caiaphas explained what had happened. "When the crowd discovered you have been recaptured, they started chanting for your release, but Pilate refused. If you remain here, we fear a rebellion."

"And you fear that you would be blamed for it?"

"We don't need trouble like this right now, Barabbas."

"I would be no trouble, Caiaphas. My intent is to stay out of trouble, but I cannot control the crowds any better than you—or Pilate."

"I'll see what I can do," Caiaphas said.

There were many things Pilate would rather do than meet once more with the High Priest on the portico. The sun burned the air and baked the stones of the plaza, making the meeting into an inferno. He wanted to get back to Caesarea, away from the heat and stench of this city, or at least go into his inner chambers, where it would be darker and cool.

"What did he tell you?"

"He would rather not be in prison, of course," Caiaphas explained.

"And?"

"Well, we have to be careful."

"We?" Pilate tried to inject disdain for the implication they were in league with one another. It had never worked out well.

"The decision to release Barabbas would not be good for either of us."

"What?" Pilate scowled. "I thought you wanted him free."

"We would rather have him free than the Nazarene, but that one is dead now, and it's probably just as well to keep Barabbas confined. He's leaning into the cause of the blasphemer as we speak."

"You heard about the confrontation in the street this morning, Caiaphas?"

"Yes, Prefect. Ephraim was there and told us what happened."

"My wife had another dream last night; that the Jews would rebel if I did not let Barabbas go; that Romans soldiers would die."

"If you let him go, he may *inspire* the rebellion."

Pilate's face betrayed his feeling of being in the middle again. He hated this place. He couldn't win. "Why are you so keenly interested in keeping him in prison? I thought you wanted him free. You certainly did last week."

"The lesser of two evils, Pilate."

"Why does it always come down to that? Do you suppose that we'll ever come to a place, you and I, where the choice is between the greater of two goods?"

Caiaphas hesitated.

"You don't need to answer that, Caiaphas. Just think about it. I have no intention to release Barabbas. He has done far too much damage to me already."

"I think that's best, Pilate."

Pilate watched as the High Priest and his guards retreated to the street in front of the palace. He didn't move. He didn't *want* to move. What could be best about the choice between two bad options?

Chapter Twenty-Eight

FUTURE

Would that I could know the future!
Would I gladly change the present?

Dispath of Tophan

"Where are we now?" Mael's disorientation always lingered after jumps like this.

"Just watch," Ransom said as he dropped Mael's hand.

The huge hall was made mostly of stone, with majestic sweeping arches that soared upward to a ceiling at least twenty paces above them. All around them, tall windows of colored light depicted stylized scenes of men and women, frozen in time, with sad faces that shone in on them from the brightness outside.

In front of them, an older man in a white robe stood before an ornate lectern looking out over a sparse collection of individuals who sat on the stiff benches that filled the hall. They sat as if they might catch some disease if they dared come too close to one another.

"What is he saying?" Mael said.

"Just listen."

The man trundled on and the attendees occasionally mumbled something in response.

Ransom slid into one of the aisles between the benches and sat down, motioning to Mael to join him.

"Can they see us?" Mael whispered.

"Of course!" Ransom leaned in close. "And they can hear us." He winked.

Mael nodded—time to remain quiet. He had a thousand questions.

The man in front droned on, accenting his words with flourishes of his hands and raising his voice with drama to try to make whatever he was saying interesting. Mael couldn't understand a word of it, and the people in the benches didn't seem to care, except to respond every once in while with a mechanistic echo of something the man said.

The man finished with some grand final statement, then bowed his head. He mumbled some more and then with a sudden clarity, finished his words with the statement "In Chaisus name."

When he looked up, everyone on the benches stood up and started filing out of the hall. No one spoke. They nodded to one another occasionally. The man disappeared through a door in the side of the hall and the great room fell deathly silent.

Ransom moved. Mael looked over to see him wiping tears from his eyes with the back of his forehand. "Come with me!" his husky voice rattled with emotion. He took Mael's hand and they passed through the brilliant passage of light to land again in the cool morning shades of the garden.

Ransom sat down on the bench and motioned for Mael to join him as he continued to wipe his eyes. He sniffed deeply as he faced Mael, but remained silent as he stared into his eyes.

"What was that?" Mael asked.

The master dropped his hand. "*That* is what happens when the mankind takes my words, and the words of Mah'Eladra, the words of Yahweh, and turns them into a religion."

Mael looked down. "How long—how far in the future?"

"That was two thousand years, but the seeds of it started very soon after I left. The mankind loves to make rules. It's much easier than thinking—much easier than true devotion. The rules eventually kill the vorn, but people fear to admit that it means almost nothing to them anymore."

"Why did you show me this? This isn't my world."

"This is the mankind, Mael. It will be the same on every world. It will happen on Tessalindria if they don't fight against it."

"If you were not able to make it happen here, how will you make it happen on Tessalindria?"

Mael became suddenly aware of the intensity of Ransom's gaze. "Mael!" Ransom said.

Mael looked up into Ransom's eyes, and just as suddenly, it became clear. He pointed at himself. "Me?"

"Why do you think you are here, Mael?"

"I am Mael, and nothing more," he said defensively.

"Look at me, Mael!"

Mael looked up again. The intense dark eyes bore into him. "You must never say that again, Mael. For a time and half a time, it was appropriate and even right, but it will never be right again.

You must accept that you are Mael and so much more. That is why you are here, do you understand?"

Mael understood. It was new—and sudden—but ever so clear.

Ransom grabbed his hand and they vanished into the light again, emerging onto a small dirty street somewhere in time and space. "Come with me!" Ransom pulled him forward toward some crumbling steps that led down to a door in the side of the towering brick building. "There will always be a few, Mael; a few that will hold to the teachings without wavering, but it will be only a few."

The door opened by itself and they entered a small hall, filled with people sitting on simple wooden chairs that faced one another, with an open space in the middle. Ransom led Mael to a pair of empty seats against one of the walls near the entrance. People nodded and smiled as they sat, but kept their attention riveted to the man in the group who stood reading from a small book. The Tessarandin!

"Are we—?" Mael whispered.

Ransom nodded and held his finger to his lips.

The reader sat down and the room fell silent as people reflected on his admonition. Someone started singing and everyone in the room joined them. It was beautiful.

When the singing ended, they sat in silence again until a woman stood to read another excerpt from her copy of the Tessarandin.

Mael looked around again. The forty people sat in rapt attention, nodding and smiling occasionally. The woman sat down. Several people adjusted themselves in the wooden chairs, and then everyone waited. Mael sat patiently beside Ransom, expecting that someone else would rise to read. No one did.

The door to the hall burst open. Four surly young men strode in, cursing loudly as they looked around at the seated audience. Each carried a short stick in his right hand.

"I have something to read." The leader strode to the center of the assembly. The others with him took up stations facing the audience, pacing back and forth and slapping their sticks into the open palms of their left hands.

Mael looked at Ransom. He remained calm and unmoving.

The young brute in the front pulled a piece of paper out of his back pocket and unfolded it. Then with mock ceremony, started reading.

"I now declare this meeting adjourned," he read, "so that all you yevil Sessashians can get out of here and get back to work. You are pig vomit, staining our cities with your lies. You're not fit to live and your gatherings are like dog urine in our streets. Everyone must leave immediately."

He paused and looked around. "Did you hear what I said?" he snarled as he roved his eyes over the group. No one moved. Mael froze, breathless in the face of the weighted silence that hung over the room.

"Get out, Scum!" the young man yelled.

Silence.

An older man rose slowly in the front row to Mael's left. All eyes turned to him. He paused before he spoke, addressing the young man at the front directly, without fear. "We appreciate your coming here this morning," he said, "but what you read isn't fitting to the purpose of our gathering."

The leader strode over to the old man, shoving one of his cohorts out of the way. "Not fittingп" he yelled. "Do I need to read it again?"

The old man stared him in the eyes. "There's no such need," he said.

The leader's face turned red. He raised his stick and swung it at the old man's head, stopping short of striking him. The old man didn't flinch. Then just as suddenly, the leader slapped the man in the face with his left hand.

The old man recoiled from the blow but turned to face the young aggressor. "My name is Jeshwa," he said, "What's yours?"

The young man slapped him again.

The old man turned back to him and simply said, "What is your name?" his voice filled with deep compassion and gentleness.

The young man raised his stick again and then turned away. "Let's go," he said, "these scum aren't even worth hitting." He started toward the door and the others fell in line behind him. "Except for this one..." He slapped a young woman in the front row. "and this one...and this one." Four others received violent slaps to the sides of their heads.

He was almost to the door when another voice called out, "Wait!" A young man rose in the second row opposite Jeshwa.

The leader froze and turned in exasperation. "For whatⁿ"

"You still haven't told us your name."

The leader strode back toward his new challenger. "Why do you want to know my name, Ashtemba!"

"Will you listen to my full answer?"

The room fell silent. Nothing stirred except the three anxious followers. The leader looked around, his mouth twisted into a sneer. "Maybe," he said.

The man sat down.

"Stand up and speak you coward!" yelled the leader. "What is *your* name?"

The man stood up again and stared steadily into the leader's eyes. "Cordez Kallen," he said.

The leader faltered. He looked around at the passive intense audience. "Let's go." he said again and waved his stick toward the door.

Cordez Kallen spoke. "You come here with your friends and violently enter a private meeting space..."

The leader stopped but didn't turn to face his challenger. His face flushed with rage.

"You then abuse several people you don't know for some reason that *they* don't know—and perhaps *you* don't even know..."

The leader turned to face Cordez.

Cordez continued: "Then, you threaten *us* with accusations
of wrong doing, yet you are too much of a coward to even give
us your name."

Mael guessed the leader had never been in a situation where
his violence had had this effect, and he had no idea how to
handle it. "Why do you want my name?" he raged. He beat his
stick repeatedly into the palm of his left hand.

"We have forgiven you of these offenses, but we want to
bring your name before Mah'Eladra, that they may consider the
same forgiveness."

The stick stopped. Everything stopped. All eyes fixed themselves on the leader as his eyes fell to the floor. This fleeting image burned itself into Mael's memory before the leader
erupted into profanity. "Sesh, Ashtemba. I don't need your yevil
forgiveness!" He whirled toward the door. "C'mon—let's get
outta here." he growled.

They turned toward the door. Just before they left, the
leader lashed out with his club and hit a man in the head who
sat near the door. The congregants stood in unison as the last
of the thugs filed out, uncontested.

Ransom took Mael's hand, and in a flash of light, they were
back in the garden.

"Sessashians?" Mael asked.

Ransom nodded.

"Was he the anthara that we have sought?"

Ransom's face showed a peculiar intensity as Mael once
again looked into his eyes. "Wait!—Me?"

Ransom smiled. "Mael, and something much more!" he said and
vanished with a hiss. Mael sat down heavily on the bench under the
tree, the weight of understanding, pressing him onto the stone so

that he couldn't move. How could this be? How could he be the anthara?

A sudden exhaustion descended on his vorn, like the weight of Tessalindria itself settling over him like a blanket he couldn't resist. He curled up on the bench and collapsed into sleep.

Chapter Twenty-Nine

ARREST

Marcus found Mael in the garden where they arrested Jesus, fast asleep on a bench under an ancient olive tree. It was just as the commander had suggested, but how he knew Mael would be here wasn't clear. Perhaps it was a guess.

He shook the little man gently. No response. "Mael?" He shook him again.

"We could always just carry him," Cassius suggested.

Marcus nodded. "Better if he were awake. Mael?"

The little man stirred and opened his eyes suddenly, then bolted upright.

Marcus grabbed his arm. "It's me, Mael!" He could see the fog of sleep crumbling as Mael looked up into his eyes.

"Marcus?"

Marcus nodded. "And Cassius," he said as he nodded to his friend.

"Why are you here?"

"We came to find you. Pilate ordered that you be arrested."

A bewildered look flooded Mael's face. "Why?"

"It seems your presence is disturbing the crowds."

Mael looked down. "You do not have to hold me, Marcus. I'll come with you."

The mid-morning sun beat down on them as they rode back into Jerusalem. Mael rode behind Marcus on the black stallion he had been given in the fortress. Marcus had expected more resistance, but Mael seemed content to offer no trouble.

"Why does Pilate want to see me?" Mael asked.

"There are rumors of a rebellion that is festering among your people, Mael."

"My people?"

"The Jews."

They rode in silence until Marcus spoke. "The notorious criminal, Barabbas is at the center of the conflict, which I don't completely understand. Apparently, the High Priest thinks he will cause a revolt, which he has tried several times in the past."

"Pilate should free Barabbas," Mael said quietly.

"Why?"

"The people will revolt if he *isn't* freed."

"How do you know?"

"I have told Pilate this, but he is hard with pride and fear."

"You've talked to Pilate?"

"Three times."

"He wants to talk to you again, apparently."

"If he does not relent, he'll be broken."

The certainty of Mael's words gave Marcus chills. They rode on in silence. "Be careful, Mael," he said at length. "Pilate wields the power of Rome in this city. It's not insignificant."

"Pilate has no power that was not given him from Mah'Eladra."

"Who?"

"Yahweh."

"Why doesn't your god free Barabbas himself."

"They don't work that way very often. They're testing Pilate."

"They?"

"Mah'Eladra—Elohim. They are one, and they are many."

Marcus was sure he didn't understand. "Your people—"

"They're *not* my people!"

"What do you mean?"

"I am from another place. I am only here for a short time before I return home."

"Where are you from?"

"Farhantra, across the Vorsian Sea."

"Never heard of it."

Cassius snickered.

"If you are not from here, why are you so involved with the Jewish people. Seems a strange lot with whom you throw in your fate."

"I am here to learn, Marcus. Then I'll go home."

The finality of Mael's tone silenced the whole group. They passed through the gates without further conversation. The guards stared at Mael, but made no move to interfere. At the fortress they stopped. Marcus dismounted and swung Mael down to the ground. "Follow me."

"Mael!" A hoarse whisper floated in through the small grated window of his cell door. Mael sat up. He knew it must be close to midnight.

"Mael!" The urgency increased. He rose and walked to the door. The height of the window prevented him from seeing through it, and there was nothing in the cell to stand on. He put his hands against the locked door. It swung open silently.

He stepped out into the torch-lit hall in the lower level of the fortress.

"Mael! Over here!" He looked up to see Barabbas peering through the grate of the cell opposite his own. He approached the door and it swung open to let him pass. Barabbas stood back in astonishment. The door clicked behind him. Barabbas launched his shoulder into it, crumpling to the ground in pain when it didn't yield.

"How did you do that?" Barabbas asked as he winced over his bruised shoulder.

"I don't know. How did you know I was in that cell?"

"We saw the soldiers bring you in early this afternoon. I waited till now, because I thought perhaps the guards are asleep."

"Are you all alright?" Mael looked back and forth between the astonished faces of Abner and Joseph.

"We're fine," said Joseph. "Frustrated, but fine."

"Frustrated?"

"Being in a prison cell is miserable, in case you haven't noticed," Abner groused.

"What brought you here?" Barabbas said as he stood up, still rubbing his shoulder.

"I got arrested. Then I confronted Pilate on your freedom for the fourth time. He wasn't happy about it. He thinks I am fomenting a rebellion."

"We heard a bit about that," Barabbas smiled.

"Pilate knows it's going to happen—his wife told him about a dream she had." Mael said. "He just doesn't know when, how or who. It certainly isn't me."

"Well, we know less than you," Barabbas chuckled. "At least he can't blame me—us."

"He's *already* blaming you, Barabbas. The crowds now know you are here and they're calling for your release. Pilate is stubborn. He's afraid of you—afraid of the crowds—afraid of the priests, but most of all you, and now me."

Barabbas sat down on the straw mat in the middle of the room where the light of the single lamp in the cell illuminated his face. "He's not afraid of Chaisus? He saw him when he arrested us."

"I'm not sure he completely understood what he saw or maybe he's refusing to believe. I think the Ermans have no way to think about someone rising from the dead."

"What are we supposed to do?"

"How much do you know about the teaching of the master, Barabbas?" Mael looked at all three of them in turn.

Barabbas shook his head. "Not much. Some we have heard, but mostly what we have seen in those who follow—like you. It's clear that we need to know more."

"I've only been here a few days," Mael continued, "but what I have seen says the same to me. Where I come from, there are teachings that are very similar, but I have never seen anyone live them out the way the master does, from the stories I have heard. What he teaches is what I learned growing up, but here is it real—it's raw and undamaged by the mankind."

Barabbas nodded. Abner stretched. Joseph looked at the floor. Mael was about to continue ...

"Teach them to Pray."

The voice startled him. He glanced up.

Barabbas followed his eyes to the corner of the room where it met the ceiling. "What?"

Mael looked back down. "It might seem that the time here, imprisoned by the Ermans is wasted time, but while you are waiting, you can use the time for prayer."

Abner shook his head and he stared at the floor in disgust. Barabbas looked up into Mael's eyes. "Never been much of a praying man. I wouldn't know where to start."

"Tell us more," Joseph said softly.

A sudden wave of energy surged through Mael, like a wind that swept up from his feet and spiraled up around him, finally engulfing his head and vanishing into the air above him. Visions and teachings flashed through his mind. He shuddered and it was gone. He opened his eyes.

"Mael?" Barabbas reached out and grabbed his hand. "Are you alright?"

Mael looked back into his eyes. "Yes," he muttered, "The El of Mah'Eladra."

"You looked like you had seen a ghost—a spirit!"

Suddenly, his mind overflowed with what he needed to teach the men who sat before him. He opened his mouth and began to teach them all the master had taught about prayer.

Thomas sat in the small circle as they listened to Jesus. Peter, James, John, Matthias, Andrew and Bartholomew were all there in the clearing nestled against the base of the temple wall under the bridge to the western gate.

"Where is Mael?" Thomas asked.

"Mael is in jail because he confronted Pilate again," Jesus said.

The brothers looked around at each other.

"This is the way it is in my kingdom, brothers. The war you wage will be in battles against the authorities of this world who seek to suppress the truth about Yahweh. It is not physical war, but a war over the hearts of men, and these authorities have no power over you, nor the kingdom that we are teaching.

"This is different than any image you have of warfare," Jesus said. "This kingdom will conquer all the others by the loving hand of Yahweh, even as you are imprisoned for it. You will go out among the people, without means to support or defend yourself, but in each city where you tread, those who have been called will give you what you need, and Yahweh will defend you."

They sat cross-legged on the grass. Jesus leaned back on the wall. Andrew stirred and looked up. "There's something I don't understand about the swords—in the garden."

Jesus nodded. "Ask, Andrew—always ask."

"That night, before we went to the garden—when you were betrayed, you charged us to buy swords."

Jesus's face turned grave. He nodded.

"Well," Andrew continued as he looked around at the group. "When Peter said we had two, you said it was enough." The others nodded. Thomas knew what the question was. It had been on all their minds. "What did you mean, two was enough? Enough for what?"

"The swords had a purpose, Andrew." Jesus's voice was gentle, like a father explaining to a child.

"But what was the purpose?" Bartholomew interrupted. "When Peter actually used his, you rebuked him—and then you healed the man he injured."

Jesus nodded and pursed his lips. He looked into the eyes of each man in the group before answering. The compassion of the master bore into them through his eyes.

"There is a prophecy about the purpose of my death in the book of the great prophet. Every detail of that prophecy had to be fulfilled as a testimony to the children of the law, that I am the one that it speaks of. Does this make sense?"

Everyone nodded.

"In that writing, Isaiah noted that the man of prophecy would be identified with the transgressors." Jesus looked around again. "We've been accused of many things by the priests and the teachers of the law.

"In their eyes we have broken their laws of Shabbat, we have eaten with those they would declare unclean; we have not observed several of their numerous ceremonial cleansings. We have rescued the victims of their self-righteous judgment and defended the poor and the weak as well as accepting the prostitutes and sinners without participating in their sin.

"They know that these actions are truly righteous and have found no basis for my arrest in their laws. Their fear overcame their reserve when I raised Lazarus from four days in the tomb and they plotted to arrest me. The swords were props so that they could charge me with insurrection against the leaders of the people."

"But you let me use it!" Peter blurted out. "Why didn't you tell us?"

Jesus looked at him. "Peter!"

Peter looked up through the tears in his eyes.

Jesus reached over and took Peter's hand. "In the end, no one was hurt, but the fulfillment of this prophecy helped complete the fullness of the text."

Jesus stared into the eyes of each man in turn. "You have each seen the fulfillment of many prophecies concerning me, and you will be great in the kingdom of Elohim. Sometimes you won't understand and there will be more prophecy for which you will be the completion, but it is by this faith that you will be saved.

"If you had known the purpose beforehand, you may not have fulfilled the prophecy. This is the way it often will be. Now that you know, you must understand that no sword has a place in my kingdom. You will suffer by the swords of others, even to death, but as I spoke to you before, you must love your enemies with the uncommon love and pray for those who persecute you, that you may continue to be sons of Yahweh. You must not retaliate, but leave room for Yahweh's wrath. He will bring all things to light and justify those who live by this faith."

Jesus paused.

Andrew looked down as he spoke. "This is another hard teaching."

"Many will reject me, and you, on account of this, but many who are called will join you. They will die in the hands of the unrighteous, but will live in fullness because of it. Many will claim to follow me, but by their lives, they will reject me, for salvation is not in the claim, but in obedience to my word. This is how each of you and all the others will show your uncommon love to me, by obeying my words and loving all others as I have loved you."

The brothers looked from one to another. Thomas's own thoughts contained a mixture of fear and challenge, stirred together into determination that they would go out into the world with strength. The world would change around them, as it always did around Jesus.

Thomas had another question, one he was sure others had pondered. "What role does Mael have in all this? He's only recently joined us. Will you send him out with us?"

Jesus smiled. "Mael will be sent out like each of you, to different places. Do not trouble yourselves over what each of the others will be called to do. Just as you have had different roles in my kingdom, so it is with Mael. Where he is going you cannot go. You will never see him again nor remember his journey among us."

"I will never forget him," Thomas said. He looked around at the other brothers, who nodded.

A slight hiss called his eyes back to the place where Jesus had been sitting. He'd vanished, as he always did after sessions like this.

Chapter Thirty

INSURRECTION

"The stars tell us we are alive, but not how to live."

On Beings
Mortag of Horrinaine

"Do you believe in what they say about the stars, Claudius?" Marcus asked. He didn't know Claudius well, except that he was a decorated soldier who had fought in Asia Minor before his assignment to this post in Palestine.

"What about them?"

"Well, that they tell us how our lives will develop—if you know how to read them."

"Never thought much about it."

"Look at them, Claudius."

Claudius looked up.

"We seldom see them this bright, without the moon—or perhaps it's just that we never bother to look."

Claudius grunted. "Or maybe you're never up this late."

Marcus nodded. "Haven't been on a midnight watch for a long time, not since I've been here."

"They're very quiet." Claudius's voice hushed as he said it.

"Do you suppose that the gods put them about deliberately, the patterns I mean, so that we would see them a certain way?"

Claudius shook his head. "I've never thought much about the gods, honestly. Always seemed to me that if they were really gods, they would be a lot different."

"Different? In what way."

"Well, they argue a lot—and fight with each other—more like men than gods. They are just more powerful, so their fights are nastier."

Marcus pursed his lips and nodded. "Never thought about it that way."

They fell silent as they stared upward. The cool quiet of midnight offered them a sense of retreat. Ordinarily, these streets teemed with people, all of whom had some agenda that was typically not the agenda of Rome. The stars had no agenda. They just were.

"Do you know much about the Hebrew god?" Marcus asked.

"Not really, but if he is being exampled by the Hebrews, I'm not interested."

"Not even curious?"

"Not even curious."

"We are occupying their land—they consider us infidels," Marcus continued. "It's likely that what we see is jaded by their disdain for us."

"Yeah, well what god would teach them such disdain? They think themselves so much better, but they are as ruthless as they think us to be."

Marcus pondered that for a moment. "Do you consider yourself ruthless, Claudius?"

"Me? Not really. I'm a soldier. I swore allegiance to Rome, so I obey my commander. To some that makes me ruthless."

"You have a family?"

"Never had the time—yet. And you?"

"Wife and two young ones," Marcus said. "Boy six—girl three and a half."

"You miss them?"

"Of course. This should be my last tour, and I will retire to the family vineyard."

"Where are they?"

"Just north of Rome."

"Where you—"

A shriek ripped the air not five paces away and suddenly the steps of the fortress were swarming with men in black tunics and head scarves. Marcus reached for his sword, but three men bowled him over by before he got it out of his sheath.

They shouted in Aramaic; meaningless phrases laced with hate and anger.

Claudius managed to strike the gong before he disappeared from view under a wave of black cloth and muscle.

"Roman Pig," someone muttered. The first knife found its way between Marcus's ribs under his armor. He tried to shout but someone punched his face so hard the words never emerged.

Another knife slashed his thigh. A dagger plunged into his shoulder. His adrenalin surged, but they pressed him to the ground, helplessly outnumbered. Someone kicked his head. He couldn't see. His own weapons were out of reach as angry hands pinned him to the stone pavers.

"Free Barabbas!" The shout echoed from twenty voices all around.

Where were the other soldiers? They should be here by now.

More knives found their way between the plates of his armor. It hurt, everything hurt. They slashed his arms and legs. Everywhere there were knives and grunts and curses.

He could taste his blood and the pain. The pain ...

Shouts rang out in the darkness—Roman voices!

The black creatures loosed their grips and started yelling in panic. Marcus couldn't see. He couldn't move. Consciousness receded from him in waves with short periods of utter darkness.

"Marcus! Marcus!" Someone held his head. "Marcus!" The voice was distant and urgent. "Marcus!" it echoed. "Wake up!"

He knew the voice, but could not remember...darkness...he tried to speak but all he could taste was blood...darkness .... He couldn't breathe ... darkness .... "Marcus" ... darkness ...."Irenia". He could not be sure if he said it or just imagined his wife ... darkness ....

Pilate sat on the chair, numb to what transpired around him except for the two guards that escorted the little man up the stairs in front of him. He hadn't asked for this post in Jerusalem. It was more like a death sentence than the duty of a Roman prefect.

He had sent to the prison to have one final talk with the foreigner. The little man stopped three paces in front of him, with the soldiers towering above him, holding him by his upper arms like a child's rag doll.

"What do you know of this?" Pilate tried to suppress the anger that swarmed his emotions, as it leaked out into his voice.

"I know nothing of it, Prefect. I have been in your prison the last two days."

"Your name is Mael, is it not?"

"It's Mael, yes."

"It's not a Jewish name."

"I am not from here." Mael's face showed no hint of any emotion that may have belied his thoughts.

Pilate waved to the guards and they released the prisoner's arms. Mael shrugged his cloak back into place on his shoulders.

"Where are you from, Mael?"

"I am from Farhantra, on the western side of the Vorsian Sea. It's far from here."

"I've never heard of it." The small talk lifted Pilate's spirit. It was refreshing to talk to someone who was not Roman or Jewish, although Mael seemed to be at the vortex of all of the trouble. "Will you join me inside?"

Pilate glanced up at the soldiers who looked puzzled. He knew that they would have already searched Mael for weapons. All Mael had on was his sandals and a simple cloak and he was too small to be of any physical threat.

"I'll go with you wherever you feel comfortable," Mael said.

Pilate hesitated for a moment as he pondered the complete lack of fear in Mael's demeanor. "Come then, have you had anything to eat?"

"I dined at the prison."

Pilate turned and moved through the large double door off the portico into the main hall. "Bring us some fruit and wine," he said to one of the men standing by the door.

"Why did you come to Jerusalem, Mael?" he asked as they passed into the dining room. He sat down at the head of the table and offered Mael a seat to his right, with a flourish of his hand. One of the soldiers pulled out the chair, and Mael sat down stiffly.

"I came here to learn."

"To learn? To learn what? How to stir up the people in revolt?"

"No."

"What then? Tell me." Pilate didn't like the mockery that crept around the corners of his words, but his anger wouldn't let him remain calm.

"I was brought here to learn from the master, so I can take his teachings back to my people."

"The master?"

"The one you call Jesus—the prophet."

Pilate startled at the frankness of Mael's answers. No one else used Jesus's name without trepidation, anger or as a joke.

"When I have learned enough, I'll go back to my people and trouble you no more."

"Jesus is dead, Mael, why don't you go back now."

Two servants appeared and laid out several plates of fresh pomegranates surrounded by dates and figs and small biscuits of sweet flatbread, with two crystal chalices half-filled with deep red wine.

"Please, help yourself." Pilate waved his hand over the fare.

Mael hesitated.

Pilate took a date and one of the biscuits and placed it on the small plate that had been set in front of him. Mael took a fig and did the same.

"I'll stay here to learn until the master returns to the deep sky."

"What are you saying?" Pilate leaned forward.

"The master came back from the dead, and is in this city, as he continues to teach his followers."

Pilate shuddered.

Mael looked up into his eyes. "You know this is true. He appeared before you—you saw him."

"Whatever it was that I saw, it didn't look like him."

Mael reached for the fig on his plate and then hesitated before turning back to look in Pilate's eyes. "Before his death, the master had been hurt by living in this world. Abused by many. The lash of your soldiers abused him further. In his resurrection, he was restored to the form which he would have had, had it not been for the cruelty of this fallen place."

"The soldiers did their job." Pilate said.

"We hold nothing against the soldiers, nor the priests who schemed to have him killed—nor you for assigning him to scourging and mockery. That is not the way of the master. They fulfilled their role in the prophecies. He has nothing but compassion for them and he is teaching his followers the same."

"Then why did they rise up last night?" Pilate snarled. "Seven of my soldiers died. Then nearly twenty-five of your people were killed before they retreated."

"Those who rebelled, Pilate, who rose up against your authority and power, are not my people, even if you consider my people to be those who follow the master."

Pilate settled back into his chair. "All Jews hate the Romans."

"If that were ever true, it is no longer."

Pilate shook his head. He was about to speak when he noticed Mael staring up over his shoulder. Pilate followed his eyes that looked into the distance beyond the eastern wall of the hall. When he looked back, Mael was staring at *him*.

"The master came to change the world. That will happen when people change, Prefect."

"This situation is beyond change," Pilate said.

"The change in the master's message is different; it starts in the person, from the inside. His message is to shun violence and to embrace an uncommon love for all others without judgment, regardless of their heritage—or history. This uncommon love is extended to the Romans as well or to anyone who would persecute the followers.

"How can someone love an enemy? Or someone who would harm them?"

"It's a decision." Mael's eyes never broke contact with him while he spoke.

"You can't just decide to love like that!"

"That is what makes it uncommon. It *is* a decision. It's a commitment to decide that over and over again—in every situation."

Pilate took a swallow of his wine. Mael took the fig off his plate and nibbled on it.

"Do you not drink wine?" Pilate asked. "This is good Roman wine, from Sicily."

"Not this morning. This fruit is enough. What do you call it?"

"That's a fig."

"It's very sweet."

Pilate nodded.

"So, Mael—what do you suggest I do about the massacre last night? Seven good men lost their lives at the hands of that rebellious mob."

"Why do you call them good?"

Pilate hesitated, stunned by the question. "They were Roman soldiers. Some of them had wives and children."

"That makes them good?"

Pilate was about to speak when Mael continued. "Those who rose up against you—they also had wives and children, are they not good? Have you heard the expression 'an eye for an eye, and a tooth for a tooth'?"

"A Jewish expression?"

"I don't know," Mael confessed, "but the master added some clarification."

Pilate raised his eyebrows and looked back at the little man.

"An eye for an eye, a tooth for a tooth and the whole world goes blind and hungry."

Pilate shook his head. "What should I do about my seven soldiers?"

"What should Jerusalem do about its twenty-five?"

Pilate's anger flared. He stood up, pushing his chair back violently, but before he could speak Mael said. "Forgive them all."

"Whatᵒ"

"Forgive them without condition."

"That's nonsense! They will perceive it as weakness."

"Some will perceive it as courage—with strength. Someone has to stop poking out eyes and smashing teeth."

"We will lose control of the city."

"It's not yours to control, Prefect."

"Guards!" Pilate shouted. Two guards ran into the room. He waved his hand to have Mael taken out.

Mael stood his ground. As the guards reached to grab him, he said, "Free Barabbas, Prefect." The guards froze. "He had no part in this rebellion and he is joining with those who follow the master. Offer this olive branch and start the healing process."

Everything moved slowly. Pilate couldn't force his attention away from the stare of this little man who challenged him.

"Forgive without condition," Mael said. "Ask for forgiveness without condition. Peacemakers who sow in peace, reap a harvest of righteousness."

Pilate watched Mael stand up, knowing he was powerless to control the situation. Mael raised both hands in front of him. The purple scars from wounds to his hands became visible for the first time. Pilate winced. All he could see in the little man was the visage of the Nazarene.

"Your Roman kingdom is shaking and will fail, Prefect. The kingdom of the master will live forever and never be shaken."

Pilate watched helplessly as Mael turned and walked between the two guards toward the door. His anger wrapped itself around some unknown truth that seemed just beyond his grasp. He wanted to shout and he wanted to cry, but most of all, he just wanted to *not* be in Palestine.

He sat down heavily in his chair and retrieved his half-empty flagon. He knew the guards were waiting to be told what to do. He drained his wine and looked up. "Let the prisoner, Barabbas, go." He said.

"Prefect?"

"I said, let Barabbas and those with him, go!"

"And the little one?"

"He is nothing."

Chapter Thirty-One

NEWS

"Gather together often, because community is of utmost importance."

Jesus of Nazareth

A palpable tension greeted Thomas as he entered the room. News of the killings traveled fast and Peter had called the meeting for everyone to be there.

Thomas entered last and Peter gave him the usual bear hug. "Glad you could make it." The slight chiding might have offended him if anyone else had done so. John closed the door behind him and locked it.

"Took me a while to find it, after I heard," Thomas offered back. "Could you have made the directions a bit more obscure?"

Bartholomew chuckled. "Can't be too careful these days."

"I suppose not," Thomas admitted. He took his seat on the floor. The second floor room, in the southern tip of the old city, near the water gate, had only one window that looked out over the wall into the Kidron Valley. The sun filtered through the window casting its long beams against the far wall. "How did you find it?"

"Belongs to a nephew of one of the sisters—not quite ready to join yet, but a sympathizer." Peter smiled.

"What do we know about all this?" Matthias asked.

Thomas glanced at each face around the room as Peter started. "It happened at midnight, or very close to it. A group of armed men attacked the guards at the fortress simultaneously. They killed several before the alarm sounded. The garrison responded in force and killed in return, but many more. We don't know the numbers."

"Were any of the brothers involved?" James asked. Thomas was still getting used to the appellations of brother and sister in their fledgling group.

"We don't know for sure," Peter replied. "We would have heard by now if they had. We're thankful for that. It wouldn't be in keeping with the master's teaching."

"We have several," Simon offered, "whose background might tempt them to be back in league with the Caucus."

"We don't even know if the Caucus was responsible," Peter said. "The rumor mill has been quiet."

"I'm sure that—" An urgent knock on the door arrested Peter's response. Everyone looked at each other. A wave of fear rippled through the faces.

The knock came again. The rhythmic pattern that all had agreed to: two knocks, a pause, two knocks, and a pause closed out with three rapid knocks.

John rose and glanced around the room. Peter nodded. John released the bolt on the door and it swung into the room.

Mael stood where the door had been with three others that Thomas didn't recognize.

"May we join you?" Mael strode through the door, beckoning the more hesitant trio to follow.

John closed the door behind them. Mael looked around the room. "I thought we might find the master here," he said.

"Not yet," Peter forced a smile. "Good to see you Mael, last we heard you were in prison."

Mael nodded.

"Who are your friends?"

Mael turned and waved to each man in turn. "This is Barabbas—*the* Barabbas—Abner and Joseph." They nodded as Mael introduced them. "They were prisoners with me, but we were freed this morning. May we sit down?"

Peter waved to the floor in the middle of the room. "Any seat you like."

They sat down awkwardly.

"How did you find us?" Peter asked.

Mael smiled. "I was told where to find you."

The master materialized with a hiss in front of him as Peter opened his mouth to respond.

Barabbas scrambled to his feet, followed quickly by Abner and Joseph. Jesus turned. "Welcome friends." He stepped forward and wrapped his arms around Barabbas. "It's been a wide chaotic road to this place, Barabbas, but now it's straight and narrow, and you'll do well to stay on it—you must walk on it, for surely death and destruction will follow you to your grave—and beyond—if you depart to the left or to the right."

The master sat down cross-legged on the floor and motioned for the others to join him. When they had taken their places, he looked around at the startled group.

"My kingdom will cast a wide net, brothers. Many will come from afar, but only a few will make the decision to the end. It's unlikely that they will be the rich or the powerful, because wealth and power blind the mankind to the true riches of the kingdom, but there will be many prostitutes and the sinners, thieves and brigands, murderers, adulterers, the lame and the blind—they will be washed—they will be sanctified, and they will be changed.

"In the blink of an eye, some will see the path and turn to walk on it. The world will not accept that this is possible, but you must never lose confidence." He stared directly at Barabbas.

"Others will turn and walk with you for a while, but they will break faith with Yahweh and turn again to the world. They will persecute you and revile you, but you must walk, always, so that such accusations are false. For blessed are you that are persecuted for my sake. You shall surely not lose your reward."

Thomas glanced around. All eyes riveted on the speaker.

"What happened last night must never be part of my kingdom. These actions—these attitudes—belong to this world. An eye for an eye, a tooth for a tooth—precious lives lost at the hands of men whose lives are then taken in turn. You must not be like this."

"You are to bring life, and light—and truth. Your lives are forfeit to the greater purpose of saving others, not destroying them in selfish, fearful rage. You must accept others, as I have accepted you, from what you *were*, to what you are becoming.

"You must love others with the uncommon love, that makes no distinction between persons, for Yahweh loves like this and causes his rain to fall on the just and the unjust. As he gives freely to his whole creation, so it must be with you.

"You will be blamed for these killings. Already the authorities are scheming, and enemies join together against my kingdom, but they cannot hurt you while I am with you. In vain they will plot, and in their anger try to imprison and kill you.

"Do not fear and do not flee. We will sojourn together for a time and then you will return to remain here in Jerusalem until the gates to the kingdom are opened to all."

"When will this be?" Thomas asked.

"It not for you to know the day or the hour, but when I am taken from you, it will be near."

"Is there something we should do while we wait?" Thaddaeus asked, "—besides waiting, I mean."

A chuckle rippled through the room.

"Gather together often, because community is of utmost importance. Pray together at all times, because prayer is your conduit to the power of the most high. Don't fast, as I explained before, but when I am gone, then you *will* fast. Don't fast like the pagans or the priests, for they fast for their own glory to be seen and applauded by others, but when you fast, keep it between you and your Father.

"*You will fast to loose the chains of injustice and untie the cords of the yoke, to set the oppressed free and to break every yoke. You will fast to share your food with the hungry and to provide the poor and the wanderer with shelter, and to clothe the naked when you see them.*

"*When you fast like this, your light will shine like the dawn and you will heal the nations. Your righteousness will go before you and the glory of Yahweh will guard you from behind. You will call, and Yahweh will answer. You will call for help and He will say, 'Here I am', and though no one is with you, you will never be alone.*"

Thomas glanced at Abner, whose eyes rested vacantly on the floor in front of him. Joseph stared at Jesus in rapt attention. Mael kept his eyes fixed on the master as if every word was being absorbed into who he was.

Mael stopped on the bottom step of the main staircase of Pilate's residence. Four guards stood at the top. Usually, there were only two. So far, they had taken no notice of him.

He started up the stairs, his eyes fixed on the guards to see when they would notice. At the fifth step from the top one of the guards drew his sword. Mael looked up into his eyes.

"Gassis?"

"Arrest him!" Gassis growled as he leapt down two steps toward Mael. The other guards were right behind him.

"Gassis, its Mael!" Mael cried out as the big Erman grabbed his arm.

"We know who you are!" Gassis said. "You incited the riot at the fortress last night."

"No, I—"

"Shut up!" Gassis slapped him across the mouth. One of the other guards had hold of his other arm. Instead of taking him down the steps, they dragged him up toward the main door.

"Where are we going?" Mael tried to think—he tried to relax and not resist. The men were nearly twice his weight.

"Pilate wants to see you."

"Pilate let me leave this morning."

"Quiet!"

Gassis pounded on the door to the residence.

It swung open slowly to reveal two more heavily armed soldiers.

"A gift for Pilate!" Gassis snarled. The soldiers nodded and stepped back.

They dragged him into and across the atrium, barely giving him opportunity to get his feet under himself. Pilate met them at the door to his dining hall.

"The trouble maker returns." His voice was bitter and cold.

Mael got his feet under himself and stood up, shaking the guards off his arms and straightening his tunic.

"Why are you here, Mael?" Pilate said.

"DO NOT FEAR, FOR THEY ARE MY SERVANTS TO DO JUSTICE."

Mael stood up to his full height and looked directly into Pilate's eyes. "I came here to thank you for releasing Barabbas."

"It was foolish of me to do so," Pilate rasped. "We'll find him—them, and when we do, they won't go free again."

"You are but a servant, to execute justice, Prefect. Where there is no crime—"

Gassis slapped him across the mouth. "How will justice be given for those who killed Margas?"

Pilate's temper boiled. "Watch yourself, soldier! This is not your job! Stand down! Now!"

Gassis glowered, but took a step back.

Tears rolled down Mael's cheeks. He choked as he watched the Prefect berate his guard. "Mar—Margas?"

"You know Margas?" Pilate asked.

Mael's hands were on his face, with tears streaming down between his fingers. Pilate's words were distant.

"No, not Margas."

"Yes, Mael, Margas was one of those killed last night; perhaps the first. You see what your treachery has brought?"

A wave of something, similar to what had happened in the jail, curled up around Mael. As it rose, he stood up straight and the tears stopped. He looked Pilate in the eyes.

"I told you this morning and I will tell you again, in the presence of these witnesses, so that all things can be attested by their presence. Neither Barabbas nor I were in any way involved in the murder of these men, on either side."

"That's not what the priests say."

"What do the priests say?"

"That you incited the crowd and they rose up in rebellion."

"They have been here this morning already to tell you this?"

Pilate didn't answer.

"I will tell you what Yahweh says. If you do not change, you will remain Prefect here for a time, until you are called back from whence you came. You'll be tried for your inhumanity and condemned to death as you have proclaimed it for others. You will die the death of the one who betrayed the master and your body will not see its grave, but be cast upon the waters where men will see it and mock your name."

Pilate's face drained white. His eyes burned with hatred and his breathing became ragged and labored. "Seize him!" he shouted.

Before the guards could move, a hiss heralded the arrival of two Eladrim warriors, both larger than either of the guards. At their appearance, Gassis crumpled to his knees before falling silently face down on the stone floor. The other guard collapsed onto the pommel of his own sword, driving it into his belly.

Mael looked back at Pilate whose anger evolved into dread. "Write it down, Pilate," he said, softly, "and do nothing to interfere with the followers of the master while you yet live, lest something greater happen to you."

Mael glanced up. "Thank you, Vishtalar." The warrior nodded to Mael and then toward the door. It was time to leave.

By the time Mael reached the door to Pilate's inner chamber, Vishtalar and his companion had vanished, but this time, their presence walked beside him. In his peripheral vision, faint lights floated along either side of him, but if he turned to look, there was nothing.

Mael didn't look back, and no one came after him. Pilate sat alone with two faithful Roman soldiers either dead or useless, lying on the floor in front of him. Mael hurt, but he was quite sure he hadn't caused all this pain.

As he passed the two guards at the front door, they moved to intercept him but stopped; terrified by something they couldn't see or understand.

He descended the front steps of the palace into the brilliant late morning light of Asolara and stepped into the anonymity of the crowd that filled the street.

"Do you understand what just happened?"

Mael startled at the voice of Ransom who suddenly walked beside him.

"Where did you come from?"

Ransom smiled. "I was waiting for you in the arch over there. Do you understand what just happened?"

"I think so."

"Do you remember the discussion we had at the pinnacle of the temple?"

"Yes."

"Don't be afraid to stand up for what is right, Mael. If you fall off the pinnacle doing what is right, the Eladra will catch you, but you must never test them for selfish gain. Your desire to thank Pilate was right. Your compassion for Margas, in his death is right; it is the fulfillment of psadeq."

"I didn't understand what I said to Pilate at the end," Mael confessed. "It seemed cruel."

"It is the word of Mah'Eladra."

"How did I know to say it? I heard no voice, but I didn't just make it up."

"There are things that you will know, Mael, that you will speak as a prophet speaks, that you won't understand. The prophets of old often wished they understood some of the things they spoke on behalf of Mah'Eladra. Many of them searched diligently, but they went to their deaths, only knowing that future generations would see and understand. So it will be with you, Mael."

"But the voice only said not to be afraid—that Pilate, too, is a servant appointed for justice."

"And so he is. Because of the things you told him, he won't interfere further with the progress of my kingdom. There will be others who will do that, but only to fulfill the will of Mah'Eladra."

Mael stopped walking. The master paused and turned to face him. "When I hear your words, Master, they make no sense, but in my vorn, in the deep parts of who I am, I know that they're true."

"Who are you, Mael?"

"I don't know." Mael looked down and continued walking. Ransom matched his stride. "But, I have another question," Mael said.

"Speak."

"When I spoke to Pilate—the words at the beginning, 'If you do not change' seemed to qualify the prophecy—that it can be different."

Ransom smiled. "It is the great hope of Mah'Eladra. They always hold out that someone—anyone—*can* change. It's always offered, and it's always true. But it's also true that if a person hardens themselves in rebellion, that Mah'Eladra will use that rebellion to their own purposes, so that Mah'Eladra will be lifted up."

"I feel a helplessness and a deep hurt for Pilate. Will he change?"

"Search deep in your vorn, Mael. You know the answer. Don't be afraid of it."

They walked a bit further as Mael pondered what Ransom said. As they approached the bridge to the western gate of the temple, he strained to listen to his inner voice. People swarmed around them; people moving to the rhythm of some unseen hope that kept them alive. The quiet desperation in their vorns reached out and touched him as they sought the answers that the master had tried to give them. He thought about Pilate. "No," he realized aloud. "He *will* refrain from pursuing your followers, but he *won't* change."

Ransom nodded gravely. "Do you feel the oppression of these people, Mael?"

Mael nodded.

"They are like sheep without a shepherd. They cry out for answers, but there are few who hear and respond. Those designated to lead the people have lost their way and, though they try, their voices die in the wind of their own hypocrisy."

Ransom continued, "It is the same on Tessalindria as it is here. Many will seek but few will find, because they seek with the wisdom of the mankind, rather than the wisdom of Mah'Eladra."

"How do your bear the weight of so many who hurt but will not allow themselves help?" Mael asked.

"Are you feeling that, Mael? Are you tasting the suffering around you that you cannot bear, yet understand that you cannot turn away from?"

"Yes." Mael's admission added to his burden. "Many times. I don't know what to do."

"Mah'Eladra have promised—it is written in the Tessarandin—that they will not allow you to suffer more than you can manage. That is why there are days and nights. Each day has just enough trouble for you to manage, but you must learn to absorb the hurt and not pass it on, except to Mah'Eladra who have no limit to the hurt they can endure."

"And how can I not pass this hurt along. It's accumulating day after day. The more I learn—the more I see and hear—the more burden it becomes."

"You must learn to lay it at the feet of Mah'Eladra. Otherwise, when it becomes too heavy, you will lay it on the shoulders of others of the mankind, and there will be no end to the cycle of hurt from even the smallest injustice."

"But how?" Mael gazed out into the crowded streets before them.

"Every morning, Mael, before it is light, before it has become today, take the burdens of yesterday that have not been swept clean by sleep, and lay them at the feet of Mah'Eladra who will take them from you without reproach. Then that day becomes new and fresh and strengthens you to its own challenges."

"Every day?"

The master nodded. "Before it becomes today."

Erolin had told him this, but it had not been as clear. He suddenly remembered a story she had spoken to him:

"A man had three sons. The firstborn never asked him for anything, but contented himself with the abundant provision of his father's house, willingly supplied because of the father's love for his firstborn.

The youngest often came to him and asked him for things he needed. The father gave generously to every need because of his unfailing love for his youngest son.

The middle son got up early and walked with his father every morning before it was light, and shared with his father his struggle and hurt, his joy and vision. He asked for little, but the father heaped upon him his presence and protection, pressed down, shaken together and overflowing into his lap, so that every need was met."

Mael turned to ask one more question. Ransom had vanished. He stood alone as the throngs of Terra's mankind surged around him. The emptiness of the sheep without a shepherd and the joy of the presence of Mah'Eladra swept over him in waves.

Chapter Thirty-Two

CONSPIRACY

"While the advice of a friend may be bitter on the palate,
And the counsel of an enemy sweet to the tongue,
Swallow only that which is discerned by wisdom."

Sessasha's way
Tarasinden Varr

Caiaphas stood before the Prefect on the portico of Pilate's residence. "What do you mean, you're not charging them with this crime?"

"I am not here to arbitrate between the sects of your religion."

"You were willing to do so last week!"

"That was different," Pilate stormed.

"Different□ Different in what way?" Something had changed, but the sudden reversal of Pilate's willingness to implicate the followers of the Nazarene didn't bode well for the temple or the city of Jerusalem.

"Don't try my patience, High Priest. I'm here to oversee the peace of this city as a prefect of Rome. I'm not interested in your religious disputes."

"Our 'religious disputes' are disturbing the peace, and you've made it clear we're not allowed to take care of this matter ourselves."

"You could, if you were willing." Pilate's disgust erupted into his voice.

Caiaphas's eyes darkened. "We're willing, Prefect, but our laws require death for blasphemers, and Rome requires that the death penalty be reserved only for you, but you don't understand or appreciate how necessary this is for the stability of our people—our laws."

"You have the prisons."

"Prisons won't contain blasphemy, Prefect. Death alone deals with that malady. You're inciting revolt by not allowing us to punish these ideas according to our law."

Pilate looked up into Caiaphas's eyes. The petulant turn of his lips betrayed his mockery. "I let you abuse, main, torture and kill one of your blasphemers, and look where we are."

"He was the tap-root. Other roots will spring up—they are already taking his place. If we don't rid ourselves of them now ..."

"These other roots—the cowardly followers of your Nazarene—where are they? They've barely shown their faces since his death. Our intelligence can hardly find them other than occasional appearances in the market place to buy very ordinary things like food and soap."

"You never see roots until they sprout. Who do you think attacked your soldiers?"

"Do you think we're stupid, Caiaphas, that we don't know who attacked us?" Pilate stood up, his posture no longer tired and bored. "We know it was the caucus, Caiaphas."

Pilate took a step closer. Caiaphas stood his ground.

"We know it was them, and we weren't able to find *one* follower of the Nazarene among the dead."

"You don't know all of them. They're growing in numbers, especially with the rumors of the Nazarene's appearances among them."

"People follow leaders, Caiaphas, you know that. Do you think the leaders of this sect would have only sent followers on such a task without being there themselves?"

"This is a dangerous and insidious group, Pilate. They do things differently. They're a cult of the worst kind and you've little appreciation for what they'll do. If you don't quell them, they'll be your undoing."

Pilate blanched at his words, before retreating to his seat. After he settled himself, he looked up and raised his hand in a gesture of final proclamation. "While I remain in this seat, Rome will no longer take sides in the disputes of your religious affairs. Rome still reserves the right to oversee matters of execution of civil offenders, including those whom you deem dangerous to your way of life. I remind you that Judea remains a province of Rome."

Caiaphas stared into Pilate's eyes for a few seconds before he looked down and nodded his head. "As you have spoken, Prefect."

"If I were you, Caiaphas, I would keep an eye on that ugly little runt, Mael."

Caiaphas looked up. "Oh?"

Pilate's eyes betrayed a sense of old confidences with Caiaphas. "*He's* your troublemaker."

"He instigated the attack?"

"Oh no—no, he had nothing to do with it. We had him in jail with Barabbas; but he's one to watch. I have no clue where he came from—he's not of your people, but he's more like your Nazarene than any of the others, mark my word."

Caiaphas sensed a break in Pilate's stubbornness. "Are you afraid of him, Pilate?"

Pilate startled and looked up. "He's no threat to Rome, if that's what you mean, but keep an eye on him."

Caiaphas nodded. "Is he a threat to *you*, prefect?"

Pilate pursed his lips and shook his head. "I don't think so, but I'll be watching. I'll let you know if I see anything suspicious."

"That would be helpful," Caiaphas smiled.

"You can arrest him if you want," Pilate said, "but any corporal punishment still belongs to Rome. Is this clear?"

"You said that before, Prefect, and it's perfectly clear."

Caiaphas hesitated while he pondered if he wanted to ask the next question.

"Something else, Caiaphas?"

"Yes, Prefect. If you *are* watching him, it might be helpful—"

"—if I let you know where he is?"

"Yes."

Pilate smiled for the first time. "I think we can work that out."

The old Pilate was back. Not exactly a friend, but cooperative with the needs of the religious leadership in a common truce for the sake of the city that they shared. Caiaphas nodded. "I think we're done, then."

"For now," Pilate said as he stood up.

Caiaphas turned and descended the steps of the mansion without turning back.

Thomas sat in the small circle of apostles in a quiet clearing west of the southern wall of the city. It was one of their favorite places. Through the grove of short olive trees, they could see the Serpent's pool below them at the head of the Hinom valley. The clearing stood off the usual trails around the city, nowhere near any main road.

James, John, Philip, Mael, Peter and Matthew sat with him.

"Who said the master told us to meet here?" he asked.

"I did," said Peter. "He sent a note last night. It came by one of the couriers. We're to meet him at noon."

"I didn't know the master could write," Bartholomew said.

"Neither did I," James and John said at the same time.

"He can read," Peter said. "We all heard him in the synagogue at Capernaum and other occasions. I am guessing he can write, don't you think?"

Everyone nodded.

"But he's never sent a note before," Thomas said.

"We were with him day and night before, remember?" Philip said. "There wouldn't have been a need."

"Yeah, but ever since the resurrection, he just appears—I think it's a bit odd." Thomas was skeptical.

"No one else would know this place." Philip observed.

"He'll be here," Mael announced.

"How do you know?" Thomas asked.

"He will."

"How do you know this stuff?" Thomas said.

"I don't know—but I know he *will* be here."

"Where are the others?" Matthew asked.

James opened his mouth to respond but clamped it shut.

"No one move!" The voice came from behind Thomas, and before any of them could respond, several men with swords surrounded them. Temple guards!

Thomas wasn't sure where they came from. They must have known about this meeting, but it didn't matter now. He sat still.

Peter stood up. "What do you want?"

Two guards threatened him with their swords. "Sit down!"

Peter eyed them carefully for a moment before he sat down.

"Wise choice," growled the apparent leader.

Mael stood up. "They want me. Nothing else."

The leader turned to face him. "How do you know?" His voice flooded with surprise, scorn and contempt."

Mael held out his hands. "I'll go with you, but leave the others, as you have been commanded."

Peter jumped up again. "No!"

"Sit down, Peter!" All eyes turned to see the master standing behind Peter just outside the circle.

"Who are you?" demanded the leader.

"I am Jesus, whom you crucified," the master said softly as he held out his arms to reveal his wrists.

The guards took a step back, faces blanched in terror.

"Take the one whom you were sent to arrest and go." The measured calm of the master's voice reassured Thomas. "Your business here is finished, but go tell your priests, *"Be ever hearing, but never understanding; be ever seeing, but never perceiving. Your people's hearts have become calloused and you hardly hear with your ears and you have closed your eyes. Otherwise you might see with your eyes, and hear with your ears, understand with your hearts and turn, and I would heal you."*

In the brief pause following the master's words, Thomas looked around. The bewildered guards' faces showed their fear. The baffled looks of the brothers revealed their awe at the master's simple instruction. Thomas wondered how he knew that the words Jesus spoke were a quote from the prophet.

"Come with us!" the leader said to Mael. Two other guards stepped forward as Mael raised his arms into their hands. Mael looked into Thomas's eyes. **"DO NOT FEAR!"**

Thomas startled at the unspoken words.

Mael turned away. The temple guards formed a small circle around him and led him up the narrow path toward the aqueduct that fed the pool.

"Should we go after them?" Thomas said as he turned to Jesus.

"No, Mael must face them alone. His faith is growing daily and this test of his faith will make it stronger. He won't die. The words he will need will be given him at the hour he needs them."

The master looked slowly around the small group. "My friends, you have seen things that many others longed to see, but only saw them from afar through faith. Each of you are called to testify to what you have seen and heard and each of you will eventually do so at the cost of your life, just as you saw it happen to the son of man."

The men listened quietly. Thomas watched their eyes as he spoke. He guessed that the others were wrestling with these words of uneasy truth just as he was.

"You will go out with compassion into a world abused by evil and filled with hurt and you will hurt with it. Trust in Yahweh, trust also in me. Listen to the words you are given and give them back to those around you. Heal the fevers and cast out demons in my name. Touch the lepers, and open the eyes of the blind and lift the lame to walk. When told to do so, call those who have died back from death, even death after a time. Then you will know for certain that the king of life, whose kingdom you are preaching, will most certainly be able to call *you* back from death to eternity with him."

"Don't be afraid. When I have gone, I will send you the counselor. He will walk with you and be in you so that you will never be alone."

"Is this already happening to Mael?" Matthew asked.

The master nodded. "His path is different than yours, for reasons you'll never understand. You should watch and listen. When he is gone, your faith will be stronger, but you won't remember why."

"Does he know this?" Thomas's curiosity about Mael exceeded that of his own fate.

"He knows in part, just as each of you knows in part. Before he leaves, he will know fully."

"Did you send the note asking us to gather here?" asked Philip.

Jesus smiled. "No, that was the High Priest."

"You knew about it?" John asked.

"I know many things, John—and so do the Romans. They know who you are, and where you are, but don't fear. Caiaphas and Pilate conspire together against those who follow me, but I have many servants among their numbers, and they can do nothing without my permission."

Jesus closed his eyes and lifted his face to the sky briefly before he spread his hands out over the ground in front of him. "Eat, my friends—my brothers. There is much yet to do today." A small linen cloth appeared on the ground. On it were three loaves of fresh bread, an earthen bowl of figs, and one of fresh dates. A small plank of dried fish lay between the bowls.

As it often was with Jesus, the appearance of food changed the conversation from learning to the familiar. Thomas smiled. It was simply time to eat.

Chapter Thirty-Three

DIFFERENCES

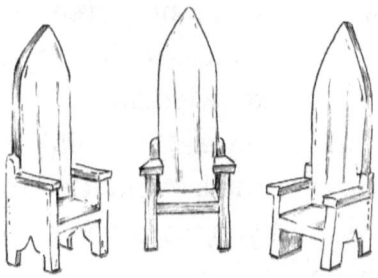

"Your knowledge should never take precedence over your uncommon love for one another."

The Middle Way
Pratoraman

Caiaphas sat with his two friends under a tree in the courtyard of his residence. The water in his flagon had become warm on the small table to his right as thoughts about his predicament kept him from enjoying his respite in the shade.

"It's just so hard to know for sure where all this is going," he said without trying to conceal the quiet desperation that overshadowed his hope. He secretly hoped that Jacob and his underlings hadn't found "the little runt", Mael, and he could relax into the afternoon work at the temple having tried, but failed, to catch the troublemaker.

Gamaliel smiled. "Being High Priest has never been easy, Caiaphas."

Caiaphas shook his head. "It seems to have been easier for a number of my predecessors. And to be honest, I've not felt much support from either of you."

Nicodemus looked down as he pursed his lips. "It's tough, Caiaphas. We know that the messiah has to come at some point, right?" He looked up for acknowledgment.

Caiaphas stared into his eyes. "You think Jesus was the messiah?" He thought back over the last month. "You've not said much in council these days, and you were one of the ones who didn't assent to his crucifixion."

"It's complicated, Caiaphas. You know that as well as any of us. Your sect and mine often disagree."

"He was so arrogant!" Caiaphas growled as he looked down into his warm glass. "He would not relent on the slightest thing—and he kept accusing *us* of being the problem."

"Maybe we are," Gamaliel said.

"What□" Caiaphas wanted his friends to be honest, but he also wanted support. "What're you talking about?"

"We've searched through the law and the prophets," said Nicodemus. "You've been part of the discussions, my friend. There are many prophecies that have been and are being fulfilled, if they are interpreted a certain way...."

"And if they are interpreted differently?" Caiaphas asked.

"That's the core issue," Nicodemus said. "Yahweh gave this all to us mostly in the form of stories. The stories help us relate—they help us see who He is through the lens of human experience and history—what He wants and what He does not want. We see the lives of those who seek Him and those who did not and it forms in us deep meanings of what righteousness is."

"He also gave us the law!" Caiaphas hated the defensive tone of his own words.

"He did," Gamaliel said quietly, "and he also gave us the prophets: Isaiah, Jeremiah... Ezekiel... Daniel ... When you put the three together, the stories, the law and the prophecies—well it's like soup—the meat, the vegetables and the spices, any one of them alone doesn't make much of a meal ..."

"You're saying I'm in the soup?" Caiaphas asked. A bit of levity seemed acceptable, given the situation.

"We're all in this soup," Nicodemus said. "And like any good soup, it's challenging to figure out what the most important part of it is."

Gamliel nodded. "Throughout history, Yahweh has brought men into the storyline that have challenged the instituted authority at the time. This was true of Abraham, Jacob, and then what happened with Joseph when his brothers strayed from the path. Moses was called to re-flavor the soup by adding the law, and we haven't done a very good job of keeping that. The judges of Israel tried for centuries to keep the people faithful and when that seemed to be failing, we tried making ourselves into a kingdom. Kingdoms relied on the king, who may have been good or bad and as the kings came and went, so did the people."

"Don't forget the priests," Caiaphas said.

"No, we can't forget the priests," Gamaliel continued, "but the priests were always beholden to the civil side of the society. They had a hard time with the judges and a harder time under the kings. Add the prophets into the mix and it became more confusing: The kings trying to keep order in society and not doing a very good job for the most part, the priests, trying to hold onto and honor the law while the prophets constantly stirred the pot with their messages about the failures of the others."

"And we believe all this was from Yahweh," Nicodemus said. "As confusing as it may be, somehow, it all has to fit. Many wise men, serious scholars of the law, the historians and the prophets have been working for centuries to put this puzzle together.

"Abraham would have been appalled that Jacob had to go live in Egypt. Moses would have shaken his head with the behavior of the people under the judges. Samuel was certainly not happy with the idea of a king and the kings didn't like the prophets for the most part. The prophets—well, they were ultimately frustrated by the discipline we went through in Babylon. They saw it coming and it hurt to see it actually happen."

"What are you trying to say?" Caiaphas drained the last drop of water from his flagon.

"Well," Gamaliel said, "if you look at this in total, the only constant is a steady evolution of our nation, with each of the steps in that process being a source of dismay for those who came before."

"Have you two been talking?" Caiaphas glanced back and forth between the others."

"It seems that that is all we do these days," Gamaliel smiled. "These are extraordinary times, we have to talk about what they mean, just as men throughout history have had to do, and if Yahweh is on the move, it's probable that it's going to be uncomfortable for all us, don't you think?"

"He's been quiet for hundreds of years!" Caiaphas argued, as he slouched back in his chair. "Why now?"

"We might as well ask 'why *not* now'?" Gamaliel chided.

"It *is* the year of jubilee," Nicodemus said.

They sat and pondered these things silently.

"The common thread through all of this is the notion of the messiah." Nicodemus spoke slowly with caution. "He's got to show up some time and when he does, it seems to me that a lot's going to have to change."

Caiaphas shook his head. "So my original question: Are you saying you think Jesus was the messiah?" He glanced up at Nicodemus. "Are you becoming one of his followers?"

"I've been trying to be honest with myself about his teachings," Nicodemus said. "If you listen carefully, he has a lot to say—new wine, so to speak, and we certainly have had a tendency to get used to the flavor of our own old wine."

Caiaphas leaned forward. "What're you saying, Nicodemus?"

"Just this, my friend. You're in the un-enviable position of having to act on this situation—to be decisive—as you know. It's easy, in that place, to be unable to listen with a truly open mind, because you have responsibilities that drive your thinking back to what is manageable from what is right."

Caiaphas shuddered. "We're all in this together, Nicodemus."

"I'm just saying that we better make sure we know what we're doing."

"The decisions about Jesus have been made," Caiaphas observed. "Now the challenge, at least for me, is what to do about his followers. They're not so sure he's still dead."

"And what about the rumors of this outsider?" Gamaliel asked. "What's his name?"

"Mael," Caiaphas said glumly. "Mael and nothing else, or something like that."

"Your tone tells me that he's more than you want to admit."

"He's still alive." Resentment crept into his tone, "He hasn't done anything I could arrest him for but ..."

One of Caiaphas's servants approached the small group. "A note, High Priest," he said as he held out his hand.

"Thank you." Caiaphas frowned as he read it while the servant backed away.

"But you arrested him anyway?" Nicodemus said.

Caiaphas looked up at Nicodemus and scowled as he nodded. "I have to go."

"Do you want us to join you?" Gamaliel asked.

"You don't have to do this alone, Caiaphas." Nicodemus said.

Caiaphas hesitated as his friends waited. He looked back and forth between them. The issues with Mael were personal but Nicodemus was right, as he often was.

He looked down into his empty mug that he had never put down. "I think that would be wise."

Mael stood still as the three men approached him: the High Priest and two others whom he recognized, but didn't know. As they came near, he became aware that he could see into their vorns—he saw the totality of who they were. He felt their motives, as if they wore different clothing that represented each one at the core of his existence.

"Good afternoon, Mael." The High Priest offered the words without any emotion, a platitude of introduction. His vorn spoke of indifference and pain, a gray confusion of anger, resentment, and unease, tinged by fear. The grayness shed off his robes like a waterfall, cascading from the linen headgear that covered his hair and ears. It clouded his face before it slipped off his shoulders and dripped down his robe onto the stone pavers of the courtyard.

Mael nodded with a slight bow. The temple guards still held the chains to his manacles.

"This is Nicodemus," the priest said, nodding to the tall man to his right. "He's a teacher of the law in Israel." Nicodemus nodded to Mael. Waves of yellow and orange light shed from him like water off a felted goat hair coat. Nicodemus was a friend of the master. Mael was sure that no one else could see what he was seeing, and he had never seen anything like it before.

"And this is Gamaliel, a trusted scholar, a learned man in the ways of Yahweh."

The man on Kiephus's left nodded. Bluish light with streaks of white flowed down his vestments; a man of honor and clear thinking—cautious but kind and not swayed by emotion—devoted to the law and its application to his people.

"Release him," Kiephus said to the guards.

The guards removed the manacles from Mael's wrists and stepped back.

"You may go," Kiephus said before turning back to Mael. "Please, sit down." He waved his hand to one of the chairs on the portico, nodding in turn to each of the others. The three of them sat down in the three chairs facing him.

"I prefer to stand," Mael said as he rubbed his wrists.

"Do you know why you're here, Mael?" The High Priest asked as he ordered his robes after sitting.

"Yes."

The priest looked up in surprise. "I had you brought here so that you could explain to us your interest in the one they call Chaisus."

"I am here to learn from him, as I've already told you."

"But he's gone—dead and buried." Anger lurked behind the words, and the gray cascade off his shoulders intensified as he said it.

"He's overcome your grave, and returns to teach those he has chosen."

"What do you mean, 'he returns to teach'?"

Mael stared at the High Priest. "He simply appears to us—in different ways, at different times—and teaches us."

"He has never appeared to any of us." The priest's scorn darkened the cascade off his shoulders.

"Perhaps he only comes to those who have listened—who will listen."

The priest darkened again.

Nicodemus spoke. "What is he teaching you that you did not learn before?"

"He is teaching us about his kingdom. He's giving more detail about its nature and how it will be and how it will come to pass."

"He's not a king!" Kiephus protested, his voice verging on a snarl.

Mael stared back at him. "He's not a king like Caesar—or Herod—or any king that has set himself up over the mankind in this world. He is not like your first king, Saul or even the great king David, or Josiah or Hezekiah." Mael did not know how he knew any of these names. They poured out of his mouth. "His kingdom will not be found 'here' or 'there'". He gestured to the right and left. "It will be found in the midst of a community of the righteous, who know him and are obedient to his commands."

Kiephus's eyes raged and he was about to speak when Gamaliel interrupted him with a wave of his hand. "How do you know these things? You yourself say you have only been here but a short while."

Mael lowered his eyes to the genuine question. "I don't know all things, only that which I am given."

"He's blasphemi—"

Gamaliel silenced Kiephus with another gesture. Kiephus retreated from his words, but his eyes burned.

"Are you a prophet?"

Mael looked up at the scholar. "I am Mael and—from Farhantra, across the Vorsian Sea."

"Yet you know our history—you know our people—our traditions."

"I am here to learn, and then I will return to teach my people."

Nicodemus spoke thoughtfully. "Tell us more of what you know of this kingdom then."

Mael looked at Nicodemus. The question was genuine, with no hint of guile. His robe pulsed with a warm, reddish light. "This is the kingdom that was foretold by your prophet, Daniel—a rock cut from the mountain that will smash the kingdoms of this world. Elohim of heaven will set it up; a kingdom that will never be destroyed. It will crush all those kingdoms and bring them to an end, but it will itself endure forever."

"This is outrageous!" Kiephus erupted.

"Is it so outrageous?" Mael turned to face the priest's anger. "Have you not an uneasy truce with these Romans who oppress you? Would you not have them crushed and forced to leave this land so that you could worship Yahweh freely—without their presence—without their prejudice? Would you not want this prophecy to be true?—to be part of a kingdom where Yahweh is truly the king and that your worship would be in truth and in spirit?"

Kiephus's eyes burned into Mael. An intense compassion for Kiephus rolled over Mael. He felt the weight of the priest's role, as the one appointed to lead the people. He felt his jealous confusion mixed with anger.

"You've been stewards, High Priest—waiting for this time—waiting for this kingdom to return to your people. You are the High Priest, not the king, and it's your stewardship to lead this people into the arms of the true king."

"Jesus could not have been the king!" Kiephus blurted out. "Where is he now? Dead and in his grave where he belongs."

"Worldly kings are cowards, Kiephus," Mael said gently. "They command others to die for them in their vainglory. Jesus died for his people, a true king, and has been raised to sit at the right hand of Yahweh, where he will reign over his kingdom in justice and truth."

"Hear his blasphemy!" Kiephus snarled as he looked back and forth between the two others.

"It is only blasphemy if it's not true, Kiephus." Nicodemus said.

"It cannot be true. You saw for yourself his disregard of the law, his breaking of the traditions for Shabbat, his liaison with the sinners—with the tax collectors and the prostitutes. Such be-havior would not ascribe to the messiah of Israel. He was a law-breaker, with no formal training."

Gamaliel shook his head. "This is a conversation we need to have in private, as it doesn't concern the prisoner."

Kiephus looked down. "You are ever wise, my friend. Guards!"

The two guards who brought Mael to the courtyard hurried back from the shade of the portico.

"Take him to one of the cells in the east wall until we've decided what to do with him."

Mael moved his hands behind his back so the guards could re-attach the manacles.

Kiephus continued, "Post two guards and make sure he has no visitors and does not leave under any circumstances. Water, but no food until I say."

The guards saluted. "Come along then," one said.

They took Mael by his upper arms and led him across the courtyard through the residence's gate. He didn't try to look back.

Nicodemus waited until the trio had left the courtyard. "It seems unnecessary to keep him in prison, Caiaphas. He's done nothing wrong."

"He's challenging our authority as leaders of this nation. Many are following."

"Following what?" Gamaliel countered.

Caiaphas's eyes darkened. "That's just the problem. This Jesus taught them to rebel against the traditions that hold our society together. Perhaps he *was* teaching a new way, but now that he's gone, whatever order or sense he may have been making is now in the hands of untrained, ordinary men—and who knows what happens next. History has shown that this kind of rebellion never works out well."

"Yes," said Gamaliel, "but what shall we do? We cannot just arrest all of those who have followed him. There might be hundreds or even thousands."

"We need to find the leaders," Caiaphas responded.

"But there are no leaders, as you just pointed out." Nicodemus was struggling along with Gamaliel. "We don't know who is teaching what to whom. If Jesus is making appearances to teach them as Mael insists—if he just appears and disappears..."

"You believe that⊓" Caiaphas said.

"It's hard to know what to believe, Caiaphas," Gamaliel replied. "There have been many claims to have seen Jesus, and without proof that it is not happening, we need to be very wise. If it is the case, we have to know for sure. Surely if Jesus is coming and going as Mael suggests, then we have a very different situation on our hands, one that's going to be difficult to manage and requires careful attention as to it spiritual basis."

Caiaphas shook his head. "We've seen demons do that."

"You don't even believe in demons," Gamaliel said, "or angels, for that matter."

"From all the stories," Nicodemus interjected, "Jesus had control of the demons. Jesus claimed he was god. We judged this as blasphemy, but if it were true, certainly there would be no limit on what he can do."

The others fell silent. Nicodemus tread carefully. From what he had seen and the extended personal conversation he'd had with Jesus, he couldn't rule out what Gamaliel had just said. He was glad he was not in Caiaphas's sandals, and he wasn't sure what Gamaliel was thinking.

Gamaliel broke the silence as he looked up. "Perhaps we should let Mael go and have him followed. He'll lead us back to the others and we can question them."

Caiaphas pursed his lips and shook his head. "He's the only lead we have."

"Yes, the only one to lead us to the truth."

Caiaphas looked up and stared at Gamaliel. "Perhaps I should just ask him. He is forthright about his answers. Maybe he'll tell us where to find the others."

"Is your intent honest?" Nicodemus asked.

"What?" Caiaphas turned on him.

"He's sensitive to the heart behind the questions—like he can read our minds," Nicodemus observed.

"And?"

"Well, if you go to him and ask because you want to know and understand him, he will answer truly. If you go because you seek understanding for your own determined agenda, I'm not sure you will get much from him."

"Then he will stay in his cell," Caiaphas growled.

"He's an unusual young man, Caiaphas," Nicodemus said. "He doesn't seem to mind staying in his cell,"

"When he gets hungry enough, he'll talk."

"If you recall, when you imprisoned him, an angel brought him water and manna." Gamaliel spoke gently, "and we haven't seen manna since Yahweh fed our people in the desert."

Caiaphas looked down again. "He's stays in prison until we have a path forward!" It was a command decision. "I will go to him tomorrow after morning prayers and see if he will be more forthcoming."

Chapter Thirty-Four

CELL

"The Wastes are a testimony to greed and pride and should serve a warning to the mankind."

Outworlds
Colloran

Mael found himself in the same cell that he had been in for his first arrest. It was just as dark and clean with the straw mat in the center. The only light filtered in through the small grated window in the door from the torches in the hall. Mael knew there were two guards. They remained quiet, but their presence beyond the door was palpable.

He sat cross-legged on the mat. Understandings of his presence on Terra and about his journey here fell together slowly, like a vast puzzle taking shape with each encounter, with each new insight, and with more time with Ransom. He was in this world for a time, brought here by Mah'Eladra, who watched over him and spoke to him when they wanted. With each hearing of the voice he learned something new; with each simple obedience he became stronger—more confident of the path he walked on.

He knew for certain that no prison cell, no matter how deep or dark, no matter how well guarded, could contain him when Mah'Eladra wanted him free, and no moment of freedom was secure if Mah'Eladra wanted him in custody.

He sat, fully submitted to a situation that gave the powers of Terra an illusion of control in their self-delusion. He waited, oblivious to the darkness or the hardness of the stone floor, or the cold walls, or the two silent guards who believed that they restrained his coming and going.

Three times a day, the guards changed. There were no words, no voices. With each change, they opened the hatch at the bottom of the door and shoved a small flask of water into the cell. He drank the water as he watched the mice coming and going through two holes in the corner of the cell.

Mael dosed in and out of consciousness on some schedule that he couldn't rationalize in time, moving in and out of dreamscapes that often felt more like alternate realities.

"Come, Mael!"

Mael startled from unconsciousness to full alertness. Ransom stood in front of him with his hand stretched down, bidding him to take it and stand.

"Ransom," he said as he took his hand.

"It is time," Ransom said.

Mael rose with the help of his hand and suddenly they were standing in the bright sunlight overlooking a vast emptiness, as far as he could see. He shielded his eyes from the burning light. Asolara was behind him, and before him the landscape undulated between deep canyons and striated walls of rock, forbidding and empty. On the distant horizon, faintly visible behind the curtains of the sky, a magnificent, snow covered mountain, with several peaks, rose from the edge of the desert.

Mael turned to face Asolara. They were standing on a ridge. The land in front of him sloped down to meet the sea, perhaps a daysmarch away. Far out toward the horizon, a thin wedge of land interrupted the line between the sea and sky for only a short distance. Nothing moved in the vast world around them. No sound met his ears. The pure and undefiled smell of stone and sand surrounded him in the brilliant light. Ransom still held his hand.

"Do you know this place?" Ransom asked.

"It feels like home—but I don't think I've been here before."

"Look north again, Mael."

Ransom dropped his hand as he turned.

"Can you see the crown?"

A shudder ran from his neck to his toes. The Crown of Tessalindria! "I only dreamed that I would ever see it."

Ransom nodded.

Mael stared at the distant peaks. "Is the Grand Elia Margah as beautiful as the legends say?"

"The legends fail to do it justice."

"Can we go there?"

"When it is time."

Mael looked down into the burning, tortured landscape that lay before him. The NarEl Wastes. "Are the legends about the Wastes true?"

Ransom smiled. "Depends, of course."

"From the Vishtoenvar rebellion?" Mael asked as he looked up at Ransom.

Ransom nodded.

"Can you tell me what is true?"

"You know the truth, Mael." Ransom spoke through clenched teeth as he stared out over the barren land before them. A tear formed in his eye. Mael waited.

"It was envy, Mael—a lust for power, a dissatisfaction with the glories that the eladra shared in the creation of this world. When Vishtoenvar realized that this creation, and the beauty that the eladra had built into it, were destined for the pleasure of the mankind, whom Mah'Eladra had placed in it, he rebelled. He incited the mankind into disobedience, as he also did on Terra. He drew others with him and rampaged through the land south of the crown, scorching what they had built down to the rocks and sand.

"The great war followed, as Mah'Eladra sent out the faithful legions to put an end to the madness. Vishtoenvar and his followers were finally driven out across the sea to Mooriman, where they built their stronghold surrounded by the ocean on all sides. Mah'Eladra let them stay, and forbade their travel to any other lands on Tessalindria for a time. The mankind, driven from the Wastes, travelled north and settled the city of Fazdeen."

"Fazdeen is real?"

"Yes. From there they spread out. Wise men kept order in Fazdeen to keep the remnants of obedience to Mah'Eladra intact. Those who disliked the confinement of order, were allowed to leave, but never allowed to return. From there, the mankind spread to all of Tessalindria. Today, they await the arrival of the anthara from the prophecies."

"I know the prophecies."

Ransom nodded. "I know you do."

Mael stared out over the Wastes. "Am I to cross them today?"

"No, Mael—when you return."

A slight breeze rose up the warm slopes behind them, to warm his back, driven by the heat of Asolara on the south facing slopes. It smelled of sand, stone, and the ocean. He suddenly noticed the hints of wild lavender and cypress. Mael breathed deeply.

As he gazed across the Wastes, a slight movement caught his eye. "Look!" he pointed down into the wastes and glanced sideways to see if Ransom had noticed.

Ransom was gone! Mael whirled a full turn. Ransom was nowhere. He turned his eyes back into the Wastes.

The movement he had noticed was a man, and now he was standing on a large stone, waving both arms. Mael glanced around again—still no sign of Ransom. When he looked back, the man was beckoning him to come.

Mael tried to guess how far away he was. Distances were deceiving in the brilliantly clear air. Mael waited. The man made no effort to move toward him, but beckoned again when Mael caught his eye.

Unease crept into his vorn. Where had Ransom gone? Was that him on the rock? Had he not just explained that Mael wouldn't cross the Wastes today?

The man cupped his hands to his mouth. "Come!" he shouted. His voice echoed through the deep canyons and arrived in Mael's ears as a faint call of many voices, not unlike the voice that told him to obey, but it was different.

"Come!" the man shouted again.

The echoes rattled through Mael's mind. Indecision was cowardice. He was here for a reason; there always was a reason with Ransom, and he was alone—also for a reason.

Mael started his descent into the Wastes. What should have been a trail was little used and neglected, covered with loose stones the size of his fist and washed with sand that made it slippery on the hard packed clay. He looked up. The man hadn't moved from his perch on the stone, but he squatted on his heels as he watched Mael approach.

It was farther than Mael expected—hot and dry, and he had no water. The rocks around him shimmered in the blistering rays of Asolara. Sweat on his back and arms gathered the dust from his hurried descent. His footsteps echoed in the empty Wastes, as showers of sand and pebbles cascaded down the rocks below his path. Nothing else moved. Even the man on the rock.

Who could this be—in this forsaken wilderness in the mid-day sun? Where had Ransom gone? Why was he drawn to this stranger? What would he say when he met him?

The ground leveled out, the path twisting and turning between the boulders and shallow canyon walls that were high enough that he could not see over them. The man remained unmoving as he moved closer, in and out of his sight as he wound along the path, until finally he emerged into an opening in front of the large boulder. The man was standing now. He was huge.

Mael stopped. The man stared at him. "Why have you come here?" Dark tones of anger and malice rippled through his voice. A black cloak wrapped around him with the hood pulled over his head as he towered above Mael from the stone that was twice Mael's height.

"You beckoned me come, from the ridge." Mael flung his hand backward without taking his eyes off the man.

"You were surveying my domain."

"I've never seen the Wastes before."

"Do you know who I am?" The man's voice rumbled with the same thick darkness as the robe parted to reveal his hands. In his left was a large hammer and in his right was a black whip.

Suddenly Mael knew. "You are darkness, and nothingness. You are waste. You are the Fallen One. They call you Vishtoen-var."

The giant leapt from his perch on the stone and landed on the ground five paces in front of Mael. The ground shook from the impact and Mael nearly lost his balance.

"Why have you come here, Mael from Farhantra? It is not yet time." The voice reeked of anger. Without warning, the whip curled out in front of him and snapped hard, barely a hand's breadth in front of Mael's nose, and the hammer spun down, hitting the ground like thunder.

Mael startled and stumbled back as the enemy took another step forward.

"Answer me!"

The words of Vishtalar percolated up through his memory—Vishtalar his friend and guardian. "*He cannot touch you, Mael. He will threaten you, and move upon you, but hold your ground. He has no power that you do not give to him!*"

Mael trembled, but stood up straight. "I was brought here—to see this place that I must cross."

"And who brought you here?"

Mael hesitated. Vishtoenvar had apparently not seen Ransom on the ridge.

"Who brought you here□" the whip snapped in front of his face again, dangerously close. Mael stepped forward.

"Ransom, the ancient one, who was and is and will be!" Mael wasn't sure how he knew to say that.

Vishtoenvar seemed to grow larger. "The liar! The imposter. He who is the father of all lies!" The hammer thundered to the ground again, shifting the stone under Mael from the hammer's impact. Vishtoenvar leapt forward as Mael fought for his balance.

Mael held up his hand. "No closer! You cannot touch me, for my time is not come!"

Vishtoenvar reared back, looking to the sky and shaking his hammer toward it. The whip writhed back and forth on the ground as it if were alive. He roared into the nothingness. "Vakatar insa mendar!" and vanished with a burst of foul smoke that roiled outward, rolling over Mael to suffocate him for a brief moment.

Mael closed his eyes and coughed several times before rising from his knees. There was no sign of his adversary. He shivered in the hot sun, surrounded by the brilliant, deathly stillness of the NarEl Waste.

He stood without moving. His hands trembled. Tears rolled down his cheek. He wanted to run, but there was no reason, and no direction that made sense. He waited.

His senses cleared. He needed to go back to the ridge. He turned back to the path and suddenly he was somewhere else, and Ransom stood beside him again and they were walking through a city whose radiance he could not have imagined. Everything glowed. The colors burned brilliant to where he had to shield his eyes.

Layers upon layers of depth seemed to pulse before him, and the streets rose upward in all directions from where they walked.

"Do you remember this?" Ransom's voice was like the sound of a waterfall.

Mael was about to say no, when a glimmer of some ancient memory surfaced briefly and vanished. "I don't know," he said.

Then it happened again. He had been here, somehow, some-time.

Ransom was quiet, as if he knew what was happening.

Another wave, more intense than the first two swept over Mael. He was sure he had been here now, but the memories were not connected to a time.

A fourth wave washed over him; a fifth, more complete and more detailed.

They turned a corner and before them, an enormous spiral staircase of gold rose out of the glittering pavement. Mael stopped. "The Golden Stair!" he uttered without knowing where it came from.

Ransom smiled.

"The Grand Elia Margah!" Mael's eyes drifted up the spiral. The eight peaks of the crown surrounded its base as it rose up and vanished into the deep sky.

Ransom turned to him and grasped both his upper arms with his strong hands. "Never forget to remember, Mael!"

The vision vanished. They stood in the dark temple prison cell, Ransom still holding his arms. "Never forget to remember!" was left to hang in the air as Ransom vanished from the cell, plunging Mael into near darkness.

Mael turned to face the slit of soft light that filtered through high up on the door. He walked to the door and knocked on it. "Open this door," he said.

A face appeared at the small window as if the guard were checking on his presence.

"Open this door!"

A jangle of keys, a screech of the lock, and the squeal of rusty hinges opened the door before him. He walked out. The two guards stood like dead men, unaware that they could no longer restrain their small prisoner.

Chapter Thirty-Five

ESCAPE

"The marriage covenant is as strong as death."

It Is Said

Sessasha

Mael's journey up from the temple cells had been unimpeded, as if the way had been cleared just for him, but the frenetic courtyard of the temple smothered Mael with its busyness as he weaved through the throngs gathered there.

Coupled with the sense of freedom, was the awareness that for the first time since arrival in the tomb, he was profoundly alone in the crowd, and a hostility pervaded the court that he hadn't felt before. The fresh memory of his encounter with the lord of darkness in the NarEl Wastes was real and present. Vishtoenvar wasn't here, but his minions and those trapped in his schemes were. He'd been banished from Terra when Ransom died, though Mael didn't understand how he could know that.

Two days in the prison left him bewildered about what might have happened to the brothers, and where they might be. Instinct told him to go to the garden, so he headed toward the Golden Gate.

The unease heightened as he approached the gate, an unease that he had only felt once before.

Mael stopped in the shade of the east portico and looked up. The cloudless, morning sky divulged no hint of gulls. He had no idea how close he was to the ocean, where he might expect messenger gulls but perhaps a different bird served the darkness here. He could feel their presence but could not see any source for his uneasiness.

He moved toward the gate in the relative calm of the portico, eyeing his surroundings, but even in the deep shade against the eastern wall, the feeling wouldn't go away. Perhaps it wasn't birds, but something else.

Twenty paces from the gate he stopped and backed up against the wall, looking out into the crowds in the temple court. He wondered if it would be safer in the throngs than standing alone where he was.

"You there!" The tone of the voice told Mael everything. He bolted from the wall and into the crowds.

"Stop!"

Mael wouldn't stop. He knew he couldn't. He dodged into the crowds, weaving between the people, changing direction frequently and ducking under the tables of the moneychangers to emerge on the other side in a full run. He headed south across the open courtyard. Several voices joined in the pursuit. He dared not look back.

In front of him, the gate with the staircase led down to the street. As he approached the gate, he slowed, not wanting to cause suspicion by his haste. Midway through the gate, the bugles sounded. The guards jumped to the gate, pushing travelers aside in their haste to shut it. They pushed Mael through with several others, and the gates rumbled shut behind him. The heavy bars dropped in place on the far side. Mael stayed with the slug of those outside the gate. Their faces showed their frustration at being shut out.

"Wonder what that's all about!"

"I dunno—the Ermans messing with us again."

"Must be serious."

"Kiephus will be furious."

"How long do you s'pose it will be this time."

"I'm not waitin'..."

The enclave of those at the gate turned down the staircase. Mael breathed deeply. Whatever it was, it was on the other side of the gate. He turned with the crowd.

A hand gripped his upper arm and adrenaline snapped through his startled body. He tried to pull free, but the hold was too strong.

"Mael! It's me!" Bieter's voice. "I was sent here to find you."

Mael shuddered and relaxed into the grip of the friendly hands. "How did you know...?"

"The Master told me to wait outside the gate and to bring you with me when you came."

"Where are we going?"

Bieter bent over and whispered. "The others are there already, waiting for you."

"Where?"

Bieter relaxed his grip and dropped his hands into an easy saunter. "You'll see." He said with a smile.

"I missed several days with the brothers."

"We know—we prayed for you."

"Did you know where I was?"

"Yes."

"Did the Master tell you about our visit to Tessa?"

"Nobody was able to visit you in prison."

Mael nodded. Times like this became more frequent and no-
ticeable, as if Bieter hadn't heard his question. He decided not to
pursue it.

As the clump of travelers from the temple thinned in different
directions, Bieter led Mael down a road through a shallow valley
heading south. They left the walls of the city behind them and the
buildings thinned. Dust rose off the dry road from the shuffling of
many feet. Asolara scorched the air that cascaded down the rising
ground to either side of them.

"Why can't you tell me where we are going?"

"Would you even know if I told you?"

Bieter moved fast and Mael struggled to keep up . "Well, no,
actually."

"You'll see."

Bieter injected a humor into his voice, and Mael suddenly
noticed once again that he could see the light that flowed down
Bieter's tunic. It was blue with yellow streaks, cascading down
like a spring waterfall, like the light surrounding Nicodemus, but
brighter. Those that were still in the path were not like this at all.
Most of them shed an uninteresting gray brown, as if there were
no light in them at all. The visible state of the vorns of these men
and woman pulled on him with a weight of compassion he'd never
felt before.

He looked down. He could see no such aura on himself, but
felt the pull of those around him, weighing on his shoulders and
clinging to his cloak, pulling him down. He wanted to stop and
touch them, to talk with them, to lift them up and give them light,

but Bieter marched on in front of him, oblivious to the burdens that assaulted him from all sides.

"Bieter ... do you feel the people all around you?"

"What do you mean?

"The people, those in front of us, and behind—the ones that come toward us and pass us. Do you feel the grayness of their lives—the emptiness?"

Bieter stopped and turned to look at Mael. His eyes brightened in astonishment and glanced quickly at a woman and her son that were passing him. He closed his eyes and shook his head slightly before opening them again. He didn't move.

"What?" Mael asked.

"For a second—just an instant," Bieter said, "you were shedding light, like the master does since his resurrection—and the people on the road, I saw... I saw... nothing."

"Nothing?"

"They were gray—empty, 'like sheep without a shepherd' as the master says—and then it was gone." Bieter closed his eyes and shook his head again. "Come, we'll have to hurry now. We don't want to miss the brothers."

Mael walked along beside Bieter, pondering what Bieter had just said. Apparently, here on Terra, the followers of Ransom would start to see the world through Ransom's eyes. Mael first saw this when he met with Kiephus and the other two teachers. That Bieter saw it but only briefly, was curious. For Mael, it was now a continuous spectacle. Bieter's body still shed the warm yellow and blue cascade as they walked. Mael had never noticed Ransom shedding such light.

The silence of their southward journey ended abruptly as they approached a bend in the road, obscured by a thicket of dense brush. A cry of pain, followed by wailing, erupted into the otherwise still landscape.

Mael's skin tingled and Bieter straightened and started running toward the bend. As they came around the thicket, the wail erupted again. "Please...Please...No..."

In the middle of the road stood a man, holding the hair of a woman on the top and he was beating her with his fist. She tried to back away, but he held fast, swearing in the name of Elohim and striking her again.

Bieter ran forward without a word, and with the full force of his running body struck the man just below the shoulders, sending him tumbling to the ground as he released the woman's hair. She backed away, her hands covering her face, searching to find the cloth that had covered her hair.

The man scrambled to his feet, his fists raised either to defend himself or perhaps to strike back at Bieter who now stood, calm, but breathing heavily between the man and the woman. The man was considerably smaller than Bieter, apparently restrained by the presence of his oversized adversary. "You have no right!" he snapped at Bieter.

"But you have the right to beat this woman?" Bieter countered.

"She's my wife!"

The woman fell to the ground on her knees, and sobbed as she continued to cover her face with her hands.

"Is this true?" Bieter asked over his shoulder as he kept his eyes fastened on the man.

"Yes," the woman said between sobs.

Bieter shook his head. "What has she done to deserve such treatment?" he asked.

The man held his posture of opportunistic aggression. "We're on our way to see the priests to get a divorce. I have the papers in my tunic."

Bieter shook his head in disbelief. "What has she done to deserve this?"

"She is refusing to come with me. I've had to drag her this far—seven leagues already, and I'm tired of her rebellion."

"What has she done to deserve divorce?"

"In four years she has born me no children—and she doesn't know how to cook or keep our domestic affairs. I have many justified complaints."

"Has she been unfaithful to you?"

The man hesitated. "Not that I know. But what would you know about it?" his face turned dark again. Dark gray strands cascaded from his ears and chin, rolling down to vanish into the ground.

"I am married," said Bieter. "I know a lot about it."

"You are not married to *her*!" the man growled as he pointed at his wife.

"You're right. I am married to my own wife, whom I chose, as you must have this woman. My wife isn't perfect—we also have no children after seven years. She is also not the greatest cook, but I am not starving because of it, and neither are you."

The man hesitated. "Get out of my way!"

"No!"

"The Law says I can divorce her—if I am not pleased with her."

"I am sure you have heard that, but it has not been that way from the beginning."

"Who says otherwise?"

"Mosess—Yahweh—that should be enough."

"The priests say that I can divorce her for any reason, as long as I serve papers. The priests speak for Yahweh."

"What is your name?"

"That doesn't matter."

"His name is Samuel—Mirabel."

Mael started at the clarity of the intrusion. "Names always matter, Samuel," he said as stepped up beside Bieter. "Mirabel has done nothing to warrant your divorce serving. Was not Sarah barren for many years before she had Isaac? As was Hannah, the mother of your namesake? There are others too. It's the province of Elohim to provide children."

Samuel took a step backward, glancing quickly back and forth between Mael and Bieter, who looked down at Mael. Samuel's face flickered with surprise before it turned dark again, as the gray cascade on his cloak became a shade darker and intensified. "You, a foreigner, would judge me?"

"It is Yahweh who judges, those who have given you the law. Moses allowed divorce because the hearts of the people were hard, like yours. He preferred divorce to the horrors of abuse and neglect, but this was never the preference of Yahweh."

"And just what *does* Yahweh want?" Samuel sneered. He had lowered his hands, but his belligerent posture framed his words.

"Yahweh wants you to honor the covenant you made with Mirabel to be her husband—to take her and protect her in the same way that Yahweh has been the covenant husband and protector of your nation, even when your people were rebellious and imperfect. Yahweh chose your people, not because you would be a perfect bride, but because he loved you, as you once loved Mirabel. He loved you even when your people played the harlot with the Baals and other false gods of the nations surrounding you."

Samuel scowled.

Mael continued. "Yet Mirabel has remained faithful to you, even while you cavort with the young women you meet in the market, with whom you lay before returning to your bride to accuse her of ruining dinner! When they are with child, you pay to have the child hidden or destroyed."

Bieter took a step back, a look of astonishment sweeping over his face. The gray cascade falling off Samuel's shoulders, changed to a shade of light purple and his eyes fell. Mael heard Mirabel struggling to rise to her feet behind him. Samuel fell to his knees, weeping, with tears of agony coursing down his face between fits of rage and despair.

"You are a prophet!" Mirabel gasped as she wiped tears from her eyes.

Mael stepped forward and stood looking down at Samuel who buried his face in his hands. "By all rights, she could be the one divorcing you, but even this is not the way of Yahweh. The way of Yahweh is forgiveness and acceptance. Rise up, Samuel. Go and sin no more."

Samuel rose, but not in repentance. He launched himself up against Mael, striking him hard on the side of his head with his clenched fist. Mael stumbled and fell backward. Samuel pounced on him, pounding with his fists. Mirabel shrieked. Bieter leapt forward, grabbed Samuel's cloak at the back of his neck with both hands and lifted him off Mael to toss him to the side like a rag doll. He crumbled to the ground sobbing hysterically.

Bieter bent and lifted Mael. Mael felt the swelling on his cheeks and a gash where one of the strikes had broken open the old wound from the Mooriman official's ring.

"Are you alright?" Bieter asked

Mael nodded and straightened his cloak, before walking over to Samuel.

"Mael!" Bieter's voice overflowed with panic.

"Stand up, Samuel!" Mael ordered. "You can be forgiven if you change. Mirabel will accept you in love. A year from now she will be with child, a handsome son, who will fear Yahweh and honor the true Israel with his life. You will name him Mael."

Samuel looked up, his eyes flowing with tears. He nodded. He stood up and looked at Mirabel. He opened his arms as he approached her. She hesitated.

"It's alright, Mirabel," Mael said.

Samuel embraced his wife. He wept and sobbed between bouts of profuse apologies. "I'm sorry... I'm so sorry...so sorry ..."

Mirabel stared at Mael over Samuel's shoulder through her tears. "Thank you," she mouthed silently. Mael nodded.

Chapter Thirty-Six

BETHLEHEM

"'But you, Bethlehem Ephrathah, though you are small among the clans of Judah, out of you will come for me one who will be ruler over Israel, whose origins are from of old, from ancient times.'"

Micah, Prophet to Israel.

Peter tugged on Mael's sleeve. "Time to move on," he whispered as he bent over to Mael's ear.

Mael watched the couple as they embraced, nodding to Mirabel as she stared at him. He turned toward Peter as he nodded down the road. His eyes were shot with tears that swelled his cheeks. "Why is the mankind so cruel—so unfaithful to the ways of Yahweh?"

Peter didn't have an answer—at least one that satisfied him. "I guess they have been left to wander. The shepherds of Yahweh have been false, tolerating misdeeds and explaining away the love of the father of life for their false rules."

Mael nodded as he stared down the road in front of them. "One of your prophets was told to marry a prostitute, which he did in obedience to Yahweh."

"Hosea. How do you know about Hosea?"

"When she left him, he could have divorced her, for her infidelity."

Peter nodded.

Mael continued: "But Yahweh told him to go find her and pay silver to bring her back to live with him. This is the force of the marriage covenant. It's not something to be trifled with."

"How do you learn these things, Mael?"

"I don't know, Peter. I find myself learning as I speak."

"You were brilliant back there. I wish I had your courage."

Mael nodded and fell silent for a few steps. "You'll have courage when you need it, Peter."

"What do you mean?"

"You will be given the spirit of Yahweh, to live in you."

"How do you know?—when?"

"Do you remember seeing the gray lines falling off people on the road, as we walked along?"

"Yes, that was very strange."

"As much as I understand, that is the spirit, guiding your mind to see spiritual realities. It will become more real."

"Do you see it also?"

"All the time now. In my world we call it the El of Mah'Eladra."

"Your world?"

"I am not from here, Peter."

Peter hesitated and Mael turned to stare at him.

"A whole other world?"

Mael nodded.

"Impossible."

"Perhaps—Perhaps not. Where are we going, by the way?"

Peter wanted to pursue the conversation, but was just as happy to get back to the objective of their journey after the interruption by Samuel and Mirabel. "South, to meet with the brothers and sisters. The Master wants to meet us for more teaching about his kingdom. Jerusalem is getting hot and he thought we might meet away for a few days."

"You can't tell me?"

"I have never been there myself."

"But you know where you are going?"

Peter nodded. "I have instructions." They were easy enough, but not to somewhere he knew. They would pass through Bethlehem before finding the road Jesus had told him to follow to their destination.

Mael nodded. He had spoken little since the confrontation with Samuel, as if the encounter weighed heavy on him. "What are you thinking, Mael?"

"Samuel and Mirabel—perhaps they should never have married." Mael kept his eyes straight ahead, as Peter glanced at him.

"We asked the master about that," Peter reflected.

"And what did he say?"

"He said that marriage is not for everyone—that there would be some who would remain unmarried for the sake of his kingdom. Marriage takes time and commitment and that sacred commitment would challenge a person's commitment to the purposes of his kingdom."

"I can see where that would be true."

"Are you? Were you ever married?"

"No."

"What is it like where you come from? Similar to here?"

"Very similar, I think. If a man treated his wife as Samuel did—"

"Mirabel."

"Yes, Mirabel... he would be beaten by the priests. It seems harsh, but marriage is highly honored."

"Are there no divorces?"

Mael paused. "In a few cases, but it is very rare—certainly not allowed for the reasons that Samuel cited. Even the civil courts uphold this as a requirement for social order. So marriage is taken very seriously."

The traverses up and down the frequent wadis in the bleak desert extended the walking distance considerably. Peter was feeling the effects in his legs and back. They needed to get to Bethlehem before the gates closed, or it would be a long, cold night in the desert.

"Don't worry, Peter," Mael said. "The town you seek is just beyond the top of this gully. We will be there soon."

"How do you know?"

Mael had his head down and was shuffling now, obviously tired from the walk and from the beating by Samuel. "It's there," was all he said.

Peter pressed on. He had not seen any town in front of them from the far side of the wadi, but in the desert, not noticing something was meaningless to reality. Mael may have seen it, but then Mael had peculiar insight into many things that baffled him. How he knew Samuel's and Mirabel's names was beyond him.

The temperature had dropped as the sun made its way lower with each descent in the landscape, but as they came over the southern crest of the wadi, Bethlehem came into view, nestled into the desert about three hundred paces in front of them. The gates were still open but not for long. The sun hung just above the skyline to the west.

"We should hurry!" he said to Mael.

Mael nodded and broke into a slow jog. Peter joined him. They would shut the gates when the last hint of the sun fell out of sight.

As they approached the gates, the guards started waving at them to hurry. Mael sped up. Peter had to run to keep up with him. By the time they got there, the guards were already pulling the gates shut with enough room for them to get through. "You just made it!" The guard smiled.

Peter bent over with his hands on his knees to catch his breath.

"Glad we made it," Mael said.

Peter looked up. Mael showed no shortness of breath or any other indication that he had strained. Peter shook his head and looked down. "Now we need to find a place to stay for the night."

"We've made a mistake." Bieter's voice was hushed in the din of the dining room in the inn they had chosen.

Mael was happy to be inside, out of the chill of the night that had settled around them as they sought out some place to stay. It was inexpensive, as they had been told, but Mael understood Bieter. This was Bethlehem's brothel, subtle but clear. All the women serving food would later be serving the desires of the men sitting at the tables. There were few women patrons.

Dinner was simple and hearty: a lamb stew, flavored with savory herbs with a thick dark sauce with turnip cubes and raisins. Bread was plentiful and wine; seemingly as much as one wanted. Small bowls of olives and savory nuts adorned every table, each with a small flickering oil lamp that helped light the room.

"We have to be careful," Bieter continued, "this is a dangerous place for those like you and I. Cheap but dangerous."

Mael nodded. "The food is good," he said as he took another spoonful of the stew.

"It always is. It's part of the hook."

"The hook?"

"They draw people in with good food, then the women do their thing."

"What's your name?" Bieter asked the young woman who came to their table.

"Miriam."

"Nice name."

She smiled, "Do you need anything else?"

"Some water," Mael suggested.

"Water?" Her dark eyes flashed and she cocked her head as if she had not heard.

"Just water." Mael repeated.

"Is something wrong with the wine?"

Mael looked at her again. "I don't know. I've not tasted it."

Miriam shook her head.

Peter nodded. "The wine is fine. My friend doesn't always drink wine."

Miriam bobbed her head. The long curly locks of auburn that hung down over her shoulders bounced. They pulled Mael's eyes downward from her face to her chest where they came to rest for a moment before he turned them quickly away. Miriam turned away to get their drinks.

Something flickered in his vorn and he looked up at Peter. "Careful, Mael."

Mael's eyes fell. He nodded.

"These girls are professionals, Mael. Their job is to make you look. When you look, you wonder. When you wonder you wander. When you wander, you fall. They're very good at it."

"What does the master teach about this?"

Bieter broke one of the small loaves and handed half to Mael. "In remembrance of his body."

Mael nodded. "His body," he said.

"When the master taught about this, most people thought he was making somewhat of a joke. He told us that if you have a problem controlling your eyes, gouge them out, because it's better to enter the eternal kingdom blind than to have both eyes and not enter at all."

"Seems severe."

Bieter nodded as he chewed his bread. "We all chuckled. Nice hyperbole to make a point. The master was serious. He later explained to us that this failure to treat women respectfully, flooding your mind with selfish human desire, is so serious that if you have to lose an eye over it, you should. If you took out one of your eyes, you would probably think twice about looking again. Then he went on to point out, that you always have a choice. If you want to save your eye, simply do not allow it to wander."

"That could be hard." Mael stirred his stew with his spoon.

"Self-discipline is hard. It's *always* hard, but it will save you an eye or two, and your vorn in eternity.

"A good way to look at it, for sure." Mael knew this was true. It was the same teaching from the Kirrinath, but the brief encounter of his eyes with Miriam's breasts, even under her tunic swirled before him. It was no longer a passing thought, but a burning image, seeking to master his mind.

Bieter stared at him. "You have to master it, Mael, or it will master you. There's always a master when you are being tempted, but you always have a choice about whom it will be: your passion, your lust—or your mind centered on the will of Yahweh. It's *your* choice, and *you* are always responsible for the choice you make."

Bieter sopped the bottom of his bowl with the last bit of bread.

Mael watched Bieter, as he tried to suppress the images that pursued his attention. This had happened before, but it was several years in the past:

"Have you ever thought about getting married, Ma?" Yander didn't make eye contact, but continued her hoeing around the young potato plants in the garden plot behind her house.

Mael paused his mind but not his hands, as he gently packed the loose soil up over the fledgling potatoes. "I don't know—"

"How can you not know?"

"It's crossed my mind. Do you like being married?"

"Four years now—I'm getting used to it."

Mael laughed. "Getting used to it▫"

"Well, it's a bigger commitment than I thought when it happened."

"You better explain that."

Yander paused to wipe the sweat off her face, then leaned on her hoe. "You've heard the stories about how amazing it is—two people who say they love one another and get married."

Mael sat on the ground between the potato rows, crossed his legs and leaned forward to listen.

"Many mistake the passion for love—that passion and desire to be with this other person. To sleep in the same bed, if you know what I mean."

Mael nodded.

"But love has to be a decision, not a passion."

"What do you mean?"

Yander wiped her brow again and returned to her hoeing.

"I had to discover this because the passion can be very fleeting, short episodes. When one is not married, one can feel that passion when they are with someone, and create the illusion in their mind that it will be like this continuously if I get married."

"And?"

"There is little passion in hoeing in the potatoes," she laughed, "or making bread, or feeding the family three times a day or when Salua is busy being a tailor and comes home angry, because some

Mooriman highborn kept him late sewing thirty gold buttons on his undershirt."

Mael smiled. "Happens to all of us, now and then."

"Right and that is when you realize that love is not passion. It's commitment. It's covenant—a promise."

Mael rocked forward and crawled to the next set of young plants. "And to be honest, it's distracting."

"Distracting?"

"There are so many things I could be doing, if I had not made this commitment." Yander stopped and leaned on her hoe again. "Look at you! You are free to do what you want. You can come over here and help me, which is great, and you can spend hours at the temple talking to the priests about—whatever—"

"You're convincing me that being married might not be best," Mael laughed.

"I asked you if you ever considered it."

"Well, once—at least I think I felt that passion that you speak of."

"Who was it?" Yander's voice floated a tease across a couple rows of green.

"Not telling."

"Don't be foolish. Erolin?" Yander chuckled.

Marrying Erolin had honestly never ever crossed his mind. "What☐ No!—but still not telling."

"I'm your sister, Ma. This is ridiculous!"

"It was fleeting."

"And?

Mael hesitated. She had a point. There would be no harm done … "It was Inoa."

"The baker's daughter☐"

The incredulity in Yander's voice caused him to pause. "You want to hear this or not☐"

Yander nodded. "Sorry," she leaned into her hoeing again. Mael pushed more dirt. This was harder than he thought.

"This was before she was married, of course—I'm guessing we were sixteen" he started. "We were good friends, but there had never been any passion. I was working late at the smithy and she came to pick up a bread knife that Fada had refurbished and sharpened; the handle was loose."

Yander remained silent. Mael knew she was listening.

"She came in—I was alone—we exchanged pleasantries. I gave her the knife, wrapped safely in a parcel skin and when I looked up, she was staring into my eyes. Suddenly, she seemed to be the most beautiful young woman in the whole city of Farhantra, with her long black hair tied back with a purple ribbon. Her eyes were on fire. I wanted to touch her. I didn't want her to leave—it seemed as if she felt the same.

"Then she dropped her eyes and flushed. 'Thanks for the knife,' she mumbled and turned away. 'My father will pay for it tomorrow.' She vanished out the door.

"I didn't know what to do. I wanted to go after her, but could not leave the fire." He paused—more lose dirt around the potatoes.

"And then?"

Mael continued, slowly. "For about a week, I could not escape the desire to see Inoa again. I went by the bakery. She was pleasant, but furtively distant, as if she'd been told to stay away from me. It hurt. I was sure there was more—over time it faded. She got engaged to Ranaas, and that was the end."

"No others?"

"No, that was enough. I am so busy at the forge with Fada, and spend as much time as I can at the temple. That all seems so much more important. And now I have this sense that there is something big—something much bigger for my life, I cannot imagine being married."

"As long as you are not just being lazy."

Mael looked up. "What□"

"A lot of other men your age aren't married because they are just lazy. They know the commitment and are afraid of it. They would not make good husbands anyway. They go to the Mooriman brothels and waste themselves there instead of doing the hard work of being married."

Thoughts of Erolin now flooded Mael's mind, intermingled with the images of Miriam that he was trying to displace. Mael was surprised at the difficulty of getting control over either of them.

He looked up. "You're married, Bieter—does being married help?

"Some, but not as much as people claim, I still have to be careful—but yes, it does help to have a wife to go home to—that I can remember and think about."

"What about out here, away from home—does that make it harder."

Bieter nodded as he chewed the last bite of bread and stared into Mael's eyes. "It never goes away—the challenge of thinking rightly about women."

"We might have tried to stay somewhere else." Mael said.

"We tried several places, right?" Bieter noted.

"Yes. Do you really think this is the only place with vacancies?"

"Seems that way—" Bieter leaned across the table and lowered his voice. "When I realized what this was, I got two rooms. It would not look good for you and me to be sharing a room here."

Mael didn't like the suspicion that crept in behind his eyes as he stared back at Bieter. Bieter was a strong man, admired for his commitment to the teachings of the master, but Mael, feeling his own weakness, projected that weakness onto Bieter. He knew it wasn't right. Bieter's comment that he would take responsibility for his own thoughts and attitudes—his actions, felt hollow. Whether Bieter could read his thoughts, Mael didn't know.

"We need to rise very early," Bieter said, "the others were expecting us tonight and I want to get there as early as possible."

"How early?"

"It's been a long day. We should get to sleep early we can be on our way when they open the gates half an hour before Asolara is up to trouble us with her heat."

"That would be wise." Mael pushed his stool back and stood up. Bieter fished in his cloak and drew out three copper coins. "That's a lot, isn't it?"

Bieter nodded. "The extra may dissuade our friend from trying to visit us."

"Maybe it will encourage her."

Beiter stared down. "Keep your door locked, Mael. That would be the best discouragement."

Sleep eluded Mael. The single latticed window in his tiny room was slightly open, but afforded little light. It didn't need to be darker to sleep, but the discussion at dinner and the images of Miriam tormented Mael's vorn. Flickering memories of Erolin flitted in and out between his tossing and turning on the hard bed. It all seemed too preposterous.

He thought back to Inoa and what would have happened to her if they had married. Right now, she was with Ranaas. They had a boy and a girl. The world they lived in was oppressive but safe. Mael could not say the same for the path he was traveling, unfettered, but dangerous.

He rolled over again, tortured by his errant mind as it wandered aimlessly from one fantasy to another. Where was sleep? He should be exhausted ...

The knock on the door was so slight, he thought twice before he concluded that it was real. He stood up beside the bed. The second knock was more definitive.

Bieter's warming swam before him. '*Keep your door locked, Mael*'.

"**OPEN THE DOOR, MAEL!**" The words knifed through the confusion.

Mael hesitated. The knock came a third time.

"OPEN THE DOOR, MAEL!"

He breathed deeply and lifted the hook on the lock as quietly as he could. He cracked the door to look out. Miriam didn't wait. She pushed the door open enough to come through, then stepped in front and backed up to close the door behind her.

Fear flickered through her eyes, illuminated by the single candle that she carried. She wore a pale blue hooded robe, pulled around her and held closed by her arms that pulled tight against her body. The long locks of curly auburn hair cascaded down over her chest and her crimson lips glistened in the flame.

Mael stepped back. "Why are you here, Miriam?"

She hesitated. "I have come to be with you," she whispered.

"You look afraid."

"I am."

"I cannot be with you in that way, Miriam."

"Cannot or will not?"

"Both—either."

"Why did you open the door?"

"I was told to."

Miriam's eyes shifted. "Told to?"

"By Yahweh."

Fear darted across Miriam's face.

"You can leave if you like."

"I can't."

"Can't leave?"

Miriam's eyes fell and she pulled her arms tighter around her body. The candle flickered with the movement. "The master will beat me if I don't bring back money."

"I have no money. Bieter, the big man from dinner has what money there is."

Miriam's head fell forward as one hand came up to her face to wipe back the tears.

A wave of compassion swept over Mael. "Come, sit down on the bed."

Miriam shook her head and sniffed as she looked up.

"Don't go yet—we should talk." Mael stepped aside and motioned again to the cot. "Please—let me have the candle."

Miriam handed the candle to Mael as she moved to the bed and sat down. She stared back at Mael.

Mael set the candle carefully on the floor, and then sat cross-legged on the floor opposite her.

They stared silently at one another.

"Why did you and Bieter come here, to this place, if you didn't want the company of a woman?"

"We are passing through. This was the only place we found for the night."

"Where are you going?"

"We're following the Nazarene prophet. We're hope to find him in the desert to the south."

Miriam startled. "Chaisus from Nazaretha"

Mael nodded.

"He passed through here with his disciples two days ago."

"We're on our way to join him," Mael said.

"There was lots of talk about him."

"Talk?"

"They say he was born here. In a stable not far from here at the end of the street."

"I didn't know."

"There are lots of stories. Some of them—well, I don't know."

"What stories?"

Miriam seemed to relax. Her eyes glittered in the candle light. "They say that rich men came from far to the east to give him gifts. They say that shepherds left their flocks in the field to come see this new baby."

"I have not heard these stories," Mael said.

"Herod heard that he might be a king, and tried to destroy him. He came here with his soldiers and they killed many babies, but he wasn't here."

"Where did he go?"

"His family ended up in Nazareth, they say. I have never been there, but Herod didn't know. Then suddenly he appears all over the place, talking about his kingdom."

Mael nodded. "That is what I want to know more about. That's why we're traveling to find him."

Miriam looked down. She sniffed as she wiped her eyes with the back of her hand.

Mael wanted to reach out and touch her.

"**Tell her.**"

Mael looked up at the ceiling. "Tell her what?"

Miriam followed his gaze up into the corner of the room. "What did you say?"

Mael looked down into her eyes. "How many men have you served here at the inn?"

"You will be the fourth." She cast her eyes down.

"Perhaps the third was the last."

"What do you mean?"

"You don't need to have this life."

Miriam started shaking. "I have no choice."

"We always have a choice."

"What choice do I have?"

"Come with us, to learn from the master—from Chaisus."

"My master would not allow it. He saved me from ruin when the Romans killed my parents. He took me in. He taught me how to be with a man to make money for him when there was nowhere for me to go."

"He taught you?"

"Yes." It was more of a whimper.

"You must leave this life, Miriam."

"I cannot."

"Cannot or will not?"

She looked up, tears brimming in her eyes and rolling down her cheeks. "Both—either. There is no forgiveness for someone like me, who has sold herself into slavery for survival."

Mael leaned forward. "There's always forgiveness—for any-thing—if you change. Chaisus teaches that."

"I can't."

"Come with us, Miriam. The master will forgive you."

"How can I come with you?"

"We are leaving before dawn, as soon as the gates open. Your cloak has a hood. When the time comes, you can climb out this window. We will meet you outside and take you with us to the master."

Miriam shook her head.

"You have to believe, to have faith, Miriam."

Her whole body shook with sobs, rising up from deep within.

Mael raised his hand to comfort her.

"**Don't touch her!**"

He pulled his hand back.

Miriam turned on the bed and simply laid down. Within seconds, she was fast asleep, curled up in a tight ball in the middle of his bed.

Mael nodded as he stood up and refastened the hook on the door. He blew out the candle and lay down on the small rug in front of the bed. It wasn't long ...

Peter knocked quietly, hoping not to wake any other visitors at the inn. A hurried scuffle came from inside. Voices? Sure-ly not! He knocked again. More hurried shuffling. "Mael?" he whispered.

More silence followed, then a crisp click as the hook was released from inside. Mael opened the door.

"I thought I heard voices."

"You did. I'm ready to go."

Peter looked over Mael's head into the empty room.

"What's going on, Mael◻"

"Outside." Mael pushed past him and walked silently toward the single window at the end of the hall. Peter followed. He had paid the night before, so there was nothing to settle with the inn. As they exited to the street, the faintest hint of color decorated the sky to the east—light compared to the darkness inside.

As they emerged, a cloaked figure rose from the bench beside the door.

"We need to hurry." Mael's voice lofted urgent.

"Who is this?" Peter said.

"Let's move," Mael said as he started down the street toward the city gate.

A woman! Her size and movement gave her away. Mael held her hand and pulled her along with unnatural urgency.

When they arrived at the gate, it was still closed. The guards looked up at the trio as they prepared the gate. "Eager to get out?" one of them asked.

Peter nodded. "Long trip ahead of us today."

"Jerusalem?" The guard organized the ropes that would lift the heavy bar that held the gate locked.

"Going south."

"Into the desert?"

Peter nodded.

"I've heard that Jesus and some of his followers are hiding out down there."

Peter nodded again.

Mael and the hooded woman remained silent.

"You going to find them?"

"If we can."

The guard turned to the three others that stood by watching. "Almost time," he said. They moved to the ropes that hung down from above. "Seldom have visitors trying to get out so early. Thanks for your patience."

"We will wait till you're ready," Peter said.

"No harm in opening a bit early." The guard smiled and nodded to the other.

"Thanks."

They pulled on their ropes. The heavy bar swung upward, pivoting on one end until it was clear of the huge gates. They tied off the ropes and moved quickly, to push the gates open, two guards on each side. "May your day be blessed," the head guard said. The other nodded.

Peter led through the gate, with Mael and the woman behind him. They walked in silence to where the road broke south, and headed into the desert toward the brightening sky.

They walked without speaking until they had rounded the city and headed south. Peter stopped abruptly and turned to face Mael. The woman pulled back her hood. Miriam!

"What is going on◻" The pent up irritation crept through Peter's voice.

"She is coming with us, to find Jesus."

"She can't."

"Why?"

Peter wasn't expecting this question. "She lives here."

"You live in Capernaum."

"You cannot just kidnap a young woman, Mael."

"I didn't kidnap her."

Peter shook his head.

"She came to my room last night—"

"I told you not to open the door."

"Yahweh said otherwise."

"What□"

"She needs to escape, Peter. The innkeeper is harsh—there's no life for her back there." Mael swung his arm back toward the walls of Bethlehem. "The master is promising freedom."

"From sin…"

"Sin includes slavery," Mael said.

They stared at each other.

"Jesus can send her back if he will not have her with us," Mael said.

"Better that she not even come."

"How can you say that?"

Peter stared down at Mael, who met his gaze with unwavering eyes. "We will let Jesus decide. Let's go."

Miriam, who had stood with her head down, awaiting the verdict, spoke for the first time. "Thank you, Peter."

Chapter Thirty-Seven

OASIS

"To those who have eyes, let them see.
To those who have ears, let them hear.
Those who do so will turn and be healed."

Jesus of Nazareth

Mael and Bieter traveled south. The desert deepened and they met fewer travelers on the road. Bieter had described the place they were looking for: a retreat in the desert where Chaisus had been before and thought was suitable as a place to spend time unhindered by the crowds. Chaisus wanted time to talk in more depth about his kingdom.

Mael wasn't sure if Bieter was fully convinced that Miriam should be allowed to come along. They had argued briefly after they were some distance from the gate. Bieter seemed angry that Mael had allowed Miriam to come into his room, even broaching the idea that the voice may have been false. He also did not seem convinced that nothing had happened between Miriam and Mael in the room. After a few rounds of arguing, they fell silent.

Miriam was quiet. She walked softly, a glowing, silent presence that Mael felt by his side. His feelings reflected those he had felt for Inoa, but he knew now, clearer than ever before, that their connection had to remain one of friendship—that Miriam had to walk a path that would forever be without him. He was going home to Tessalindria at some point. He doubted she could come with him, even if they both wanted that.

The path before her led safely out of Bethlehem, but who could know what might be in store for her in the small band that followed Chaisus. The other women would adopt her and take care of her, probably the best caretakers for any woman on Terra who needed care.

The road they traveled seemed ancient and barren.

"Domas told me it's not on any map," Bieter said.

"How will we find it?" Mael asked.

"He said it would be clear."

The departure onto the path they wanted from the main road *was* obvious. It veered off to the left into the barren, forbidding wasteland of the desert where no road should have been. Its comfortable width and unpacked surface said it had been there a long time, unused by most who traveled past it. It wound through the barren landscape without a hint that it could possibly lead anywhere except to further burning sand. Asolara had risen hot, scorching the tops of the orange rocks that poked up through the drifts of sand. The only respite from the heat was in the empty canyons as the path dipped into them.

They were in a deep chasm between two towering sentinels of rock when suddenly, the landscape opened before them into a luscious grove of palms. The ground rolled out before them with flowering plants and thick grasses that swayed in a gentle breeze that flowed toward them, enveloping them in rich scents that Mael had never encountered.

Bieter gasped and stopped.

Mael looked at Miriam. She stood staring, her mouth open in disbelief.

"Bieter! Mael!" Domas ran toward them from the path entering the grove. He ran headlong into Bieter who embraced him with the usual crushing hug that only a man the size of Bieter could deliver. "We expected you last night. Is everything alright?"

Domas hugged Mael, then turned to Miriam.

"We were delayed in Bethlehem," Bieter said. "This is Miriam."

Domas bowed. "Welcome, Miriam." He stepped forward to hug her and she shied back, lowering her head in fear.

Domas stopped.

"Miriam decided to come with us from Bethlehem, but she knows little of our ways." Mael smiled. "I'm sure she will learn more while she's here."

Domas turned. "Come," he said. "We're preparing lunch."

They followed Domas down the path through the trees and came around a corner to an opening that was a hundred paces across. It was round, ringed about the perimeter with small mud brick buildings with grass roofs. In the center was a small lake, shimmering like crystal as the breeze played across its surface.

Small cooking fires dotted its shore surrounded by many people, most of whom Mael could not remember seeing before. He guessed that there were seventy in all. He stood frozen by the sight.

Chaisus rose from the nearest fire. "Welcome friends," he said as he stepped toward them. "Bieter," he said as he hugged the big fisherman, "Your delay in Bethlehem was necessary to fulfill all righteousness. Mael, my friend. You've done well." His hug was powerful, radiating with confidence, as showers of bright yellow light cascaded off his robe.

"And Miriam!" he stepped forward to embrace her. She did not shy back. Tears ran down her cheeks as Chaisus pulled her into his hug. The faint orange streams flowing from her cloak brightened as they embraced. "You are safe here now, Miriam, daughter of Abraham." Chaisus stepped back. Miriam wept with both hands covering her face.

Mael felt the tears welling in his own eyes. Chaisus looked at him. "No tears, Mael. This is a place of refuge. Come. Lunch is served."

They joined the small group where Chaisus had been sitting. The only other persons Mael recognized were Natanial and Mary of Magdala. She rose as they approached, fixing her eyes on Miriam as if she were a long displaced friend. "Come," she said as she took Miriam's hand.

Miriam glanced at Mael with eyes that said, "Thank you", then turned to follow Mary away from the group. Two other women rose and followed. Mael wanted to go with them.

"No, Mael." Mael startled at Chaisus's words. "Come sit with us, my friend. There is lunch—and then there is much we have to do."

The afternoon brought another round of teaching by Jesus. Thomas sat with the seventy, gathered at the edge of the water on the thick green grass that lined its banks. Jesus stood with the water behind him, facing into the sun's light that illuminated him with unnatural brilliance. He told them many things about his kingdom, reminding them of things he had taught before but they had not fully understood.

Somehow, now, it was clearer—sharper, as if the retelling burned into him a memory that he was sure he would never forget.

Some of what he taught was new.

"My kingdom is like a large harbor, sheltered from the ocean, where ships come from afar, bringing their wealth into the city. Some ships bring spices, gold and myrrh, enriching the city with wealth from far away. Others bring with them pestilence, vermin and corruption. The harbor keepers begged the king to burn these ships so their pestilence would not contaminate the city.

"The king refused. 'Burning them may catch others afire and, after seeing the city, they may go out and come back with gifts. But the day will come, when we will close the harbor, and I will send out my soldiers to burn those who have not repented, and they will burn with unquenchable fire.'"

He reminded them about the light they would bring to Terra. The city, high on a hill, whose light cannot be hidden. A city that would draw everyone to gaze upon it and desire to be within its walls where there is feasting and joyous celebration of life that is life indeed.

He spoke about the pursuit of happiness, and the emptiness of seeking happiness for the sake of being happy—that happiness would be found in emptying oneself in the righteous service of others. Happiness would come from genuine mourning over the state of the world around them—that it would be found in humility rather than self-aggrandizement.

Revenge couldn't bring happiness. Revenge leads only to the ever-expanding circle of vengeance and retribution. Happiness would be found in showing mercy without judgement. It would be found in genuine forgiveness.

This kingdom was different at every level...

A sudden thunder of galloping horses arrested the discourse. Jesus looked up as all heads turned to witness the intrusion. The crowd stood up.

Seven horses galloped toward them, mounted by fierce men, in dark robes. They reigned in abruptly, about ten paces from the attendants. Jesus made his way through the group as the leader swung down from his saddle.

The leader approached, his hand resting on the hilt of a sword that hung in its scabbard from his belt, his head wrapped in a black turban. He strode up to Jesus as the other horsemen dismounted. "We have come to reclaim that which two of your followers stole from me."

Mael looked around quickly. Miriam had stepped behind Mary of Magdala, and cowered under the onslaught of the man's words.

Jesus stood up straight. "Drop your swords. You are standing on hallowed ground!" His voice rolled like thunder. Seven swords dropped from the belts of the dark men and vanished in the grass at their feet. Terror swept across their faces. "Name the theft," Jesus said, "and if what you say is true, you will be recompensed."

"Two of your disciples stole one of my women from my inn."

"Stole?—Peter! Mael! Come. Let us know of your thievery."

Mael stepped up beside the master, protected by the very force of his presence. Peter made his way to join them.

"Those are the men!"

Jesus turned to face them. His eyes burned with passion. "What did you steal from this man?"

Mael looked down. "We stole nothing, Master. We paid more than was asked for our meal and the rooms for the night. In the night, Miriam came to me, a prostitute offered by the owner of the inn—"

"I'm the owner of the inn," the man snarled.

Jesus silenced him with a wave of his hand.

"She came to my room, distressed by being offered to me for money. I talked to her about the hope of your kingdom and asked her to join us, to find refuge with your followers."

"He's a liar." The man's face flooded with rage. "He had his way with her and decided to take her along for more."

Jesus turned to the man. "Do you have proof of this?"

"It's obvious. Why else would she go with him?"

"Simeon!"

The man startled and stepped back.

"Miriam, come here," Jesus said.

Miriam stepped out from Mary's shadow and approached Jesus.

"That's her!" Simeon pointed his finger.

Jesus looked at the man. "Simeon bar Naphtali! You who capture and enslave women to sell their bodies to the lust of men. You who teach them yourself how to be with other men. You who mistreat these same women to keep them in your debt. Dare you to accuse this one who has rescued Miriam from your snare? Stand forth, pick up the stones, and start the stoning now with the woman of your own adultery, and then the thief."

Jesus pushed Miriam forward. She cried out and buried her face in her hands. Mael stepped forward to stand with her, staring into the eyes of his accuser.

Simeon fell to his knees and looked up briefly before bowing his head. "I am a sinful man."

Jesus stepped forward. "Stand up, Simeon." He gently lifted Simeon up by the chin. "Go back home; sell your possessions; set the captives free. Burn your inn, that it may never more be a source of sin for the city. Then come and join us here."

Simeon stared into his eyes for a brief moment. "I cannot."

"Will not." Jesus spoke firmly, but with compassion.

"Why would I come to live in this wasteland, with the scorpions and snakes, without water or food, to be burned by the sun? This is no kingdom! Its insanity—and we would like our swords back."

"Your swords are gone," Jesus said. "Go then, and find out what this means, 'He who lives by the sword, will die by the sword'. May you find peace."

"You're a thief like your disciples! May you die in your kingdom of sand!" Simeon retorted.

The riders mounted their horses. Simeon wheeled his horse around. The others followed him out of the oasis.

Thomas looked back toward the Oasis and, for just a moment, he saw what Simeon had seen: a barren bowl in the sand—not a hint of green as far as he could see. In the foreground stood a ragged band of men and women, baking in the heat of the sun with a few dilapidated mudbrick huts around the perimeter of a dry lakebed. Then, in a moment, in the blink of his eyes, the oasis returned, flooding his senses with its fragrance.

Thomas looked at the Master, who smiled and swept his hand over the greenery before them. "The kingdom of Elohim, Thomas. My kingdom of sand. For him who has eyes, let him see."

The next two days passed quickly in the oasis. Chaisus taught the followers in more depth about the daily life of those who would follow him. He challenged them about their devotion and the trials and persecutions that would be levied against them out of envy and jealousy, particularly by the religious leaders, both from those in Jerusalem and beyond.

On the third day, another woman straggled into the oasis. She was also from Bethlehem. She had almost made it to the water when she collapsed. Her dress was torn and burned in some areas and the hair on one side of her head had been burned off. Bruises adorned her cheeks and one eye was swollen shut. Mael was the first to see her lying on the ground, unconscious. He called for help.

A small crowd had surrounded them, watching and praying audibly. Miriam pushed through the crowd. "Adiana!"

She knelt by the woman, as tears flowed down her cheeks. "No," she sobbed, rocking back and forth on her heels. "No—Adiana!"

Chaisus arrived and walked to the front. "Do not fear. She's only sleeping." He knelt down and gently took Adiana in his arms and raised her from the ground. "She needs a bed," he said softly as he walked toward one of the buildings. "Wake up, Adiana!"

The woman's eyes fluttered open in terror.

"Bring some water," Chaisus said over his shoulder. Several women ran from the group to do as he asked.

He laid her on a small cot in the first shelter. She tried to talk. "Shhhhh," said Chaisus. "Not now." He turned to those who had followed them into the shelter. "She needs rest and water. Everyone should leave. Mael stay here with us...and Miriam."

The onlookers filed out into Asolara's light.

"She is your friend, Miriam?"

Miriam was drying her eyes with the back of her hand. "She served with me at the inn—she's a good person."

Chaisus stood and wrapped his arms around Miriam. "I am confident that she is."

"But what happened? Who would do this to her?" Miriam said.

Chaisus held her tightly. "We'll find out when she can tell us. For now we need to wait."

They sat and waited. Chaisus closed his eyes and said nothing more. Miriam wept as she held Adiana's limp hand, gently daubing her face with a wet cloth she had been given. Mael stood and watched. He wondered what Chaisus was thinking. He wondered what Miriam was feeling. Orange light flowed down her tunic and skirt, splashing onto the ground and disappearing in the sand beneath the cot. Adiana's cloak flowed with purple and luminous blue. He wondered what it meant.

Suddenly the color changed. It brightened slightly and warmed to a dull red as Adiana sat up in surprise.

"Welcome back, Adiana." Chaisus smiled. Adiana's eyes flashed in panic until she saw Miriam.

"Miriam!"

Miriam launched from her seat, discarding the daubing cloth and falling into Adiana's arms. Chaisus wiped tears from his eyes with the back of his hand. "I'll be outside," He said, his voice made husky by emotion. He rose and moved out through the door.

"Adiana, Adiana!" Miriam hugged her friend and wept. "What happened?"

Adiana shook her head as she pulled back from Miriam. "You remember Hulda? From Jerusalem?"

"Of course—is she alright?"

"I don't know—she—" Adiana looked down and moved her hands to her face. "It was horrible—"

"What happened, Adiana?"

"After you disappeared—we didn't know what happened. The master got mean. He thought we helped you escape. We didn't know, so we couldn't tell, so he beat us." She touched her face gently, feeling for the bruises. "They're gone!" She looked up at Mael, surprise fleeting through her dark brown eyes.

"What happened with Hulda?"

"He scoured the town—when he couldn't find you—the guards told him that it might have been you that left so early with two men. He beat us again until we told him what we knew—only that you had gone to one of the rooms for the night."

Miriam looked down at her hands as they twisted around one another.

"The master had us chained to our beds, while he went looking for you. He came back angry and he beat us again before the evening meal. He yelled at us that we owed him more money for a sword that he lost—he didn't explain."

Miriam shook her head. Suddenly Mael knew exactly what happened. He could visualize it as Adiana recounted the story:

"Master bought a new sword. He brought it to dinner and laid it on the table before him while he ate. When Hulda brought his dinner, and set it before him, she grabbed the sword and ran it through his heart."

Miriam gasped and leaned back, her hands covering her mouth in disbelief.

"Hulda lost control and rampaged through the dining room, smashing the oil lamps with the bloody sword. No one was armed to stop her. Everything caught fire. We ran for the doors, but they were locked. We broke the windows—the wind fanned the flames. Everyone was shouting, shoving—pushing. I climbed through one of the windows as the fire caught up with me and singed my cloak. A blast of flame burned my hair." She turned to expose the side of her face where the hair was missing.

"We stood outside and watched it all burn. Men from the town tried to put it out, but it was too hot. I didn't know that a mudbrick building could burn to the ground. There is nothing left."

"What happened to the other women?" Miriam's voice was a hoarse whisper behind the tears.

"I don't know."

"What did you do?"

"I tried to find a place to stay. No one would take me in—the reputation, you know."

Miriam nodded and sighed.

Adiana continued. "I slept on the street two nights, stealing food from gardens and paddocks. This morning, I decided to take my chances. I asked the guards which way you had gone and headed south—into the desert. I collapsed on the road from the heat, but was awakened by an angel, I think, who gave me water and told me how to find you here."

Miriam launched forward into a hug. Adiana's eyes met Mael's gaze as she looked over Miriam's shoulder from the embrace.

"You're safe here now," Mael said without breaking eye contact. "Welcome to the kingdom of Elohim."

More people came to the oasis every day—men and women. Two more refugees from the brothel in Bethlehem arrived. They told the same story, with other details. Hulda had died in the fire, trapped in the tragedy of her own making. The innkeeper's wife committed suicide two days later. The Elders of Bethlehem proposed an ordinance to ban the rebuilding of the brothel, or any other such establishment in the town.

Chaisus taught every day, new things and reminders of things already said. New parables surfaced from the deep reserves of knowledge he had.

Mostly, the disciples learned to live together, to share everything they had, to celebrate with gladness and joy of being together, away from the terrifying cultural influence of a cruel world that the mankind had made for itself on Terra.

Chaisus taught them that they would have to go back and live in this world again, but how to preserve the oasis in their hearts—how to be a kingdom that would be in the world, but called out and separate at the same time.

He did miracles among them, healed all the diseases and taught them that they could do the same with "faith", what Mael understood as armatan. Chaisus convinced them of the one he would send to them to guide them, a voice in the spiritual wind that they could listen to, a presence living inside them that they could rely on for guidance and courage.

The number grew to nearly a hundred, living together in community and the presence of Elohim that lived among them.

One day, after teaching, when the group had left for evening chores and preparation for the evening meal, Chaisus sat alone by the edge of the lake, facing into the rays of Asolara as she hovered low over the dunes to the west.

Mael approached. "Master?"

"Come sit with me Mael."

Mael sat beside him.

"Do you see Asolara, hovering low? Do you know what that means?"

"I think I do."

"The day is at an end, Mael. Asolara sets and night settles on Terra and darkness reigns."

Mael nodded, but wasn't sure that Ransom noticed.

"I am sending out my followers like sheep among the wolves into this darkness. They will be tested and killed for their knowledge of the light that will shine in the darkness, but cannot be overcome by it. They will die with an eye on the light and enter into the eternal light of what you call the deep sky. Do you think they are ready?"

"You alone know that."

"Ready or not, the time has come."

They sat for a while in silence. Asolara fell behind the dunes and deep green-azure of twilight filled the sky to the west.

"And you, Mael, do you now know who you are?"

"I think I do."

Ransom smiled. "And you know that you will go back to Tessalindria alone, and there you must do what I have done here."

Mael nodded. "Must I go alone?"

"You came to this world alone, and so you must return. You must be a light to your world, in spite of ignorance, fear, jealousy, envy...there is no other way."

Mael shook his head. "I'm not sure I'm ready."

"Ready or not, the time has come. We will travel from here in a few days when the desert reclaims this oasis. We will pass through Bethlehem and Jerusalem one last time. From there we will go to a hill I will designate and be taken back to my father—Elohim—Mah'Eladra."

"We will be with you, Mael, even on Tessalindria. There you will find those who hearts yearn for the kingdom, which is beyond Tessa. You will bring the kingdom there. You must listen to the voice on all occasions—never fail in this and do not fear, for where the voice is spoken, it does not return empty or void of power."

They spoke no more that night. Mael sat with Ransom until the last traces of Asolara were gone and the thin crescent of Terra's moon fell into luminance just above her. The stars spread out their canopy in full splendor, as they reflected off the surface of the lake like a perfect mirror.

Ransom rose and left. Mael sat and listened in the overwhelming stillness of eternity for the rest of the night.

Two days later, the time came. "We will leave this place forever after the morning meal," Ransom announced in his teaching that evening. There was little to pack since most people had come with almost nothing, and everything they needed had been provided perfectly by the oasis. That which had been promised: food, shelter and clothing, had been more than adequate yet there was nothing left to take.

"Take what you need for the day. We will bake our bread for the journey in haste in the morning, without waiting for the yeast. Make enough for one day, but no more. When you enter a town, seek those who will welcome you according to the law and stay with them."

A man in the back of the group called out. "What about your kingdom? Are you now restoring it to Israel?"

The Master shook his head and smiled. "When we get to Jerusalem, stay there and wait for the gift that I have promised, he who will be with you. Meet together as you have here, as you will in my kingdom, because the kingdom will not be here, or there, but it will be in your very midst."

"What shall we eat? And where shall we stay?" another asked.

"Remember the birds of the air and the flowers of the field, as I told you. Elohim will take care of your needs as they take care of the sparrow and the lily. The rest of the world chases after what they need: food, shelter and clothing, and they will get them in that chase, but if you seek the welfare of my kingdom and the way of Elohim, all these will be provided, just as they were provided here."

Mael rose early for his morning walk, but the oasis was already fully alive, well before Asolara rose above the dunes to the east. Something had stirred the encampment to action. He smelled the roasting bread, baked with savory herbs. Many fires burned around the lake, perhaps for the last time. He left his shelter to find that the tables, normally beside each fire, had been moved to one place and were already set; the wine already poured.

Domas approached him as he stretched and shook the sleep out of his eyes. "We're traveling in sixes. You and I, Bieter, Mary, Miriam and Adiana are together."

"When was this decided?"

"The master made the assignments. You slept late, Mael." Domas winked. "Come. The morning meal is upon us. We've been told to leave before Asolara breaches the dunes."

"Do you suppose there's a reason?"

Domas laughed. "You, of all people, know there is always a reason, Mael. You also know that you don't need to know the reason when the Master speaks."

Mael nodded.

"Come." Domas waved his hand toward the lake. The group moved toward the cluster of tables.

The traveling groups sat together.

"Are you afraid to go back through Bethlehem?" Domas asked Miriam.

"I want to see the inn—burned to the ground."

"So do I," Adiana said. Her hair was growing back, but other than that, there was no remnant of hurt.

Peter looked up from the table. "We did not see much of the town. Perhaps now we will see it in daylight."

"And maybe not in so much of a hurry." Mael noted.

The master's voice rose above the hum of multiple conversations. "Today we leave this place. We can never come back here, but what we had here, we will take with us. You must never forget. What we had here was not the place, the food, the water or the wine. What we had here was each other; what we had here was learning about how we are to be out there." He swept his hand backward toward the path leading back to the road.

"Whenever you are together," he lifted one of the unleavened cakes that adorned the tables, "break bread together with gladness and sincerity, and remember my death—together."

"In remembrance of you!" The whole assembly chanted in unison before they broke the loaves and passed them around the tables.

Chaisus then lifted his cup of wine. "Remember the covenant you made with Yahweh, a covenant ratified by my blood, a covenant that binds you together in the eternal kingdom."

"In remembrance of you!" Glasses lifted and clinked together.

"Leave everything as it is and take only your packed things." The master turned to the path and started the journey. Everyone stood up and followed, coalescing into their traveling groups.

As they neared the rise where they would lose sight of the oasis, Chaisus stopped and faced the entourage. "Turn and look one last time."

Everyone turned. The circular oasis stood green and inviting in the gathering light of dawn.

"Behold your refuge!" As Ransom spoke, a single bolt of lightning materialized in the empty sky and hurtled downward into the middle of the lake. An explosion, followed by a wave of fire, moved outward from the lake, reducing everything to cinders. Several onlookers cried out in fear and shied back from the approaching flames, but as quickly as it consumed the oasis, it withdrew back to the lake and then shot into the sky taking every trace of their presence with it. The crowd gasped. Nothing remained but sand and four of the brick buildings, burned clean of any trace of habitation.

"Behold the value of things—destined to be burned, consumed by fire. What remains is us, and what we have built."

The crowd turned to face him. "We will follow you anywhere!"

"Come!" Chaisus said.

Chapter Thirty-Eight

NORTHWARD

"Steel burns and wood is turned to dust, but the vorn is refined by fire."

Timanneaus

Mael stood in the street facing the burned inn. Miriam, Adiana and Mary stood in a huddle with their arms around one another, weeping. He watched helplessly, giving them space as he stood to the side with Bieter and Domas. Nothing remained but a layer of cinder as fine as dust on a closet shelf and as deep at the width of his hand.

Bieter had his hands on his hips, shaking his head. "Never seen anything like this—even the stones—the iron work."

People walking down the road gave the women wide berth. Maybe they noted the strangers, but some might have recognized the woman as employees of the brothel.

"Must have been quite a fire, to consume all the iron," Mael said.

Bieter smiled. "You are a smith, after all, right?"

Mael nodded. "And I have burned my share of iron and steel. It takes an inferno to do that. Even the earthenware is reduced to dust."

"Was it a tall building?" Thomas asked.

"Two levels," Bieter noted, "but not small."

A man walking by on the street stopped near them. "Worst fire we've ever had in Bethlehem."

"Do you know if many people were hurt?"

"You're not from around here."

Bieter nodded. "Up north."

"Passing through?"

Bieter smiled. "Yes, heading to Chershalem."

"Are you in the entourage with the prophet?"

"Yes, we were just two weeks in the desert."

"We know—the rumor is that he passed through here just a few days before the fire, and that he called down the fire on the inn, because of the evil there."

"We heard that the fire was started by one of the women who worked here." Domas said.

The man turned and pointed at the lot where the inn stood. "This was no ordinary fire!" His brow furrowed and he scowled. "It was so hot we could not get close to it to throw water on it! Several men tried, and were burned. And look! None of the other buildings near it are even charred." He waved his hand around the square.

Mael looked. It was true. "How long did it burn?"

"It was fast. People barely got out. It reduced the inn to nothing and then vanished. It was holy fire—not of this earth! Everyone got out except the inn keeper and one of the women—the one who started the fire."

"Will anyone rebuild here?" Bieter asked.

"Probably not. People are afraid of the prophet now."

"He's is not one to be afraid of." Mael said.

"The Romans and the Sanhedrin are afraid of him, for sure."

"How do you know?" Bieter asked.

"They arrived together about a week or so ago. Twenty Roman soldiers and ten from the temple guard in Jerusalem. They were looking for him—the prophet. They heard that he was hiding out down here with his followers."

The man shook his head. "We heard that they had crucified him—dead and buried. They said that there were rumors of his resurrection and they were trying to find his followers mostly, since they weren't convinced."

"What happened?" Domas asked.

"We sent them south into the desert. You know—rumors about where he might be. They were also looking for one of his followers in particular, a short foreigner with ..." He looked at Mael. "Like you," he said pointing his finger.

"Why me?" Mael asked.

"They didn't say, but they did say that if we saw him we should report to them at once."

"Will you do that?" Mael asked.

"We hate the Romans. The Sanhedrin in Chershalem is not much better. But right now, most people are more afraid of the Nazarene." He nodded toward the inn. "I doubt anyone would cooperate with any of them."

Mael stared at the man. "You didn't answer my question."

"What?"

"Will you inform the Sanhedrin or the Romans that we are here?"

"You say you are headed to Chershalem?"

Mael nodded—the evasion was clear.

"You better be careful. They are looking for you—they seem very determined."

"They didn't find us in the desert."

"No, and they were some upset by that. Thought we had deceived them. Threatened the town with retribution, but they eventually left."

"We'll be careful," Bieter said. "Thanks for the warnings."

"No trouble," the man said. "Shalom and Safe journeys."

All three of them nodded.

The man scowled as he passed the women, and muttered something that Mael could not here. All three of the women turned, obviously startled and embarrassed by his statement.

"We need to be very careful here," Peter said, "and get on the road as quickly as possible. Probably the safest place of all is right in Chershalem, in the middle of all the people."

Mael nodded. "Should we leave tonight? If we spend the night on the road, it may even be safer than here."

"If we go out through the gate at this time, the guards will take note," Domas said. "No one would leave for Chershalem at this hour of the day.

"Go to Pethny."

Mael hesitated. "We should leave for Chershalem. Two hours north of here, a road cuts east toward Pethny. We will find a place to stay on that road. If anyone comes looking for us, they will not know we took that route."

Bieter frowned. "How do you know these things?"

"I know many things, but we should leave now. There is nothing for us in this place."

"Chaisus told us to go to Chershalem," Thomas said.

"We will head straight to Chershalem without stopping in Pethny."

Thomas sighed and turned to inform the women.

"I didn't want to stay in this place anyway," Mary said.

Miriam and Adiana nodded. "Neither did we. We were going to ask you if we could move on," Miriam said.

"You seem downcast, Mael," Domas said at they left Bethlehem behind them in the desert. Mael knew Domas was trying to make conversation to lighten the mood.

"It's hard to think that there is more trouble ahead for me in Chershalem—maybe even on the road before we get there."

"It's odd that they have singled you out." Bieter said. "Perhaps it's because you challenged Pilate. Maybe because you escaped Caiaphas's jail..."

"I think I remind him of the Master. He sees me as the next threat."

Mael knew that part of his sadness came with the knowledge that he would be leaving. His sojourn on Terra had not been easy. Different customs and culture, the political and spiritual turmoil of these people, and the constant reminder that he was not fully part of it weighed on his vorn.

The idea of returning to Tessalindria filled him with unknowns. He left in tragedy and troubling circumstances, with no sure understanding of what may have happened to his family or Erolin. Where and when he would return hung over him, a dark shadow of the unknown.

The uncertainty about the intervening journey here on Terra and his return to Tessa, played against the quiet surety that this was all in the hands of Mah'Eladra. Whatever they had in store for him would work out, though the path for following them had been hard with pain and apparent failure.

The women walked in front of them, talking quietly. Images of Miriam still plagued his thoughts, invading at unexpected times.

He knew there was no path forward for him and Miriam, but even in that surety, he could not escape his thoughts about her presence. Even the selection of the traveling teams from the oasis, that put them together for this journey, burdened him. Was this a test? Was there some greater purpose? Even the futility of dwelling on the situation pressed against him, stealing his joy. How would he escape?

The last words of the innkeeper rang in his ears as they trudged along in the desert. The wasteland, the scorpions and snakes, without water or food ... burned by Asolara. Was it insanity? Perhaps it was a metaphor for the spiritual world that the disciples were walking into that plagued him. Was it an illusion that Ransom's hundred or so followers could recreate and spread the vision of the kingdom? It differed little from the illusion that this dessert could become a beautiful garden, but the oasis was just that. Though the innkeeper could not see it, the disciples had. It was real and, in spite of the apparent illusion, it had sustained and nourished them for two weeks.

"Is this the road to Pethny?" A voice broke into Mael's meditation. "Mael?"

Mael looked up. Miriam was standing in front of him pointing to the right. "Is this the road to Pethny?"

Mael shuddered and shook his head. "Sorry, I was lost in my thoughts."

Bieter laughed.

Mael looked around. He wasn't sure. How could he not know? He was the one who had known so surely that they should go to Pethny—that there was a road and they would find it.

Bieter laughed again. "Of course this is the road!"

"How do you know?" Mael said.

"The sign, my little friend. The sign."

Mael shook his head.

"Oh," Miriam said.

"Then I suppose it is," Mael said. The sign was obvious, but he had been deep in thought.

Domas slapped him on the back. "You should get your eyes out of your head and enjoy this scenery. When we get to Pethny, and then Chershalem, you'll wish you could be back here where it is quiet and beautiful. Elohim made all this for us. So many others would like to see this."

Mael wasn't sure. It reminded him of the NarEl Wastes on Tessalindria. His memory swept back to his encounter with Vishtoenvar. Maybe it wasn't supposed to be this way. Surely, Elohim wanted Terra to be more like the oasis, and not this kingdom of sand.

"Let's go to Pethny," Bieter said.

The women nodded. Thomas laughed. Mael looked down the branch in the road. "To Pethny—and Chershalem."

As they started to walk, Miriam dropped back beside him and took his hand. "Walk with me, Mael."

Mael shuddered. He wasn't afraid. He wasn't nervous, and he had no good reason to refuse. He simply nodded.

"There is no reason to be afraid, Mael."

"I'm not."

"I have never had the opportunity to thank you for your kindness in rescuing me."

Mael stared straight ahead.

"You had the courage to let me come into your room, and the courage not to indulge in the temptations I offered you. You had the courage to stand up to Bieter and take me to the oasis. There are few men like this."

Her hand played with his as they walked. Mael liked it. It made him feel warm and close, something he hadn't felt before.

"Domas told me about you—many things—mysteries about how you came here, and where you are from. I trust that Domas isn't lying, but it's hard to believe."

Miriam's other hand came across and joined onto the back of his. Two hands. "I also know that you will have to return to this place. Tessa, he called it?"

Mael nodded.

"And I know that I cannot come with you. It's a journey like that of the Master—that you must walk alone."

Mary and Adiana walked in front of them. Bieter and Domas were engaged in some distant conversation, far enough back that it remained private.

Miriam squeezed his hand. "But I would go with you if I could."

"Please don't say that." Mael squeezed the words out as his throat tightened.

"I've seen the way you have looked at me and I was not afraid. I have never felt that from a man."

"Please..."

"You need to know, Mael. Domas asked me to tell you."

"Why?" Mael still could not bring himself to look at her.

Miriam hesitated. "Because he's your friend—he knows you—he knows you need to feel safe with me."

Mael clenched his teeth as tears formed in his eyes.

Miriam waited.

"I feel safe with you," he said through his teeth. "I don't feel safe with *me*, when I am thinking about you."

They kept walking. Thoughts swirled around him. "I asked the master if it was possible for you to come with me—he said no—I asked Yahweh if you would be safe here without me."

Miriam squeezed his hand and drew up closer beside him.

"They made it clear that I could not know such things, but that I would have to trust their goodness in this matter. That's hard for me. I don't understand my feelings."

"I feel safe with the others, even if you are not here. I'll miss you, of course."

Mael nodded. They walked on together, hand in hand. Mael didn't feel compelled to explain further. She seemed to understand the situation and to be content with his silence, as he was with hers. He loved the feel of her hand as she held his. No matter what the future, he wanted moments like this to last.

Chapter Thirty-Nine

HOME

*"The journey through a portal is but a few small steps that take
us a long way."*

Passages
Oratanga

They approached Chershalem from the east on the road from
Pethny. The sight left a lasting impression—one that Mael would
never forget. Asolara cast her late morning shadows in front of
them as they came up the rise in the road south of Ransom's

garden. Chershalem's temple walls shone with a rose tint in the full light on their stone faces.

They traveled the road, parallel to the massive walls, past the garden and up to the serpentine road that led to the Golden Gate into the temple courts.

"Do you think it wise," Domas said, "to enter the city through the temple? Should we go north around Bethesda and the fortress?"

Bieter shook his head. "You have any idea what is best, Mael?"

"Either way we are putting our hand in the adder's nest," Mael said, "but there's more likely to be a lot of people in the temple courts. More distraction, and the Golden gate is not guarded by the Ermans."

"Good point," Domas said.

They headed up the serpentine ascent to the Golden Gate. The women walked behind, more in keeping with the customs of the city. Their safety was not as much an issue as it was on the desert road.

"What should we do when we get into the city?" Domas asked.

"Not sure," Bieter said. "Chaisus left us no specifics. We will need a place to stay."

"How long will we be here?" Mael asked.

"What do you mean, 'we'?" Bieter said.

Mael knew what he meant. The eleven whom Chaisus had chosen had been asked to move on to some place that Chaisus had designated where he would meet them privately. Mael knew his path would be different, but he didn't know the timing or the places that Chaisus had specified. He would wait for the voice, or some event that would drive his direction. He assumed that it involved the portal, but did not know how that would work.

"We'll stay with some women we know here," Mary said. "We've been here before for feasts and always managed to work it out."

"We don't have to stick together?" Mael asked.

"Chaisus only asked us to get here—to Chershalem," Bieter said, "then the instructions are vague. Domas and I will go to the mountain Chaisus indicated.

"We'll stay here and wait for the promise as he told us." Miriam said.

Mael's inner parts turned. He seemed to be the only one with an unsettled plan for his immediate future.

They walked through the Golden Gate together. As they passed the guards, Mael noticed one of them staring at him. The guard leaned over and whispered something to a second guard.

A sudden awareness overwhelmed him. He had to get away from the others—for their sake. He was in danger and had to be sure that he did not endanger them.

He dropped back, and took a couple quick steps to the right into a group of merchants that were arguing about something. He ducked low, under the table where they stood, and scrambled along on the paving stones to emerge at the other end, darting between the legs of one man, "Hey!" he shouted, but Mael was already two paces behind him.

The tingling on the back of his neck continued, but he couldn't identify the source. He moved quickly along the pillars of the colonnade, skirting the crowds that filled the northern court of the temple. There was another gate in the north wall, east of the fortress, where he had entered several times.

He headed into the crowds, toward the northern portico. The sense of danger heightened. He turned left, dodging through the people toward the back corner of the temple. The gate behind the temple now seemed the objective. He entered the west portico, hugging the back wall.

Mael broke into a run as he approached the gate. The guards saw him coming and braced to stop him, but he ducked to the ground and rolled between them under their crossed spears. They cursed and yelled to the crowd to stop him.

The startled visitors to the temple tried to react as Mael darted between them. Someone tripped him. He sprawled onto the stone deck of the bridge outside the gate. Before he had time to stand, several strong hands pinned him to the ground. Mael stopped struggling.

The guards made their way through the crowd. When they reached him, they hauled him to his feet. "Kiephus wants to see you!" one of them said.

"Take me to Kiephus."

They led him back through the gate and across the temple courts, a spectacle for all to see as he stumbled along, trying to keep up with the brisk pace of the guards.

Kiephus paced back and forth, as two guards held Mael's arms. Mael didn't resist, but their grips were painful, as if they had to restrain him as a threat.

"Why did you come back?" Kiephus scowled as he spoke.

"Because the master told me to."

"He told you to come here?"

"To Chershalem, yes."

"You must have known it was dangerous to do so.

"Yes."

"You burned the inn in Bethlehem—and you eluded my guard that was sent there to find you."

"I didn't burn the inn."

"They say you can do miracles."

"I don't do miracles. Elohim do the miracles."

"Through you?" Sarcasm laced Kiephus's words.

"Only when I hear their voice."

Kiephus looked up at the other priests. "Hear his blasphemy!"

"Would that you would hear their voice, obey and see the miracles yourself. But you cannot hear their voice because of your hard heart." Mael wasn't sure where the words came from.

The priest's eyes stormed and the scowl on his face darkened. The outflow of his robe darkened to almost black. Kiephus looked around the room. "Do we need to hear more? The man must die for his blasphemies."

"You cannot execute me without Erman consent, is this not so?"

"Pilate will consent, you fool. We've already agreed."

"DO NOT FEAR, MAEL. YOUR TIME HAS NOT YET COME."

"You will call attention to my death if you crucify me."

"What do you mean?"

"Wouldn't you rather see me just disappear?"

"Death would make you disappear."

"Crucifixion would make my death public—death in the hands of injustice. You crucified the Master and many rallied to him."

Kiephus hesitated. He faced the guards. "Don't let him escape." He turned to the other priests. "We need to talk."

Mael smiled at the guards. "I am not going anywhere. May I sit down?" The guards looked at one another. One of them nodded. "Right here!" they shoved him to the pavers. Mael crossed his legs, closed his eyes and waited to see the will of Mah'Eladra.

Mael sat once again in the small, cold cell with only the feeble light from the torches filtering through the barred window in the door. He knew the guards were outside, as usual, but they said nothing.

The voice of Mah'Eladra assured him that there was more for him to do. He knew he would return to Tessa. Kiephus clearly wanted to kill him, but Kiephus didn't know many things. Perhaps his death would be the portal back to Tessa where he would be resurrected to fulfill his purpose there as Ransom had described.

The time in the oasis had solidified his understanding of the kingdom as it would form on Terra. That the hundred or so that

had gathered there could effect this transformation was a matter
of armatan. They were weak and immature, but they had been
with Chaisus and that alone held many surprises. He had breathed
his El onto them, what they called the 'spirit'. Though Mael did
not fully understand that, he would not underestimate its effect.
Chaisus had described it like the wind that came and went as it
willed, but left change in its path, like the shifting sands of the
desert, or the waves on the sea, its effect never to be predicted or
minimized.

Miriam came to mind. He wondered if she would ever know
what happened to him. He hoped that Kiephus would not make
his death public, partly to protect her from having to see it, but
he didn't want her to know nothing of what happened to him.

Mael dozed. He fell in and out of sleep consciousness as he
sat waiting. His shallow dreams swam with images of his experi-
ences on Terra, interlaced with memories of family and his life in
Farhantra. Erolin faded into his awareness and spoke to him: "I will
see you soon," she whispered before she vanished. He didn't know
how long it had been when Kiephus came with guards to take him.

"Where are we going?" Mael asked as the guards hauled him
to his feet.

"We are taking you to your death, as is fitting for all blasphemers." Kiephus said.

"And the Ermans?"

"They'll never know about this."

The hurried ascent to the temple courts in the hands of the
guards was painful. The courts were dark, with the crescent moon
half way to its zenith.

"I thought the temple gates are shut after Asolara sets."

"Shut up!" one of the guards said in a low voice. Kiephus said
nothing.

In addition to the High Priest, four other priests trailed behind
the four guards. They remained silent. Mael decided to be quiet

also. The darkness was their domain and it was obvious that they wanted to keep the secret of his fate.

They moved quickly as he stumbled to keep up with their pace. The rough guards showed no mercy. The entourage exited through the gate where Mael had tried to escape. Kiephus obviously held sway over the shut gates that opened for them as they approached.

They marched down the long bridge. No one spoke. At the end of the bridge, they paused as the guards lit torches and then descended some stairs into a passage below ground. They emerged from the tunnel onto a small plaza surrounding a large pool, reflecting the light of Terra's moon like a mirror. The guards extinguished their torches as they skirted the pool, taking a road that led up a small rise.

Suddenly, Mael knew where they were. He bit his lip. They descended into the Garden of the Dead with the moon behind them, weaving among the tombs until they stopped in front of the tomb where the master had been laid. Emotion flooded Mael. The portal...

Kiephus stopped in front of the entrance to the tomb. The stone had been restored to its place; rolled up the slight incline, and held by a wooden chock. With a nod from the priest, the guards shoved Mael forward to the ground in front of Kiephus. "Stand up, Mael!"

Mael stood up and brushed the dust off his tunic as he faced Kiephus.

"Tonight, little man, you will truly become—how did you say it?—'Mael and nothing more'?"

Mael looked into the priest's eyes. "I have never claimed to be anything else."

Kiephus stormed. "Put him in the tomb!"

One of the guards lit another torch and entered the tomb. Two others grabbed Mael's arms and hauled him to the entrance, struggling to hold onto him as they squeezed through the small opening together. They pulled him around the burial slab and pushed him up against the solid black rock of the back wall.

Kiephus entered, standing at the opposite end of the burial slab as the other priests crowded in behind him. The tomb was never meant to hold this many people.

Kiephus's face grew dark. The cascade off his robes went to black, a shivering spectacle of evil. "You will die here, 'Mael and nothing more'. No one will know and no one will care. No one will mourn your death, and no one will find you until they open this tomb to house its rightful owner. There will be no one to roll back the stone. It's a shame you chose death in this way."

Mael looked in the priest's eyes. "I choose life!"

Kiephus scowled and motioned with his hand as two guards drew their swords. "Kill him!"

As the guards stepped forward, Mael felt the warmth of the wall as it changed. He stepped back into the darkness as a single flick of a sword grazed his left shoulder. He stumbled backward. The wound wasn't serious, but it hurt. He lost his balance, just as he had in the Kana portal on Tessa and somersaulted backward into the darkness.

Caiaphas cursed. "What happened?"

The guards stepped back in terror. "We don't know your Highness."

"Give me your sword!" One of the guards handed his sword to Caiaphas.

Caiaphas hurled the sword at the wall. The sword vanished without a trace and without a sound as the cold, inky wall swirled in anger. As suddenly as it all happened, the wall turned back to solid rock.

No one moved. Each stood frozen in terror or wonder, such times requiring no distinction between the two. "Out! Get out!" Caiaphas yelled. The priests and guards scrambled to get out of the small opening, stumbling over one another in their hurry. Caiaphas came out last. He grabbed the heavy mallet that stood by the door and, overcome with anger, struck the chock that held the stone from the door.

The stone hesitated then slowly ground down the ramp, settling against the wall where it had been the day before he had ordered the tomb opened.

Caiaphas looked around and then looked up at the moon. It must be the middle of the night. Why was he here? Why had the other priests come—and the temple guard—what was happening? He recognized the location—the tomb of the blasphemer, but could not account for his presence there.

The baffled look on the faces of the guards and the priests spoke of a similar confusion. They looked to him for an answer.

His pride took over. "Thank you all for your help. Go home and get some sleep. Tomorrow will be a busy day."

For the rest of his life, Caiaphas would never be able to remember why he was there in the tombs. In his embarrassment, he never talked about it with the priests or the guards and none of them ever mentioned the event again.

All knowledge of the strange little man, 'Mael and nothing more' was mercifully erased from his memory and experience. He would now have his hands full with the followers of Jesus of Nazareth.

Chapter Forty

EMERGENCE

Mael stood in the utter darkness on solid ground. The bleeding seemed to have stopped, but his shoulder ached as he held it tightly with his right hand. He walked forward and, just like in the tomb, the air changed. It was cool, and fragrant with Willara flowers. Tessa!

He banged his head on a low hanging stone. He knelt and crawled. The ceiling lowered. The tunnel turned to the left and sloped up, becoming smaller and lower.

Faint light filtered in from above as he wriggled forward on his belly. As he swept leaves and small stones out of the way, he could tell that someone else had passed through this passage recently.

He emerged onto a shallow ledge in full light, stood up straight, brushed off his tunic, and squinted in the brightness.

Far below, the sea stretched out before him as far as he could see, sparkling in the light of Asolara, half risen on the far water horizon. Thirty paces below him, huge rolling waves crashed against the solid rock of the ledge he stood on. Several ravens rode eddies that rose up the face of the cliffs. Willara vines trailed over the edge of the cliff edge above him, resplendent in the morning light with their brilliant red, fragrant flowers.

He moved along the ledge to where a narrow cleft in the cliff face allowed him to clamber up to the top of the escarpment. The land rolled out before him like a quilted carpet of open green fields dotted with clumps of small trees and snaked with blue ribbons of water in the valleys. At the horizon, the land rose into the haze of blue, snow-capped mountains. No houses, no roads, no fences—no sign of the mankind interrupted the view.

To his right, across several fields, something moved. Mael shaded his eyes and stared. There was nothing. Then, a small figure appeared coming up over a hill. He walked slowly, as if there were no hurry in all the world, but moving toward Mael though the field. He descended into a dip in the rolling landscape and then appeared again, but now traveling to the left around the hill, as if following some path.

Mael squinted. The traveler disappeared again behind a small clump of dense trees. When he appeared again, he was traveling south.

Mael had no agenda. To meet this person in this otherwise empty world was as good an idea as he had, so he moved toward him, skirting along the edge of the trees to the right of the field of golden flowers on a trajectory that might intersect his path. Mael couldn't see him.

When Mael crested a small hill in the field, he paused and looked again, waiting for any movement. Nothing.

He trotted down into the low swale below the hill hoping to make it to the next rise quickly. When he came to the top, he could see the traveler again, walking away from him, about five hundred paces in front of him.

He cupped his hands to his mouth and shouted. "Hey!"

The figure paused and turned, shading his eyes as he faced almost directly into the glare of Asolara, scanning for the source of Mael's shout. Mael waved his arms and jumped. "Here!" he yelled.

The figure moved toward him and broke into a trot as he disappeared into a depression behind a clump of trees.

Mael launched himself down the hill in the direction that he guessed would intersect the stranger's path. He ran beside a stream into the valley, with the land rising on either side of him. Mael guessed that he would find him shortly. He could not be far now.

A large boulder in the side of the hill obscured the path of the stream. He headed toward it and as he rounded the corner, he pulled up short at the surprised person who came to a stop two paces in front of him.

Her hands covered her mouth but there was no mistaking her copper hair that fell down just below her collar.

Mael froze.

"Mael!"

"Erolin!"

Neither moved—their eyes locked in wonder.

"How in Tessa..." they said simultaneously.

Mael shook his head and rubbed his eyes.

Erolin launched herself at him without restraint, toppling him to the ground then rolled off him onto the grass.

"What are you doing here?" they said at the same time.

Mael laughed for the first time in days.

"I arrived in the portal just this morning—perhaps two hours ago," Erolin said, "and have been wandering these fields for clues. I didn't want to get too far from it."

"Where are we?"

"I can only guess. There's no sign of the mankind as far as I have been able to see."

"When?"

Erolin shook her head.

Mael sat up and faced her. She rolled toward him onto her side and propped her head on her hand, elbow on the ground.

"You look younger!" The words came out without thought, before Mael had even had time to process his own realization.

"I feel younger—stronger, like I should be twenty, not forty, but I've not found a glass or still water to see myself yet."

"You look *much* younger," Mael repeated. "Last I saw, you were being dismembered by the priests—the last memory I carried into the portal and since."

Erolin nodded. "A painful ordeal. It was only this morning." She pursed her lips. "I remember the pain. They stabbed me many times. They cut off my hand." She held her left hand up.

"I remember life fading away in the pain, and being pulled from my body to stand and watch as the priests argued over their failure to kill *you*. They picked my body up and tossed it into the portal. A great rushing wind picked me up and took me to the base of the golden stair. There were thousands there, climbing the stairs—singing and laughing.

"I started up. I hadn't gone far when suddenly one of the Eladra came up beside me and pushed me off the stair. I fell, head over heels, plunging out of the light into darkness again.

"I fell and fell, and when I stopped falling, I found myself standing in the darkness. I came out of the portal to this. Even my hand!" She held out her left hand and flexed her wrist in a small circle. "Hard to believe it was completely severed off."

"Perhaps other things were healed also. I saw this happen to another—wait! We're on Tessa, right?"

Erolin laughed. "Where else would we be?

Mael blinked and shook his head. "I was forty days in a different world, Erolin. Not sure where or when, but forty days."

"A different world?"

"Somewhere out there." Mael swept his hand toward the Deep Sky. "The eighth portal. They called it Terra. They're like us, but different."

Erolin stared at the ground. "You'll have to tell me more."

Mael nodded. They paused as they each reflected on new things they just learned.

"From the movement of Asolara I am guessing we are far north, but I won't know for sure without the stars. From my studies of the portals—there's one on the northeast coast of Mythinia, but I won't know until I can see the stars."

"And when?"

"It's early morning—late spring—all the water—the flowers and the snow on the mountains and—it's *now.*" Erolin smirked as she waved her hand toward the western horizon. "That's all I have."

Mael picked at the grass in front of him. "How far is it to the NarEl Wastes?"

"What?"

"The NarEl Wastes."

"I've never been there, but many daysmarch to be sure—other side of the continent if I am right about where we are. They're south of Tessamandria."

"I have to go there."

"Seriously?"

Mael nodded. "I've learned who I am, Erolin—what I have to do starts in the wastes."

Erolin's face sobered and she sat up. "It'll be a hard journey, Mael."

"To the wastes? Or through them."

"Both."

Mael rose to his feet and held out his hand to help Erolin stand. "I need your help to get there, but I'll have to cross them alone..."

Erolin took his hand. "I know."

Mael looked into her eyes. "You know?"

"Come," she said. "We'll talk along the way."

~ The End ~

(of this part of the story)

ABOUT THE AUTHOR

About the Author

F. W. Faller was born on Cape Cod in 1955. As a busy child, there was never time for reading until after college. When he discovered the power of fiction to change the world, he began his quest for a writing that would encompass his worldview with good fiction.

The original efforts were sidelined by reading *Lord of the Rings*. Being completely derailed from any original thought by these books for a number of years, other aspects of life took over: work in the church, marriage, children, a demanding job...

In the summer of 1998 he settled down and wrote the opening scenes of his first novel, A *Sword for the Immerland king*.

Since that time he has written five novels in the Portals of Tessalindria Collection as well as a number of satellite shorts and the backstory for the collection. In addition, he has written many non-fiction articles related to spiritual life issues that he publishes on his website for the curious to peruse.

Currently, he is retired and living in Portland, Maine with his wife of forty years and focusing on his family, the strength of the church, and writing his legacy of thought into the best fiction he can muster for future generations to enjoy.

ALSO BY ...

Thank you for reading this book.

Book reviews are very helpful to authors in their craft and their careers.

- If you are my personal friend on Facebook, it is better to write a review on Goodreads

- Please take the time to write a review on Amazon.com if you can.

www.immerland.com

Newsletter Signup

A Bit about the Books

The "Portals of Tessalindria" Collection is a growing number of books that I like to characterize as "historical fiction from another planet".

They are about Tessalindria, a small planet on the other side of the universe, created by the one creator god, Mah'Eladra, but in the farthest reaches of the science fiction world, no human from earth will ever find Tessalindria or be able to go there. Tessalindria is a lot like earth. The mankind, whom Mah'Eladra created, are basically the same as us, but they have a different history, of course, a different culture and different ways of thinking.

On Tessalindria there are space/time portals that transport people throughout history with Mah'Eladra's message. God is still God, but since He never does the same thing twice, there are other differences between Tessalindria and Earth that are revealed throughout the novels.

The books take place at all different times in the history of Tessalindria so some of them border on medieval fantasy, others more on urban fantasy and some that are futuristic, but all of them develop a view of Tessalindria from their own perspective in time.

Some would classify them as fantasy, but they would not be considered high fantasy, involving magic, swords, dragons, elves, dwarfs etc. There is spiritual power, but no magic per se. Others would like to call them science fiction, but hardcore sci-fi buffs would be disappointed at the very ordinary world that Tessalindria is.

For many years I struggled to find the niche genre for these books. The closest analogy is *The Chronicles of Narnia* and the space trilogy by C. S. Lewis. While this may seem presumptuous, they are much the same: the postulation that there are other places and times where God is working differently than on Earth and how it might be different if God still has to be the same.

The books purposefully challenge many basic and lazy assumptions that we often make about God because of our somewhat Christian culture. These books are for thinkers and ruminators, who are willing to "*Think beyond the horizon and color outside the lines*".

While the books *were* written in a certain order, I prefer to call this a "collection", not a "series". A series implies order. A collection can be read in any order. While the stories overlap, they are separate, but each giving color and understanding to all the others as they are read. The *Chronicles of Narnia* is like this, as well as Lewis's space trilogy, *Out of the Silent Planet*, *Perelandra* and *That Hideous Strength*.

All of the books are written in the new sub-genre called *nobelbright*. Basically, this assumes that while there is evil, most people are mostly good, but they make mistakes and bad decisions that challenge them and others around them to rise up and become better. In the books, as in real life, there's violence and hatred, anger, bitterness, mistrust, envy, greed and the like, but we can rise above it if we work at it.

When I first started writing, I wanted to create a cross-over collection that would inspire non-religious people to seek God. I have discovered that this is too broad to find my tribe, and have come to see that these books are for believers who are willing to be challenged and encouraged in faith, admitting that they are basically religious in nature.

At the end of the day, with the help of others, I have settled on my genre as *religious soft science fiction*.

I hope that you will find these stories and the world of Tessalindria inspiring and challenging to your thinking, to make your faith more robust and provocative.

Please visit my website and sign up for my newsletter for continued ongoing information about the release of other books in the collection.

www.immerland.com

Newsletter Signup

Other Books

Please visit www.immerland.com for more in depth and up-to-date information about the release of these books.

A Sword for the Immerland King – The story of a blacksmith who defies a king's command to make a sword for his fiftieth birthday and the twisted paths to truth that culminate in a significant shift in the history of the kingdom of Immerland.

Lonama's Map – The story of two teen friends who discover new challenges in life, as they are accidentally transported back in time to discover that the legends of their times are true and how their friendship is continually challenged as they discover truth from the fiction of history.

Mankar's Bane (Formerly *Tveeling*) – The story about the twins of Huravag who are separated for a time as their lives weave into an intriguing tale that leads to the overthrow of the evil king Mankar.

Bitterleaf – This is an urban fantasy about a biochemist who has developed a drug that can offset the effects of aging. But there is trouble when the drug is released to the public early, and Wilner and his family must seek refuge with the Sessashian cult to hide from the reaches of his corporation, that seeks his help in the chaos of the drug's failure.

Earthbound – The story of Mael, destined to be the savior figure for Tessalindria, as he grows to discover who he is, after being transported to a place to learn personally from the master of life, before returning to Tessalindria.

Contact

If you would like to contact F. W. Faller you can reach him in the following ways:

- Home web page –Immerland.com

- Author email address – f.w.faller@gmail.com

- Facebook – Friends of Immerland group

- Instagram – @valradica

If you would like to hear regularly about what is happening in Tessalindria and get other special opportunities, please sign up for my monthly newsletter.

I never share my email list or individual emails with anyone else and you can always unsubscribe with the link at the bottom of each newsletter.

www.immerland.com

Newsletter Signup

www.ingramcontent.com/pod-product-compliance
Lightning Source LLC
Chambersburg PA
CBHW021122260626
47169CB00005B/1397